What's Mine's Mine

George MacDonald

DEDICATION

To all who aspire to be who they were created to be.

What's Mine's Mine

George MacDonald

Table of Contents

IN THREE VOLUMES

VOL. I.

CONTENTS OF VOL. I.

CHAPTER

WHAT'S MINE'S MINE.

CHAPTER I.

HOW COME THEY THERE?

The room was handsomely furnished, but such as I would quarrel with none for calling common, for it certainly was uninteresting. Not a thing in it had to do with genuine individual choice, but merely with the fashion and custom of the class to which its occupiers belonged. It was a dining-room, of good size, appointed with all the things a dining-room "ought" to have, mostly new, and entirely expensive—mirrored sideboard in oak; heavy chairs, just the dozen, in fawn-coloured morocco seats and backs— the dining-room, in short, of a London-house inhabited by rich middle-class people. A big fire blazed in the low round-backed grate, whose flashes were reflected in the steel fender and the ugly fire-irons that were never used. A snowy cloth of linen, finer than ordinary, for there was pride in the housekeeping, covered the large dining-table, and a company, evidently a family, was eating its breakfast. But how come these people THERE?

For, supposing my reader one of the company, let him rise from the well-appointed table—its silver, bright as the complex motions of butler's elbows can make it; its china, ornate though not elegant; its ham, huge, and neither too fat nor too lean; its game-pie, with nothing to be desired in composition, or in flavour natural or artificial;—let him rise from these and go to the left of the two windows, for there are two opposite each other, the room having been enlarged by being built out: if he be such a one as I would have for a reader, might I choose—a reader whose heart, not merely his eye, mirrors what he sees—one who not merely beholds the outward shows of things, but catches a glimpse of the soul that looks out of them, whose garment and revelation they are;—if he be such, I say, he will stand, for more than a moment, speechless with something akin to that which made the morning stars sing together.

He finds himself gazing far over western seas, while yet the sun is in the east. They lie clear and cold, pale and cold, broken with islands scattering thinner to the horizon, which is jagged here and there with yet another. The ocean looks a wild, yet peaceful mingling of lake and land. Some of the islands are green from shore to shore, of low yet broken surface; others are mere rocks, with a bold front to the sea, one or two of them strange both in form and character. Over the pale blue sea hangs the pale blue sky, flecked with a few cold white clouds that look as if they disowned the earth they had got so high—though none the less her children, and doomed to descend again to her bosom. A keen little wind is out, crisping the surface of the sea in patches—a pretty large crisping to be seen from that height, for the window looks over hill above hill to the sea. Life, quiet yet eager, is all about; the solitude itself is alive, content to be a solitude because it is alive. Its life needs nothing from beyond—is independent even of the few sails of fishing boats that here and there with their red brown break the blue of the water.

If my reader, gently obedient to my thaumaturgy, will now turn and cross to the other window, let him as he does so beware of casting a glance on his right towards the place he has left at the table, for the room will now look to him tenfold commonplace, so that he too will be inclined to ask, "How come these and their belongings HERE —just HERE?"—let him first look from the window. There he sees hills of heather rolling away eastward, at middle distance beginning to rise into mountains, and farther yet, on the horizon, showing snow on their crests—though that may disappear and return several times before settling down for the winter. It is a solemn and very still region—not a PRETTY country at all, but great—beautiful with the beauties of colour and variety of surface; while, far in the distance, where the mountains and the clouds have business together, its aspect rises to grandeur. To his first glance probably not a tree will be discoverable; the second will fall upon a solitary clump of firs, like a mole on the cheek of one of the hills not far off, a hill steeper than most of them, and green to the top.

Is my reader seized with that form of divine longing which wonders what lies over the nearest hill? Does he fancy, ascending the other side to its crest, some sweet face of highland girl, singing songs of the old centuries while yet there was a people in these wastes? Why should he imagine in the presence of the actual? why dream when the eyes can see? He has but to return to the table to reseat himself by the side of one of the prettiest of girls!

She is fair, yet with a glowing tinge under her fairness which flames out only in her eyes, and seldom reddens her skin. She has brown hair with just a suspicion of red and no more, and a waviness that turns to curl at the ends. She has a good forehead, arched a little, not without a look of habitation, though whence that comes it might be hard to say. There are no great clouds on that sky of the face, but there is a soft dimness that might turn to rain. She has a straight nose, not too large for the imperfect yet decidedly Greek contour; a doubtful, rather straight, thin-lipped mouth, which seems to dissolve into a bewitching smile, and reveals perfect teeth —and a good deal more to the eyes that can read it. When the mouth smiles, the eyes light up, which is a good sign. Their shape is long oval— and their colour when unlighted, much that of an unpeeled almond; when she smiles, they grow red. She has an object in life which can hardly be called a mission. She is rather tall, and quite graceful, though not altogether natural in her movements. Her dress gives a feathery impression to one who rather receives than notes the look of ladies. She has a good hand—not the doll hand so much admired of those who can judge only of quantity and know nothing of quality, but a fine sensible hand,—the best thing about her: a hand may be too small just as well as too large.

Poor mother earth! what a load of disappointing women, made fit for fine things, and running all to self and show, she carries on her weary old back! From all such, good Lord deliver us!—except it be for our discipline or their awaking.

Near her at the breakfast table sits one of aspect so different, that you could ill believe they belonged to the same family. She is younger and taller— tall indeed, but not ungraceful, though by no means beautiful. She has all the features that belong to a face—among them not a good one. Stay! I am wrong: there were in truth, dominant over the rest, TWO good features— her two eyes, dark as eyes well could be without being all pupil, large, and rather long like her sister's until she looked at you, and then they opened wide. They did not flash or glow, but were full of the light that tries to see —questioning eyes. They were simple eyes—I will not say without arriere pensee, for there was no end of thinking faculty, if not yet thought, behind them,—but honest eyes that looked at you from the root of eyes, with neither attack nor defence in them. If she was not so graceful as her sister, she was hardly more than a girl, and had a remnant of that curiously lovely mingling of grace and clumsiness which we see in long-legged growing girls. I will give her the advantage of not being further described, except so far as this—that her hair was long and black, that her complexion was dark, with something of a freckly unevenness, and that her hands were larger and yet better than her sister's.

There is one truth about a plain face, that may not have occurred to many: its ugliness accompanies a condition of larger undevelopment, for all ugliness that is not evil, is undevelopment; and so implies the larger material and possibility of development. The idea of no countenance is yet carried out, and this kind will take more developing for the completion of its idea, and may result in a greater beauty. I would therefore advise any young man of aspiration in the matter of beauty, to choose a plain woman for wife—IF THROUGH HER PLAINNESS SHE IS YET LOVELY IN HIS EYES; for the loveliness is herself, victorious over the plainness, and her face, so far from complete and yet serving her loveliness, has in it room for completion on a grander scale than possibly most handsome faces. In a handsome face one sees the lines of its coming perfection, and has a glimpse of what it must be when finished: few are prophets enough for a plain face. A keen surprise of beauty waits many a man, if he be pure enough to come near the transfiguration of the homely face he loved.

This plain face was a solemn one, and the solemnity suited the plainness. It was not specially expressive—did not look specially intelligent; there was more of latent than operative power in it—while her sister's had more expression than power. Both were lady-like; whether they were ladies, my reader may determine. There are common ladies and there are rare ladies; the former MAY be countesses; the latter MAY be peasants.

There were two younger girls at the table, of whom I will say nothing more than that one of them looked awkward, promised to be handsome, and was apparently a good soul; the other was pretty, and looked pert.

The family possessed two young men, but they were not here; one was a partner in the business from which his father had practically retired; the other was that day expected from Oxford.

The mother, a woman with many autumnal reminders of spring about her, sat at the head of the table, and regarded her queendom with a smile a little set, perhaps, but bright. She had the look of a woman on good terms with her motherhood, with society, with the universe—yet had scarce a shadow of assumption on her countenance. For if she felt as one who had a claim upon things to go pleasantly with her, had she not put in her claim, and had it acknowledged? Her smile was a sweet white-toothed smile, true if shallow, and a more than tolerably happy one—often irradiating THE GOVERNOR opposite—for so was the head styled by the whole family from mother to chit.

He was the only one at the table on whose countenance a shadow—as of some end unattained—was visible. He had tried to get into parliament, and had not succeeded; but I will not presume to say that was the source of the shadow. He did not look discontented, or even peevish; there was indeed a certain radiance of success about him-only above the cloudy horizon of his thick, dark eyebrows, seemed to hang a thundery atmosphere. His forehead was large, but his features rather small; he had, however, grown a trifle fat, which tended to make up. In his youth he must have been very nice-looking, probably too pretty to be handsome. In good health and when things went well, as they had mostly done with him, he was sweet-tempered; what he might be in other conditions was seldom conjectured. But was that a sleeping thunder-cloud, or only the shadow of his eyebrows?

He had a good opinion of himself-on what grounds I do not know; but he was rich, and I know no better ground; I doubt if there is any more certain soil for growing a good opinion of oneself. Certainly, the more you try to raise one by doing what is right and worth doing, the less you succeed.

Mr. Peregrine Palmer had finished his breakfast, and sat for a while looking at nothing in particular, plunged in deep thought about nothing at all, while the girls went on with theirs. He was a little above the middle height, and looked not much older than his wife; his black hair had but begun to be touched with silver; he seemed a man without an atom of care more than humanity counts reasonable; his speech was not unlike that of an Englishman, for, although born in Glasgow, he had been to Oxford. He spoke respectfully to his wife, and with a pleasant playfulness to his daughters; his manner was nowise made to order, but natural enough; his grammar was as good as conversation requires; everything was respectable about him-and yet-he was one remove at least from a gentleman. Something hard to define was lacking to that idea of perfection.

Mr. Peregrine Palmer's grandfather had begun to make the family fortune by developing a little secret still in a remote highland glen, which had acquired a reputation for its whisky, into a great superterrene distillery. Both he and his son made money by it, and it had "done well" for Mr. Peregrine also. With all three of them the making of money had been the great calling of life. They were diligent in business, fervent in spirit, serving Mammon, and founding claim to consideration on the fact. Neither Jacob nor John Palmer's worst enemy had ever called him a hypocrite: neither had been suspected of thinking to serve Mammon and God. Both had gone regularly to church, but neither had taught in a Sunday school, or once gone to a week-day sermon. Peregrine had built a church and a school. He did not now take any active part in the distillery, but worked mainly in money itself.

Jacob, the son of a ship-chandler in Greenock, had never thought about gentleman or no gentleman; but his son John had entertained the difference, and done his best to make a gentleman of Peregrine; and neither Peregrine nor any of his family ever doubted his father's success; and if he had not quite succeeded, I would have the blame laid on Peregrine and not on either father or grandfather. For a man to GROW a gentleman, it is of great consequence that his grandfather should have been an honest man; but if a man BE a gentleman, it matters little what his grandfather or grandmother either was. Nay—if a man be a gentleman, it is of the smallest consequence, except for its own sake, whether the world counts him one or not.

Mr. Peregrine Palmer rose from the table with a merry remark on the prolongation of the meal by his girls, and went towards the door.

"Are you going to shoot?" asked his wife.

"Not to-day. But I am going to look after my guns. I daresay they've got them all right, but there's nothing like seeing to a thing yourself!"

Mr. Palmer had this virtue, and this very gentlemanlike way—that he always gave his wife as full an answer as he would another lady. He was not given to marital brevity.

He was there for the grouse-shooting—not exactly, only "as it were." He did not care VERY much about the sport, and had he cared nothing, would have been there all the same. Other people, in what he counted his social position, shot grouse, and he liked to do what other people did, for then he felt all right: if ever he tried the gate of heaven, it would be because other people did. But the primary cause of his being so far in the north was the simple fact that he had had the chance of buying a property very cheap—a fine property of mist and cloud, heather and rock, mountain and moor, and with no such reputation for grouse as to enhance its price. "My estate" sounded well, and after a time of good preserving he would be able to let it well, he trusted. No sooner was it bought than his wife and daughters were eager to visit it; and the man of business, perceiving it would cost him much less if they passed their autumns there instead of on the continent, proceeded at once to enlarge the house and make it comfortable. If they should never go a second time, it would, with its perfect appointments, make the shooting there more attractive!

They had arrived the day before. The journey had been fatiguing, for a great part of it was by road; but they were all in splendid health, and not too tired to get up at a reasonable hour the next day.

CHAPTER II.

A SHORT GLANCE OVER THE SHOULDER.

Mr. Peregrine was the first of the Palmer family to learn that there was a Palmer coat of arms. He learned it at college, and on this wise.

One day a fellow-student, who pleased himself with what he called philology, remarked that his father must have been a hit of a humorist to name him Peregrine:—"except indeed it be a family name!" he added.

"I never thought about it," said Peregrine. "I don't quite know what you mean."

The fact was he had no glimmer of what he meant.

"Nothing profound," returned the other. "Only don't you see Peregrine means pilgrim? It is the same as the Italian pellegrino, from the Latin, peregrinus, which means one that goes about the fields,—what in Scotland you call a LANDLOUPER."

"Well, but," returned Peregrine, hesitatingly, "I don't find myself much wiser. Peregrine means a pilgrim, you say, but what of that? All names mean something, I suppose! It don't matter much."

"What is your coat of arms?"

"I don't know."

"Why did your father call you Peregrine?"

"I don't know that either. I suppose because he liked the name."

"Why should he have liked it?" continued the other, who was given to the Socratic method.

"I know no more than the man in the moon."

"What does your surname mean?"

"Something to do with palms, I suppose."

"Doubtless."

"You see I don't go in for that kind of thing like you!"

"Any man who cares about the cut of his coat, might have a little curiosity about the cut of his name: it sits to him a good deal closer!"

"That is true—so close that you can't do anything with it. I can't pull mine off however you criticize it!"

"You can change it any day. Would you like to change it?"

"No, thank you, Mr. Stokes!" returned Peregrine dryly.

"I didn't mean with mine," growled the other. "My name is an historical one too—but that is not in question.—Do you know your crest ought to be a hairy worm?"

"Why?"

"Don't you know the palmer-worm? It got its name where you got yours!"

"Well, we all come from Adam!"

"What! worms and all?"

"Surely. We're all worms, the parson says. Come, put me through; it's time for lunch. Or, if you prefer, let me burst in ignorance. I don't mind."

"Well, then, I will explain. The palmer was a pilgrim: when he came home, he carried a palm-branch to show he had been to the holy land."

"Did the hairy worm go to the holy land too?"

"He is called a palmer-worm because he has feet enough to go any number of pilgrimages. But you are such a land-louper, you ought to blazon two hairy worms saltier-wise."

"I don't understand."

"Why, your name, interpreted to half an ear, is just PILGRIM PILGRIM!"

"I wonder if my father meant it!"

"That I cannot even guess at, not having the pleasure of knowing your father. But it does look like a paternal joke!"

His friend sought out for him the coat and crest of the Palmers; but for the latter, strongly recommended a departure: the fresh family-branch would suit the worm so well!—his crest ought to be two worms crossed, tufted, the tufts ouched in gold. It was not heraldic language, but with Peregrine passed well enough. Still he did not take to the worms, but contented himself with the ordinary crest. He was henceforth, however, better pleased with his name, for he fancied in it something of the dignity of a doubled surname.

His first glance at his wife was because she crossed the field of his vision; his second glance was because of her beauty; his third because her name was SHELLEY. It is marvellous how whimsically sentimental commonplace people can be where their own interesting personality is concerned: her name he instantly associated with SCALLOP-SHELL, and began to make inquiry about her. Learning that her other name was Miriam, one also of the holy land—

"A most remarkable coincidence!—a mere coincidence of course!" he said to himself. "Evidently that is the woman destined to be the companion of my pilgrimage!"

When their first child was born, the father was greatly exercised as to a fitting name for him. He turned up an old botany book, and sought out the scientific names of different palms. CHAMAEROPS would not do, for it was a dwarf-palm; BORASSUS might do, seeing it was a boy—only it stood for a FAN-PALM; CORYPHA would not be bad for a girl, only it was the name of a heathen goddess, and would not go well with the idea of a holy palmer. COCOA, PHOENIX, and ARECA, one after the other, went in at his eyes and through his head; none of them pleased him. His wife, however, who in her smiling way had fallen in with his whim, helped him out of his difficulty. She was the daughter of nonconformist parents in Lancashire, and had been encouraged when a child to read a certain old-fashioned book called The Pilgrim's Progress, which her husband had never seen. He did not read it now, but accepting her suggestion, named the boy Christian. When a daughter came, he would have had her Christiana, but his wife persuaded him to be content with Christina. They named their second son Valentine, after Mr. Valiant-for-truth. Their second daughter was Mercy; and for the third and fourth, Hope and Grace seemed near enough. So the family had a cool glow of puritanism about it, while nothing was farther from the thoughts of any of them than what their names signified. All, except the mother, associated them with the crusades for the rescue of the sepulchre of the Lord from the pagans; not a thought did one of them spend on the rescue of a live soul from the sepulchre of low desires, mean thoughts, and crawling selfishness.

CHAPTER III.

THE GIRLS' FIRST WALK.

The Governor, Peregrine and Palmer as he was, did not care about walking at any time, not even when he HAD to do it because other people did; the mother, of whom there would have been little left had the sweetness in her moral, and the house-keeping in her practical nature, been subtracted, had things to see to within doors: the young people must go out by themselves! They put on their hats, and issued.

The temperature was keen, though it was now nearly the middle of August, by which time in those northern regions the earth has begun to get a little warm: the house stood high, and the atmosphere was thin. There was a certain sense of sadness in the pale sky and its cold brightness; but these young people felt no cold, and perceived no sadness. The air was exhilarating, and they breathed deep breaths of a pleasure more akin to the spiritual than they were capable of knowing. For as they gazed around them, they thought, like Hamlet's mother in the presence of her invisible husband, that they saw all there was to be seen. They did not know nature: in the school to which they had gone they patronized instead of revering her. She wrought upon them nevertheless after her own fashion with her children, unheedful whether they knew what she was about or not. The mere space, the mere height from which they looked, the rarity of the air, the soft aspiration of earth towards heaven, made them all more of children.

But not one of them being capable of enjoying anything by herself, together they were unable to enjoy much; and, like the miser who, when he cannot much enjoy his money, desires more, began to desire more company to share in the already withering satisfaction of their new possession—to help them, that is, to get pleasure out of it, as out of a new dress. It is a good thing to desire to share a good thing, but it is not well to be unable alone to enjoy a good thing. It is our enjoyment that should make us desirous to share. What is there to share if the thing be of no value in itself? To enjoy alone is to be able to share. No participation can make that of value which in itself is of none. It is not love alone but pride also, and often only pride, that leads to the desire for another to be present with us in possession.

The girls grew weary of the show around them because it was so quiet, so regardless of their presence, so moveless, so monotonous. Endless change was going on, but it was too slow for them to see; had it been rapid, its motions were not of a kind to interest them. Ere half an hour they had begun to think with regret of Piccadilly and Regent street—for they had passed the season in London. There is a good deal counted social which is merely gregarious. Doubtless humanity is better company than a bare hill-side; but not a little depends on how near we come to the humanity, and how near we come to the hill. I doubt if one who could not enjoy a bare hill-side alone, would enjoy that hill-side in any company; if he thought he did, I suspect it would be that the company enabled him, not to forget himself in what he saw, but to be more pleasantly aware of himself than the lone hill would permit him to be;—for the mere hill has its relation to that true self which the common self is so anxious to avoid and forget. The girls, however, went on and on, led mainly by the animal delight of motion, the two younger making many a diversion up the hill on the one side, and down the hill on the other, shrieking at everything fresh that pleased them.

The house they had just left stood on the projecting shoulder of a hill, here and there planted with firs. Of the hardy trees there was a thicket at the back of the house, while toward the south, less hardy ones grew in the shrubbery, though they would never, because of the sea-breezes, come to any height. The carriage-drive to the house joined two not very distant points on the same road, and there was no lodge at either gate. It was a rough, country road, a good deal rutted, and seldom repaired. Opposite the gates rose the steep slope of a heathery hill, along the flank of which the girls were now walking. On their right lay a piece of rough moorland, covered with heather, patches of bracken, and coarse grass. A few yards to the right, it sank in a steep descent. Such was the disposition of the ground for some distance along the road—on one side the hill, on the other a narrow level, and abrupt descent.

As they advanced they caught sight of a ruin rising above the brow of the descent: the two younger darted across the heather toward it; the two elder continued their walk along the road, gradually descending towards a valley.

"I wonder what we shall see round the corner there!" said Mercy, the younger of the two.

"The same over again, I suppose!" answered Christina. "What a rough road it is! I've twice nearly sprained my ankle!"

"I was thinking of what I saw the other day in somebody's travels—about his interest in every turn of the road, always looking for what was to come next."

"Time enough when it comes, in my opinion!" rejoined Christina.

For she was like any other mirror—quite ready to receive what was thrown upon her, but incapable of originating anything, almost incapable of using anything.

As they descended, and the hill-side, here covered with bracken and boulders, grew higher and higher above them, the valley, in front and on the right, gradually opened, here and there showing a glimpse of a small stream that cantered steadily toward the sea, now tumbling over a rock, now sullen in a brown pool. Arriving at length at a shoulder of the hill round which the road turned, a whole mile of the brook lay before them. It came down a narrow valley, with scraps of meadow in the bottom; but immediately below them the valley was of some width, and was good land from side to side, where green oats waved their feathery grace, and the yellow barley was nearly ready for the sickle. No more than the barren hill, however, had the fertile valley anything for them. Their talk was of the last ball they were at.

The sisters were about as good friends as such negative creatures could be; and they would be such friends all their lives, if on the one hand neither of them grew to anything better, and on the other no jealousy, or marked difference of social position through marriage, intervened. They loved each other, if not tenderly, yet with the genuineness of healthy family-habit—a thing not to be despised, for it keeps the door open for something better. In itself it is not at all to be reckoned upon, for habit is but the merest shadow of reality. Still it is not a small thing, as families go, if sisters and brothers do not dislike each other.

They were criticizing certain of the young men they had met at the said ball. Being, in their development, if not in their nature, commonplace, what should they talk about but clothes or young men? And why, although an excellent type of its kind, should I take the trouble to record their conversation? To read, it might have amused me—or even interested, as may a carrot painted by a Dutchman; but were I a painter, I should be sorry to paint carrots, and the girls' talk is not for my pen. At the same time I confess myself incapable of doing it justice. When one is annoyed at the sight of things meant to be and not beautiful, there is danger of not giving them even the poor fair-play they stand in so much the more need of that it can do so little for them.

But now they changed the subject of their talk. They had come to a point of the road not far from the ruin to which the children had run across the heather.

"Look, Chrissy! It IS an old castle!" said Mercy. "I wonder whether it is on our land!"

"Not much to be proud of!" replied the other. "It is nothing but the walls of a square house!"

"Not just a common square house! Look at that pepper-pot on one of the corners!—I wonder how it is all the old castles get deserted!"

"Because they are old. It's well to desert them before they tumble down."

"But they wouldn't tumble down if they weren't neglected. Think of Warwick castle! Stone doesn't rot like wood! Just see the thickness of those walls!"

"Yes, they are thick! But stone too has its way of rotting. Westminster palace is wearing through, flake by flake. The weather will be at the lords before long."

"That's what Valentine would call a sign of the times. I say, what a radical he is, Chrissy!—Look! the old place is just like an empty egg-shell! I know, if it had been mine, I wouldn't have let it come to that!"

"You say so because it never was yours: if it had been, you would know how uncomfortable it was!"

"I should like to know," said Mercy, after a little pause, during which they stood looking at the ruin, "whether the owners leave such places because they get fastidious and want better, or because they are too poor to keep them up! At all events a man must be poor to SELL the house that belonged to his ancestors!—It must be miserable to grow poor after being used to plenty!—I wonder whose is the old place!"

"Oh, the governor's, I suppose! He has all hereabout for miles."

"I hope it is ours! I SHOULD like to build it up again! I would live in it myself!"

"I'm afraid the governor won't advance your share for that purpose!"

"I love old things!" said Mercy.

"I believe you take your old doll to bed with you yet!" rejoined Christina. "I am different to you!" she continued, with Frenchified grammar; "I like things as new as ever I can have them!"

"I like new things well enough, Chrissy—you know I do! It is natural. The earth herself has new clothes once a year. It is but once a year, I grant!"

"Often enough for an old granny like her!"

"Look what a pretty cottage!—down there, half-way to the burn! It's like an English cottage! Those we saw as we came along were either like a piece of the earth, or so white as to look ghastly! This one looks neat and comfortable, and has trees about it!"

The ruin, once a fortified house and called a castle, stood on a sloping root or spur that ran from the hill down to the bank of the stream, where it stopped abruptly with a steep scaur, at whose foot lay a dark pool. On the same spur, half-way to the burn, stood a low, stone-built, thatched cottage, with a little grove about it, mostly of the hardy, contented, musical fir—a tree that would seem to have less regard to earthly prosperity than most, and looks like a pilgrim and a stranger: not caring much, it thrives where other trees cannot. There might have been a hundred of them, mingled, in strangest contrast, with a few delicate silver birches, about the cottage. It stood toward the east side of the sinking ridge, which had a steep descent, both east and west, to the fields below. The slopes were green with sweet grass, and apparently smooth as a lawn. Not far from where the cottage seemed to rest rather than rise or stand, the burn rushed right against the side of the spur, as if to go straight through it, but turned abruptly, and flowed along the side to the end of it, where its way to the sea was open. On the point of the ridge were a few more firs: except these, those about the cottage, the mole on the hill-cheek, and the plantation about the New House, up or down was not a tree to be seen. The girls stood for a moment looking.

"It's really quite pretty!" said Christina with condescension. "It has actually something of what one misses here so much—a certain cosy look! Tidy it is too! As you say, Mercy, it might be in England —only for the poverty of its trees.—And oh those wretched bare hills!" she added, as she turned away and moved on.

"Wait till the heather is quite out: then you will have colour to make up for the bareness."

"Tell true now, Mercy: that you are Scotch need not keep you from speaking the truth:—don't you think heather just—well—just a leetle magentaish?—not a colour to be altogether admired?—just a little vulgar, don't you know? The fashion has changed so much within the last few years!"

"No, I don't think so; and if I did I should be ashamed of it. I suppose poor old mother Earth ought to go to the pre-Raphaelites to be taught how to dress herself!"

Mercy spoke with some warmth, but Christina was not sufficiently interested to be cross. She made no answer.

They were now at the part of the road which crossed the descending spur as it left the hill-side. Here they stopped again, and looked down the rocky slope. There was hardly anything green betwixt them and the old ruin—little but stones on a mass of rock; but immediately beyond the ruin the green began: there it seemed as if a wave of the meadow had risen and overflowed the spur, leaving its turf behind it. Catching sight of Hope and Grace as they ran about the ruin, they went to join them, the one drawn by a vague interest in the exuviae of vanished life, the other by mere curiosity to see inside the care-worn, protesting walls. Through a gap that might once have been a door, they entered the heart of the sad unhoping thing dropt by the Past on its way to oblivion: nothing looks so unlike life as a dead body, nothing so unfit for human dwelling as a long-forsaken house.

Finding in one corner a broken stair, they clambered up to a gap in the east wall; and as they reached it, heard the sound of a horse's feet. Looking down .the road, they saw a gig approaching with two men. It had reached a part not so steep, and was coming at a trot.

"Why!" exclaimed Christina, "there's Val!—and some one with him!"

"I heard the governor say to mamma," returned Mercy, "that Val was going to bring a college friend with him,—'for a pop at the grouse,' he said. I wonder what he will be like!"

"He's a good-big-looking fellow," said Christina.

They drew nearer.

"You might have said a big, good-looking fellow!" rejoined Mercy.

"He really is handsome!—Now mind, Mercy, I was the first to discover it!" said Christina.

"Indeed you were not!—At least I was the first to SAY it!" returned Mercy. "But you will take him all to yourself anyhow, and I am sure I don't care!"

Yet the girls were not vulgar—they were only common. They did and said vulgar things because they had not the sensitive vitality to shrink from them. They had not been well taught—that is roused to LIVE: in the family was not a breath of aspiration. There was plenty of ambition, that is, aspiration turned hell-ward. They thought themselves as far from vulgar as any lady in any land, being in this vulgar—that they despised the people they called vulgar, yet thought much of themselves for not being vulgar. There was little in them the world would call vulgar; but the world and its ways are vulgar; its breeding will not pass with the ushers of the high countries. The worst in that of these girls was a FAST, disagreeable way of talking, which they owed to a certain governess they had had for a while.

They hastened to the road. The gig came up. Valentine threw the reins to his companion, jumped out, embraced his sisters, and seemed glad to see them. Had he met them after a like interval at home, he would have given them a cooler greeting; but he had travelled so many miles that they seemed not to have met for quite a long time.

"My friend, Mr. Sercombe," he said, jerking his head toward the gig.

Mr. Sercombe raised his POT-LID—the last fashion in head-gear—and acquaintance was made.

"We'll drive on, Sercombe," said Valentine, jumping up. "You see, Chris, we're half dead with hunger! Do you think we shall find anything to eat?"

"Judging by what we left at breakfast," replied Christina, "I should say you will find enough for—one of you; but you had better go and see."

CHAPTER IV.

THE SHOP IN THE VILLAGE.

Two or three days have passed. The sun had been set for an hour, and the night is already rather dark notwithstanding the long twilight of these northern regions, for a blanket of vapour has gathered over the heaven, and a few stray drops have begun to fall from it. A thin wind now and then wakes, and gives a feeble puff, but seems immediately to change its mind and resolve not to blow, but let the rain come down. A drearier-looking spot for human abode it would be difficult to imagine, except it were as much of the sandy Sahara, or of the ashy, sage-covered waste of western America. A muddy road wound through huts of turf—among them one or two of clay, and one or two of stone, which were more like cottages. Hardly one had a window two feet square, and many of their windows had no glass. In almost all of them the only chimney was little more than a hole in the middle of the thatch. This rendered the absence of glass in the windows not so objectionable; for, left without ordered path to its outlet, the smoke preferred a circuitous route, and lingered by the way, filling the air. Peat-smoke, however, is both wholesome and pleasant, nor was there mingled with it any disagreeable smell of cooking. Outside were no lamps; the road was unlighted save by the few rays that here and there crept from a window, casting a doubtful glimmer on the mire.

One of the better cottages sent out a little better light, though only from a tallow candle, through the open upper half of a door horizontally divided in two. Except by that same half-door, indeed, little light could enter the place, for its one window was filled with all sorts of little things for sale. Small and inconvenient for the humblest commerce, this was not merely the best, it was the only shop in the hamlet.

There were two persons in it, one before and one behind the counter. The latter was a young woman, the former a man.

He was leaning over the counter—whether from weariness, listlessness, or interest in his talk with the girl behind, it would not have been easy, in the dim light and deep shadow, to say. He seemed quite at home, yet the young woman treated him with a marked, though unembarrassed respect. The candle stood to one side of them upon the counter, making a ghastly halo in the damp air; and in the light puff that occasionally came in at the door, casting the shadow of one of a pair of scales, now on this now on that of the two faces. The young woman was tall and dark, with a large forehead: —so much could be seen; but the sweetness of her mouth, the blueness of her eyes, the extreme darkness of her hair, were not to be distinguished. The man also was dark. His coat was of some rough brown material, probably dyed and woven in the village, and his kilt of tartan. They were more than well worn—looked even in that poor light a little shabby. On his head was the highland bonnet called a glengarry. His profile was remarkable—hardly less than grand, with a certain aquiline expression, although the nose was not roman. His eyes appeared very dark, but in the daylight were greenish hazel. Usually he talked with the girl in Gaelic, but was now speaking English, a far purer English than that of most English people, though with something of the character of book-English as distinguished from conversation-English, and a very perceptible accent.

"And when was it you heard from Lachlan, Annie?" he asked.

After a moment's pause, during which she had been putting away things in a drawer of the counter—not so big as many a kitchen dresser—

"Last Thursday it was, sir," answered the girl. "You know we hear every month, sometimes oftener."

"Yes; I know that.—I hope the dear fellow is well?"

"He is quite well and of good hope. He says he will soon come and see us now."

"And take you away, Annie?"

"Well, sir," returned Annie, after a moment's hesitation, "he does not SAY so!"

33

"If he did not mean it, he would be a rascal, and I should have to kill him. But my life on Lachlan's honesty!"

"Thank you, sir. He would lay down his for you."

"Not if you said to him, DON'T!-eh, Annie?"

"But he would, Macruadh!" returned the young woman, almost angrily. "Are not you his chief?"

"Ah, that is all over now, my girl! There are no chiefs, and no clans any more! The chiefs that need not, yet sell their land like Esau for a mess of pottage—and their brothers with it! And the Sasunnach who buys it, claims rights over them that never grew on the land or were hid in its caves! Thank God, the poor man is not their slave, but he is the worse off, for they will not let him eat, and he has nowhere to go. My heart is like to break for my people. Sometimes I feel as if I would gladly die."

"Oh, sir! don't say that!" expostulated the young woman, and her voice trembled. "Every heart in Glenruadh is glad when it goes well with the Macruadh."

"Yes, yes; I know you all love my father's son and my uncle's nephew; but how can it go well with the Macruadh when it goes ill with his clan? There is no way now for a chief to be the father of his people; we are all poor together! My uncle—God rest his soul!—they managed it so, I suppose, as to persuade him there was no help for it! Well, a man must be an honest man, even if there be no way but ruin! God knows, as we've all heard my father say a hundred times from the pulpit, there's no ruin but dishonesty! For poverty and hard work, he's a poor creature would crouch for those!"

"He who well goes down hill, holds his head up!" said Annie, and a pause followed.

"There are strangers at the New House, we hear," she said.

"From a distance I saw some young ladies, and one or two men. I don't desire to see more of them. God forbid I should wish them any manner of harm! but—I hardly understand myself—I don't like to see them there. I am afraid it is pride. They are rich, I hear, so we shall not be troubled with attention from them; they will look down upon us."

"Look down on the Macruadh!" exclaimed Annie, as if she could not believe her ears.

"Not that I should heed that!" he went on. "A cock on the barn-ridge looks down on you, and you don't feel offended! What I do dread is looking down on them. There is something in me that can hate, Annie, and I fear it. There is something about the land—I don't care about money, but I feel like a miser about the land!—I don't mean ANY land; I shouldn't care to buy land unless it had once been ours; but what came down to me from my own people—with my own people upon it—I would rather turn the spigot of the molten gold and let it run down the abyss, than a rood of that slip from me! I feel it even a disgrace to have lost what of it I never had!"

"Indeed, Macruadh," said Annie, "it's a hard time! There is no money in the country! And fast the people are going after Lachlan!"

"I shall miss you, Annie!"

"You are very kind to us all, sir."

"Are you not all my own! And you have to take care of for Lachlan's sake besides. He left you solemnly to my charge—as if that had been necessary, the foolish fellow, when we are foster-brothers!"

Again came a pause.

"Not a gentleman-farmer left from one end of the strath to the other!" said the chief at length. "When Ian is at home, we feel just like two old turkey-cocks left alone in the yard!"

"Say two golden eagles, sir, on the cliff of the rock."

"Don't compare us to the eagle, Annie. I do not love the bird. He is very proud and greedy and cruel, and never will know the hand that tames him. He is the bird of the monarch or the earl, not the bird of the father of his people. But he is beautiful, and I do not kill him."

"They shot another, the female bird, last week! All the birds are going! Soon there will be nothing but the great sheep and the little grouse. The capercailzie's gone, and the ptarmigan's gone!—Well, there's a world beyond!"

"Where the birds go, Annie?—Well, it may be! But the ptarmigan's not gone yet, though there are not many; and for the capercailzie—only who that loves them will be here to see!—But do you really think there is a heaven for all God's creatures, Annie? Ian does."

"I don't know what I said to make you think so, sir! When the heart aches the tongue mistakes. But how is my lady, your mother?"

"Pretty well, thank you—wonderfully cheerful. It is time I went home to her. Lachlan would think I was playing him false, and making love to you on my own account!"

"No fear! He would know better than that! He would know too, if she was not belonging to Lachlan, her father's daughter would not let her chief humble himself."

"You're one of the old sort, Annie! Good night. Mind you tell Lachlan I never miss a chance of looking in to see how you are getting on."

"I will. Good night, Macruadh."

They shook hands over the counter, and the young chief took his departure.

As he stood up, he showed a fine-made, powerful frame, over six feet in height, and perfectly poised. With a great easy stride he swept silently out of the shop; nor from gait any more than look would one have thought he had been all day at work on the remnant of property he could call his own.

To a cit it would have seemed strange that one sprung from innumerable patriarchal ancestors holding the land of the country, should talk so familiarly with a girl in a miserable little shop in a most miserable hamlet; it would have seemed stranger yet that such a one should toil at the labour the soul of a cit despises; but stranger than both it would seem to him, if he saw how such a man is tempted to look down upon HIM.

If less CLEVERNESS is required for country affairs, they leave the more room for thinking. There are great and small in every class; here and there is a ploughman that understands Burns, here and there a large-minded shopkeeper, here and there perhaps an unselfish duke. Doubtless most of the youth's ancestors would likewise have held such labour unworthy of a gentleman, and would have preferred driving to their hills a herd of lowland cattle; but this, the last Macruadh, had now and then a peep into the kingdom of heaven.

CHAPTER V.

THE CHIEF.

The Macruadh strode into the dark, and down the village, wasting no time in picking his way—thence into the yet deeper dark of the moorland hills. The rain was beginning to come down in earnest, but he did not heed it; he was thoroughbred, and feared no element. An umbrella was to him a ludicrous thing: how could a little rain—as he would have called it had it come down in torrents—hurt any one!

The Macruadh, as the few who yet held by the sore-frayed, fast-vanishing skirt of clanship, called him, was the son of the last minister of the parish-a godly man, who lived that which he could ill explain, and was immeasurably better than those parts of his creed which, from a sense of duty, he pushed to the front. For he held devoutly by the root of which he spoke too little, and it supplied much sap to his life and teaching—out of the pulpit. He was a genial, friendly, and by nature even merry man, always ready to share what he had, and making no show of having what he had not, either in wisdom, knowledge, or earthly goods. His father and brother had been owners of the property and chiefs of the clan, much beloved by the poor of it, and not a little misunderstood by most of the more nourishing. For a great hunger after larger means, the ambition of the mammon-ruled world, had arisen in the land, and with it a rage for emigration. The uncle of the present Macruadh did all he could to keep his people at home, lived on a couple of hundreds a year himself, and let many of his farms to his gentlemen-tacksmen, as they were called, at lower rents; but it was unavailing; one after another departed, until his land lay in a measure waste, and he grew very poor, mourning far more over his clan and his country than his poverty. In more prosperous times he had scraped together a little money, meaning it, if he could but avoid spending it in his old age, for his brother, who must soon succeed him; for he was himself a bachelor—the result of a romantic attachment and sorrow in his youth; but he lent it to a company which failed, and so lost it. At length he believed himself compelled, for the good of his people, to part with all but a mere remnant of the property. From the man to whom he sold it, Mr. Peregrine

Palmer bought it for twice the money, and had still a good bargain. But the hopes of the laird were disappointed: in the sheep it fed, and the grouse it might be brought to breed, lay all its value in the market; there was no increase in the demand for labour; and more and more of the peasantry emigrated, or were driven to other parts of the country. Such was the present treatment of the land, causing human life to ebb from it, and working directly counter to the creative God.

The laird retired to the humble cottage of his brother the pastor, just married rather late in life—where every comfort love could give waited for him; but the thought that he could have done better for his people by retaining the land soon wore him out; and having made a certain disposition of the purchase-money, he died.

What remained of the property came to the minister. As for the chieftainship, that had almost died before the chief; but, reviving by union with the reverence felt for the minister, it took thereafter a higher form. When the minister died, the idea of it transmitted to his son was of a peculiarly sacred character; while in the eyes of the people, the authority of the chief and the influence of the minister seemed to meet reborn in Alister notwithstanding his youth. In himself he was much beloved, and in love the blessed rule, blessed where understood, holds, that to him that hath shall be given, he only who has being fit to receive. The love the people bore to his father, both pastor and chief, crowned head and heart of Alister. Scarce man or woman of the poor remnant of the clan did not love the young Macruadh.

On his side was true response. With a renewed and renovating conscience, and a vivid sense that all things had to be made new, he possessed an old strong heart, clinging first to his father and mother, and then to the shadow even of any good thing that had come floating down the ages. Call it a dream, a wild ideal, a foolish fancy—call it what you please, he was filled with the notion of doing something in his own person and family, having the remnant of the clan for the nucleus of his endeavour, to restore to a vital reality, let it be of smallest extent, that most ancient of governments, the patriarchal, which, all around, had rotted into the feudal, in its turn rapidly disintegrating into the mere dust and ashes of the kingdom of the dead, over which Mammon reigns supreme. There may have been youthful presumption and some folly in the notion, but it sprang neither from presumption nor folly, but from simple humanity, and his sense of the responsibility he neither could nor would avoid, as the person upon whom had devolved the headship, however shadowy, of a house, ruinous indeed, but not yet razed.

The castle on the ridge stood the symbol of the family condition. It had, however, been a ruin much longer than any one alive could remember. Alister's uncle had lived in a house on the spot where Mr. Peregrine Palmer's now stood; the man who bought it had pulled it down to build that which Mr. Palmer had since enlarged. It was but a humble affair—a great cottage in stone, much in the style of that in which the young chief now lived—only six times the size, with the one feature indispensable to the notion of a chief's residence, a large hall. Some would say it was but a huge kitchen; but it was the sacred place of the house, in which served the angel of hospitality. THERE was always plenty to eat and drink for any comer, whether he had "claim" or not: the question of claim where was need, was not thought of. When the old house had to make room for the new, the staves of the last of its half-pipes of claret, one of which used always to stand on tap amidst the peat-smoke, yielded its final ministration to humanity by serving to cook a few meals for mason and carpenter.

The property of Clanruadh, for it was regarded as clan-property BECAUSE belonging to the chief, stretched in old time away out of sight in all directions—nobody, in several, could tell exactly how far, for the undrawn boundary lines lay in regions of mist and cloud, in regions stony, rocky, desert, to which a red deer, not to say a stray sheep, rarely ascended. At one time it took in a portion at least of every hill to be seen from the spot where stood the ruin. The chief had now but a small farm, consisting of some fair soil on the slope of a hill, and some very good in the valley on both sides of the burn; with a hill-pasture that was not worth measuring in acres, for it abounded in rocks, and was prolific in heather and ling, with patches of coarse grass here and there, and some extent of good high-valley grass, to which the small black cattle and black-faced sheep were driven in summer. Beyond periodical burnings of the heather, this uplifted portion received no attention save from the mist, the snow, the rain, the sun, and the sweet air. A few grouse and black game bred on it, and many mountain-hares, with martens, wild cats, and other VERMIN. But so tender of life was the Macruadh that, though he did not spare these last, he did not like killing even a fox or a hooded crow, and never shot a bird for sport, or would let another shoot one, though the poorest would now and then beg a bird or two from him, sure of having their request. It seemed to him as if the creatures were almost a part of his clan, of which also he had to take care against a greedy world. But as the deer and the birds ranged where they would, it was not much he could do for them—as little almost as for the men and women that had gone over the sea, and were lost to their country in Canada.

Regret, and not any murmur, stirred the mind of Alister Macruadh when he thought of the change that had passed on all things around him. He had been too well taught for grumbling—least of all at what was plainly the will of the Supreme—inasmuch as, however man might be to blame, the thing was there. Personal regrets he had none beyond those of family feeling and transmitted SENTIMENT. He was able to understand something of the signs of the times, and saw that nothing could bring back the old way—saw that nothing comes back—at least in the same form; saw that there had been much that ought not to come back, and that, if patriarchal ways were ever to return, they must rise out of, and be administered upon loftier principles—must begin afresh, and be wrought out afresh from the bosom of a new Abraham, capable of so bringing up his children that a new development of the one natural system, of government should be possible with and through them. Perhaps even now, in the new country to which so many of his people were gone, some shadowy reappearance of the old fashion might have begun to take shape on a higher level, with loftier aims, and in circumstances holding out fewer temptations to the evils of the past!

Alister could not, at his years, have generated such thoughts but for the wisdom that had gone before him—first the large-minded speculation of his father, who was capable even of discarding his prejudices where he saw they might mislead him; and next, the response of his mother to the same: she was the only one who entirely understood her husband. Isobel Macruadh was a woman of real thinking-power. Her sons being but boys when their father died, she at once took the part of mediator between the mind of the father and that of his sons; and besides guiding them on the same principles, often told them things their father had said, and talked with them of things they had heard him say.

One of the chief lessons he left them wrought well for the casting out of all with which the feudal system had debased the patriarchal; and the poverty shared with the clan had powerfully helped: it was spoken against the growing talionic regard of human relations—that, namely, the conditions of a bargain fulfilled on both sides, all is fulfilled between the bargaining parties.

"In the possibility of any bargain," he had said, "are involved eternal conditions: there is relationship—there is brotherhood. Even to give with a denial of claim, to be kind under protest, is an injury, is charity without the love, is salt without the saltness. If we spent our lives in charity we should never overtake neglected claims—claims neglected from the very beginning of the relations of men. If a man say, 'I have not been unjust; I owed the man nothing;' he sides with Death—says with the typical murderer, 'Am I my brother's keeper?' builds the tombs of those his fathers slew."

In the bosom of young Alister Macruadh, the fatherly relation of the strong to the weak survived the disappearance of most of the outward signs of clan-kindred: the chieftainship was SUBLIMED in him. The more the body of outer fact died, the stronger grew in him the spirit of the relation. As some savage element of a race will reappear in an individual of it after ages of civilization, so may good old ways of thinking and feeling, modes long gone out of fashion and practice, survive and revive modified by circumstance, in an individual of a new age. Such a one will see the customs of his ancestors glorified in the mists of the past; what is noble in them will appeal to all that is best in his nature, spurring the most generous of his impulses, and stirring up the conscience that would be void of offence. When the operative force of such regards has been fostered by the teaching of a revered parent; when the influences he has left behind are nourished and tended, with thorough belief and devoted care, by her who shared his authority in life, and now bears alone the family sceptre, there can be no bound set to their possible potency in a mind of high spiritual order. The primary impulse became with Alister a large portion of his religion: he was the shepherd of the much ravaged and dwindled Macruadh-fold; it was his church, in which the love of the neighbour was intensified in the love of the relation and dependent. To aid and guard this his flock, was Alister's divine service. It was associated with a great dislike of dogma, originating in the recoil of the truth within him from much that was commonly held and taught for true.

Call the thing enthusiasm or what you will, so you believe it there, and genuine.

It was only towards the poor of a decayed clan he had opportunity of exercising the cherished relation; almost all who were not poor had emigrated before the lands were sold; and indeed it was only the poor who set store by their unity with the old head. Not a few of the clan, removed elsewhither, would have smiled degenerate, and with scorn in their amusement, at the idea of Alister's clinging to any supposed reality in the position he could claim. Among such nevertheless were several who, having made money by trade, would each have been glad enough to keep up old traditions, and been ready even to revive older, had the headship fallen to him. But in the hands of a man whom, from the top of their wealth, they regarded as but a poor farmer, they forgot all about it—along with a few other more important and older-world matters; for where Mammon gets in his foot, he will soon be lord of the house, and turn not merely Rank, his rival demon, out of doors, but God himself. Alister indeed lived in a dream; he did not know how far the sea of hearts had ebbed, leaving him alone on the mount of his vision; but he dreamed a dream that was worth dreaming; comfort and help flowed from it to those about him, nor did it fail to yield his own soul refreshment also. All dreams are not false; some dreams are truer than the plainest facts. Fact at best is but a garment of truth, which has ten thousand changes of raiment woven in the same loom. Let the dreamer only do the truth of his dream, and one day he will realize all that was worth realizing in it—and a great deal more and better than it contained. Alister had no far-reaching visions of anything to come out of his; he had, like the true man he was, only the desire to live up to his idea of what the people looked up to in him. The one thing that troubled him was, that his uncle, whom he loved so dearly, should have sold the land.

Doubtless there was pride mingled with his devotion, and pride is an evil thing. Still it was a human and not a devilish pride. I would not be misunderstood as defending pride, or even excusing it in any shape; it is a thing that must be got rid of at all costs; but even for evil we must speak the truth; and the pride of a good man, evil as it is, and in him more evil than in an evil man, yet cannot be in itself such a bad thing as the pride of a bad man. The good man would at once recognize and reject the pride of a bad man. A pride that loves cannot be so bad as a pride that hates. Yet if the good man do not cast out his pride, it will sink him lower than the bad man's, for it will degenerate into a worse pride than that of any bad man. Each must bring its own divinely-ordained consequence.

There is one other point in the character of the Macruadh which I must mention ere I pass on; in this region, and at this time, it was a great peculiarity, one that yielded satisfaction to few of the clan, and made him even despised in the strath: he hated whisky, and all the drinking customs associated with it. In this he was not original; he had not come to hate it from noting the degradation and crime that attended it, or that as poverty grew, drunkenness grew, men who had used it in moderation taking more and more as circumstances became more adverse, turning sadness into slavery: he had been brought up to hate it. His father, who, as a clergyman doing his endeavour for the welfare of his flock, found himself greatly thwarted by its deadening influences, rendering men callous not only to the special vice itself, but to worse vices as well, had banished it from his table and his house; while the mother had from their very childhood instilled a loathing of the national weakness and its physical means into the minds of her sons. In her childhood she had seen its evils in her own father: by no means a drunkard, he was the less of a father because he did as others did.

Never an evening passed without his drinking his stated portion of whisky-toddy, growing more and more subject to attacks of had temper, with consequent injustice and unkindness. The recollection may have made her too sweeping in her condemnation of the habit, but I doubt it; and anyhow a habit is not a man, and we need not much condemn that kind of injustice. We need not be tender over a habit which, though not all bad, yet leads to endless results that are all bad. I would follow such to its grave without many tears!

Isobel Macruadh was one of those rare women who preserve in years the influence gained in youth; and the thing that lay at the root of the fact was her justice. For though her highland temper would occasionally burst out in hot flame, everyone knew that if she were in the wrong, she would see it and say it before any one else would tell her of it. This justice it was, ready against herself as for another, that fixed the influence which her goodness and her teaching of righteousness gained.

Her eldest child, a girl, died in infancy. Alister and Ian were her whole earthly family, and they worshipped her.

CHAPTER VI.

WORK AND WAGE.

Alister strode through the night, revolving no questions hard to solve, though such were not strangers to him. He had not been to a university like his brother, but he had had a good educational beginning—who ever had more than a beginning?—chiefly from his father, who for his time and opportunity was even a learned man—and better, a man who knew what things were worth a man's human while, and what were not: he could and did think about things that a man must think about or perish; and his son Alister had made himself able to think about what he did not know, by doing the thing he did know. But now, as he walked, fighting with the wind, his bonnet of little shelter pulled down on his forehead, he was thinking mostly of Lachlan his foster-brother, whose devotion had done much to nourish in him the sense that he was head of the clan. He had not far to go to reach his home—about a couple of miles.

He had left the village a quarter of the way behind him, when through the darkness he spied something darker yet by the roadside. Going up to it, he found an old woman, half sitting, half standing, with a load of peats in a creel upon her back, unable, apparently, for the moment at least, to proceed. Alister knew at once by her shape and posture who she was.

"Ah, mistress Conal!" he said, "I am sorry to see you resting on such a night so near your own door. It means you have filled your creel too full, and tired yourself too much."

"I am not too much tired, Macruadh!" returned the old woman, who was proud and cross-tempered, and had a reputation for witchcraft, which did her neither much good nor much harm.

"Well, whether you are tired or not, I believe I am the stronger of the two!"

"Small doubt of that, Alister!" said mistress Conal with a sigh.

"Then I will take your creel, and you will soon be home. Come along! It is going to be a wild night!"

So saying he took the rope from the neck of the old woman right gently, and threw the creel with a strong swing over his shoulder. This dislodged a few of the topmost of the peats which the poor old thing had been a long way to fetch. She heard them fall, and one of them struck her foot. She started up, almost in a rage.

"Sir! sir! my peats!" she cried. "What would you be throwing away the good peats into the dark for, letting that swallow them they should swallow!"

These words, as all that passed between them, were spoken neither in Scotch nor English, but in Gaelic—which, were I able to write it down, most of my readers would no more understand than they would Phoenician: we must therefore content ourselves with what their conversation comes to in English, which, if deficient compared with Gaelic in vowel-sounds, yet serves to say most things capable of being said.

"I am sorry, mistress Conal; but we'll not be losing them," returned the laird gently, and began to feel about the road for the fallen peats.

"How many were there, do you think, of them that fell?" he asked, rising after a vain search.

"How should I be knowing! But I am sure there would be nigh six of them!" answered the woman, in a tone of deep annoyance—nor was it much wonder; they were precious to the cold, feeble age that had gone so far to fetch so few.

The laird again stooped his long back, and searched and searched, feeling on all sides around him. He picked up three. Not another, after searching for several minutes, could he find.

"I'm thinking that must be all of them, but I find only three!" he said. "Come, let us go home! You must not make your cough worse for one or two peats, perhaps none!"

"Three, Macruadh, three!" insisted the old woman in wavering voice, broken by coughing; for, having once guessed six, she was not inclined to lower her idea of her having.

"Well, well! we'll count them when we get home!" said Alister, and gave his hand to her to help her up.

She yielded grumbling, and, bowed still though relieved from her burden, tottered by his side along the dark, muddy, wind-and-rain-haunted road.

"Did you see my niece to-night at the shop?" she asked; for she was proud of being so nearly related to those who kept the shop of the hamlet.

"That I did," answered the chief; and a little talk followed about Lachlan in Canada.

No one could have perceived from the way in which the old woman accepted his service, and the tone in which she spoke to him while he bent under her burden, that she no less than loved her chief; but everybody only smiled at mistress Conal's rough speech. That night, ere she went to bed, she prayed for the Macruadh as she never prayed for one of her immediate family. And if there was a good deal of superstition mingled with her prayer, the main thing in it was genuine, that is, the love that prompted it; and if God heard only perfect prayers, how could he be the prayer-hearing God?

Her dwelling stood but a stone's-throw from the road, and presently they turned up to it by a short steep ascent. It was a poor hut, mostly built of turf; but turf makes warm walls, impervious to the wind, and it was a place of her own!—that is, she had it to herself, a luxury many cannot even imagine, while to others to he able to be alone at will seems one of the original necessities of life. Even the Lord, who probably had not always a room to himself in the poor houses he staid at, could not do without solitude; therefore not unfrequently spent the night in the open air, on the quiet, star-served hill: there even for him it would seem to have been easier to find an entrance into that deeper solitude which, it is true, he did not need in order to find his Father and his God, but which apparently he did need in order to come into closest contact with him who was the one joy of his life, whether his hard life on earth, or his blessed life in heaven.

The Macruadh set down the creel, and taking out peat after peat, piled them up against the wall, where already a good many waited their turn to be laid on the fire; for, as the old woman said, she must carry a few when she could, and get ahead with her store ere the winter came, or she would soon be devoured: there was a death that always prowled about old people, she said, watching for the fire to go out. Many of the Celts are by nature poets, and mistress Conal often spoke in a manner seldom heard from the lips of a lowland woman. The common forms of Gaelic are more poetic than those of most languages, and could have originated only with a poetic people, while mistress Conal was by no means an ordinary type of her people; maugre her ill temper and gruffness, she thought as well as spoke like a poetess. This, conjoined with the gift of the second sight, had helped to her reputation as a witch.

As the chief piled the peats, he counted them. She sat watching him and them from a stone that made part of a rude rampart to the hearth.

"I told you so, Macruadh!" she said, the moment she saw his hand return empty from the bottom of the creel. "I was positive there should be three more!—But what's on the road is not with the devil."

"I am very sorry!" said the chief, who thought it wiser not to contradict her.

He would have searched his sporan for a coin to make up to her for the supposed loss of her peats; but he knew well enough there was not a coin in it. He shook hands with her, bade her good night, and went, closing the door carefully behind him against a great gust of wind that struggled to enter, threatening to sweep the fire she was now blowing at with her wrinkled, leather-like lips, off the hearth altogether—a thing that had happened before, to the danger of the whole building, itself of the substance burning in the middle of its floor.

The Macruadh ran down the last few steep steps of the path, and jumped into the road. Through the darkness came the sound of one springing aside with a great start, and the click of a gun-lock.

"Who goes there?" cried a rather tremulous voice.

"The Macruadh," answered the chief.

The utterance apparently conveyed nothing.

"Do you belong to these parts?" said the voice.

A former Macruadh might have answered, "No; these parts belong to me;" Alister curtly replied,

"I do."

"Here then, my good fellow! take my game-bag, and carry it as far as the New House—if you know where I mean. I will give you a shilling."

One moment the chief spent in repressing a foolish indignation; the next he spent in reflection.

Had he seen how pale and tired was the youth with the gun, he would have offered to carry his bag for him; to offer and to be asked, however, most people find different; and here the offer of payment added to the difficulty. But the word SHILLING had raised the vision of the old woman in her lonely cottage, brooding over the loss, real or imaginary mattered nothing, of her three far-borne peats. What a happy night, through all the wind and the rain, would a silver shilling under her chaff pillow give her! The thought froze the chief's pride, and warmed his heart. What right had he to deny her such a pleasure! It would cost him nothing! It would even bring him a little amusement! The chief of Clanruadh carrying his game-bag for a Sasunnach fellow to earn a shilling! the idea had a touch of humorous consolation in it. I will not assert the consolation strong enough to cast quite out a certain feeling of shame that mingled with his amusement—a shame which—is it not odd!—he would not have felt had his sporan been full of sovereigns. But the shame was not altogether a shameful one; a fanciful fear of degrading the chieftainship, and a vague sense of the thing being an imposition, had each a part in it. There could be nothing dishonest, however, in thus earning a shilling for poor mistress Conal!

"I will carry your bag," he said, "but I must have the shilling first, if you please."

"Oh!" rejoined Valentine Palmer. "You do not trust me! How then am I to trust you?"

"Sir!" exclaimed Alister—and, again finding himself on the point of being foolish, laughed.

"I will pay you when the job is done," said Valentine.

"That is quite fair, but it does not suit my purpose," returned Alister.

They were walking along the road side by side, but each could scarcely see anything of the other. The sportsman was searching his pockets to find a shilling. He succeeded, and, groping, put it in Alister's hand, with the words—

"All right! it is only a shilling! There it is! But it is not yours yet: here is the bag!"

Alister took the bag, turned, and ran back.

"Hillo!" cried Valentine.

But Alister had disappeared, and as soon as he turned up the soft path to the cottage, his steps became inaudible through the wind.

He opened the door, went in, laid the shilling on the back of the old woman's hand, and without a word hurried out again, and down to the road.

The stranger was some distance ahead, tramping wearily on through the darkness, and grumbling at his folly in bribing a fellow with a shilling to carry off his game-bag. Alister overtook him.

"Oh, here you are after all!" exclaimed Valentine. "I thought you had made off with work and wages both! What did you do it for?"

"I wanted to give the shilling to an old woman close by."

"Your mother—eh?"

"No."

"Your grandmother?"

"No."

"SOME relation then!" insisted the stranger.

"Doubtless," answered the laird, and Valentine thought him a surly fellow.

They walked on in silence. The youth could hardly keep up with Alister, who thought him ill bred, and did not care for his company.

"Why do you walk so fast?" said Valentine.

"Because I want to get home," replied Alister.

"But I paid you to keep me company!"

"You paid me to carry your bag. I will leave it at the New House."

His coolness roused the weary youth.

"You rascal!" he said; "you keep alongside of me, or I'll pepper you."

As he spoke, he shifted his gun. But Alister had already, with a few long strides, put a space of utter darkness between them. He had taken the shilling, and must carry the bag, but did not feel bound to personal attendance. At the same time he could not deny there was reason in the man's unwillingness to trust him. What had he about him to give him in pledge? Nothing but his watch, his father's, a gift of THE PRINCE to the head of the family!—he could not profane that by depositing it for a game-bag! He must yield to his employer, moderate his pace, and move side by side with the Sasunnach!

Again they walked some distance in silence. Alister began to discover that his companion was weary, and his good heart spoke.

"Let me carry your gun," he said.

"See you damned!" returned Valentine, with an angry laugh.

"You fancy your gun protects your bag?"

"I do."

The same instant the gun was drawn, with swift quiet force, through the loop of his arm from behind. Feeling himself defenceless, he sprang at the highlander, but he eluded him, and in a moment was out of his reach, lost in the darkness. He heard the lock of one barrel snap: it was not loaded; the second barrel went off, and he gave a great jump, imagining himself struck. The next instant the gun was below his arm again.

"It will be lighter to carry now!" said the Macruadh; "but if you like I will take it."

"Take it, then. But no!—By Jove, I wish there was light enough to see what sort of a rascal you look!"

"You are not very polite!"

"Mind your own politeness. I was never so roughly served in my life!—by a fellow too that had taken my money! If I knew where to find a magistrate in this beastly place,—"

"You would tell him I emptied your gun because you threatened me with it!"

"You were going off with my bag!"

"Because I undertook to carry your bag, was I bound to endure your company?"

"Alister!" said a quiet voice out of the darkness.

The highlander started, and in a tone strangely tremulous, yet with a kind of triumph in it, answered—

"Ian!"

The one word said, he stood still, but as in the act to run, staring into the darkness. The next moment he flung down the game-bag, and two men were in each other's arms.

"Where are you from, Ian?" said the chief at length, in a voice broken with gladness.

All Valentine understood of the question, for it was in Gaelic, was its emotion, and he scorned a fellow to show the least sign of breaking down.

"Straight from Moscow," answered the new-comer. "How is our mother?"

"Well, Ian, thank God!"

"Then, thank God, all is well!"

"What brought you home in such haste?"

"I had a bad dream about my mother, and was a little anxious. There was more reason too, which I will tell you afterwards."

"What were you doing in Moscow? Have you a furlough?"

"No; I am a sort of deserter. I would have thrown up my commission, but had not a chance. In Moscow I was teaching in a school to keep out of the way of the police. But I will tell you all by and by."

The voice was low, veiled, and sad; the joy of the meeting rippled through it like a brook.

The brothers had forgotten the stranger, and stood talking till the patience of Valentine was as much exhausted as his strength.

"Are you going to stand there all night?" he said at last. "This is no doubt very interesting to you, but it is rather a bore to one who can neither see you, nor understand a word you say."

"Is the gentleman a friend of yours, Alister?" asked Ian.

"Not exactly.—But he is a Sasunnach," he concluded in English, "and we ought not to be speaking Gaelic."

"I beg his pardon," said Ian. "Will you introduce me?"

"It is impossible; I do not know his name. I never saw him, and don't see him now. But he insists on my company."

"That is a great compliment. How far?"

"To the New House."

"I paid him a shilling to carry my bag," said Valentine. "He took the shilling, and was going to walk off with my bag!"

"Well?"

"Well indeed! Not at all well! How was I to know—"

"But he didn't—did he?" said Ian, whose voice seemed now to tingle with amusement. "—Alister, you were wrong."

It was an illogical face-about, but Alister responded at once.

"I know it," he said. "The moment I heard your voice, I knew it.—How is it, Ian,"—here he fell back into Gaelic—"that when you are by me, I know what is right so much quicker? I don't understand it. I meant to do right, but—"

"But your pride got up. Alister, you always set out well—nobly—and then comes the devil's turn! Then you begin to do as if you repented! You don't carry the thing right straight out. I hate to see the devil make a fool of a man like you! Do YOU not know that in your own country you owe a stranger hospitality?"

"My own country!" echoed Alister with a groan.

"Yes, your own country—and perhaps more yours than it was your grandfather's! You know who said, 'The meek shall inherit the earth'! If it be not ours in God's way, I for one would not care to call it mine another way."—Here he changed again to English.—"But we must not keep the gentleman standing while we talk!"

"Thank you!" said Valentine. "The fact is, I'm dead beat."

"Have you anything I could carry for you?" asked Ian.

"No, I thank you.—Yes; there! if you don't mind taking my gun?—you speak like a gentleman!"

"I will take it with pleasure."

He took the gun, and they started.

"If you choose, Alister," said his brother, once more in Gaelic, "to break through conventionalities, you must not expect people to allow you to creep inside them again the moment you please."

But the young fellow's fatigue had touched Alister.

"Are you a big man?" he said, taking Valentine gently by the arm.

"Not so big as you, I'll lay you a sovereign," answered Valentine, wondering why he should ask.

"Then look here!" said Alister; "you get astride my shoulders, and I'll carry you home. I believe you're hungry, and that takes the pith out of you!— Come," he went on, perceiving some sign of reluctance in the youth, "you'll break down if you walk much farther!—Here, Ian! you take the bag; you can manage that and the gun too!"

Valentine murmured some objection; but the brothers took the thing so much as a matter of course, and he felt so terribly exhausted—for he had lost his way, and been out since the morning—that he yielded.

Alister doubled himself up on his heels; Valentine got his weary legs over his stalwart shoulders; the chief rose with him as if he had been no heavier than mistress Conal's creel, and bore him along much relieved in his aching limbs.

So little was the chief oppressed by his burden, that he and his brother kept up a stream of conversation, every now and then forgetting their manners and gliding off into Gaelic, but as often recollecting themselves, apologizing, and starting afresh upon the path of English. Long before they reached the end of their journey, Valentine, able from his perch to listen in some measure of ease, came to understand that he had to do, not with rustics, but, whatever their peculiarities, with gentlemen of a noteworthy sort.

The brothers, in the joy of their reunion, talked much of things at home and abroad, avoiding things personal and domestic as often as they spoke English; but when they saw the lights of the New House, a silence fell upon them. At the door, Alister set his burden carefully down.

"There!" he said with a laugh, "I hope I have earned my shilling!"

"Ten times over," answered Valentine; "but I know better now than offer to pay you. I thank you with all my heart."

The door opened, Ian gave the gun and the bag to the butler, and the brothers bade Valentine good night.

Valentine had a strange tale to tell. Sercombe refused to accept his conclusions: if he had offered the men half a crown apiece, he said, they would have pocketed the money.

CHAPTER VII.

MOTHER AND SON.

The sun was shining bright, and the laird was out in his fields. His oats were nearly ready for the scythe, and he was judging where he had best begin to cut them.

His fields lay chiefly along the banks of the stream, occupying the whole breadth of the valley on the east side of the ridge where the cottage stood. On the west side of the ridge, nearly parallel to, and not many yards from it, a small brook ran to join the stream: this was a march betwixt the chief's land and Mr. Peregrine Palmer's. Their respective limit was not everywhere so well defined.

The air was clear and clean, and full of life. The wind was asleep. A consciousness of work approaching completion filled earth and air—a mood of calm expectation, as of a man who sees his end drawing nigh, and awaits the saving judgment of the father of spirits. There was no song of birds—only a crow from the yard, or the cry of a blackcock from the hill; the two streams were left to do all the singing, and they did their best, though their water was low. The day was of the evening of the year; in the full sunshine was present the twilight and the coming night, but there was a sense of readiness on all sides. The fruits of the earth must be housed; that alone remained to be done.

When the laird had made up his mind, he turned towards the house—a lowly cottage, more extensive than many farmhouses, but looking no better. It was well built, with an outside wall of rough stone and lime, and another wall of turf within, lined in parts with wood, making it as warm a nest as any house of the size could be. The door, picturesque with abundant repair, opened by a latch into the kitchen.

For long years the floor of the kitchen had been an earthen one, with the fire on a hearth in the middle of it, as in all the cottages; and the smoke rose into the roof, keeping it very dry and warm, if also very sooty, and thence into the air through a hole in the middle. But some ten years before this time, Alister and Ian, mere lads, had built a chimney outside, and opening the wall, removed the hearth to it—with the smoke also, which now had its own private way to liberty. They then paved the floor with such stones as they could find, in the fields and on the hill, sufficiently flat and smooth on one side, and by sinking them according to their thickness, managed to get a tolerably even surface. Many other improvements followed; and although it was a poor place still, it would at the time of Dr. Johnson's visit to the highlands have been counted a good house, not to be despised by unambitious knight or poor baronet. Nor was the time yet over, when ladies and gentlemen, of all courtesy and good breeding, might be found in such houses.

In the kitchen a deal-dresser, scoured white, stood under one of the tiny windows, giving light enough for a clean-souled cook—and what window-light would ever be enough for one of a different sort? There were only four panes in it, but it opened and closed with a button, and so was superior to many windows. There was a larger on the opposite side, which at times in the winter nights when the cold was great, they filled bodily with a barricade of turf. Here, in the kitchen, the chief takes his meals with his lady-mother. She and Ian have just finished their breakfast, and gone to the other end of the house. The laird broke his fast long ago.

A fire is burning on the hearth—small, for the mid-day-meal is not yet on its way. Everything is tidy; the hearth is swept up, and the dishes are washed: the barefooted girl is reaching the last of them to its place on the rack hehind the dresser. She is a red-haired, blue-eyed Celt, with a pretty face, and a refinement of motion and speech rarer in some other peasantries.

The chief enters, and takes from the wall an old-fashioned gun. He wants a bird or two, for Ian's home-coming is a great event.

"I saw a big stag last night down by the burn, sir," said the girl, "feeding as if he had been the red cow."

"I don't want him to-day, Nancy," returned her master. "Had he big horns?"

"Great horns, sir; but it was too dark to count the tines."

"When was it? Why did you not tell me?"

"I thought it was morning, sir, and when I got up it was the middle of the night. The moon was so shiny that I went to the door and looked out. Just at the narrow leap, I saw him plain."

"If you should see him again, Nancy, scare him. I don't want the Sasunnachs at the New House to see him."

"Hadn't you better take him yourself, Macruadh? He would make fine hams for the winter!"

"Mind your own business, Nancy, and hold your tongue," said the chief, with a smile that took all the harshness from the words. "Don't you tell any one you saw him. For what you know he may be the big stag!"

"Sure no one would kill HIM, sir!" answered the girl aghast.

"I hope not. But get the stoving-pot ready, Nancy; I'm going to find a bird or two. Lest I should not succeed, have a couple of chickens at hand."

"Sir, the mistress has commanded them already."

"That is well; but do not kill them except I am not back in time."

"I understand, sir."

Macruadh knew the stag as well as the horse he rode, and that his habit had for some time been to come down at night and feed on the small border of rich grass on the south side of the burn, between it and the abrupt heathery rise of the hill. For there the burn ran so near the hill, and the ground was so covered with huge masses of grey rock, that there was hardly room for cultivation, and the bank was left in grass.

The stalking of the stag was the passion of the highlander in that part of the country. He cared little for shooting the grouse, black or red, and almost despised those whose ambition was a full bag of such game; he dreamed day and night of killing deer. The chief, however, was in this matter more of a man without being less of a highlander. He loved the deer so much, saw them so much a part of the glory of mountain and sky, sunshine and storm, that he liked to see them living, not dead, and only now and then shot one, when the family had need of it. He felt himself indeed almost the father of the deer as well as of his clan, and mourned greatly that he could do so little now, from the limited range of his property, to protect them. His love for live creatures was not quite equal to that of St. Francis, for he had not conceived the thought of turning wolf or fox from the error of his ways; but even the creatures that preyed upon others he killed only from a sense of duty, and with no pleasure in their death. The heartlessness of the common type of sportsman was loathsome to him. When there was not much doing on the farm, he would sometimes be out all night with his gun, it is true, but he would seldom fire it, and then only at some beast of prey; on the hill-side or in the valley he would lie watching the ways and doings of the many creatures that roam the night—each with its object, each with its reasons, each with its fitting of means to ends. One of the grounds of his dislike to the new possessors of the old land was the raid he feared upon the wild animals.

The laird gone, I will take my reader into the PARLOUR, as they called in English their one sitting-room. Shall I first tell him what the room was like, or first describe the two persons in it? Led up to a picture, I certainly should not look first at the frame; but a description is a process of painting rather than a picture; and when you cannot see the thing in one, but must take each part by itself, and in your mind get it into relation with the rest, there is an advantage, I think, in having a notion of the frame first. For one thing, you cannot see the persons without imagining their surroundings, and if those should be unfittingly imagined, they interfere with the truth of the persons, and you may not be able to get them right after.

The room, then, was about fifteen feet by twelve, and the ceiling was low. On the white walls hung a few frames, of which two or three contained water-colours—not very good, but not displeasing; several held miniature portraits—mostly in red coats, and one or two a silhouette. Opposite the door hung a target of hide, round, and bossed with brass. Alister had come upon it in the house, covering a meal-barrel, to which service it had probably been put in aid of its eluding a search for arms after the battle of Culloden. Never more to cover man's food from mice, or his person from an enemy, it was raised to the WALHALLA of the parlour. Under it rested, horizontally upon two nails, the sword of the chief—a long and broad ANDREW FERRARA, with a plated basket-hilt; beside it hung a dirk—longer than usual, and fine in form, with a carved hilt in the shape of an eagle's head and neck, and its sheath, whose leather was dry and flaky with age, heavily mounted in silver. Below these was a card-table of marquetry with spindle-legs, and on it a work-box of ivory, inlaid with silver and ebony. In the corner stood a harp, an Erard, golden and gracious, not a string of it broken. In the middle of the room was a small square table, covered with a green cloth. An old-fashioned easy chair stood by the chimney; and one sat in it whom to see was to forget her surroundings.

In middle age she is still beautiful, with the rare beauty that shines from the root of the being. Her hair is of the darkest brown, almost black; her eyes are very dark, and her skin is very fair, though the soft bloom, as of reflected sunset, is gone from her cheek, and her hair shows lines of keen silver. Her features are fine, clear, and regular—the chin a little strong perhaps, not for the size, but the fineness of the rest; her form is that of a younger woman; her hand and foot are long and delicate. A more refined and courteous presence could not have been found in the island. The dignity of her carriage nowise marred its grace, or betrayed the least consciousness; she looked dignified because she was dignified. That form of falsehood which consists in assuming the look of what one fain would be, was, as much as any other, impossible to Isobel Macruadh. She wore no cap; her hair was gathered in a large knot near the top of her head. Her gown was of a dark print; she had no ornament except a ring with a single ruby. She was working a bit of net into lace.

She could speak Gaelic as well as any in the glen—perhaps better; but to her sons she always spoke English. To them indeed English was their mother-tongue, in the sense that English only came addressed to themselves from her lips. There were, she said, plenty to teach them Gaelic; she must see to their English.

The one window of the parlour, though not large, was of tolerable size; but little light entered, so shaded was it with a rose-tree in a pot on the sill. By the wall opposite was a couch, and on the couch lay Ian with a book in his hand—a book in a strange language. His mother and he would sometimes be a whole morning together and exchange no more than a word or two, though many a look and smile. It seemed enough for each to be in the other's company. There was a quite peculiar hond between the two. Like so many of the young men of that country, Ian had been intended for the army; but there was in him this much of the spirit of the eagle he resembled, that he passionately loved freedom, and had almost a gypsy's delight in wandering. When he left college, he became tutor in a Russian family of distinction, and after that accepted a commission in the household troops of the Czar. But wherever he went, he seemed, as he said once to his mother, almost physically aware of a line stretching between him and her, which seemed to vibrate when he grew anxious about her. The bond between him and his brother was equally strong, but in feeling different. Between him and Alister it was a cable; between him and his mother a harpstring; in the one case it was a muscle, in the other a nerve. The one retained, the other drew him. Given to roaming as he was, again and again he returned, from pure love-longing, to what he always felt as the PROTECTION of his mother. It was protection indeed he often had sought—protection from his own glooms, which nothing but her love seemed able to tenuate.

He was tall—if an inch above six feet be tall, but not of his brother's fine proportion. He was thin, with long slender fingers and feet like his mother's. His small, strong bones were covered with little more than hard muscle, but every motion of limb or body was grace. At times, when lost in thought and unconscious of movement, an observer might have imagined him in conversation with some one unseen, towards whom he was carrying himself with courtesy: plain it was that courtesy with him was not a graft upon the finest stock, but an essential element. His forehead was rather low, freckled, and crowned with hair of a foxy red; his eyes were of the glass-gray or green loved of our elder poets; his nose was a very eagle in itself—large and fine. He more resembled the mask of the dead Shakspere than any other I have met, only in him the proportions were a little exaggerated; his nose was a little too large, and his mouth a little too small for the mask; but the mingled sweetness and strength in the curves of the latter prevented the impression of weakness generally given by the association of such a nose and such a mouth. On his short upper lip was a small light moustache, and on his face not a hair more. In rest his countenance wore a great calmness, but a calmness that might seem rooted in sadness.

While the mother might, more than once in a day, differ to fault-finding from her elder-born—whom she admired, notwithstanding, as well as loved, from the bottom of her heart—she was never KNOWN to say a word in opposition to the younger. It was even whispered that she was afraid of him. It was not so; but her reverence for Ian was such that, even when she felt bound not to agree with him, she seldom had the confidence that, differing from HIM, she was in the right. Sometimes in the middle of the night she would slip like a ghost into the room where he lay, and sit by his bed till the black cock, the gray cock, the red cock crew. The son might be awake all the time, and the mother suspect him awake, yet no word pass between them. She would rise and go as she came. Her feeling for her younger son was like that of Hannah for her eldest—intensest love mixed with strangest reverence. But there were vast alternations and inexplicable minglings in her thoughts of him. At one moment she would regard him as gifted beyond his fellows for some great work, at another be filled with a horrible fear that he was in rebellion against the God of his life. Doubtless mothers are far too ready to think THEIR sons above the ordinary breed of sons: self, unpossessed of God, will worship itself in its offspring; yet the sons whom HOLY mothers have regarded as born to great things and who have passed away without sign, may have gone on toward their great things. Whether this mother thought too much of her son or not, there were questions moving in his mind which she could not have understood—even then when he would creep to her bed in the morning to forget in her arms the terrible dreams of the night, or when at evening he would draw his little stool to her knee, unable or unwilling to enjoy his book anywhere but by her side.

What gave him his unconscious power over his mother, was, first, the things he said, and next, the things he did not say; for he seemed to her to dwell always in a rich silence. Yet throughout was she aware of a something between them, across which they could not meet; and it was in part her distress at the seeming impossibility of effecting a spiritual union with her son, that made her so desirous of personal proximity to him. Such union is by most thinking people presumed impossible without consent of opinion, and this mistake rendered her unable to FEEL near him, to be at home with him. If she had believed that they understood each other, that they were of like OPINION, she would not have been half so unhappy when he went away, would not have longed half so grievously for his return. Ian on his part understood his mother, but knew she did not understand him, and was therefore troubled. Hence it resulted that always after a time came the hour—which never came to her—when he could endure proximity without oneness no longer, and would suddenly announce his departure. And after a day or two of his absence, the mother would be doubly wretched to find a sort of relief in it, and would spend wakeful nights trying to oust it as the merest fancy, persuading herself that she was miserable, and nothing but miserable, in the loss of her darling.

Naturally then she would turn more to Alister, and his love was a strengthening tonic to her sick motherhood. He was never jealous of either. Their love for each other was to him a love. He too would mourn deeply over his brother's departure, but it became at once his business to comfort his mother. And while she had no suspicion of the degree to which he suffered, it drew her with fresh love to her elder born, and gave her renewal of the quiet satisfaction in him that was never absent, when she saw how he too missed Ian. Their mutual affection was indeed as true and strong as a mother could desire it. "If such love," she said to herself, "had appeared in the middle of its history instead of now at its close, the transmitted affection would have been enough to bind the clan together for centuries more!"

It was with a prelusive smile that shone on the mother's heart like the opening of heaven, that Ian lowered his book to answer her question. She had said—

"Did you not feel the cold very much at St. Petersburg last winter, Ian?"

"Yes, mother, at times," he answered. "But everybody wears fur; the peasant his sheep-skin, the noble his silver fox. They have to fight the cold! Nose and toes are in constant danger. Did I never tell you what happened to me once in that way? I don't think I ever did!"

"You never tell me anything, Ian!" said his mother, looking at him with a loving sadness.

"I was suddenly stopped in the street by what I took for an unheard-of insult: I actually thought my great proboscis was being pulled! If I had been as fiery as Alister, the man would have found his back, and I should have lost my nose. Without the least warning a handful of snow was thrust in my face, and my nose had not even a chance of snorting with indignation, it found itself so twisted in every direction at once! But I have a way, in any sudden occurrence, of feeling perplexed enough to want to be sure before doing anything, and if it has sometimes hindered me from what was expedient, it has oftener saved me from what would have been wrong: in another instant I was able to do justice to the promptitude of a fellow Christian for the preservation of my nose, already whitening in frosty death: he was rubbing it hard with snow, the orthodox remedy! My whole face presently sharpened into one burning spot, and taking off my hat, I thanked the man for his most kind attention. He pointed out to me that time spent in explaining the condition of my nose, would have been pure loss: the danger was pressing, and he attacked it at once! I was indeed entirely unconscious of the state of my beak—the worst symptom of any!"

"I trust, Ian, you will not go back to Russia!" said his mother, after a little more talk about frost-biting. "Surely there is work for you at home!"

"What can I do at home, mother? You have no money to buy me a commission, and I am not much good at farm-work. Alister says I am not worth a horseman's wages!"

"You could find teaching at home; or you could go into the church. We might manage that, for you would only have to attend the divinity classes."

"Mother! would you put me into one of the priests' offices that I may eat a piece of bread? As for teaching, there are too many hungry students for that: I could not take the bread out of their mouths! And in truth, mother, I could not endure it—except it were required of me. I can live on as little as any, but it must be with some liberty. I have surely inherited the spirit of some old sea-rover, it is so difficult for me to rest! I am a very thistle-down for wandering! I must know how my fellow-creatures live! I should like to BE one man after another—each for an hour or two!"

"Your father used to say there was much Norse blood in the family."

"There it is, mother! I cannot help it!"

"I don't like your holding the Czar's commission, Ian—somehow I don't like it! He is a tyrant!"

"I am going to throw it up, mother."

"I am glad of that! How did you ever get it?"

"Oddly enough, through the man that pulled my nose. I had a chance afterwards of doing him a good turn, which he was most generous in acknowledging; and as he belonged to the court, I had the offer of a lieutenant's commission. The Scotch are in favour."

A deep cloud had settled on the face of the young man. The lady looked at him for a moment with keenest mother-eyes, suppressed a deep sigh, and betook herself again to her work.

Ere she thought how he might take it, another question broke from her lips.

"What sort of church had you to go to in St. Petersburg, Ian?" she said.

Ian was silent a moment, thinking how to be true, and not hurt her more than could not be helped.

"There are a thousand places of worship there, mother," he returned, with a curious smile.

"Any presbyterian place?" she asked.

"I believe so," he replied.

"Ian, you haven't given up praying?"

"If ever I prayed, mother, I certainly have not given it up."

"Ever prayed, Ian! When a mere child you prayed like an aged Christian!"

"Ah, mother, that was a sad pity! I asked for things of which I felt no need! I was a hypocrite! I ought to have prayed like a little child!"

The mother was silent: she it was who had taught him to pray thus—making him pray aloud in her hearing! and this was the result! The premature blossom had withered! she said to herself. But it was no blossom, only a muslin flower!

"Then you didn't go to church!" she said at length.

"Not often, mother dear," he answered. "When I do go, I like to go to the church of the country I happen to be in. Going to church and praying to God are not the same thing."

"Then you do say your prayers? Oh, do not tell me you never bow down before your maker!"

"Shall I tell you where I think I did once pray to God, mother?" he said, after a little pause, anxious to soothe her suffering. "At least I did think then that I prayed!" he added.

"It was not this morning, then, before you left your chamber?"

"No, mother," answered Ian; "I did not pray this morning, and I never say prayers."

The mother gave a gasp, but answered nothing. Ian went on again.

"I should like to tell you, mother, about that time when I am almost sure I prayed!"

"I should like to hear about it," she answered, with strangest minglings of emotion. At one and the same instant she felt parted from her son by a gulf into which she must cast herself to find him, and that he stood on a height of sacred experience which she never could hope to climb. "Oh for his father to talk to him!" she said to herself. He was a power on her soul which she almost feared. If he were to put forth his power, might he not drag her down into unbelief?

It was the first time they had come so close in their talk. The moment his mother spoke out, Ian had responded. He was anxious to be open with her so far as he could, and forced his natural taciturnity, the prime cause of which was his thoughtfulness: it was hard to talk where was so much thinking to be done, so little time to do it in, and so little progress made by it! But wherever he could keep his mother company, there he would not leave her! Just as he opened his mouth, however, to begin his narration, the door of the room also opened, flung wide by the small red hand of Nancy, and two young ladies entered.

CHAPTER VIII.

A MORNING CALL.

Had Valentine known who the brothers were, or where they lived, he would before now have called to thank them again for their kindness to him; but he imagined they had some distance to go after depositing him, and had not yet discovered his mistake. The visit now paid had nothing to do with him.

The two elder girls, curious about the pretty cottage, had come wandering down the spur, or hill-toe, as far as its precincts—if precincts they may be called where was no fence, only a little grove and a less garden. Beside the door stood a milk-pail and a churn, set out to be sweetened by the sun and wind. It was very rural, they thought, and very homely, but not so attractive as some cottages in the south:—it indicated a rusticity honoured by the most unceremonious visit from its superiors. Thus without hesitation concluding, Christina, followed by Mercy, walked in at the open door, found a barefooted girl in the kitchen, and spoke pleasantly to her. She, in simple hospitality forgetting herself, made answer in Gaelic; and, never doubting the ladies had come to call upon her mistress, led the way, and the girls, without thinking, followed her to the parlour.

As they came, they had been talking. Had they been in any degree truly educated, they would have been quite capable of an opinion of their own, for they had good enough faculties; but they had never been really taught to read; therefore, with the utmost confidence, they had been passing judgment upon a book from which they had not gathered the slightest notion as to the idea or intention of the writer. Christina was of that numerous class of readers, who, if you show one thing better or worse than another, will without hesitation report that you love the one and hate the other. If you say, for instance, that it is a worse and yet more shameful thing for a man to break his wife's heart by systematic neglect, than to strike her and be sorry for it, such readers give out that you approve of wife-beating, and perhaps write to expostulate with you on your brutality. If you express pleasure that a poor maniac should have succeeded in escaping through the door of death from his haunting demon, they accuse you of advocating suicide. But Mercy was not yet afloat on the sea of essential LIE whereon Christina swung to every wave.

One question they had been discussing was, whether the hero of the story was worthy the name of lover, seeing he deferred offering his hand to the girl because she told her mother a FIB to account for her being with him in the garden after dark. "It was cowardly and unfair," said Christina: "was it not for HIS sake she did it?" Mercy did not think to say "WAS IT?" as she well might. "Don't you see, Chrissy," she said, "he reasoned this way: 'If she tell her mother a lie, she may tell me a lie some day too!'?" So indeed the youth did reason; but it occurred to neither of his critics to note the fact that he would not have minded the girl's telling her mother the lie, if he could have been certain she would never tell HIM one! In regard to her hiding from him certain passages with another gentleman, occurring between this event and his proposal, Christina judged he had no right to know them, and if he had, their concealment was what he deserved.

When the girl, who would have thought it rude to ask their names—if I mistake not, it was a point in highland hospitality to entertain without such inquiry—led the way to the parlour, they followed expecting they did not know what: they had heard of the cowhouse, the stable, and even the pigsty, being under the same roof in these parts! When the opening door disclosed "lady" Macruadh, every inch a chieftain's widow, their conventional breeding failed them a little; though incapable of recognizing a refinement beyond their own, they were not incapable of feeling its influence; and they had not yet learned how to be rude with propriety in unproved circumstances—still less how to be gracious without a moment's notice. But when a young man sprang from a couch, and the stately lady rose and advanced to receive them, it was too late to retreat, and for a moment they stood abashed, feeling, I am glad to say, like intruders. The behaviour of the lady and gentleman, however, speedily set them partially at ease. The latter, with movements more than graceful, for they were gracious, and altogether free of scroll-pattern or Polonius-flourish, placed chairs, and invited them to be seated, and the former began to talk as if their entrance were the least unexpected thing in the world. Leaving them to explain their visit or not as they saw fit, she spoke of the weather, the harvest, the shooting; feared the gentlemen would be disappointed: the birds were quite healthy, but not numerous—they had too many enemies to multiply! asked if they had seen the view from such and such a point;—in short, carried herself as one to whom cordiality to strangers was an easy duty. But she was not taken with them. Her order of civilization was higher than theirs; and the simplicity as well as old-fashioned finish of her consciousness recoiled a little —though she had not experience enough of a certain kind to be able at once to say what it was in the manner and expression of the young ladies that did not please her.

Mammon, gaining more and more of the upper hand in all social relations, has done much to lower the PETITE as well as the GRANDE MORALE of the country—the good breeding as well as the honesty. Unmannerliness with the completest self-possession, is a poor substitute for stiffness, a poorer for courtesy. Respect and graciousness from each to each is of the very essence of Christianity, independently of rank, or possession, or relation. A certain roughness and rudeness have usurped upon the intercourse of the century. It comes of the spread of imagined greatness; true greatness, unconscious of itself, cannot find expression other than gracious. In the presence of another, a man of true breeding is but faintly aware of his own self, and keenly aware of the other's self. Before the human—that bush which, however trodden and peeled, yet burns with the divine presence—the man who thinks of the homage due to him, and not of the homage owing by him, is essentially rude. Mammon is slowly stifling and desiccating Rank; both are miserable deities, but the one is yet meaner than the other. Unrefined families with money are received with open arms and honours paid, in circles where a better breeding than theirs has hitherto prevailed: this, working along with the natural law of corruption where is no aspiration, has gradually caused the deterioration of which I speak. Courtesy will never regain her former position, but she will be raised to a much higher; like Duty she will be known as a daughter of the living God, "the first stocke father of gentilnes;" for in his neighbour every man will see a revelation of the Most High.

Without being able to recognize the superiority of a woman who lived in a cottage, the young ladies felt and disliked it; and the matron felt the commonness of the girls, without knowing what exactly it was. The girls, on the other hand, were interested in the young man: he looked like a gentleman! Ian was interested in the young women: he thought they were shy, when they were only "put out," and wished to make them comfortable —in which he quickly succeeded. His unconsciously commanding air in the midst of his great courtesy, roused their admiration, and they had not been many minutes in his company ere they were satisfied that, however it was to be accounted for, the young man was in truth very much of a gentleman. It was an unexpected discovery of northern produce, and "the estate" gathered interest in their eyes. Christina did the greater part of the talking, hut both did their best to be agreeable.

Ian saw quite as well as his mother what ordinary girls they were, but, accustomed to the newer modes in manner and speech, he was not shocked by movements and phrases that annoyed her. The mother apprehended fascination, and was uneasy, though far from showing it.

When they rose, Ian attended them to the door, leaving his mother anxious, for she feared he would accompany them home. Till he returned, she did not resume her seat.

The girls took their way along the ridge in silence, till the ruin was between them and the cottage, when they burst into laughter. They were ladies enough not to laugh till out of sight, but not ladies enough to see there was nothing to laugh at.

"A harp, too!" said Christina. "Mercy, I believe we are on the top of mount Ararat, and have this very moment left the real Noah's ark, patched into a cottage! Who CAN they be?"

"Gentlefolk evidently," said Mercy, "—perhaps old-fashioned people from Inverness."

"The young man must have been to college!—In the north, you know," continued Christina, thinking with pride that her brother was at Oxford, "nothing is easier than to get an education, such as it is!

It costs in fact next to nothing. Ploughmen send their sons to St. Andrew's and Aberdeen to make gentlemen of them! Fancy!"

"You must allow this case a successful one!"

"I didn't mean HIS father was a ploughman! That is impossible! Besides, I heard him call that very respectable person MOTHER! She is not a ploughman's wife, but evidently a lady of the middle class."

Christina did not count herself or her people to belong to the middle class. How it was it is not quite easy to say—perhaps the tone of implied contempt with which the father spoke of the lower classes, and the quiet negation with which the mother would allude to shopkeepers, may have had to do with it—but the young people all imagined themselves to belong to the upper classes! It was a pity there was no title in the family—but any of the girls might well marry a coronet! There were indeed persons higher than they; a duke was higher; the queen was higher—but that was pleasant! it was nice to have a few to look up to!

On anyone living in a humble house, not to say a poor cottage, they looked down, as the case might be, with indifference or patronage; they little dreamed how, had she known all about them, the respectable person in the cottage would have looked down upon THEM! At the same time the laugh in which they now indulged was not altogether one of amusement; it was in part an effort to avenge themselves of a certain uncomfortable feeling of rebuke.

"I will tell you my theory, Mercy!" Christina went on. "The lady is the widow of an Indian officer—perhaps a colonel. Some of their widows are left very poor, though, their husbands having been in the service of their country, they think no small beer of themselves! The young man has a military air which he may have got from his father; or he may be an officer himself: young officers are always poor; that's what makes them so nice to flirt with. I wonder whether he really IS an officer! We've actually called upon the people, and come away too, without knowing their names!"

"I suppose they're from the New House!" said Ian, returning after he had bowed the ladies from the threshold, with the reward of a bewitching smile from the elder, and a shy glance from the younger.

"Where else could they be from?" returned his mother; "—come to make our poor country yet poorer!"

"They're not English!"

"Not they!—vulgar people from Glasgow!"

"I think you are too hard on them, mother! They are not exactly vulgar. I thought, indeed, there was a sort of gentleness about them you do not often meet in Scotch girls!"

"In the lowlands, I grant, Ian; but the daughter of the poorest tacksman of the Macruadhs has a manner and a modesty I have seen in no Sasunnach girl yet. Those girls are bold!"

"Self-possessed, perhaps!" said Ian.

Upon the awkwardness he took for shyness, had followed a reaction. It was with the young ladies a part of good breeding, whatever mistake they made, not to look otherwise than contented with themselves: having for a moment failed in this principle, they were eager to make up for it.

"Girls are different from what they used to be, I fancy, mother!" added Ian thoughtfully.

"The world changes very fast!" said the mother sadly. She was thinking, like Rebecca, if her sons took a fancy to these who were not daughters of the land, what good would her life do her.

"Ah, mother dear," said Ian, "I have never"—and as he spoke the cloud deepened on his forehead—"seen more than one woman whose ways and manners reminded me of you!"

"And what was she?" the mother asked, in pleased alarm.

But she almost repented the question when she saw how low the cloud descended on his countenance.

"A princess, mother. She is dead," he answered, and turning walked so gently from the room that it was impossible for his mother to detain him.

CHAPTER IX.

ME. SERCOMBE.

The next morning, soon after sunrise, the laird began to cut his barley. Ian would gladly have helped, but Alister had a notion that such labour was not fit for him.

"I had a comical interview this morning," said the chief, entering the kitchen at dinner-time. "I was out before my people, and was standing by the burn-side near the foot-bridge, when I heard somebody shouting, and looked up. There was a big English fellow in gray on the top of the ridge, with his gun on his shoulder, hollo-ing. I knew he was English by his hollo-ing. It was plain it was to me, but not choosing to be at his beck and call, I took no heed. 'Hullo, you there! wake up!' he cried. 'What should I wake up for?' I returned. 'To carry my bag. You don't seem to have anything to do! I'll give you five shillings.'"

"You see to what you expose yourself by your unconventlonalities, Alister!" said his brother, with rnock gravity.

"It was not the fellow we carried home the other night, Ian; it was one twice his size. It would take all I have to carry HIM as far!"

"The other must have pointed you out to him!"

"It was much too dark for him to know me again!"

"You forget the hall-lamp!" said Ian.

"Ah, yes, to be sure! I had forgotten!" answered Alister. "To tell the truth, I thought, when I took his shilling, he would never know me from Nebuchadnezzar: that is the one thing I am ashamed of in the affair—I did in the dark what perhaps I should not have done in the daylight!—I don't mean I would not have carried him and his bag too! I refer only to the shilling! Now, of course, I will hold my face to it; but I thought it better to be short with a fellow like that."

"Well?"

"'You'll want prepayment, no doubt!' he went on, putting his hand in his pocket. Those Sasunnach fellows think every highlandman keen as a hawk after their dirty money!"

"They have but too good reason in some parts!" said the mother. "It is not so bad here yet, but there is a great difference in that respect. The old breed is fast disappearing. What with the difficulty of living by the hardest work, and the occasional chance of earning a shilling easily, many have turned both idle and greedy."

"That's for you and your shilling, Alister!" said Ian.

"I confess," returned Alister, "if I had foreseen what an idea of the gentlemen of the country I might give, I should have hesitated. But I haven't begun to be ashamed yet!"

"Ashamed, Alister!" cried Ian. "What does it matter what a fellow like that thinks of you?"

"And mistress Conal has her shilling!" said the mother.

"If the thing was right," pursued Ian, "no harm can come of it; if it was not right, no end of harm may come. Are you sure it was good for mistress Conal to have that shilling, Alister? What if it be drawing away her heart from him who is watching his old child in her turf-hut? What if the devil be grinning at her from, that shilling?"

"Ian! if God had not meant her to have the shilling, he would not have let Alister earn it."

"Certainly God can take care of her from a shilling!" said Ian, with one of his strangely sweet smiles. "I was only trying Alister, mother."

"I confess I did not like the thought of it at first," resumed Mrs. Macruadh; "but it was mere pride; for when I thought of your father, I knew he would have been pleased with Alister."

"Then, mother, I am glad; and I don't care what Ian, or any Sasunnach under the sun, may think of me."

"But you haven't told us," said Ian, "how the thing ended."

"I said to the fellow," resumed Alister, "that I had my shearing to do, and hadn't the time to go with him. 'Is this your season for sheep-shearing?' said he.'We call cutting the corn shearing,' I answered, 'because in these parts we use the reaping hook.' 'That is a great waste of labour!' he returned. I did not tell him that some of our land would smash his machines like toys. 'How?' I asked. 'It costs so much more,' he said. 'But it feeds so many more!' I replied. 'Oh yes, of course, if you don't want the farmer to make a living!' 'I manage to make a living,' I said. 'Then you are the farmer?' 'So it would appear.' 'I beg your pardon; I thought—' 'You thought I was an idle fellow, glad of an easy job to keep the life in me!' 'You were deuced glad of a job the other night, they tell me!' 'So I was. I wanted a shilling for a poor woman, and hadn't one to give her without going home a mile and a half for it!' By this time he had come down, and I had gone a few steps to meet him; I did not want to seem unfriendly. 'Upon my word, it was very good of you! The old lady ought to be grateful!' he said. 'So ought we all,' I answered, '—I to your friend for the shilling, and he to me for taking his bag. He did me one good turn for my poor woman, and I did him another for his poor leg!' 'So you're quits!' said he. 'Not at all,' I answered; 'on the contrary, we are under mutual obligation.' 'I don't see the difference!—Hillo, there's a hare!' And up went his gun to his shoulder. 'None of that!' I cried, and knocked up the barrel. 'What do you mean?' he roared, looking furious. 'Get out of the way, or I'll shoot you.' 'Murder as well as poaching!' I said. 'Poaching!' he shouted. 'That rabbit is mine,' I answered; 'I will not have it killed.' 'Cool!—on Mr. Palmer's land!' said he. 'The land is mine, and I am my own gamekeeper!' I rejoined. 'You look like it!' he said. 'You go after your birds!—not in this direction though,' I answered, and turned and left him."

"You were rough with him!" said Ian.

"I did lose my temper rather."

"It was a mistake on his part."

"I expected to hear him fire," Alister continued, "for there was the rabbit he took for a hare lurching slowly away! I'm glad he didn't: I always feel bad after a row!—Can a conscience ever get too fastidious, Ian?"

"The only way to find that out is always to obey it."

"So long as it agrees with the Bible, Ian!" interposed the mother.

"The Bible is a big book, mother, and the things in it are of many sorts," returned Ian. "The Lord did not go with every thing in it."

"Ian! Ian! I am shocked to hear you!"

"It is the truth, mother."

"What WOULD your father say!"

"'He that loveth father or mother more than me is not worthy of me.'"

Ian rose from the table, knelt by his mother, and laid his head on her shoulder.

She was silent, pained by his words, and put her arm round him as if to shelter him from the evil one. Homage to will and word of the Master, apart from the acceptance of certain doctrines concerning him, was in her eyes not merely defective but dangerous. To love the Lord with the love of truest obedience; to believe him the son of God and the saver of men with absolute acceptance of the heart, was far from enough! it was but sentimental affection!

A certain young preacher in Scotland some years ago, accused by an old lady of preaching works, took refuge in the Lord's sermon on the mount:

"Ow ay!" answered the partisan, "but he was a varra yoong mon whan he preacht that sermon!"

Alister rose and went: there was to him something specially sacred in the communion of his mother and brother. Heartily he held with Ian, but shrank from any difference with his mother. For her sake he received Sunday after Sunday in silence what was to him a bushel of dust with here and there a bit of mouldy bread in it; but the mother did not imagine any great coincidence of opinion between her and Alister any more than between her and Ian. She had not the faintest notion how much genuine faith both of them had, or how it surpassed her own in vitality.

But while Ian seemed to his brother, who knew him best, hardly touched with earthly stain, Alister, notwithstanding his large and dominant humanity, was still in the troublous condition of one trying to do right against a powerful fermentation of pride. He held noblest principles; but the sediment of generations was too easily stirred up to cloud them. He was not quite honest in his attitude towards some of his ancestors, judging them far more leniently than he would have judged others. He loved his neighbour, but his neighbour was mostly of his own family or his own clan. He MIGHT have been unjust for the sake of his own—a small fault in the eyes of the world, but a great fault indeed in a nature like his, capable of being so much beyond it. For, while the faults of a good man cannot be such evil things as the faults of a bad man, they are more blameworthy, and greater faults than the same would be in a bad man: we must not confuse the guilt of the person with the abstract evil of the thing.

Ian was one of those blessed few who doubt in virtue of a larger faith. While its roots were seeking a deeper soil, it could not show so fast a growth above ground, He doubted most about the things he loved best, while he devoted the energies of a mind whose keenness almost masked its power, to discover possible ways of believing them. To the wise his doubts would have been his best credentials; they were worth tenfold the faith of most. It was truth, and higher truth, he was always seeking. The sadness which coloured his deepest individuality, only one thing could ever remove —the conscious presence of the Eternal. This is true of all sadness, but Ian knew it.

He overtook Alister on his way to the barley-field.

"I have been trying to find out wherein lay the falseness of the position in which you found yourself this morning," he said. "There could be nothing wrong in doing a small thing for its reward any more than a great one; where I think you went wrong was in ASSUMING your social position afterwards: you should have waited for its being accorded you. There was no occasion to be offended with the man. You ought to have seen how you must look to him, and given him time. I don't perceive why you should be so gracious to old mistress Conal, and so hard upon him. Certainly you would not speak as he did to any man, but he has been brought up differently; he is not such a gentleman as you cannot help being. In a word, you ought to have treated him as an inferior, and been more polite to him."

CHAPTER X.

THE PLOUGH-BULLS.

Partly, it may be, from such incidents at the outset of their acquaintance, there was for some time no further meeting betwixt any of the chief's family and that of the new laird. There was indeed little to draw them together except common isolation. Valentine would have been pleased to show gratitude to his helpers on that stormy night, but after his sisters' account of their call, he felt not only ashamed, which was right, but ashamed to show his shame, which was a fresh shame. The girls on their part made so much of what they counted the ridiculous elements of their "adventure," that, natural vengeance on their untruthfulness, they came themselves to see in it almost only what was ridiculous. In the same spirit Mr. Sercombe recounted his adventure with Alister, which annoyed his host, who had but little acquaintance with the boundaries of his land. From the additional servants they had hired in the vicinity, the people of the New House gathered correct information concerning the people at the cottage, but the honour in which they were held only added to the ridicule they associated with them. On the other side also there was little inclination towards a pursuit of intercourse. Mrs. Macruadh, from Nancy's account and the behaviour of the girls, divined the explanation of their visit; and, as their mother did not follow it up, took no notice of it. In the mind of Mercy, however, lurked a little thorn, with the bluntest possible sting of suspicion, every time she joined in a laugh at the people of the cottage, that she was not quite just to them.

The shooting, such as it was, went on, the sleeping and the eating, the walking and the talking. Long letters were written from the New House to female friends—letters with the flourishes if not the matter of wit, and funny tales concerning the natives, whom, because of their poor houses and unintelligibility, they represented as semi-savages. The young men went back to Oxford; and the time for the return of the family to civilization seemed drawing nigh.

It happened about this time, however, that a certain speculation in which Mr. Peregrine Palmer was very materially interested, failed utterly, depriving him of the consciousness of a good many thousands, and producing in him the feeling of a lady of moderate means when she loses her purse: he must save it off something! For though he spent freely, he placed a great value on money—as well he might, seeing it gave him all the distinction which before everything else he prized. He did not know what a poor thing it is to be distinguished among men, therefore did not like losing his thousands. Having by failure sinned against Mammon, he must do something to ease the money-conscience that ruled his conduct; and the first thing that occurred to him was, to leave his wife and daughters where they were for the winter. None of them were in the least delicate; his wife professed herself fond of a country life; it would give the girls a good opportunity for practice, drawing, and study generally, and he would find them a suitable governess! He talked the matter over with Mrs. Palmer. She did not mind much, and would not object. He would spend Christmas with them, he said, and bring down Christian, and perhaps Mr. Sercombe.

The girls did not like the idea. It was so cold in the country in winter, and the snow would be so deep! they would be starved to death! But, of course —if the governor had made up his mind to be cruel!

The thing was settled. It was only for one winter! It would be a new experience for them, and they would enjoy their next SEASON all the more! The governor had promised to send them down new furs, and a great boxful of novels! He did not apprise them that he meant to sell their horses. Their horses were his! He was an indulgent father and did not stint them, but he was not going to ask their leave! At the same time he had not the courage to tell them.

He took his wife with him as far as Inverness for a day or two, that she might lay in a good stock of everything antagonistic to cold.

When father and mother were gone from the house, the girls felt LARKY. They had no wish to do anything they would not do if their parents were at home, but they had some sense of relief in the thought that they could do whatever they liked. A more sympathetic historian might say, and I am nowise inclined to contradict him, that it was only the reaction from the pain of parting, and the instinct to make the best of their loneliness. However it was, the elder girls resolved on a walk to the village, to see what might be seen, and in particular the young woman at the shop, of whom they had heard their brother and Mr. Sercombe speak with admiration, qualified with the remark that she was so proper they could hardly get a civil word out of her. She was in fact too scrupulously polite for their taste.

It was a bright, pleasant, frosty morning, perfectly still, with an air like wine. The harvest had vanished from the fields. The sun shone on millions of tiny dew-suns, threaded on forsaken spider-webs. A few small, white, frozen clouds flecked the sky. The purple heather was not yet gone, and not any snow had yet fallen in the valley. The burn was large, for there had been a good deal of rain, but it was not much darker than its usual brown of smoke-crystal. They tripped gaily along. If they had little spiritual, they had much innocent animal life, which no great disappointments or keen twinges of conscience had yet damped. They were hut human kittens—and not of the finest breed.

As they crossed the root of the spur, and looked down on the autumn fields to the east of it, they spied something going on which they did not understand. Stopping, and gazing more intently, they beheld what seemed a contest between man and beast, but its nature they could not yet distinguish. Gradually it grew plain that two of the cattle of the country, wild and shaggy, were rebelling against control. They were in fact two young bulls, of the small black highland breed, accustomed to gallop over the rough hills, jumping like goats, which Alister had set himself the task of breaking to the plough—by no means an easy one, or to be accomplished single-handed by any but a man of some strength, and both persistence and patience. In the summer he had lost a horse, which he could ill afford to replace: if he could make these bulls work, they would save him the price of the horse, would cost less to keep, and require less attention! He bridled them by the nose, not with rings through the gristle, but with nose-bands of iron, bluntly spiked inside, against which they could not pull hard without pain, and had made some progress, though he could by no means trust them yet: every now and then a fit of mingled wildness and stubbornness would seize them, and the contest would appear about to begin again from the beginning; but they seldom now held out very long. The nose-band of one of them had come off, Alister had him by a horn in each hand, and a fierce struggle was going on between them, while the other was pulling away from his companion as if determined to take to the hills. It was a good thing for them that share and coulter were pretty deep in the ground, to the help of their master; for had they got away, they would have killed, or at least disabled themselves. Presently, however, he had the nose-band on, and by force and persuasion together got the better of them; the staggy little furies gave in; and quickly gathering up his reins, he went back to the plough-stilts, where each hand held at once a handle and a rein. With energetic obedience the, little animals began to pull—so vigorously that it took nearly all the chief's strength to hold at once his plough and his team.

It was something of a sight to the girls after a long dearth of events. Many things indeed upon which they scarce cast an eye when they came, they were now capable of regarding with a little feeble interest. Nor, although ignorant of everything agricultural, were they quite unused to animals; having horses they called their own, they would not unfrequently go to the stables to give their orders, or see that they were carried out.

They waited for some time hoping the fight would begin again, and drew a little nearer; then, as by common consent, left the road, passed the ruin, ran down the steep side of the ridge, and began to toil through the stubble towards the ploughman. A sharp straw would every now and then go through a delicate stocking, and the damp soil gathered in great lumps on their shoes, but they plodded on, laughing merrily as they went.

The Macruadh was meditating the power of the frost to break up the clods of the field, when he saw the girls close to him. He pulled in his cattle, and taking off his bonnet with one hand while the other held both reins—

"Excuse me, ladies," he said; "my animals are young, and not quite broken."

They were not a little surprised at such a reception, and were driven to conclude that the man must be the laird himself. They had heard that he cultivated his own land, but had not therefore imagined him labouring in his own person.

In spite of the blindness produced by their conventional training, vulgarly called education, they could not fail to perceive something in the man worthy of their regard. Before them, on the alert toward his cattle, but full of courtesy, stood a dark, handsome, weather-browned man, with an eagle air, not so pronounced as his brother's. His hair was long, and almost black, —in thick, soft curls over a small, well-set head. His glance had the flash that comes of victorious effort, and his free carriage was that of one whom labour has nowise subdued, whose every muscle is instinct with ready life. True even in trifles, he wore the dark beard that nature had given him; disordered by the struggle with his bulls, it imparted a certain wild look that contrasted with his speech. Christina forgot that the man was a labourer like any other, but noted that he did not manifest the least embarrassment in their presence, or any consciousness of a superfluity of favour in their approach: she did not know that neither would his hired servant, or the poorest member of his clan. It was said of a certain Sutherland clan that they were all gentlemen, and of a certain Argyll clan that they were all poets; of the Macruadhs it was said they were both. As to Mercy, the first glance of the chiefs hazel eyes, looking straight into hers with genial respect, went deeper than any look had yet penetrated.

Ladies in Alister's fields were not an everyday sight. Hardly before had his work been enlivened by such a presence; and the joy of it was in his eyes, though his behaviour was calm. Christina thought how pleasant it would be to have him for a worshipping slave—so interpenetrated with her charms that, like Una's lion, he would crouch at her feet, come and go at her pleasure, live on her smiles, and be sad when she gave him none. She would make a gentleman of him, then leave him to dream of her! It would be a pleasant and interesting task in the dullness of their winter's banishment, with the days so short and the nights so unendurably long!

The man was handsome!—she would do it!—and would proceed at once to initiate the conquest of him!

The temptation to patronize not unfrequently presents an object for the patronage superior to the would-be patron; for the temptation is one to which slight persons chiefly are exposed; it affords an outlet for the vague activity of self-importance. Few have learned that one is of no value except to God and other men. Miss Palmer worshipped herself, and therefore would fain be worshipped—so dreamed of a friendship de haut en bas with the country fellow.

She put on a smile—no difficult thing, for she was a good-natured girl. It looked to Alister quite natural. It was nevertheless, like Hamlet's false friends, "sent for."

"Do you like ploughing?" she asked.

Had she known the manners of the country, she would have added "laird," or "Macruadh."

"Yes I do," Alister answered; "but I should plough all the same if I did not. It has to be done."

"But why should YOU do it?"

"Because I must," laughed the laird.

What ought she to answer? Should she condole with the man because he had to work? It did not seem prudent! She would try another tack!

"You had some trouble with your oxen! We saw it from the road, and were quite frightened. I hope you are not hurt."

"There was no danger of that," answered Alister with a smile.

"What wild creatures they are! Ain't it rather hard work for them? They are so small!"

"They are as strong as horses," answered the laird. "I have had my work to break them! Indeed, I can hardly say I have done it yet! they would very much like to run their horns into me!"

"Then it MUST be dangerous! It shows that they were not meant to work!"

"They were meant to work if I can make them work."

"Then you approve of slavery!" said Mercy

She hardly knew what made her oppose him. As yet she bad no opinions of her own, though she did catch a thought sometimes, when it happened to come within her reach. Alister smiled a curious smile.

"I should," he said, "if the right people were made slaves of. I would take shares in a company of Algerine pirates to rid the social world of certain types of the human!"

The girls looked at each other. "Sharp!" said Christina to herself.

"What sorts would you have them take?" she asked.

"Idle men in particular," answered Alister.

"Would you not have them take idle ladies as well?"

"I would see first how they behaved when the men were gone."

"You believe, then," said Mercy, "we have a right to make the lower animals work?"

"I think it is our duty," answered Alister. "At all events, if we do not, we must either kill them off by degrees, or cede them this world, and emigrate. But even that would be a bad thing for my little bulls there! It is not so many years since the last wolf was killed—here, close by! and if the dogs turned to wolves again, where would they be? The domestic animals would then have wild beasts instead of men for their masters! To have the world a habitable one, man must rule."

"Men are nothing but tyrants to them!" said Christina.

"Most are, I admit."

Ere he could prevent her, she had walked up to the near bull, and begun to pat him. He poked a sharp wicked horn sideways at her, catching her cloak on it, and grazing her arm. She started back very white. Alister gave him a terrible tug. The beast shook his head, and began to paw the earth.

"It wont do to go near him," he said. "—But you needn't be afraid; he can't touch you. That iron band round his nose has spikes in it."

"Poor fellow!" said Christina; "it is no wonder he should be out of temper! It must hurt him dreadfully!"

"It does hurt him when he pulls against it, but not when he is quiet."

"I call it cruel!"

"I do not. The fellow knows what is wanted of him—just as well as any naughty child."

"How can he when he has no reason!"

"Oh, hasn't he!"

"Animals have no reason; they have only instinct!"

"They have plenty of reason—more than many men and women. They are not so far off us as pride makes most people think! It is only those that don't know them that talk about the instinct of animals!"

"Do you know them?"

"Pretty well for a man; but they're often too much for me."

"Anyhow that poor thing does not know better."

"He knows enough; and if he did not, would you allow him to do as he pleased because he didn't know better? He wanted to put his horn into you a moment ago!"

"Still it must be hard to want very much to do a thing, and not be able to do it!" said Mercy.

"I used to feel as if I could tear my old nurse to pieces when she wouldn't let me do as I wanted!" said Christina.

"I suppose you do whatever you please now, ladies?"

"No, indeed. We wanted to go to London, and here we are for the winter!"

"And you think it hard?"

"Yes, we do."

"And so, from sympathy, you side with my cattle?"

"Well—yes!"

"You think I have no right to keep them captive, and make them work?"

"None at all," said Christina.

"Then it is time I let them go!"

Alister made for the animals' heads.

"No, no! please don't!" cried both the girls, turning, the one white, the other red.

"Certainly not if you do not wish it!" answered Alister, staying his step. "If I did, however, you would be quite safe, for they would not come near me. They would be off up that hill as hard as they could tear, jumping everything that came in their way."

"Is it not very dull here in the winter?" asked Christina, panting a little, but trying to look as if she had known quite well he was only joking.

"I do not find it dull."

"Ah, but you are a man, and can do as you please!"

"I never could do as I pleased, and so I please as I do," answered Alister.

"I do not quite understand you."

"When you cannot do as you like, the best thing is to like what you have to do. One's own way is not to be had in this world. There's a better, though, which is to be had!"

"I have heard a parson talk like that," said Mercy, "but never a layman!"

"My father was a parson as good as any layman. He would have laid me on my back in a moment—here as I stand!" said Alister, drawing himself to his height.

He broke suddenly into Gaelic, addressing the more troublesome of the bulls. No better pleased to stand still than to go on, he had fallen to digging at his neighbour, who retorted with the horn convenient, and presently there was a great mixing of bull and harness and cloddy earth. Turning quickly towards them, Alister dropped a rein. In a moment the plough was out of the furrow, and the bulls were straining every muscle, each to send the other into the wilds of the unseen creation. Alister sprang to their heads, and taking them by their noses forced them back into the line of the furrow. Christina, thinking they had broken loose, fled; but there was Mercy with the reins, hauling with all her might!

"Thank you, thank you!" said the laird, laughing with pleasure. "You are a friend indeed!"

"Mercy! Mercy! come away directly," cried Christina.

But Mercy did not heed her. The laird took the reins, and administering a blow each to the animals, made them stand still.

There are tender-hearted people who virtually object to the whole scheme of creation; they would neither have force used nor pain suffered; they talk as if kindness could do everything, even where it is not felt. Millions of human beings but for suffering would never develop an atom of affection. The man who would spare DUE suffering is not wise. It is folly to conclude a thing ought not to be done because it hurts. There are powers to be born, creations to be perfected, sinners to be redeemed, through the ministry of pain, that could be born, perfected, redeemed, in no other way. But Christina was neither wise nor unwise after such fashion. She was annoyed at finding the laird not easily to be brought to her feet, and Mercy already advanced to his good graces. She was not jealous of Mercy, for was she not beautiful and Mercy plain? but Mercy had by her PLUCK secured an advantage, and the handsome ploughman looked at her admiringly! Partly therefore because she was not pleased with him, partly that she thought a little outcry would be telling,—

"Oh, you wicked man!" she cried, "you are hurting the poor brutes!"

"No more than is necessary," he answered.

"You are cruel!"

"Good morning, ladies."

He just managed to take off his bonnet, for the four-legged explosions at the end of his plough were pulling madly. He slackened his reins, and away it went, like a sharp knife through a Dutch cheese.

"You've made him quite cross!" said Mercy.

"What a brute of a man!" said Christina.

She never restrained herself from teasing cat or puppy for her amusement —did not even mind hurting it a little. Those capable of distinguishing

94

between the qualities of resembling actions are few. There are some who will regard Alister as capable of vivisection.

On one occasion when the brothers were boys, Alister having lost his temper in the pursuit of a runaway pony, fell upon it with his fists the moment he caught it. Ian put himself between, and received, without word or motion, more than one blow meant for the pony.

"Donal was only in fun!" he said, as soon as Alister's anger had spent itself. "Father would never have punished him like that!"

Alister was ashamed, and never again was guilty of such an outbreak. From that moment he began the serious endeavour to subjugate the pig, tiger, mule, or whatever animal he found in himself. There remained, however, this difference between them—that Alister punished without compunction, while Ian was sorely troubled at having to cause any suffering.

CHAPTER XI.

THE FIR-GROVE.

As the ladies went up the ridge, regarded in the neighbourhood as the chief's pleasure-ground where nobody went except to call upon the chief, they must, having mounted it lower down than where they descended, pass the cottage. The grove of birch, mountain-ash, and fir which surrounded it, was planted quite irregularly, and a narrow foot-path went winding through it to the door. Against one of the firs was a rough bench turned to the west, and seated upon it they saw Ian, smoking a formless mass of much defiled sea-foam, otherwise meer-schaum. He rose, uncovered, and sat down again. But Christina, who regarded it as a praiseworthy kindness to address any one beneath her, not only returned his salutation, but stopped, and said,

"Good morning! We have been learning how they plough in Scotland, but I fear we annoyed the ploughman."

"Fergus does sometimes LOOK surly," said Ian, rising again, and going to her; "he has bad rheumatism, poor fellow! And then he can't speak a word of English, and is ashamed of it!"

"The man we saw spoke English very well. Is Fergus your brother's name?"

"No; my brother's name is Alister—that is Gaelic for Alexander."

"He was ploughing with two wild little oxen, and could hardly manage them."

"Then it must have been Alister—only, excuse me, he could manage them perfectly. Alister could break a pair of buffaloes."

"He seemed rather vexed, and I thought it might be that we made the creatures troublesome.—I do not mean he was rude—only a little rough to us."

Ian smiled, and waited for more.

"He did not like to be told he was hard on the animals. I only said the poor things did not know better!"

"Ah—I see!—He understands animals so well, he doesn't like to be meddled with in his management of them. I daresay he told you that, if they didn't know better, he had to teach them better! They are troublesome little wretches.—Yes, I confess he is a little touchy about animals!"

Somehow Christina felt herself rebuked, and did not like it. He had almost told her that, if she had quarrelled with his ploughman-brother, the fault must be hers!

"But indeed, Captain Macruadh," she said—for the people called him captain, "I am not ignorant about animals! We have horses of our own, and know all about them.—Don't we, Mercy?"

"Yes," said Mercy; "they take apples and sugar from our hands."

"And you would have the chief's bulls tamed with apples and sugar!" returned Ian, laughing. "But the horses were tamed before ever you saw them! If you had taken them wild, or even when they were foals, and taught them everything, then you would know a little about them. An acquaintance is not a friendship! My brother loves animals and understands them almost like human beings; he understands them better than some human beings, for the most cunning of the animals are yet simple. He knows what they are thinking when I cannot read a word of their faces. I remember one terrible night, winters ago—there had been a blinding drift on and off during the day, and my father and mother were getting anxious about him—how he came staggering in, and fell on the floor, and a great lump in his plaid on his back began to wallow about, and forth crept his big colley! They had been to the hills to look after a few sheep, and the poor dog was exhausted, and Alister carried him home at the risk of his life."

"A valuable animal, I don't doubt," said Christina.

"He had been, but was no more what the world calls valuable. He was an old dog almost past work—but the wisest creature! Poor fellow, he never recovered that day on the hills! A week or so after, we buried him—in the hope of a blessed resurrection," added Ian, with a smile.

The girls looked at each other as much as to say, "Good heavens!" He caught the look, but said nothing, for he saw they had "no understanding."

The brothers believed most devoutly that the God who is present at the death-bed of the sparrow does not forget the sparrow when he is dead; for they had been taught that he is an unchanging God; "and," argued Ian, "what God remembers, he thinks of, and what he thinks of, IS." But Ian knew that what misses the heart falls under the feet! A man is bound to SHARE his best, not to tumble his SEED-PEARLS into the feeding-trough, to break the teeth of them that are there at meat. He had but lifted a corner to give them a glimpse of the Life eternal, and the girls thought him ridiculous! The human caterpillar that has not yet even begun to sicken with the growth of her psyche-wings, is among the poorest of the human animals!

But Christina was not going to give in! Her one idea of the glory of life was the subjugation of men. As if moved by a sudden impulse, she went close up to him.

"Do not be angry with me," she said, almost coaxingly, but with a visible mingling of boldness and shyness, neither of them quite assumed; for, though conscious of her boldness, she was not frightened; and there was something in the eagle-face that made it easy to look shy. "I did not mean to be rude. I am sorry."

"You mistake me," he said gently. "I only wanted you to know you misjudged my brother."

"Then, if you have forgiven me, you will let me sit for a few minutes! I am SO tired with walking in the sticky earth!"

"Do, pray, sit down," responded Ian heartily, and led the way.

But she sank gracefully at the foot of the next fir, while Mercy sat down on the bench.

"Do go on with your pipe," she said, looking up as she arranged her dress; "I am quite used to smoke. Papa would smoke in church if he dared!"

"Chrissy! You KNOW he NEVER smokes in the drawing-room!" cried Mercy, scandalized.

"I have seen him—when mamma was away."

Ian began to be a little more interested in the plain one. But what must his mother think to see them sitting there together! He could not help it! if ladies chose to sit down, it was not for him to forbid them! And there WAS a glimmer of conscience in the younger!

Most men believe only what they find or imagine possible to themselves. They may be sure of this, that there are men so different from them that no judgment they pass upon them is worth a straw, simply because it does not apply to them. I assert of Ian that neither beauty nor intellect attracted him. Imagination would entice him, but the least lack of principle would arrest its influence. The simplest manifestation of a live conscience would draw him more than anything else. I do not mean the conscience that proposes questions, but the conscience that loves right and turns from wrong.

Notwithstanding the damsel's invitation, he did not resume his pipe. He was simple, but not free and easy—too sensitive to the relations of life to be familiar upon invitation with any girl. If she was not one with whom to hold real converse, it was impossible to blow dandelions with her, and talk must confine itself to the commonplace. After gentlest assays to know what was possible, the result might be that he grew courteously playful, or drew back, and confined himself to the formal.

In the conversation that followed, he soon found the younger capable of being interested, and, having seen much in many parts of the world, had plenty to tell her. Christina smiled sweetly, taking everything with over-gentle politeness, but looking as if all that interested her was, that there they were, talking about it. Provoked at last by her persistent lack of GENUINE reception, Ian was tempted to try her with something different: perhaps she might be moved to horror! Any feeling would be a FIND! He thought he would tell them an adventure he had read in a book of travels.

In Persia, alone in a fine moonlit night, the traveller had fallen asleep on his horse, but woke suddenly, roused by something frightful, he did not know what. The evil odour all about him explained, however, his bewilderment and terror. Presently he was bumped on this side, then bumped on that; first one knee, then the other, would be struck; now the calf of one leg was caught, now the calf of the other; then both would be caught at once, and he shoved nearly over his pommel. His horse was very uneasy, but could ill help himself in the midst of a moving mass of uncertain objects. The traveller for a moment imagined himself in a boat on the sea, with a huge quantity of wrecked cargo floating around him, whence came the frequent collisions he was undergoing; but he soon perceived that the vague shapes were boxes, pannierwise on the backs of mules, moving in caravan along the desert. Of not a few the lids were broken, of some gone altogether, revealing their contents—the bodies of good Mussulmans, on their way to the consecrated soil of Mecca for burial. Carelessly shambled the mules along, stumbling as they jogged over the uneven ground, their boxes tilting from side to side, sorely shaken, some of them, in frustration of dying hopes, scattering their contents over the track —for here and there a mule carried but a wreck of coffins. On and on over the rough gravelly waste, under the dead cold moon, weltered the slow stream of death!

"You may be sure," concluded Ian, "he made haste out of the ruck! But it was with difficulty he got clear, happily to windward—then for an hour sat motionless on his horse, watching through the moonlight the long dark shadow flitting toward its far-off goal. When at length he could no longer descry it, he put his horse to his speed—but not to overtake it."

As he spoke, Mercy's eyes grew larger and larger, never leaving his face. She had at least imagination enough for that! Christina curled her pretty lip, and looked disgusted. The one at a horrible tale was horrified, the other merely disgusted! The one showed herself capable of some reception; the other did not.

"Something might be done with that girl!" thought Ian.

"Did he see their faces?" drawled Christina.

Mercy was silent, but her eyes remained fixed on him. It was Ian's telling, more than the story, that impressed her.

"I don't think he mentions them," answered Ian. "But shall I tell you," he went on, "what seems to me the most unpleasant thing about the business?"

"Do," said Christina.

"It is that the poor ghosts should see such a disagreeable fuss made with their old clothes."

Christina smiled.

"Do you think ghosts see what goes on after they are dead?" asked Mercy.

"The ghosts are not dead," said Ian, "and I can't tell. But I am inclined to think some ghosts have to stay a while and look on."

"What would be the good of that?" returned Mercy.

"Perhaps to teach them the little good they were in, or got out of the world," he answered. "To have to stick to a thing after it is dead, is terrible, but may teach much."

"I don't understand you," said Mercy. "The world is not dead!"

"Better and better!" thought Ian with himself. "The girl CAN understand! —A thing is always dead to you when you have done with it," he answered her. "Suppose you had a ball-dress crumpled and unsightly—the roses on it withered, and the tinsel shining hideously through them—would it not be a dead dress?"

"Yes, indeed."

"Then suppose, for something you had done, or for something you would not stop being, you had to wear that ball-dress till something came about— you would be like the ghosts that cannot get away.—Suppose, when you were old and wrinkled,—"

"You are very amusing, Captain Macruadh!" said Christina, with a bell-like laugh. But Ian went on.

"Some stories tell us of ghosts with the same old wrinkled faces in which they died. The world and its uses over, they are compelled to haunt it still, seeing how things go but taking no share in them beholding the relief their death is to all, feeling they have lost their chance of beauty, and are fixed in ugliness, having wasted being itself! They are like a man in a miserable dream, in which he can do nothing, but in which he must stay, and go dreaming, dreaming on without hope of release. To be in a world and have nothing to do with it, must be awful! A little more imagination would do some people good!"

"No, please!—no more for me!" said Christina, laughing as she rose.

Mercy was silent. Though she had never really thought about anything herself, she did not doubt that certain people were in earnest about something. She knew that she ought to be good, and she knew she was not good; how to be good she did not know, for she had never set herself, to be good. She sometimes wished she were good; but there are thousands of wandering ghosts who would be good if they might without taking trouble: the kind of goodness they desire would not be worth a life to hold it.

Fear is a wholesome element in the human economy; they are merely silly who would banish it from all association with religion. True, there is no religion in fear; religion is love, and love casts out fear; but until a man has love, it is well he should have fear. So long as there are wild beasts about, it is better to be afraid than secure.

The vague awe ready to assail every soul that has not found rest in its source, readier the more honest the soul, had for the first time laid hold of Mercy. The earnest face of the speaker had most to do with it. She had never heard anybody talk like that!

The lady of the house appeared, asking, with kind dignity, if they would not take some refreshment: to a highlander hospitality is a law where not a passion. Christina declined the offer.

"Thanks! we were only a little tired, and are quite rested now," she said. "How beautifully sheltered your house is!"

"On the side of the sea, yes," answered Mrs. Macruadh; "but not much on the east where we want it most. The trees are growing, however!"

When the sisters were out of sight of the cottage—

"Well!" remarked Christina, "he's a nice young man too, is he not? Exceedingly well bred! And what taste he has! He knows how to amuse ladies!"

Mercy did not answer.

"I never heard anything so disgusting!" pursued Christina.

"But," suggested Mercy, "you like to READ horrid stories, Chrissy! You said so only yesterday! And there was nothing in what he told us that oughtn't to be spoken about."

"What!—not those hideous coffins—and the bodies dropping out of them —all crawling, no doubt?"

"That is your own, Chrissy! You KNOW he did not go so far as that! If Colonel Webberly had told you the story, you would have called it charming—in fun, of course, I mean!"

But Christina never liked the argumentum ad feminam.

"I would not! You know I would not!" she exclaimed. "I do believe the girl has fallen in love with the horrid man! Of the two, I declare, I like the ploughman better. I am sorry I happened to vex him; he is a good stupid sort of fellow! I can't bear this man! How horribly he fixed his eyes on you when he was talking that rubbish about the ball-dress!"

"He was anxious to make himself understood. I know he made me think I must mind what I was about!"

"Oh, nonsense! We didn't come into this wilderness to be preached to by a lay John the Baptist! He is an ill-bred fellow!"

She would not have said so much against him, had not Mercy taken his part.

Mercy rarely contradicted her sister, but even this brief passage with a real man had roused the justice in her.

"I don't agree with you, Chrissy," she said. "He seems to me VERY MUCH of a gentleman!"

She did not venture to say all she felt, not choosing to be at absolute variance, and the threatened quarrel blew over like a shower in spring.

But some sort of impression remained from the words of Ian on the mind of Mercy, for the next morning she read a chapter in the book of Genesis, and said a prayer her mother had taught her.

CHAPTER XII.

AMONG THE HILLS.

When Mr. and Mrs. Palmer reached Inverness, they found they could spend a few days there, one way and another, to good purpose, for they had friends to visit as well as shopping to do. Mr. Palmer's affairs calling him to the south were not immediately pressing, and their sojourn extended itself to a full week of eight days, during which the girls were under no rule but their own. Their parents regarded them as perfectly to be trusted, nor were the girls themselves aware of any reason why they should not be so regarded.

The window of Christina's bedroom overlooked a part of the road between the New House and the old castle; and she could see from it all the ridge as far as the grove that concealed the cottage: if now they saw more of the young men their neighbours, and were led farther into the wilds, thickets, or pasturage of their acquaintance, I cannot say she had no hand in it.

She was depressed by a sense of failure; the boor, as she called him, was much too thick-skinned for any society but that of his bulls! and she had made no progress with the Valentine any more than with the Orson; he was better pleased with her ugly sister than with her beautiful self!

She would have given neither of tie men another thought, but that there was no one else with whom to do any of that huckster business called flirting, which to her had just harm enough in it to make it interesting to her. She was one of those who can imagine beauty nor enjoyment in a thing altogether right. She took it for granted that bad and beautiful were often one; that the pleasures of the world owed their delight to a touch, a wash, a tincture of the wicked in them. Such have so many crooked lines in themselves that they fancy nature laid down on lines of crookedness. They think the obliquity the beauty of the campanile, the blurring the charm of the sketch.

I tread on delicate ground—ground which, alas! many girls tread boldly, scattering much feather-bloom from the wings of poor Psyche, gathering for her hoards of unlovely memories, and sowing the seed of many a wish that they had done differently. They cannot pass over such ground and escape having their nature more or less vulgarized. I do not speak of anything counted wicked; it is only gambling with the precious and lovely things of the deepest human relation! If a girl with such an experience marry a man she loves—with what power of loving may be left such a one —will she not now and then remember something it would be joy to discover she had but dreamed? will she be able always to forget certain cabinets in her brain which "it would not do" to throw open to the husband who thinks her simple as well as innocent? Honesty and truth, God's essentials, are perhaps more lacking in ordinary intercourse between young men and women than anywhere else. Greed and selfishness are as busy there as in money-making and ambition. Thousands on both sides are constantly seeking more than their share—more also than they even intend to return value for. Thousands of girls have been made sad for life by the speeches of a man careful all the time to SAY nothing that amounted to a pledge! I do not forget that many a woman who would otherwise have been worth little, has for her sorrow found such consolation that she has become rich before God; these words hold nevertheless: "It must needs be that offences come, but woe to that man by whom the offence cometh!"

On a morning two days later, Christina called Mercy, rather imperiously, to get ready at once for their usual walk. She obeyed, and they set out. Christina declared she was perishing with cold, and they walked fast. By and by they saw on the road before them the two brothers walking slow; one was reading, the other listening. When they came nearer they descried in Alister's hand a manuscript volume; Ian carried an old-fashioned fowling-piece. It was a hard frost, which was perhaps the cause of Alister's leisure so early in the day.

Hearing the light steps of the girls behind them, the men turned. The laird was the first to speak. The plough and the fierce bulls not there to bewilder their judgment, the young women immediately discovered their perception in the matter of breeding to be less infallible than they had imagined it: no well bred woman could for a moment doubt the man before them a gentleman—though his carriage was more courteous and more natural than is often seen in a Mayfair drawing-room, and his English, a little old-fashioned. Ian was at once more like and more unlike other people. His manner was equally courteous, but notably stiffer: he was as much at his ease, but more reserved. To use a figure, he did not step out so far to meet them.

They walked on together.

"You are a little earlier than usual this morning, ladies!" remarked the chief.

"How do you know that, Mr. Macruadh?" rejoined Christina.

"I often see you pass—and till now always at the same hour."

"And yet we have never met before!"

"The busy and the"—he hesitated a moment—"unbusy seldom meet," said the chief.

"Why don't you say the IDLE?" suggested Christina.

"Because that would be rude."

"Why would it be rude? Most people, suppose, are more idle than busy!"

"IDLE is a word of blame; I had no right to use it."

"I should have taken you for one of those who always speak their minds!"

"I hope I do when it is required, and I have any to speak."

"You prefer judging with closed doors!"

The chief was silent: he did not understand her. Did she want him to say he did not think them idle? or, if they were, that they were quite right?

"I think it hard," resumed Christina, with a tone of injury, almost of suffering, in her voice, "that we should be friendly and open with people, and they all the time thinking of us in a way it would be rude to tell us! It is enough to make one vow never to speak to—to anybody again!"

Alister turned and looked at her. What could she mean?

"You can't think it hard," he said, "that people should not tell you what they think of you the moment they first see you!"

"They might at least tell us what they mean by calling us idle!"

"I said NOT BUSY."

"Is EVERYBODY to blame that is idle?" persisted Christina.

"Perhaps my brother will answer you that question," said Alister.

"If my brother and I tell you honestly what we thought of you when first we saw you," said Ian, "will you tell us honestly what you thought of us?"

The girls cast an involuntary glance at each other, and when their eyes met, could not keep them from looking conscious. A twitching also at the corners of Mercy's mouth showed they had been saying more than they would care to be cross-questioned upon.

"Ah, you betray yourselves, ladies!" Ian said. "It is all very well to challenge us, but you are not prepared to lead the way!"

"Girls are never allowed to lead!" said Christina. "The men are down on them the moment they dare!"

"I am not that way inclined," answered Ian. "If man or woman lead TO anything, success will justify the leader. I will propose another thing!"

"What is it?" asked Christina.

"To agree that, when we are about to part, with no probability of meeting again in this world, we shall speak out plainly what we think of each other!"

"But that will be such a time!" said Christina.

"In a world that turns quite round every twenty-four hours, it may be a very short time!"

"We shall be coming every summer, though I hope not to stay through another winter!"

"Changes come when they are least expected!"

"We cannot know," said Alister, "that we shall never meet again!"

"There the probability will be enough."

"But how can we come to a better—I mean a FAIRER opinion of each other, when we meet so seldom?" asked Mercy innocently.

"This is only the second time we have met, and already we are not quite strangers!" said Christina.

"On the other hand," said Alister, "we have been within call for more than two months, and this is our second meeting!"

"Well, who has not called?" said Christina.

The young men were silent. They did not care to discuss the question as to which mother was to blame in the matter.

They were now in the bottom of the valley, had left the road, and were going up the side of the burn, often in single file, Alister leading, and Ian bringing up the rear, for the valley was thickly strewn with lumps of gray rock, of all shapes and sizes. They seemed to have rolled down the hill on the other side of the burn, but there was no sign of their origin: the hill was covered with grass below, and with heather above. Such was the winding of the way among the stones—for path there was none—that again and again no one of them could see another. The girls felt the strangeness of it, and began to experience, without knowing it, a little of the power of solitary places.

After walking thus for some distance, they found their leader halted.

"Here we have to cross the burn," he said, "and go a long way up the other side."

"You want to be rid of us!" said Christina.

"By no means," replied Alister. "We are delighted to have you with us. But we must not let you get tired before turning to go back."

"If you really do not mind, we should like to go a good deal farther. I want to see round the turn there, where another hill comes from behind and closes up the view. We haven't anybody to go with us, and have seen nothing of the country. The men won't take us shooting; and mamma is always so afraid we lose ourselves, or fall down a few precipices, or get into a bog, or be eaten by wild beasts!"

"If this frost last, we shall have time to show you something of the country. I see you can walk!"

"We can walk well enough, and should so like to get to the top of a mountain!"

"For the crossing then!" said Alister, and turning to the burn, jumped and re-jumped it, as if to let them see how to do it.

The bed of the stream was at the spot narrowed by two rocks, so that, though there was little of it, the water went through with a roar, and a force to take a man off his legs. It was too wide for the ladies, and they stood eyeing it with dismay, fearing an end to their walk and the pleasant companionship.

"Do not be frightened, ladies," said Alister: "it is not too wide for you."

"You have the advantage of us in your dress!" said Christina.

"I will get you over quite safe," returned the chief.

Christina looked as if she could not trust herself to him.

"I will try," said Mercy.

"Jump high," answered Alister, as he sprang again to the other side, and held out his hand across the chasm.

"I can neither jump high nor far!" said Mercy.

"Don't be in a hurry. I will take you—no, not by the hand; that might slip— but by the wrist. Do not think how far you can jump; all you have to do is to jump. Only jump as high as you can."

Mercy could not help feeling frightened—the water rushed so fast and loud below.

"Are you sure you can get me over?" she asked.

"Yes."

"Then I will jump."

She sprang, and Alister, with a strong pull on her arm, landed her easily.

"It is your turn now," he said, addressing Christina.

She was rather white, but tried to laugh.

"I—I—I don't think I can!" she said.

"It is really nothing," persuaded the chief.

"I am sorry to be a coward, but I fear I was born one."

"Some feelings nobody can help," said Ian, "but nobody need give way to them. One of the bravest men I ever knew would always start aside if the meanest little cur in the street came barking at him; and yet on one occasion, when the people were running in all directions, he took a mad dog by the throat, and held him. Come, Alister! you take her by one arm and I will take her by the other."

The chief sprang to her side, and the moment she felt the grasp of the two men, she had the needful courage. The three jumped together, and all were presently walking merrily along the other bank, over the same kind of ground, in single file—Ian bringing up the rear.

The ladies were startled by a gun going off close behind them.

"I beg your pardon," said Ian, "but I could not let the rascal go."

"What have you killed?" his brother asked.

"Only one of my own family—a red-haired fellow!" answered Ian, who had left the path, and was going up the hill.

The girls looked, but saw nothing, and following him a few yards, came to him behind a stone.

"Goodness gracious!" exclaimed Christina, with horror in her tone, "it's a fox!—Is it possible you have shot a fox?"

The men laughed.

"And why not?" asked Alister, as if he had no idea what she could mean. "Is the fox a sacred animal in the south?"

"It's worse than poaching!" she cried.

"Hardly!" returned Alister. "No doubt you may get a good deal of fun out of Reynard, but you can't make game of him! Why—you look as if you had lost a friend! I admire his intellect, but we can't afford to feed it on chickens and lambs."

"But to SHOOT him!"

"Why not? We do not respect him here. He is a rascal, to be sure, but then he has no money, and consequently no friends!"

"He has many friends! What WOULD Christian or Mr. Sercombe say to shooting, actually shooting a fox!"

"You treat him as if he were red gold!" said the chief. "We build temples neither to Reynard nor Mammon here. We leave the men of the south to worship them!"

"They don't worship them!" said Mercy.

"Do they not respect the rich man because he is rich, and look down on the poor man because he is poor?" said Ian. "Though the rich be a wretch, they think him grand; though the poor man be like Jesus Christ, they pity him!"

"And shouldn't the poor be pitied?" said Christina.

"Not except they need pity."

"Is it not pitiable to be poor?"

"By no means. It is pitiable to be wretched—and that, I venture to suspect, the rich are oftener than the poor.—But as to master Reynard there—instead of shooting him, what would you have had us do with him?"

"Hunt him, to be sure."

"Would he like that better?"

"What he would like is not the question. The sport is the thing."

"That will show you why he is not sacred here: we do not hunt him. It would be impossible to hunt this country; you could not ride the ground.

Besides, there are such multitudes of holes, the hounds would scarcely have a chance. No; the only dog to send after the fellow is a leaden one."

"There's another!" exclaimed the chief; "—there, sneaking away!—and your gun not loaded, Ian!"

"I am so glad!" said Christina. "He at least will escape you!"

"And some poor lamb in the spring won't escape him!" returned Alister.

"Lambs are meant to be eaten!" said Christina.

"Yes; but a lamb might think it hard to feed such a creature!"

"If the fox is of no good in the world," said Mercy, "why was he made?"

"He can't be of no good," answered the chief. "What if some things are, just that we may get rid of them?"

"COULD they be made just to be got rid of?"

"I said—that WE might get rid of them: there is all the difference in that. The very first thing men had to do in the world was to fight beasts."

"I think I see what you mean," said Mercy: "if there had been no wild beasts to fight with, men would never have grown able for much!"

"That is it," said Alister. "They were awful beasts! and they had poor weapons to fight them with—neither guns nor knives!"

"And who knows," suggested Ian, "what good it may be to the fox himself to make the best of a greedy life?"

"But what is the good to us of talking about such things?" said Christina. "They're not interesting!"

The remark silenced the brothers: where indeed could be use without interest?

But Mercy, though she could hardly have said she found the conversation VERY interesting, felt there was something in the men that cared to talk about such things, that must be interesting if she could only get at it. They were not like any other men she had met!

Christina's whole interest in men was the admiration she looked for and was sure of receiving from them; Mercy had hitherto found their company stupid.

CHAPTER XIII.

THE LAKE.

Silence lasted until they reached the shoulder of the hill that closed the view up the valley. As they rounded it, the sun went behind a cloud, and a chill wind, as if from a land where dwelt no life, met them. The hills stood back, and they were on the shore of a small lake, out of which ran the burn. They were very desolate-looking hills, with little heather, and that bloomless, to hide their hard gray bones. Their heads were mostly white with frost and snow; their shapes had little beauty; they looked worn and hopeless, ugly and sad—and so cold! The water below was slaty gray, in response to the gray sky above: there seemed no life in either. The hearts of the girls sank within them, and all at once they felt tired. In the air was just one sign of life: high above the lake wheeled a large fish-hawk.

"Look!" said Alister pointing; "there is the osprey that lives here with his wife! He is just going to catch a fish!"

He had hardly spoken when the bird, with headlong descent, shot into the water, making it foam up all about. He reappeared with a fish in his claws, and flew off to find his mate.

"Do you know the very bird?" asked Mercy.

"I know him well. He and his wife have built on that conical rock you see there in the middle of the water many years."

"Why have you never shot him? He would look well stuffed!" said Christina.

She little knew the effect of her words; the chief HATED causeless killing; and to hear a lady talk of shooting a high-soaring creature of the air as coolly as of putting on her gloves, was nauseous to him. Ian gave him praise afterwards for his unusual self-restraint. But it was a moment or two ere he had himself in hand.

"Do you not think he looks much better going about God's business?" he said.

"Perhaps; but he is not yours; you have not got him!"

"Why should I have him? He seems, indeed, the more mine the higher he goes. A dead stuffed thing—how could that be mine at all? Alive, he seems to soar in the very heaven of my soul!"

"You showed the fox no such pity!" remarked Mercy.

"I never killed a fox to HAVE him!" answered Alister. "The osprey does no harm. He eats only fish, and they are very plentiful; he never kills birds or hares, or any creature on the land. I do not see how any one could wish to kill the bird, except from mere love of destruction! Why should I make a life less in the world?"

"There would be more lives of fish—would there not?" said Mercy. "I don't want you to shoot the poor bird; I only want to hear your argument!"

The chief could not immediately reply, Ian came to his rescue.

"There are qualities in life," he said. "One cannot think the fish-life so fine, so full of delight as the bird-life!"

"No. But," said Mercy, "have the fishes not as good a right to their life as the birds?"

"Both have the right given them by the maker of them. The osprey was made to eat the fish, and the fish, I hope, get some good of being eaten by the osprey."

"Excuse me, Captain Macruadh, but that seems to me simple nonsense!" said Christina.

"I hope it is true."

"I don't know about being true, but it must be nonsense."

"It must seem so to most people."

"Then why do you say it?"

"Because I hope it is true."

"Why should you wish nonsense to be true?"

"What is true cannot be nonsense. It looks nonsense only to those that take no interest in the matter. Would it be nonsense to the fishes?"

"It does seem hard," said Mercy, "that the poor harmless things should be gobbled up by a creature pouncing down upon them from another element!"

"As the poor are gobbled up everywhere by the rich!"

"I don't believe that. The rich are very kind to the poor."

"I beg your pardon," said Ian, "but if you know no more about the rich than you do about the fish, I can hardly take your testimony. The fish are the most carnivorous creatures in the world."

"Do they eat each other?"

"Hardly that. Only the cats of Kilkenny can do that."

"I used a common phrase!"

"You did, and I am rude: the phrase must bear the blame for both of us. But the fish are even cannibals—eating the young of their own species! They are the most destructive of creatures to other lives."

"I suppose," said Mercy, "to make one kind of creature live on another kind, is the way to get the greatest good for the greatest number!"

"That doctrine, which seems to content most people, appears to me a poverty-stricken and selfish one. I can admit nothing but the greatest good to every individual creature."

"Don't you think we had better be going, Mercy? It has got quite cold; I am afraid it will rain," said Christina, drawing her cloak round her with a little shiver.

"I am ready," answered Mercy.

The brothers looked at each other. They had come out to spend the day together, but they could not leave the ladies to go home alone; having brought them across the burn, they were bound to see them over it again! An imperceptible sign passed between them, and Alister turned to the girls.

"Come then," he said, "we will go back!"

"But you were not going home yet!" said Mercy.

"Would you have us leave you in this wild place?"

"We shall find our way well enough. The burn will guide us."

"Yes; but it will not jump over you; it will leave you to jump over it!"

"I forgot the burn!" said Christina.

"Which way were you going?" asked Mercy, looking all around for road or pathway over the encircling upheaved wildernesses.

"This way," answered Ian. "Good-bye."

"Then you are not coming?"

"No. My brother will take care of you."

He went straight as an arrow up the hill. They stood and watched him go. At what seemed the top, he turned and waved his cap, then vanished.

Christina felt disappointed. She did not much care for either of the very peculiar young men, but any company was better than none; a man was better than a woman; and two men were better than one! If these were not equal to admiring her as she deserved, what more remunerative labour than teaching them to do so?

The thing that chiefly disappointed her in them was, that they had so little small talk. It was so stupid to be always speaking sense! always polite! always courteous!—"Two sir Charles Grandisons," she said, "are two too many!" And indeed the History of Sir Charles Grandison had its place in the small library free to them from childhood; but Christina knew nothing of him except by hearsay.

The young men had been brought up in a solemn school—had learned to take life as a serious and lovely and imperative thing. Not the less, upon occasions of merry-making, would they frolic like young colts even yet, and that without the least reaction or sense of folly afterwards. At the same time, although Ian had in the village from childhood the character, especially in the workshops of the carpenter, weaver, and shoemaker, of being 'full of humour, he was in himself always rather sad, being perplexed with many things: his humour was but the foam of his troubled sea.

Christina was annoyed besides that Mercy seemed not indifferent to the opinion of the men. It was from pure inexperience of the man-world, she said to herself, that the silly child could see anything interesting in them! GENTLEMEN she must allow them—but of such an old-fashioned type as to be gentlemen but by courtesy—not gentlemen in the world's count! She was of the world; they of the north of Scotland! All day Mercy had been on their side and against her! It might be from sheer perversity, but she had never been like that before! She must take care she did not make a fool of herself! It might end in some unhappiness to the young goose! Assuredly neither her father nor mother would countenance the thing! She must throw herself into the breach! But which of them was she taking a fancy to?

She was not so anxious about her sister, however, as piqued that she had not herself gathered one expression of homage, surprised one look of admiration, seen one sign of incipient worship in either. Of the two she liked better the ploughman! The other was more a man of the world—but he was not of her world! With him she was a stranger in a very strange land!

Christina's world was a very small one, and in its temple stood her own image. Ian belonged to the universe. He was a gentleman of the high court. Wherever he might go throughout God's worlds, he would be at home. How could there be much attraction between Christina and him?

Alister was more talkative on the way back than he had been all day. Christina thought the change caused by having them, or rather her, to himself alone; but in reality it sprang from the prospect of soon rejoining his brother without them. Some of the things he said, Mercy found well worth hearing; and an old Scotch ballad which he repeated, having learned it of a lowland nurse, appeared to her as beautiful as it was wild and strange. For Christina, she despised the Scotch language: it was vulgar! Had Alister informed her that Beowulf, "the most important of all the relics of the Pagan Anglo-Saxon, is written in undeniable Scotch, the English of the period," it would have made no difference to Christina! Why should it? She had never yet cared for any book beyond the novels of a certain lady which, to speak with due restraint, do not tend to profitable thought. At the same time, it was not for the worst in them that she liked them; she did not understand them well enough to see it. But there was ground to fear that, when she came to understand, shocked at first, she would speedily get accustomed to it, and at length like them all the better for it.

In Mercy's unawakened soul, echoed now and then a faint thrill of response to some of the things Alister said, and, oftener, to some of the verses he repeated; and she would look up at him when he was silent, with an unconscious seeking glance, as if dimly aware of a beneficent presence. Alister was drawn by the honest gaze of her yet undeveloped and homely countenance, with its child-look in process of sublimation, whence the woman would glance out and vanish again, leaving the child to give disappointing answers. There was something in it of the look a dog casts up out of his beautiful brown eyes into the mystery of his master's countenance. She was on the edge of coming awake; all was darkness about her, but something was pulling at her! She had never known before that a lady might be lovely in a ballad as well as in a beautiful gown!

Finding himself so listened to, though the listener was little more than a child, the heart of the chief began to swell in his great bosom. Like a child he was pleased. The gray day about him grew sweet; its very grayness was sweet, and of a silvery sheen. When they arrived at the burn, and, easily enough from that side, he had handed them across, he was not quite so glad to turn from them as he had expected to be.

"Are you going?" said Christina with genuine surprise, for she had not understood his intention.

"The way is easy now," he answered. "I am sorry to leave you, but I have to join Ian, and the twilight will be flickering down before I reach the place."

"And there will be no moon!" said Mercy: "how will you get home through the darkness?"

"We do not mean to come home to-night."

"Oh, then, you are going to friends!"

"No; we shall be with each other—not a soul besides."

"There can't surely be a hotel up there?"

Alister laughed as he answered,

"There are more ways than one of spending a night on the hills. If you look from a window—in that direction," he said, pointing, "the last thing before you go to bed, you will see that at least we shall not perish with cold."

He sprang again over the burn, and with a wave of his bonnet, went, like Ian, straight up the hill.

The girls stood for some time watching him climb as if he had been going up a flight of stairs, until he stood clear against the sky, when, with another wave of his bonnet, he too disappeared.

Mercy did not forget to look from her window in the direction Alister had indicated. There was no room to mistake what he meant, for through the dark ran a great opening to the side of a hill, somewhere in the night, where glowed and flamed, reddening the air, a huge crescent of fire, slowly climbing, like a column of attack, up toward the invisible crest.

"What does it mean?" she said to herself. "Why do they make such a bonfire—with nobody but themselves to enjoy it? What strange men—out by themselves in the dark night, on the cold hill! What can they be doing it for? I hope they have something to eat! I SHOULD like to hear them talk! I wonder what they are saying about US! I am certain we bored them!"

The brothers did speak of them, and readily agreed in some notion of their characters; but they soon turned to other things, and there passed a good deal that Mercy could not have followed. What would she, for instance, have made of Alister's challenge to his brother to explain the metaphysical necessity for the sine, tangent, and secant of an angle belonging to its supplement as well?

When the ladies overtook them in the morning, Alister was reading, from an old manuscript volume of his brother's which he had found in a chest, a certain very early attempt at humour, and now they disputed concerning it as they watched the fire. It had abundance of faults, and in especial lacked suture, but will serve to show something of Ian's youthful ingenium.

TO A VAGRANT.

Gentle vagrant, stumping over
Several verdant fields of clover!

Subject of unnumbered knockings!
Tattered' coat and ragged stockings,
Slouching hat and roving eye,
Tell of SETTLED vagrancy!
    Wretched wanderer, can it be
The poor laws have leaguered thee?
Hear'st thou, in thy thorny den,
Tramp of rural policemen,
Inly fancying, in thy rear
Coats of blue and buttons clear,
While to meet thee, in the van
Stalks some vengeful alderman?—
Each separate sense bringing a notion
Of forms that teach thee locomotion!
    Beat and battered altogether,
By fellow-men, by wind and weather;
Hounded on through fens and bogs,
Chased by men and bit by dogs:
And, in thy weakly way of judging,
So kindly taught the art of trudging;
Or, with a moment's happier lot,
Pitied, pensioned, and forgot—
Cutty-pipe thy regium donum;
Poverty thy summum bonum;
Thy frigid couch a sandstone stratum;
A colder grave thy ultimatum;
Circumventing, circumvented;
In short, excessively tormented,
Everything combines to scare
Charity's dear pensioner!
—Say, vagrant, can'st thou grant to me
A slice of thy philosophy?
    Haply, in thy many trudgings,
Having found unchallenged lodgings,
Thy thoughts, unused to saddle-crupper,
Ambling no farther than thy supper—
Thou, by the light of heaven-lit taper,

Mendest thy prospective paper!
Then, jolly pauper, stitch till day;
Let not thy roses drop away,
Lest, begrimed with muddy matter,
Thy body peep from every tatter,
And men—a charitable dose—
Should physic thee with food and clothes!
   Nursling of adversity!
'Tis thy glory thus to be
Sinking fund of raggery!
Thus to scrape a nation's dishes,
And fatten on a few good wishes!
Or, on some venial treason bent,
Frame thyself a government,
For thy crest a brirnless hat,
Poverty's aristocrat!
   Nonne habeam te tristem,
Planet of the human system?
Comet lank and melancholic
—Orbit shocking parabolic—
Seen for a little in the sky
Of the world of sympathy—
Seldom failing when predicted,
Coming most when most restricted,
Dragging a nebulous tail with thee
Of hypothetic vagrancy—
Of vagrants large, and vagrants small,
Vagrants scarce visible at all!
   Matchless oracle of woe!
Anarchy in embryo!
Strange antipodes of bliss!
Parody on happiness!
Baghouse of the great creation!
Subject meet for strangulation,
By practice tutored to condense

The cautious inquiry for pence,
And skilful, with averted eye,
To hide thy latent roguery—
Lo, on thy hopes I clap a stopper!
Vagrant, thou shalt have no copper!
Gather thy stumps, and get thee hence,
Unwise solicitor of pence!

Alister, who all but worshipped Ian, and cherished every scrap from his pen, had not until quite lately seen this foolish production, as Ian counted it, and was delighted with it, as he would have been had it been much worse. Ian was vexed that he should like it, and now spent the greater part of an hour trying to show him how very bad in parts, even senseless it was. Profusion of epithets without applicability, want of continuity, purposelessness, silliness, heartlessness—were but a few of his denunciations. Alister argued it was but a bit of fun, and that anybody that knew Ian, knew perfectly he would never amuse himself with a fellow without giving him something, but it was in vain; Ian was bent on showing it altogether unworthy. So, not to waste the night, they dropped the dispute, and by the light of the blazing heather, turned to a chapter of Boethius.

CHAPTER XIV.

THE WOLVES.

My readers may remember that Ian was on the point of acquainting his mother with an important event in his spiritual history, when they were interrupted by the involuntary call of the girls from the New House. The mother, as will readily be believed, remained desirous of listening to her son's story, though dreading it would not be of a kind to give her much satisfaction; but partly from preventions—favoured, it must be confessed by Ian, and yet more from direct avoidance on his part, the days passed without her hearing anything more of it. Ian had in truth almost repented his offer of the narrative: a certain vague assurance that it would not be satisfactory to her, had grown upon him until he felt it unkind to lay before her an experience whose narration would seem to ask a sympathy she could not give. But the mother was unable to let the thing rest. More than by interest she was urged by anxiety. In spite of her ungodlike theories of God, it was impossible she could be in despair about her noble Ian; still, her hope was at best founded on the uncovenanted mercies of God, not on the security of his bond! She did not believe that God was doing and would do his best for every man; therefore she had no assurance that he would bring down the pride of Ian, and compel his acceptance of terms worthy of an old Roman father, half law-circumventing lawyer, half heartless tyrant. But her longing to hear what her son had proposed telling her, was chiefly inspired by the hope of getting nearer to him, of closer sympathy becoming possible between them through her learning more clearly what his views were. She constantly felt as if walking along the side of a thick hedge, with occasional thinnesses through which now and then she gained a ghostly glimpse of her heart's treasure gliding along the other side—close to her, yet so far that, when they spoke, they seemed calling across a gulf of dividing darkness. Therefore, the night after that spent by her sons on the hill, all having retired some two hours before, the mother, finding herself unable to sleep, rose as she had often done ere now, and stole to the door of the little room under the thatch where Ian lay. Listening, and judging him awake, she went softly in, and sat down by his bedside.

There had been such occasions on which, though son as well as mother was wide awake, neither spoke a word; but this time the mother could not be silent.

"You never told me, Ian, the story you began about something that made you pray!"

Ian saw he could not now draw back without causing, her more trouble than would the narration.

"Are you sure you will not take cold mother dear?" he said.

"I am warmly clad, my son; and my heart, more than I can tell you, is longing to hear all about it."

"I am afraid you will not find my story so interesting as you expect, mother!"

"What concerns you is more interesting to me than anything else in the whole world, Ian."

"Not more than God, mother?" said Ian.

The mother was silent. She was as honest as her sons. The question, dim-lucent, showed her, if but in shadow, something of the truth concerning herself—not so that she could grasp it, for she saw it as in a glimmer, a fluctuating, vanishing flash—namely, that she cared more about salvation than about God—that, if she could but keep her boy out of hell, she would be content to live on without any nearer approach to him in whom she had her being! God was to her an awe, not a ceaseless, growing delight!

There are centuries of paganism yet in many lovely Christian souls—paganism so deep, therefore so little recognized, that their earnest endeavour is to plant that paganism ineradicably in the hearts of those dearest to them.

As she did not answer, Ian was afraid she was hurt, and thought it better to begin his story at once.

"It was one night in the middle of winter—last winter, near Moscow," he began, "and the frost was very bitter—the worst night for cold I have ever known. I had gone with a companion into the depth of a great pine forest. On our way, the cold grew so intense, that we took refuge at a little public-house, frequented by peasants and persons of the lowest ranks. On entering I saw a scene which surpassed all for interest I had ever before witnessed. The little lonely house was crammed with Russian soldiers, fierce-looking fellows, and I daresay their number formed our protection from violence. Many of them were among the finest looking fellows I have ever seen. They were half drunk, and were dancing and singing with the wildest gesticulations and grimaces; but such singing for strange wildness and harmony combined I had never before listened to. One would keep up a solo for some minutes, when the whole company would join in a sort of chorus, dancing frantically about, but with the most perfect regularity of movement. One of them came up to me and with a low bow begged me in the name of the rest to give them some money. I accordingly gave them a silver ruble, upon which the whole party set up a shout, surrounded me, and in a moment a score of brawny fellows had lifted me in the air, where I was borne along in triumph. I took off my cap and gave three hip-hip-hurrahs as loud as my lungs could bawl, whereupon, with the profoundest expressions of gratitude, I was lowered from my elevation. One of them then who seemed to be the spokesman of the rest, seized me in his arms and gave me a hearty kiss on the cheek, on which I took my departure amid universal acclamation.—But all that's not worth telling you about; it was not for that I began—only the scene came up so clear before me that it drew me aside."

"I don't need to tell you, Ian," said his mother, with shining eyes, "that if it were only what you had to eat on the most ordinary day of your life, it would be interesting to me!"

"Thank you, mother dear; I seem to know that without being told; but I could never talk to you about anything that was not interesting to myself."

Here he paused. He would rather have stopped.

"Go on, go on, Ian. I am longing to hear."

"Well—where was I?—We left at the inn our carriage and horses, and went with our guns far into the forest—all of straight, tall pines, up and up; and the Little island-like tops of them, which, if there be a breath of wind, are sure to be swaying about like the motion of a dream, were as still as the big frosty stars in the deep blue overhead."

"What did you want in such a lonely place at that time of the night?" asked the mother.

She sat with firm-closed lips, and wide, night-filled eyes looking at her son, the fear of love in her beautiful face—a face more beautiful than any other that son had yet seen, fit window for a heart so full of refuge to look out of; and he knew how she looked though the darkness was between them.

"Wolves, mother," he answered.

She shuddered. She was a great reader in the long winter nights, and had read terrible stories of wolves—the last of which in Scotland had been killed not far from where they sat.

"What did you want with the wolves, Ian?" she faltered.

"To kill them, mother. I never liked killing animals any more than Alister; but even he destroys the hooded crow; and wolves are yet fairer game. They are the out-of-door devils of that country, and I fancy devils do go into them sometimes, as they did once into the poor swine: they are the terror of all who live near the forests.

"There was no moon—only star-light; but whenever we came to any opener space, there was light enough from the snow to see all about; there was light indeed from the snow all through the forest, but the trees were thick and dark. Far away, somewhere in the mystery of the black wood, we could now and then hear a faint howling: it came from the red throats of the wolves."

"You are frightening me, Ian!" said the mother, as if they had been two children telling each other tales.

"Indeed, mother, they are very horrible when they hunt in droves, ravenous with hunger. To kill one of them, if it be but one, is to do something for your kind. And just at that time I was oppressed with the feeling that I had done and was doing nothing for my people—my own humans; and not knowing anything else I could at the moment attempt, I resolved to go and kill a wolf or two: they had killed a poor woman only two nights before.

"As soon as we could after hearing the noise of them, we got up into two trees. It took us some time to discover two that were fit for our purpose, and we did not get them so near each other as we should have liked. It was rather anxious work too until we found them, for if we encountered on foot a pack of those demons, we could be but a moment or two alive: killing one, ten would be upon us, and a hundred more on the backs of those. But we hoped they would smell us up in the trees, and search for us, when we should be able to give account of a few of them at least: we had double-barrelled guns, and plenty of powder and ball."

"But how could you endure the cold—at night—and without food?"

"No, mother; we did not try that! We had plenty to eat in our pockets. My companion had a bottle of vodki, and—"

"What is that?" asked the mother with suspicion.

"A sort of raw spirit—horrible stuff—more like spirits of wine. They say it does not hurt in such cold."

"But, Ian!" cried the mother, and seemed unable to say more.

"Don't be frightened, mother!" said Ian, with a merry laugh. "Surely you do not imagine *I* would drink such stuff! True, I had my bottle, but it was full of tea. The Russians drink enormous quantities of tea—though not so strong as you make it."

"Go on, then, Ian; go on."

"We sat a long time, and there was no sign of the wolves coming near us. It was very cold, but our furs kept in our warmth. By and by I fell asleep—which was not dangerous so long as I kept warm, and I thought the cold must wake me before it began to numb me. And as 'I slept I dreamed; but my dream did not change the place; the forest, the tree I was in, all my surroundings were the same. I even dreamed that I came awake, and saw everything about me just as it was. I seemed to open my eyes, and look about me on the dazzling snow from my perch: I was in a small tree on the border of a little clearing.

"Suddenly, out of the wood to my left, issued something, running fast, but with soundless feet, over the snow. I doubted in my dream whether the object were a live thing or only a shadow. It came nearer, and I saw it was a child, a little girl, running as if for her life. She came straight to the tree I sat in, and when close to it, but without a moment's halt, looked up, and I saw a sweet little face, white with terror—which somehow seemed, however, not for herself, but for me. I called out after her to stop, and I would take her into the tree beside me, where the wolves could not reach her; but she only shook her head, and ran on over the clearing into the forest. Among the holes I watched the fleeting shape appear and disappear and appear again, until I saw it no more. Then first I heard another kind of howl from the wolves—that of pursuit. It strengthened and swelled, growing nearer and nearer, till at last, through the stillness of the night and the moveless forest and the dead snow, came to my ear a kind of soft rushing sound. I don't know how to describe it. The rustle of dry leaves is too sharp; it was like a very soft heavy rain on a window—a small dull padding padding: it was the feet of the wolves. They came nearer and grew louder and louder, but the noise was still muffled and soft. Their howling, however, was now loud and horrid. I suppose they cannot help howling; if they could, they would have too much power over poor creatures, coming upon them altogether at unawares; but as it is, they tell, whether they will or no, that they are upon the way. At length, dark as a torrent of pitch, out of the forest flowed a multitude of obscure things, and streamed away, black over the snow, in the direction the child had taken. They passed close to the foot of my tree, but did not even look up, flitting by like a shadow whose substance was unseen. Where the child had vanished they also disappeared: plainly they were after her!

"It was only a dream, mother! don't be so frightened," interrupted Ian, for here his mother gave a little cry, almost forgetting what the narration was.

"Then first," he went on, "I seemed to recover my self-possession. I saw that, though I must certainly be devoured by the wolves, and the child could not escape, I had no choice but go down and follow, do what I could, and die with her. Down I was the same instant, running as I had never run before even in a dream, along the track of the wolves. As I ran, I heard their howling, but it seemed so far off that I could not hope to be in time to kill one of them ere they were upon her. Still, by their howling, it did not appear they had reached her, and I ran on. Their noise grew louder and louder, but I seemed to run miles and miles, wondering what spell was upon me that I could not come up with them. All at once the clamour grew hideous, and I saw them. They were gathered round a tree, in a clearing just like that I had left, and were madly leaping against it, but ever falling back baffled. I looked up: in the top of the tree sat the little girl, her white face looking down upon them with a smile. All the terror had vanished from it. It was still white as the snow, but like the snow was radiating a white light through the dark foliage of the fir. I see it often, mother, so clear that I could paint it. I was enchanted at the sight. But she was not in safety yet, and I rushed into the heap of wolves, striking and stabbing with my hunting-knife. I got to the tree, and was by her in a moment. But as I took the child in my arms I woke, and knew that it was a dream. I sat in my own tree, and up against the stem of it broke a howling, surging black wave of wolves. They leaped at the tree-bole as a rock-checked billow would leap. My gun was to my shoulder in a moment, and blazed among them. Howls of death arose. Their companions fell upon the wounded, and ate them up. The tearing and yelling at the foot of the tree was like the tumult of devils full of hate and malice and greed. Then for the first time I thought whether such creatures might not be the open haunts of demons. I do not imagine that, when those our Lord drove out of the man asked permission to go into the swine, they desired anything unheard of before in the demon-world. I think they were not in the way of going into tame animals; but, as they must go out of the man, as they greatly dreaded the abyss of the disembodied, and as no ferocious animals fit to harbour them were near, they begged leave to go into such as were accessible, though unsuitable; whereupon the natural consequence followed: their presence made the poor swine miserable even to madness, and with the instinct of so many maniacs that in death alone lies their deliverance, they rushed straight into the loch."

"It may be so, Ian! But I want to hear how you got away from the wolves."

"I fired and fired; and still they kept rushing on the tree-hole, heaping themselves against it, those behind struggling up on the backs of those next it, in a storm of rage and hunger and jealousy. Not a few who had just helped to eat some of their fellows, were themselves eaten in turn, and not a scrap of them left; but it was a large pack, and it would have taken a long time to kill enough to satisfy those that remained. I killed and killed until my ammunition was gone, and then there was nothing for it but await the light. When the morning began to dawn, they answered its light with silence, and turning away swept like a shadow back into the wood. Strange to tell, I heard afterwards that a child had been killed by them in the earlier part of that same night. But even now sometimes, as I lie awake, I grow almost doubtful whether the whole was not a hideous dream.

"Not the less for that was what I went through between the time my powder came to an end and the dawn of the morning, a real spiritual fact.

"In the midst of the howling I grew so sleepy that the horrible noise itself seemed to lull me while it kept me awake, and I fell into a kind of reverie with which my dream came back and mingled. I seemed to be sitting in the tree with the little shining girl, and she was my own soul; and all the wrong things I had in me, and all the wrong things I had done, with all the weaknesses and evil tendencies of my nature, whether mine by fault or by inheritance, had taken shape, and, in the persons of the howling wolves below, were besieging me, to get at me, and devour me. Suddenly my soul was gone. Above were the still, bright stars, shining unmoved; beneath was the white, betraying snow, and the howling wolves; away through the forest was fleeting, ever fleeting, my poor soul, in the likeness of a white-faced child! All at once came a great stillness, as of a desert place, where breathed nor life of man nor life of beast. I was alone, frightfully alone—alone as I had never been before. The creatures at the foot of the tree were still howling, but their cry sounded far away and small; they were in some story I had been reading, not anywhere in my life! I was left and lost—left by whom?—lost by whom?—in the waste of my own being, without stay or comfort. I looked up to the sky; it was infinite—yet only a part of myself, and much too near to afford me any refuge from the desert of my lost self. It came down nearer; the limitless space came down, and clasped me, and held me. It came close to me—as if I had been a shape off which all nature was taking a mould. I was at once everything and nothing. I cannot tell you how frightful it was! In agony I cried to God, with a cry of utter despair. I cannot say whether I may believe that he answered me; I know this, that a great quiet fell upon me—but a quiet as of utter defeat and helplessness. Then again, I cannot tell how, the quiet and the helplessness melted away into a sense of God—a feeling as if great space all about me was God and not emptiness. Wolf nor sin could touch me! I was a wide peace—my very being peace! And in my mind—whether an echo from the Bible, I do not know—were the words:—'I, even I, am he that comforteth thee. I am God, thy saviour!' Whereas I had seemed all alone, I was with God, the only withness man can really share! I lifted my eyes; morning was in the east, and the wolves were slinking away over the snow."

How to receive the strange experience the mother did not know. She ought to say something, for she sorely questioned it! Not a word had he spoken belonging to the religion in which she had brought him up, except two—SIN and GOD! There was nothing in it about the atonement! She did not see that it was a dream, say rather a vision, of the atonement itself. To Ian her interpretation of the atonement seemed an everlasting and hopeless severance. The patience of God must surely be far more tried by those who would interpret him, than by those who deny him: the latter speak lies against him, the former speak lies for him! Yet all the time the mother felt as in the presence of some creature of a higher world—one above the ordinary race of men—whom the powers of evil had indeed misled, but perhaps not finally snared. She little thought how near she was to imagining that good may come out of evil—that there is good which is not of God! She did not yet understand that salvation lies in being one with Christ, even as the branch is one with the vine;—that any salvation short of knowing God is no salvation at all. What moment a man feels that he belongs to God utterly, the atonement is there, the son of God is reaping his harvest.

The good mother was not, however, one of those conceited, stiff-necked, power-loving souls who have been the curse and ruin of the church in all ages; she was but one of those in whom reverence for its passing form dulls the perception of unchangeable truth. They shut up God's precious light in the horn lantern of human theory, and the lantern casts such shadows on the path to the kingdom as seem to dim eyes insurmountable obstructions. For the sake of what they count revealed, they refuse all further revelation, and what satisfies them is merest famine to the next generation of the children of the kingdom. Instead of God's truth they offer man's theory, and accuse of rebellion against God such as cannot live on the husks they call food. But ah, home-hungry soul! thy God is not the elder brother of the parable, but the father with the best robe and the ring— a God high above all thy longing, even as the heavens are high above the earth.

CHAPTER XV.

THE GULF THAT DIVIDED.

When Ian ceased, a silence deep as the darkness around, fell upon them. To Ian, the silence seemed the very voice of God, clear in the darkness; to the mother it was a darkness interpenetrating the darkness; it was a great gulf between her and her boy. She must cry to him aloud, but what should she cry? If she did not, an opportunity, perhaps the last, on which hung eternal issues, would be gone for ever! Each moment's delay was a disobedience to her conscience, a yielding to love's sinful reluctance! With "sick assay" she heaved at the weight on her heart, but not a word would come. If Ian would but speak again, and break the spell of the terrible stillness! She must die in eternal wrong if she did not speak! But no word would come. Something in her would not move. It was not in her brain or her lips or her tongue, for she knew all the time she could speak if she would. The caitiff will was not all on the side of duty! She was not FOR the truth!—could she then be OF the truth? She did not suspect a divine reluctance to urge that which was not good.

Not always when the will works may we lay hold of it in the act: somehow, she knew not how, she heard herself speaking.

"Are you sure it was God, Ian?" she said.

The voice she heard was weak and broken, reedy and strained, like the voice of one all but dead.

"No, mother," answered Ian, "but I hope it was."

"Hopes, my dear hoy, are not to be trusted."

"That is true, mother; and yet we are saved by hope."

"We are saved by faith."

"I do not doubt it."

"You rejoice my heart. But faith in what?"

"Faith in God, mother."

"That will not save you."

"No, but God will."

"The devils believe in God, and tremble."

"I believe in the father of Jesus Christ, and do not tremble."

"You ought to tremble before an unreconciled God."

"Like the devils, mother?"

"Like a sinful child of Adam. Whatever your fancies, Ian, God will not hear you, except you pray to him in the name of his Son."

"Mother, would you take my God from me? Would you blot him out of the deeps of the universe?"

"Ian! are you mad? What frightful things you would lay to my charge!"

"Mother, I would gladly—oh how gladly! perish for ever, to save God from being the kind of God you would have me believe him. I love God, and will not think him other than good. Rather than believe he does not hear every creature that cries to him, whether he knows Jesus Christ or not, I would believe there was no God, and go mourning to my grave."

"That is not the doctrine of the gospel."

"It is, mother: Jesus himself says, 'Every one that hath heard and learned of the Father, cometh unto me.'"

"Why then do you not come to him, Ian?"

"I do come to him; I come to him every day. I believe in nobody but him. He only makes the universe worth being, or any life worth living!"

"Ian, I can NOT understand you! If you believe like that about him,—"

"I don't believe ABOUT him, mother! I believe in him. He is my life."

"We will not dispute about words! The question is, do you place your faith for salvation in the sufferings of Christ for you?"

"I do not, mother. My faith is in Jesus himself, not in his sufferings."

"Then the anger of God is not turned away from you."

"Mother, I say again—I love God, and will not believe such things of him as you say. I love him so that I would rather lose him than believe so of him."

"Then you do not accept the Bible as your guide?"

"I do, mother, for it tells me of Jesus Christ. There is no such teaching as you say in the Bible."

"How little you know your New Testament!"

"I don't know my New Testament! It is the only book I do know! I read it constantly! It is the only thing I could not live without!—No, I do not mean that! I COULD do without my Testament! Christ would BE all the same!"

"Oh, Ian! Ian! and yet you will not give Christ the glory of satisfying divine justice by his suffering for your sins!"

"Mother, to say that the justice of God is satisfied with suffering, is a piece of the darkness of hell. God is willing to suffer, and ready to inflict suffering to save from sin, but no suffering is satisfaction to him or his justice."

"What do you mean by his justice then?"

"That he gives you and me and everybody fair play."

The homeliness of the phrase offended the moral ear of the mother.

"How dare you speak lightly of HIM in my hearing!" she cried.

"Because I will speak for God even to the face of my mother!" answered Ian. "He is more to me than you, mother—ten times more."

"You speak against God, Ian," she rejoined, calmed by the feeling she had roused.

"No, mother. He speaks against God who says he does things that are not good. It does not make a thing good to call it good. I speak FOR him when I say lie cannot but give fair play. He knows he put rue where I was sure to sin; he will not condemn me because I have sinned; he leaves me to do that myself. He will condemn me only if I do not turn away from sin, for he has made me able to turn from it, and I do."

"He will forgive sin only for Christ's sake."

"He forgives it for his own name's sake, his own love's sake. There is no such word as FOR CHRIST'S SAKE in the New Testament—except where Paul prays us for Christ's sake to be reconciled to God. It is in the English New Testament, but not in the Greek."

"Then you do not believe that the justice of God demands the satisfaction of the sinner's endless punishment?"

"I do not. Nothing can satisfy the justice of God but justice in his creature. The justice of God is the love of what is right, and the doing of what is right. Eternal misery in the name of justice could satisfy none but a demon whose bad laws had been broken."

"I grant you that no amount of suffering on the part of the wicked could SATISFY justice; but it is the Holy One who suffers for our sins!"

"Oh, mother! JUSTICE do wrong for its own satisfaction! Did Jesus DESERVE punishment? If not, then to punish him was to wrong him!"

"But he was willing; he consented;"

"He yielded to injustice—but the injustice was man's, not God's. If Justice, insisted on punishent, it would at least insist on the guilty, not the innocent, being punished! it would revolt from the idea of the innocent being punished for the guilty! Mind, I say BEING PUNISHED, not SUFFERING: that is another thing altogether. It is an eternal satisfaction to love to suffer for the guilty, but not to justice that innocence should be punished for the guilty. The whole idea of such atonement is the merest subterfuge, a figment of the paltry human intellect to reconcile difficulties of its own invention. Once, when Alister had done something wrong, my father said, 'He must be punished—except some one will be punished for him!' I offered to take his place, partly that it seemed expected of me, partly that I was moved by vanity, and partly that I foresaw what would follow."

"And what did follow?" asked the mother, to whom the least word out of the past concerning her husband, was like news from the world beyond. At the same time it seemed almost an offence that one of his sons should know anything about him she did not know.

"He scarcely touched me, mother," answered Ian. "The thing taught me something very different from what he had meant to teach by it. That he failed to carry out his idea of justice helped me afterwards to see that God could not have done it either, for that it was not justice. Some perception of this must have lain at the root of the heresy that Jesus did not suffer, but a cloud-phantom took his place on the cross. Wherever people speculate instead of obeying, they fall into endless error."

"You graceless boy! Do you dare to say your father speculated instead of obeying?" cried the mother, hot with indignation.

"No, mother. It was not my father who invented that way of accounting for the death of our Lord."

"He believed it!"

"He accepted it, saturated with the tradition of the elders before he could think for himself. He does not believe it now."

"But why then should Christ have suffered?"

"It is the one fact that explains to me everything," said Ian. "—But I am not going to talk about it. So long as your theory satisfies you, mother, why should I show you mine? When it no longer satisfies you, when it troubles you as it has troubled me, and as I pray God it may trouble you, when you feel it stand between you and the best love you could give God, then I will share my very soul with you—tell you thoughts which seem to sublimate my very being in adoration."

"I do not see what other meaning you can put upon the statement that he was a sacrifice for our sins."

"Had we not sinned he would never have died; and he died to deliver us from our sins. He against whom was the sin, became the sacrifice for it; the Father suffered in the Son, for they are one. But if I could see no other explanation than yours, I would not, could not accept it—for God's sake I would not."

"How can you say you believe in Christ, when you do not believe in the atonement!"

"It is not so, mother. I do not believe what you mean by the atonement; what God means by it, I desire to accept. But we are never told to believe in the atonement; we are told to believe in Christ—and, mother, in the name of the great Father who hears me speak, I do believe in him."

"How can you, when you do not believe what God says about him?"

"I do. God does not say those things about him you think he says. They are mere traditions, not the teaching of those who understood him. But I might believe all about him quite correctly, and yet not believe in him."

"What do you call believing in him, then?"

"Obeying him, mother—to say it as shortly as I can. I try to obey him in the smallest things he says—only there are no small things he says—and so does Alister. I strive to be what he would have me, nor do I hold anything else worth my care. Let a man trust in his atonement to absolute assurance, if he does not do the things he tells him—the very things he said—he does not believe in him. He may be a good man, but he has not yet heard enough and learned enough of the Father to be sent to Jesus to learn more."

"Then I do not believe in him," said the mother, with a strange, sad gentleness—for his words awoke an old anxiety never quite at rest.

Ian was silent. The darkness seemed to deepen around them, and the silence grew keen. The mother began to tremble.

"GOD KNOWS," said Ian at length, and again the broken silence closed around them.

It was between God and his mother now! Unwise counsellors will persuade the half crazy doubter in his own faith, to believe that he does believe!—how much better to convince him that his faith is a poor thing, that he must rise and go and do the thing that Jesus tells him, and so believe indeed! When will men understand that it is neither thought nor talk, neither sorrow for sin nor love of holiness that is required of them, but obedience! To BE and to OBEY are one.

A cold hand grasping her heart, the mother rose, and went from the room. The gulf seemed now at last utterly, hopelessly impassable! She had only feared it before; she knew it now! She did not see that, while she believed evil things of God, and none the less that she called them good, oneness was impossible between her and any being in God's creation.

The poor mother thought herself broken-hearted, and lay down too sick to know that she was trembling from head to foot. Such was the hold, such the authority of traditional human dogma on her soul—a soul that scorned the notion of priestly interposition between God and his creature—that, instead of glorifying God that she had given birth to such a man, she wept bitterly because he was on the broad road to eternal condemnation.

But as she lay, now weeping, now still and cold with despair, she found that for some time she had not been thinking. But she had not been asleep! Whence then was this quiet that was upon her? Something had happened, though she knew of nothing! There was in her as it were a moonlight of peace!

"Can it be God?" she said to herself.

No more than Ian could she tell whether it was God or not; but from that night she had an idea in her soul by which to reach after "the peace of God." She lifted up her heart in such prayer as she had never prayed before; and slowly, imperceptibly awoke in her the feeling that, if she was not believing aright, God would not therefore cast her off, but would help her to believe as she ought to believe: was she not willing? Therewith she began to feel as if the gulf betwixt her and Ian were not so wide as she had supposed; and that if it were, she would yet hope in the Son of Man. Doubtless he was in rebellion against God, seeing he would question his ways, and refuse to believe the word he had spoken, but surely something might be done for him! The possibility had not yet dawned upon her that there could be anything in the New Testament but those doctrines against which the best in him revolted. She little suspected the glory of sky and earth and sea eternal that would one day burst upon her! that she would one day see God not only good but infinitely good—infinitely better than she had dared to think him, fearing to image him better than he was! Mortal, she dreaded being more just than God, more pure than her maker!

"I will go away to-morrow!" said Ian to himself. "I am only a pain to her. She will come to see things better without me! I cannot live in her sight any longer now! I will go, and come again."

His heart broke forth in prayer.

"O God, let my mother see that thou art indeed true-hearted; that thou dost not give us life by parings and subterfuges, but abundantly; that thou dost not make men in order to assert thy dominion over them, but that they may partake of thy life. O God, have pity when I cannot understand, and teach me as thou wouldst the little one whom, if thou wert an earthly father amongst us as thy son was an earthly son, thou wouldst carry about in thy arms. When pride rises in me, and I feel as if I ought to be free and walk without thy hand; when it looks as if a man should be great in himself, nor need help from God; then think thou of me, and I shall know that I cannot live or think without the self-willing life; that thou art because thou art, I am because thou art; that I am deeper in thee than my life, thou more to my being than that being to itself. Was not that Satan's temptation, Father? Did he not take self for the root of self in him, when God only is the root of all self? And he has not repented yet! Is it his thought coming up in me, flung from the hollow darkness of his soul into mine? Thou knowest, when it comes I am wretched. I love it not. I would have thee lord and love over all. But I cannot understand: how comes it to look sometimes as if indeinpendence must be the greater? A lie cannot be greater than the truth! I do not understand, but thou dost. I cannot see my foundations; I cannot dig up the roots of my being: that would be to understand creation! Will the Adversary ever come to see that thou only art grand and beautiful? How came he to think to be greater by setting up for himself? How was it that it looked so to him? How is it that, not being true, it should ever look so? There must be an independence that thou lovest, of which this temptation is the shadow! That must be how 'Satan fell!—for the sake of not being a slave!—that he might be a free being! Ah, Lord, I see how it all comes! It is because we are not near enough to thee to partake of thy liberty that we want a liberty of our own different from thine! We do not see that we are one with thee, that thy glory is our glory, that we can have none but in thee! that we are of thy family, thy home, thy heart, and what is great for thee is great for us! that man's meanness is to want to be great out of his Father! Without thy eternity in us we are so small that we think ourselves great, and are thus miserably abject and contemptible. Thou only art true! thou only art noble! thou wantest no glory for selfishness! thou doest, thou art, what thou requirest of thy children! I know it, for I see it in

Jesus, who casts the contempt of obedience upon the baseness of pride, who cares only for thee and for us, never thinking of himself save as a gift to give us! O lovely, perfect Christ! with my very life I worship thee! Oh, pray, Christ! make me and my brother strong to be the very thing thou wouldst have us, as thy brothers, the children of thy Father. Thou art our perfect brother—perfect in love, in courage, in tenderness! Amen, Lord! Good-night! I am thine."

He was silent for a few moments, then resumed:

"Lord, thou knowest whither my thoughts turn the moment I cease praying to thee. I dared not think of her, but that I know thee. But for thee, my heart would be as water within me! Oh, take care of her, come near to her! Thou didst send her where she could not learn fast—but she did learn. And now, God, I do not know where she is! Thou only of all in this world knowest, for to thee she lives though gone from my sight and knowledge—in the dark to me. Pray, Father, let her know that thou art near her, and that I love her. Thou hast made me love her by taking her from me: thou wilt give her to me again! In this hope I will live all my days, until thou takest me also; for to hope mightily is to believe well in thee. I will hope in thee infinitely. Amen, Father!"

CHAPTER XVI.

THE CLAN CHRISTMAS.

By slow degrees, with infinite subdivisions and apparent reversals of change, the autumn had passed into winter indeed. Cloud above, mire below, mist and rain all between, made up many days; only, like the dreariest life, they were broken through and parted, lest they should seem the universe itself, by such heavenly manifestations, such gleams and glimpses of better, as come into all lives, all winters, all evil weathers. What is loosed on earth is loosed first in heaven: we have often shared of heaven, when we thought it but a softening of earth's hardness. Every relief is a promise, a pledge as well as a passing meal. The frost at length had brought with it brightness and persuasion and rousing. In the fields it was swelling and breaking the clods; and for the heart of man, it did something to break up that clod too. A sense of friendly pleasure filled all the human creatures. The children ran about like wild things; the air seemed to intoxicate them. The mother went out walking with the girls, and they talked of their father and Christian and Mr. Sercombe, who were all coming together. For some time they saw nothing of their next neighbours.

They had made some attempts at acquaintance with the people of the glen, but unhappily were nowise courteous enough for their ideas of good breeding, and offended both their pride and their sense of propriety. The manners and address of these northern peasants were blameless—nearly perfect indeed, like those of the Irish, and in their own houses beyond criticism; those of the ladies conventional where not rudely condescending. If Mistress Conal was an exception to the rest of the clan, even she would be more civil to a stranger than to her chief whom she loved—until the stranger gave her offence. And if then she passed to imprecation, she would not curse like an ordinary woman, but like a poetess, gaining rather than losing dignity. She would rise to the evil occasion, no hag, but a largely-offended sibyl, whom nothing thereafter should ever appease. To forgive was a virtue unknown to Mistress Conal. Its more than ordinary difficulty in forgiving is indeed a special fault of the Celtic character.— This must not however be confounded with a desire for revenge. The latter is by no means a specially Celtic characteristic. Resentment and vengeance are far from inseparable. The heart that surpasses in courtesy, except indeed that courtesy, be rooted in love divine, must, when treated with discourtesy, experience the worse revulsion, feel the bitterer indignation. But many a Celt would forgive, and forgive thoroughly and heartily, with his enemy in his power, who, so long as he remained beyond his reach, could not even imagine circumstances in which they might be reconciled. To a Celt the summit of wrong is a slight, but apology is correspondingly potent with him. Mistress Conal, however, had not the excuse of a specially courteous nature.

Christina and Mercy, calling upon her one morning, were not ungraciously received, but had the misfortune to remark, trusting to her supposed ignorance of English, upon the dirtiness of her floor, they themselves having imported not a little of the moisture that had turned its surface into a muddy paste. She said nothing, but, to the general grudge she bore the possessors of property once belonging to her clan, she now added a personal one; the offence lay cherished and smouldering. Had the chief offended her, she would have found a score of ways to prove to herself that he meant nothing; but she desired no mitigation of the trespass of strangers.

The people at the New House did not get on very well with any of the clan. In the first place, they were regarded not merely as interlopers, but almost as thieves of the property—though in truth it had passed to them through other hands. In the second place, a rumour had got about that they did not behave with sufficient respect to the chief's family, in the point of whose honour the clan was the more exacting because of their common poverty. Hence the inhabitants of the glen, though they were of course polite, showed but little friendliness.

But the main obstacle to their reception was in themselves: the human was not much developed in them; they understood nothing of their own beings; they had never had any difficulty with themselves:—how could they understand others, especially in circumstances and with histories so different from their own! They had not a notion how poor people feel, still less poor people poorer than before—or how they regard the rich who have what they have lost. They did not understand any huftian feeling—not even the silliness they called LOVE—a godless, mindless affair, fit only for the doll-histories invented by children: they had a feeling, or a feeling had them, till another feeling came and took its place. When a feeling was there, they felt as if it would never go; when it was gone, they felt as if it had never been; when it returned, they felt as if it had never gone. They seldom came so near anything as to think about it, never put a question to themselves as to how a thing affected them, or concerning the phenomena of its passage through their consciousness! There is a child-eternity of soul that needs to ask nothing, because it understands everything: the ways of the spirit are open to it; but where a soul does not understand, and has to learn, how is it to do so without thinking? They knew nothing of labour, nothing of danger, nothing of hunger, nothing of cold, nothing of sickness, nothing of loneliness. The realities of life, in their lowest forms as in their highest, were far from them. If they had nearly gone through life instead of having but entered upon it, they would have had some ground for thinking themselves unfairly dealt with; for to be made, and then left to be worthless, unfit even for damnation, might be suspected for hard lines; but there is One who takes a perfect interest in his lowliest creature, and will not so spare it. They were girls notwithstanding who could make themselves agreeable, and passed for clever—Christina because she could give a sharp answer, and sing a drawingroom-song, Mercy because as yet she mostly held her tongue. That there was at the same time in each of them the possibility of being developed into something of inestimable value, is merely to say that they were human.

The days passed, and Christmas drew near. The gentlemen arrived. There was family delight and a bustling reception. It is amazing—it shows indeed how deep and divine, how much beyond the individual self are the family affections—that such gladness breaks forth in the meeting of persons who, within an hour or so of the joyous welcome, self getting the better of the divine, will begin to feel bored, and will each lay the blame of the disappointment on the other.

Coats were pulled off; mufflers were unwound; pretty hands were helping; strong hands were lifting and carrying; every room was bright with a great fire; tea was refused, and dinner welcomed. After dinner came the unpacking of great boxes; and in the midst of the resultant pleasure, the proposal came to be made—none but Christina knew how—that the inhabitants of the cottage should be invited to dinner on Christmas-eve. It was carried at once, and the next afternoon a formal invitation was sent.

At the cottage it caused conference, no discussion. The lady of the New House had not called with her girls, it was true; but then neither had the lady of the castle—for that was the clanspeople's name for the whole ridge on which the cottage stood—called on the new-comers! If there was offence, it was mutual! The unceremonious invitation MIGHT indicate that it was not thought necessary to treat them as persons who knew the ways of society; on the other hand, if it meant that they were ready to throw aside formalities and behave heartily, it would be wrong not to meet them half-way! They resolved therefore to make a counter-proposal; and if the invitation came of neighbourliness, and not of imagined patronage, they would certainly meet it in a friendly spirit! Answer was returned, sealed with no mere crest but with a coat of arms, to the effect that it had been the custom since time forgotten for the chief to welcome his people and friends without distinction on Christmas-eve, and the custom could not be broken; but if the ladies and gentlemen of the New House would favour them with their com- company on the occasion, to dine and dance, the chief and his family would gratefully accept any later offer of hospitality Mr. and Mrs. Peregrine Palmer might do them, the honour to send.

This reply gave occasion to a good deal of talk at the New House, not entirely of a sort which the friends of the chief would have enjoyed hearing. Frequent were the bursts of laughter from the men at the assumption of the title of CHIEF by a man with no more land than he could just manage to live upon. The village they said, and said truly, in which the greater number of HIS PEOPLE lived, was not his at all—not a foot of the ground on which it stood, not a stone or sod of which it was built—but belonged to a certain Canadian, who was about to turn all his territory around and adjacent into a deer forest! They could not see that, if there had ever been anything genuine in the patriarchal relation, the mere loss of the clan-property could no more cause the chieftainship to cease, than could the loss of the silver-hilted Andrew Ferrara, handed down from father to son for so many generations.

There are dull people, and just as many clever people, who look upon customs of society as on laws of nature, and judge the worth of others by their knowledge or ignorance of the same. So doing they disable themselves from understanding the essential, which is, like love, the fulfilling of the law. A certain Englishman gave great offence in an Arab tent by striding across the food placed for the company on the ground: would any Celt, Irish or Welsh, have been guilty of such a blunder? But there was not any overt offence on the present occasion. They called it indeed a cool proposal that THEY should put off their Christmas party for that of a ploughman in shabby kilt and hob-nailed shoes; but on their amused indignation supervened the thought that they were in a wild part of the country, where it would be absurd to expect the SAVOIR VIVRE of the south, and it would be amusing to see the customs of the land. By suggestion and seeming response, the clever Christina, unsuspected even of Mercy, was the motive power to bring about the acceptance of the chief's invitation.

A friendly answer was returned: they would not go to dinner, they said, as it was their custom also to dine at home on Christmas-eve; but they would dine early, and spend the evening with them.

To the laird the presence of the lowland girls promised a great addition to the merry-making. During the last thirty years, all the gentlemen-farmers of the clan, and most of the humbler tacksmen as well, had vanished, and there was a wide intellectual space between all those left and the family of the chief. Often when Ian was away, would Alister, notwithstanding his love to his people and their entire response, have felt lonely but for labour.

There being in the cottage no room equal to the reception of a large company, and the laird receiving all the members of the clan—"poor," I was going to say, "and rich," but there were no rich—as well as any neighbour or traveller who chose to appear, the father of the present chief had had good regard to the necessities of entertainment in the construction of a new barn: companionship, large feasting, and dancing, had been even more considered than the storing and threshing of his corn.

There are in these days many who will mock; but for my part I am proud of a race whose social relations are the last upon which they will retrench, whose latest yielded pleasure is their hospitality. It is a common feeling that only the WELL-TO-DO have a right to be hospitable: the ideal flower of hospitality is almost unknown to the rich; it can hardly be grown save in the gardens of the poor; it is one of their beatitudes.

Means in Glenruadh had been shrinking for many years, but the heart of the chief never shrank. His dwelling dwindled from a castle to a house, from a house to a cottage; but the hospitality did not dwindle. As the money vanished, the show diminished; the place of entertainment from a hall became a kitchen, from a kitchen changed to a barn; but the heart of the chief was the same; the entertainment was but little altered, the hospitality not in the least. When things grow hard, the first saving is generally off others; the Macruadh's was off himself. The land was not his, save as steward of the grace of God! Let it not be supposed he ran in debt: with his mother at the head, or rather the heart of affairs, that could not be. She was not one to regard as hospitality a readiness to share what you have not!

Little did good Doctor Johnson suspect the shifts to which some of the highland families he visited were driven—not to feed, but to house him: and housing in certain conditions of society is the large half of hospitality. Where he did not find his quarters comfortable, he did not know what crowding had to be devised, what inconveniences endured by the family, that he might have what ease and freedom were possible. Be it in stone hall or thatched cottage, the chief must entertain the stranger as well as befriend his own! This was the fulfilling of his office—none the less that it had descended upon him in evil times. That seldom if ever had a chief been Christian enough or strong enough to fill to the full the relation of father of his people, was nothing against the ideal fact in the existent relation; it was rather for it: now that the chieftainship had come to a man with a large notion of what it required of him, he was the more, not the less ready to aim at the mark of the idea; he was not the more easily to be turned aside from a true attempt to live up to his calling, that many had yielded and were swept along bound slaves in the triumph of Mammon! He looked on his calling as entirely enough to fill full the life that would fulfil the calling. It was ambition enough for him to be the head of his family, with the highest of earthly relations to realize toward its members. As to the vulgar notion of a man's obligation to himself, he had learned to despise it.

"Eubbish!" Ian would say. "I owe my self nothing. What has my self ever done for me, but lead me wrong? What but it has come between me and my duty—between me and my very Father in heaven—between me and my fellow man! The fools of greed would persuade that a man has no right to waste himself in the low content of making and sharing a humble living; he ought to make money! make a figure in the world, forsooth! be somebody! 'Dwell among the people!' such would say: 'Bah! Let them look after themselves! If they cannot pay their rents, others will; what is it to you if the rents are paid? Send them about their business; turn the land into a deer-forest or a sheep-farm, and clear them out! They have no rights! A man is bound to the children of his body begotten; the people are nothing to him! A man is not his brother's keeper—except when he has got him in prison! And so on, in the name of the great devil!"

Whether there was enough in Alister to have met and overcome the spirit of the world, had he been brought up at Oxford or Cambridge, I have not to determine; there was that in him at least which would have come to, repent bitterly had he yielded; but brought up as he was, he was not only able to entertain the exalted idea presented to him, but to receive and make it his. With joy he recognized the higher dignity of the shepherd of a few poor, lean, wool-torn human sheep, than of the man who stands for himself, however "spacious in the possession of dirt." He who holds dead land a possession, and living souls none of his, needs wake no curse, for he is in the very pit of creation, a live outrage on the human family.

If Alister Macruadh was not in the highest grade of Christianity, he was on his way thither, for he was doing the work that was given him to do, which is the first condition of all advancement. He had much to learn yet, but he was one who, from every point his feet touched, was on the start to go further.

The day of the holy eve rose clear and bright. Snow was on the hills, and frost in the valley. There had been a time when at this season great games were played between neighbour districts or clans, but here there were no games now, because there were so few men; the more active part fell to the women. Mistress Macruadh was busy all day with her helpers, preparing a dinner of mutton, and beef, and fowls, and red-deer ham; and the men soon gave the barn something of the aspect of the old patriarchal hall for which it was no very poor substitute. A long table, covered with the finest linen, was laid for all comers; and when the guests took their places, they needed no arranging; all knew their standing, and seated themselves according to knowledge. Two or three small farmers took modestly the upper places once occupied by immediate relatives of the chief, for of the old gentry of the clan there were none. But all were happy, for their chief was with them still. Their reverence was none the less that they were at home with him. They knew his worth, and the roughest among them would mind what the Macruadh said. They knew that he feared nothing; that he was strong as the red stag after which the clan was named; that, with genuine respect for every man, he would at the least insolence knock the fellow down; that he was the best shot, the best sailor, the best ploughman in the clan: I would have said THE BEST SWORDSMAN, but that, except Ian, there was not another left to it.

Not many of them, however, understood how much he believed that he had to give an account of his people. He was far from considering such responsibility the clergyman's only. Again and again had he expostulated with some, to save them from the slow gaping hell of drink, and in one case, he had reason to hope, with success.

As they sat at dinner, it seemed to the young fellow who, with his help, had so far been victorious, that the chief scarcely took his eyes off him. One might think there was small danger where the hostess allowed nothing beyond water and milk but small ale; the chief, however, was in dread lest he should taste even that, and caught one moment the longing look he threw at the jug as it passed. He rose and went down the table, speaking to this one and that, but stopped behind the lad, and putting his arm round his shoulders, whispered in his ear. The youth looked up in his face with a solemn smile: had not the chief embraced him before them all! He was only a shepherd-lad, but his chief cared for him!

In the afternoon the extemporized tables were cleared away, candles were fixed in rough sconces along the walls, not without precaution against fire, and the floor was rubbed clean—for the barn was floored throughout with pine, in parts polished with use. The walls were already covered with the plaids of the men and women, each kept in place by a stone or two on the top of the wall where the rafters rested. In one end was a great heap of yellow oat-straw, which, partly levelled, made a most delightful divan. What with the straw, the plaids, the dresses, the shining of silver ornaments, and the flash of here and there a cairngorm or an amethyst, there was not a little colour in the barn. Some of the guests were poorly but all were decently attired, and the shabbiest behaved as ladies and gentlemen.

The party from the New House walked through the still, star-watched air, with the motionless mountains looking down on them, and a silence around, which they never suspected as a presence. The little girls were of the company, and there was much merriment. Foolish compliments were not wanting, offered chiefly on the part of Mr. Sercombe, and accepted on that of Christina. The ladies, under their furs and hoods, were in their best, with all the jewels they could wear at once, for they had heard that highlanders have a passion for colour, and that poor people are always best pleased when you go to them in your finery. The souls of these Sasunnachs were full of THINGS. They made a fine show as they emerged from the darkness of their wraps into the light of the numerous candles; nor did the approach of the widowed chieftainess to receive them, on the arm of Alister, with Ian on her other side, fail in dignity. The mother was dressed in a rich, matronly black silk; the chief was in the full dress of his clan—

the old-fashioned coat of the French court, with its silver buttons and ruffles of fine lace, the kilt of Macruadh tartan in which red predominated, the silver-mounted sporan—of the skin and adorned with the head of an otter caught with, the bare hands of one of his people, and a silver-mounted dirk of length unusual, famed for the beauty of both hilt and blade; Ian was similarly though less showily clad. When she saw the stately dame advancing between her sons, one at least of her visitors felt a doubt whether their condescension would be fully appreciated.

As soon as their reception was over, the piper—to the discomfort of Mr. Sercombe's English ears—began his invitation to the dance, and in a few moments the floor was, in a tumult of reels. The girls, unacquainted with their own country's dances, preferred looking on, and after watching reel and strathspey for some time, altogether declined attempting either. But by and by it was the turn of the clanspeople to look on while the lady of the house and her sons danced a quadrille or two with their visitors; after which the chief and his brother pairing with the two elder girls, the ladies were astonished to find them the best they had ever waltzed with, although they did not dance quite in the London way. Ian's dancing, Christina said, was French; Mercy said all she knew was that the chief took the work and left her only the motion: she felt as in a dream of flying. Before the evening was over, the young men had so far gained on Christina that Mr. Sercombe looked a little commonplace.

CHAPTER XVII.

BETWEEN DANCING AND SUPPER.

The dancing began about six o'clock, and at ten it was time for supper. It was readjr, but there was no room for it except the barn; the dancing therefore had to cease for a while, that the table might again be covered. The ladies put on their furs and furry boots and gloves, and went out into the night with the rest.

The laird and Christina started together, but, far from keeping at her side, Alister went and came, now talking to this couple, now to that, and adding to the general pleasure with every word he spoke. Ian and Mercy walked together, and as often as the chief left her side, Christina joined them. Mrs. Palmer stayed with their hostess; her husband took the younger children by the hand; Mr. Sercombe and Christian sauntered along in the company, talking now to one, now to another of the village girls.

All through the evening Christina and Mercy noted how instantly the word of the chief was followed in the smallest matter, and the fact made its impression on them; for undeveloped natures in the presence of a force, revere it as POWER—understanding by POWER, not the strength to create, to harmonize, to redeem, to discover the true, to suffer with patience; but the faculty of having things one's own vulgar, self-adoring way.

Ian had not proposed to Mercy that they should walk together; but when the issuing crowd had broken into twos and threes, they found themselves side by side. The company took its way along the ridge, and the road eastward. The night was clear, and like a great sapphire frosted with topazes—reminding Ian that, solid as is the world under our feet, it hangs in the will of God. Mercy and he walked for some time in silence. It was a sudden change from the low barn, the dull candles, and the excitement of the dance, to the awful space, the clear pure far-off lights, and the great stillness. Both felt it, though differently. There was in both of them the quest after peace. It is not the banished demon only that wanders seeking rest, but souls upon souls, and in ever growing numbers. The world and Hades swarm with them. They long after a repose that is not mere cessation of labour: there is a positive, an active rest. Mercy was only beginning to seek it, and that without knowing what it was she needed. Ian sought it in silence with God; she in crepitant intercourse with her kind. Naturally ready to fall into gloom, but healthy enough to avoid it, she would rush at anything to do—not to keep herself from thinking, for she had hardly begun to think, but to escape that heavy sense of non-existence, that weary and restless want which is the only form life can take to the yet unliving, those who have not yet awakened and arisen from the dead. She was a human chicken that had begun to be aware of herself, but had not yet attacked the shell that enclosed her: because it was transparent, and she could see life about her, she did not know that she was in a shell, or that, if she did not put forth the might of her own life, she was sealing herself up, a life in death, in her antenatal coffin. Many who think themselves free have never yet even seen the shell that imprisons them—know nothing of the liberty wherewith the Lord of our life would set them free. Men fight many a phantom when they ought to be chipping at their shells. "Thou art the dreamer!" they cry to him who would wake them. "See how diligent we are to get on in the world! We labour as if we should never go out of it!" What they call the world is but their shell, which is all the time killing the infant Christ that houses with them.

Ian looked up to the sky, and breathed a deep breath. Mercy looked up in his face, and saw his strangely beautiful smile.

"What are you thinking of, Captain Macruadh?" she said.

"I was thinking," he answered, "that perhaps up THERE"—he waved his arm wide over his head—"might he something like room; hut I doubt it, I doubt it!"

Naturally, Mercy was puzzled. The speech sounded quite mad, and yet he could not be mad, he had danced so well! She took comfort that her father was close behind.

"Did you never feel," he resumed, "as if you could not anyhow get room enough?"

"No," answered Mercy, "never."

Ian fell a thinking how to wake in her a feeling of what he meant. He had perceived that one of the first elements in human education is the sense of space—of which sense, probably, the star-dwelt heaven is the first awakener. He believed that without the heavens we could not have learned the largeness in things below them, could not, for instance, have felt the mystery of the high-ascending gothic roof—for without the greater we cannot interpret the less; and he thought that to have the sense of largeness developed might be to come a little nearer to the truth of things, to the recognition of spiritual relations.

"Did you ever see anything very big?" he asked.

"I suppose London is as big as most things!" she answered, after a moment.

"Did you ever see London?" he asked.

"We generally live there half the year."

"Pardon me; I did not ask if you had ever been to London," said Ian; "I asked if you had ever seen London."

"I know the west end pretty well."

"Did it ever strike you as very large?"

"Perhaps not; but the west end is only a part of London."

"Did you ever see London from the top of St. Paul's?"

"No."

"Did you ever see it from the top of Hampstead heath?"

"I have been there several times, but I don't remember seeing London from it. We don't go to London for the sights."

"Then you have not seen London!"

Mercy was annoyed. Ian did not notice that she was, else perhaps he would not have gone on—which would have been a pity, for a little annoyance would do her no harm. At the same time the mood was not favourable to receiving any impression from the region of the things that are not seen. A pause followed.

"It is so delightful," said Ian at length, "to come out of the motion and the heat and the narrowness into the still, cold greatness!"

"You seemed to be enjoying yourself pretty well notwithstanding, Captain Macruadh!"

"What made you think so?" he asked, turning to her with a smile.

"You were so merry—not with me—you think me only a stupid lowland girl; but the other young persons you danced with, laughed very much at things you said to them."

"You are right; I did enjoy myself. As often as one comes near a simple human heart, one's own heart finds a little room."

Ere she knew, Mercy had said—

"And you didn't find any room with me?"

With the sound of her words her face grew hot, as with a furnace-blast, even in the frosty night-air. She would have covered what she had said, but only stammered. Ian turned, and looking at her, said with a gentle gravity—

"You must not be offended with me! I must answer you truly.—You do not give me room: have you not just told me you never longed for any yourself?"

"One ought to be independent!" said Mercy, a little nettled.

"Are you sure of that? What is called independence may really be want of sympathy. That would indicate a kind of loneliness anything but good."

"I wish you would find a less disagreeable companion then!—one that would at least be as good as nobody! I am sorry I don't know how to give you room. I would if I could. Tell me how."

Again Ian turned to her: was it possible there were tears in her voice? But her black eyes were flashing in the starlight!

"Did you ever read Zanoni?" he asked.

"I never heard of it. What is it?"

"A romance of Bulwer's."

"My father won't let us read anything of Bulwer's. Does he write very wicked books?"

"The one I speak of," said Ian, "is not wicked, though it is full of rubbish, and its religion is very false."

Whether Mercy meant to take her revenge on him with consciously bad logic, I am in doubt.

"Captain Macruadh! you astonish me! A Scotchman speak so of religion!"

"I spoke of the religion in that book. I said it was false—which is the same as saying it was not religion."

"Then religion is not all true!"

"All true religion is true," said Ian, inclined to laugh like one that thought to catch an angel, and had clutched a bat! "I was going on to say that, though the religion and philosophy of the book were rubbish, the story was fundamentally a grand conception. It puzzles me to think how a man could start with such an idea, and work it out so well, and yet be so lacking both in insight and logic. It is wonderful how much of one portion of our nature may be developed along with so little of another!"

"What is the story about?" asked Mercy.

"What I may call the canvas of it, speaking as if it were a picture, is the idea that the whole of space is full of life; that, as the smallest drop of water is crowded with monsters of hideous forms and dispositions, so is what we call space full of living creatures,—"

"How horrible!"

"—not all monsters, however. There are among them creatures not altogether differing from us, but differing much from each other,—"

"As much as you and I?"

"—some of them lovely and friendly, others frightful in their beauty and malignity,—"

"What nonsense!"

"Why do you call it nonsense?"

"How could anything beautiful be frightful?"

"I ought not to have said BEAUTIFUL. But the frightfullest face I ever saw ought to have been the finest. When the lady that owned it spoke to me, I shivered."

"But anyhow the whole thing is nonsense!"

"How is it nonsense?"

"Because there are no such creatures."

"How do you know that? Another may have seen them though you and I never did!"

"You are making game of me! You think to make me believe anything you choose!"

"Will you tell me something you do believe?"

"That you may prove immediately that I do not believe it!" she retorted, with more insight than he had expected. "—You are not very entertaining!"

"Would you like me to tell you a story then?"

"Will it be nonsense?"

"No."

"I should like a little nonsense."

"You are an angel of goodness, and as wise as you are lovely!" said Ian.

She turned upon him, and opened wide at him her great black eyes, in which were mingled defiance and question.

"Your reasoning is worthy of your intellect. When you dance," he went on, looking very solemn, "your foot would not bend the neck of a daisy asleep in its rosy crown. The west wind of May haunts you with its twilight-odours; and when you waltz, so have I seen the waterspout gyrate on the blue floor of the Mediterranean. Your voice is as the harp of Selma; and when you look out of your welkin eyes— no! there I am wrong! Allow me! —ah, I thought so!—dark as Erebus!—But what!"

For Mercy, perceiving at last that he was treating her like the silliest of small girls, lost her patience, and burst into tears.

"You are dreadfully rude!" she sobbed.

Ian was vexed with himself.

"You asked me to talk nonsense to you, Miss Mercy! I attempted to obey you, and have done it stupidly. But at least it was absolute nonsense! Shall I make up for it by telling you a pretty story?"

"Anything to put away that!" answered Mercy, trying to smile.

He began at once, and told her a wonderful tale—told first after this fashion by Bob of the Angels, at a winter-night gathering of the women, as they carded and spun their wool, and reeled their yarn together. It was one well-known in the country, but Rob had filled it after his fancy with imaginative turns and spiritual hints, unappreciable by the tall child of seventeen walking by Ian's side. There was not among the maidens of the poor village one who would not have understood it better than she. It took her fancy notwithstanding, partly, perhaps, from its unlikeness to any story she had ever heard before. Her childhood had been starved on the husks of new fairy-tales, all invention and no imagination, than which more unnourishing food was never offered to God's children.

The story Ian told her under that skyful of stars, was as Rob of the Angels had dressed it for the clan matrons and maidens, only altered a very little for the ears of the lowland girl.

END OF VOL. I.

VOL. II.

CONTENTS OF VOL. II.

CHAPTER

WHATS'S MINE'S MINE.

CHAPTER I.

THE STORY TOLD BY IAN.

"There was once a woman whose husband was well to do, but he died and left her, and then she sank into poverty. She did her best; but she had a large family, and work was hard to find, and hard to do when it was found, and hardly paid when it was done. Only hearts of grace can understand the struggles of the poor—with everything but God against them! But she trusted in God, and said whatever he pleased must be right, whether he sent it with his own hand or not.

"Now, whether it was that she could not find them enough to eat, or that she could not keep them warm enough, I do not know; I do not think it was that they had not gladness enough, which is as necessary for young things as food and air and sun, for it is wonderful on how little a child can be happy; but whatever was the cause, they began to die. One after the other sickened and lay down, and did not rise again; and for a time her life was just a waiting upon death. She would have wanted to die herself, but that there was always another to die first; she had to see them all safe home before she dared wish to go herself. But at length the last of them was gone, and then when she had no more to provide for, the heart of work went out of her: where was the good of working for herself! there was no interest in it! But she knew it was the will of God she should work and eat until he chose to take her back to himself; so she worked on for her living while she would much rather have worked for her dying; and comforted herself that every day brought death a day nearer. Then she fell ill herself, and could work no more, and thought God was going to let her die; for, able to win her bread no longer, surely she was free to lie down and wait for death! But just as she was going to her bed for the last time, she bethought herself that she was bound to give her neighbour the chance of doing a good deed: and felt that any creature dying at her door without letting her know he was in want, would do her a great wrong. She saw it was the will of God that she should beg, so put on her clothes again, and went out to beg. It was sore work, and she said so to the priest. But the priest told her she need not mind, for our Lord himself lived by the kindness of the women who went about with him. They knew he could not make a living for his own body and a living for the souls of so many as well, and the least they could do was to keep him alive who was making them alive. She said that was very true; but he was all the time doing everything for everybody, and she was doing nothing for anybody. The priest was a wise man, and did not tell her how she had, since ever he knew her, been doing the work of God in his heart, helping him to believe and trust in God; so that in fact, when he was preaching, she was preaching. He did not tell her that, I say, for he was jealous over her beauty, and would have Christ's beloved sheep enter his holy kingdom with her wool white, however torn it might be. So he left her to think she was nobody at all; and told her that, whether she was worth keeping alive or not, whether she was worth begging for or not, whether it was a disgrace or an honour to beg, all was one, for it was the will of God that she should beg, and there was no word more to be said, and no thought more to be thought about it. To this she heartily agreed, and did beg—enough to keep her alive, and no more.

"But at last she saw she must leave that part of the country, and go back to the place her husband took her from. For the people about her were very poor, and she thought it hard on them to have to help a stranger like her; also her own people would want her to bury. For you must know that in the clans, marriage was thought to be dissolved by death, so far at least as the body was concerned; therefore the body of a dead wife was generally carried back to the burial place of her own people, there to be gathered to her fathers. So the woman set out for her own country, begging her way thither. Nor had she any difficulty, for there were not a few poor people on her way, and the poor are the readiest to help the poor, also to know whether a person is one that ought to be helped or not.

"One night she came to a farm house where a rich miserly farmer dwelt. She knew about him, and had not meant to stop there, but she was weary, and the sun went down as she reached his gate, and she felt as if she could go no farther. So she went up to the door and knocked, and asked if she could have a nights lodging. The woman who opened to her went and asked the farmer. Now the old man did not like hospitality, and in particular to such as stood most in need of it; he did not enjoy throwing away money! At the same time, however, he was very fond of hearing all the country rumours; and he thought with himself he would buy her news with a scrap of what was going, and a shake-down at the foot of the wall. So he told his servant to bring her in.

"He received her not unkindly, for he wanted her to talk; and he let her have a share of the supper, such as it was. But not until he had asked every question about everybody he could think of, and drawn her own history from her as well, would he allow her to have the rest she so much needed.

"Now it was a poor house, like most in the country, and nearly without partitions. The old man had his warm box-bed, and slept on feathers where no draught could reach him, and the poor woman had her bed of short rumpled straw on the earthen floor at the foot of the wall in the coldest corner. Yet the heart of the man had been moved by her story, for, without dwelling on her sufferings, she had been honest in telling it. He had indeed, ere he went to sleep, thanked God that he was so much better off than she. For if he did not think it the duty of the rich man to share with his neighbours, he at least thought it his duty to thank God for his being richer than they.

"Now it may well seem strange that such a man should be privileged to see a vision; but we do read in the Bible of a prophet who did not even know his duty to an ass, so that the ass had to teach it him. And the man alone saw the vision; the woman saw nothing of it. But she did not require to see any vision, for she had truth in the inward parts, which is better than all visions. The vision was on this wise:—In the middle of the night the man came wide awake, and looking out of his bed, saw the door open, and a light come in, burning like a star, of a faint rosy colour, unlike any light he had ever before seen. Another and another came in, and more yet, until he counted six of them. They moved near the floor, but he could not see clearly what sort of little creatures they were that were carrying them. They went up to the woman's bed, and walked slowly round it in a hovering kind of a way, stopping, and moving up and down, and going on again; and when they had done this three times, they went slowly out of the door again, stopping for a moment several times as they went.

"He fell asleep, and waking not very early, was surprised to see his guest still on her hard couch—as quiet as any rich woman, he said to himself, on her feather bed. He woke her, told her he wondered she should sleep so far into the morning, and narrated the curious vision he had had. 'Does not that explain to you,' she said, 'how it is that I have slept so long? Those were my dead children you saw come to me. They died young, without any sin, and God lets them come and comfort their poor sinful mother. I often see them in my dreams. If, when I am gone, you will look at my bed, you will find every straw laid straight and smooth. That is what they were doing last night.' Then she gave him thanks for good fare and good rest, and took her way to her own, leaving the farmer better pleased with himself than he had been for a long time, partly because there had been granted him a vision from heaven.

"At last the woman died, and was carried by angels into Abraham's bosom. She was now with her own people indeed, that is, with God and all the good. The old farmer did not know of her death till a long time after; but it was upon the night she died, as near as he could then make out, that he dreamed a wonderful dream. He never told it to any but the priest from whom he sought comfort when he lay dying; and the priest did not tell it till after everybody belonging to the old man was gone. This was the dream:—

"He was lying awake in his own bed, as he thought, in the dark night, when the poor woman came in at the door, having in her hand a wax candle, but not alight. He said to her, 'You extravagant woman! where did you get that candle?' She answered, 'It was put into my hand when I died, with the word that I was to wander till I found a fire at which to light it.' 'There!' said he, 'there's the rested fire! Blow and get a light, poor thing! It shall never be said I refused a body a light!' She went to the hearth, and began to blow at the smouldering peat; but, for all she kept trying, she could not light her candle. The old man thought it was because she was dead, not because he was dead in sin, and losing his patience, cried, 'You foolish woman! haven't you wit enough left to light a candle? It's small wonder you came to beggary!' Still she went on trying, but the more she tried, the blacker grew the peat she was blowing at. It would indeed blaze up at her breath, but the moment she brought the candle near it to catch the flame, it grew black, and each time blacker than before. 'Tut! give me the candle,' cried the farmer, springing out of bed; 'I will light it for you!' But as he stretched out his hand to take it, the woman disappeared, and he saw that the fire was dead out. 'Here's a fine business!' he said. 'How am I to get a light?' For he was miles from the next house. And with that he turned to go back to his bed. When he came near it, he saw somebody lying in it. 'What! has the carline got into my very bed?' he cried, and went to drive her out of the bed and out of the house. But when he came close, he saw it was himself lying there, and knew that at least he was out of the body, if not downright dead. The next moment he found himself on the moor, following the woman, some distance before him, with her unlighted candle still in her hand. He walked as fast as he could to get up with her, hut could not; he called after her, but she did not seem to hear.

"When first he set out, he knew every step of the ground, but by and by he ceased to know it. The moor stretched out endlessly, and the woman walked on and on. Without a thought of turning back, he followed. At length he saw a gate, seemingly in the side of a hill. The woman knocked, and by the time it opened, he was near enough to hear what passed. It was a grave and stately, but very happy-looking man that opened it, and he knew at once it was St. Peter. When he saw the woman, he stooped and kissed her. The same moment a light shone from her, and the old man thought her candle was lighted at last; but presently he saw it was her head that gave out the shining. And he heard her say, 'I pray you, St. Peter, remember the rich tenant of Balmacoy; he gave me shelter one whole night, and would have let me light my candle but I could not.' St. Peter answered, 'His fire was not fire enough to light your candle, and the bed he gave you was of short straw!' 'True, St. Peter,' said the woman, 'but he gave me some supper, and it is hard for a rich man to be generous! You may say the supper was not very good, but at least it was more than a cup of cold water!' 'Yes, verily!' answered the saint, 'but he did not give it you because you loved God, or because you were in need of it, but because he wanted to hear your news.' Then the woman was sad, for she could not think of anything more to say for the poor old rich man. And St. Peter saw that she was sad, and said, 'But if he die to-night, he shall have a place inside the gate, because you pray for him. He shall lie there!' And he pointed to just such a bed of short crumpled straw as she had lain upon in his house. But she said, 'St. Peter, you ought to be ashamed of yourself! Is that the kind of welcome to give a poor new-dead man? Where then would he have lain if I had not prayed for him?' 'In the dog-kennel outside there,' answered St. Peter. 'Oh, then, please, let me go back and warn him what comes of loving money!' she pleaded. 'That is not necessary,' he replied; 'the man is hearing every word you and I are this moment saying to each other.' 'I am so glad!' rejoined the woman; 'it will make him repent.' 'He will not be a straw the better for it!' answered the saint. 'He thinks now that he will do differently, and perhaps when he wakes will think so still; but in a day or two he will mock at it as a foolish dream. To gather money will seem to him common sense, and to lay up treasure in heaven nonsense. A bird in the hand will be to him worth ten in the heavenly bush. And the end will be that he will not get the straw inside the gate, and there will be many worse places than the dog-kennel too good for him!' With that he woke.

"'What an odd dream!' he said to himself. 'I had better mind what I am about!' So he was better that day, eating and drinking more freely, and giving more to his people. But the rest of the week he was worse than ever, trying to save what he had that day spent, and so he went on growing worse. When he found himself dying, the terror of his dream came upon him, and he told all to the priest. But the priest could not comfort him."

By the time the story was over, to which Mercy had listened without a word, they were alone in the great starry night, on the side of a hill, with the snow high above them, and the heavens above the snow, and the stars above the heavens, and God above and below everything. Only Ian felt his presence. Mercy had not missed him yet.

She did not see much in the tale: how could she? It was very odd, she thought, but not very interesting. She had expected a tale of clan-feud, or a love-story! Yet the seriousness of her companion in its narration had made some impression upon her.

"They told me you were an officer," she said, "but I see you are a clergyman! Do you tell stories like that from the pulpit?"

"I am a soldier," answered Ian, "not a clergyman. But I have heard my father tell such a story from the pulpit."

Ian imagined himself foiled in his attempt to interest the maiden. If he was, it would not be surprising. He had not the least desire to commend HIMSELF to the girl; and he would not talk rubbish even to a child. There is sensible and senseless nonsense, good absurdity and bad.

As Mercy recounted to her sister the story Ian had told her, it certainly was silly enough. She had retained but the withered stalk and leaves; the strange flower was gone. Christina judged it hardly a story for a gentleman to tell a lady.

They returned almost in silence to find the table laid, a plentiful supper spread, and the company seated. After supper came singing of songs, saying of ballads, and telling of tales. I know with what in- credulity many highlanders will read of a merry-making in their own country at which no horn went round, no punch-bowl was filled and emptied without stint! But the clearer the brain, the better justice is done to the more etherial wine of fthe soul. Of several of the old songs Christina begged the tunes, but was disappointed to find that, as she could not take them down, so the singers of them could not set them down. In the tales she found no interest. The hostess sang to her harp, and made to revering listeners eloquent music, for her high clear tones had not yet lost their sweetness, and she had some art to come in aid of her much feeling: loud murmurs of delight, in the soft strange tongue of the songs themselves, followed the profound silence with which they were heard, but Christina wondered what there was to applaud. She could not herself sing without accompaniment, and when she left, it was with a regretful feeling that she had not distinguished herself. Naturally, as they went home, the guests from the New House had much fun over the queer fashions and poverty—stricken company, the harp and the bagpipes, the horrible haggis, the wild minor songs, and the unintelligible stories and jokes; but the ladies agreed that the Macruadh was a splendid fellow.

CHAPTER II

ROB OF THE ANGELS.

Among the peasantry assembled at the feast, were two that had neither danced, nor seated themselves at the long table where all were welcome. Mercy wondered what might be the reason of their separation. Her first thought was that they must be somehow, she could not well imagine how, in lower position than any of the rest —had perhaps offended against the law, perhaps been in prison, and so the rest would not keep company with them; or perhaps they were beggars who did not belong to the clan, and therefore, although fed, were not allowed to eat with it! But she soon saw she must be wrong in each conjecture; for if there was any avoiding, it was on the part of the two: every one, it was clear, was almost on the alert to wait upon them. They seemed indeed rather persons of distinction than outcasts; for it was with something like homage, except for a certain coaxing tone in the speech of the ministrants, that they were attended. They had to help themselves to nothing; everything was carried to them. Now one, now another, where all were guests and all were servants, would rise from the table to offer them something, or see what they would choose or might be in want of, while they partook with the same dignity and self-restraint that was to be noted in all.

The elder was a man about five-and-fifty, tall and lean, with a wiry frame, dark grizzled hair, and a shaven face. His dress, which was in the style of the country, was very poor, but decent; only his plaid was large and thick, and bright compared with the rest of his apparel: it was a present he had had from his clan-some giving the wool, and others the labour in carding, dyeing, and weaving it. He carried himself like a soldier-which he had never been, though his father had. His eyes were remarkably clear and keen, and the way he used them could hardly fail to attract attention. Every now and then they would suddenly fix themselves with a gaze of earnest inquiry, which would either grow to perception, or presently melt away and let his glance go gently roving, ready to receive, but looking for nothing. His face was very brown and healthy, with marked and handsome features. Its expression seemed at first a little severe, but soon, to reading eyes, disclosed patience and tenderness. At the same time there was in it a something indescribably unlike the other faces present-and indeed his whole person and carriage were similarly peculiar. Had Mercy, however, spent on him a little more attention, the peculiarity would have explained itself. She would have seen that, although everybody spoke to him, he never spoke in reply—only made signs, sometimes with his lips, oftener with hand or head: the man was deaf and dumb. But such was the keenness of his observation that he understood everything said to him by one he knew, and much from the lips of a stranger.

His companion was a youth whose age it would have been difficult to guess. He looked a lad, and was not far from thirty. His clothing was much like his father's—poor enough, yet with the air of being a better suit than that worn every day. He was very pale and curiously freckled, with great gray eyes like his father's, which had however an altogether different expression. They looked dreamy, and seemed almost careless of what passed before them, though now and then a certain quick, sharp turn of the head showed him not devoid of attention.

The relation between the two was strangely interesting. Day and night they were inseparable. Because the father was deaf, the son gave all his attention to the sounds of the world; his soul sat in his ears, ever awake, ever listening; while such was his confidence in his father's sight, that he scarcely troubled himself to look where he set his feet. His expression also was peculiar, partly from this cause, mainly from a deeper. It was a far-away look, which a common glance would have taken to indicate that he was "not all there." In a lowland parish he would have been regarded as little better than a gifted idiot; in the mountains he was looked upon as a seer, one in communion with higher powers. Whether his people were of this opinion from being all fools together, and therefore unable to know a fool, or the lowland authorities would have been right in taking charge of him, let him who pleases judge or misjudge for himself. What his own thought of him came out in the name they gave him: "Rob of the Angels," they called him. He was nearly a foot shorter than his father, and very thin. Some said he looked always cold; but I think that came of the wonderful peace on his face, like the quiet of a lake over which lies a thin mist. Never was stronger or fuller devotion manifested by son to father than by Rob of the Angels to Hector of the Stags. His filial love and faith were perfect. While they were together, he was in his own calm elysium; when they were apart, which was seldom for more than a few minutes, his spirit seemed always waiting. I believe his notions of God his father, and Hector his father, were strangely mingled—the more perhaps that the two fathers were equally silent. It would have been a valuable revelation to some theologians to see in those two what &lti>love</i> might mean.

So gentle was Rob of the Angels, that all the women, down to the youngest maid-child, gave him a compassionate, mother-like love. He had lost his mother when he was an infant; the father had brought him up with his own hand, and from the moment of his mother's departure had scarce let him out of his sight; but the whole woman-remnant of the clan was as a mother to the boy. And from the first they had so talked to him of his mother, greatly no doubt through the feeling that from his father he could learn nothing of her, that now his mother seemed to him everywhere: he could not see God; why should not his mother be there though he could not see her! No wonder the man was peaceful!

Many would be inclined to call the two but poachers and vagabonds— vagabonds because they lived in houses not quite made with hands, for they had several dwellings that were mostly caves—which yet they contrived to make warm and comfortable; and poachers because they lived by the creatures which God scatters on his hills for his humans. Let those who inherit or purchase, avenge the breach of law; but let them not wonder when those who are disinherited and sold, cry out against the breach of higher law!

The land here had never, partly from the troubles besetting its owners, but more from their regard for the poor, of the clan, been with any care preserved; little notice was ever taken of what game was killed, or who killed it. At the same time any wish of the chief with regard to the deer, of which Rob's father for one knew every antlered head, was rigidly respected. As to the parts which became the property of others-the boundaries between were not very definite, and sale could ill change habits, especially where owners were but beginning to bestir themselves about the deer, or any of the wild animals called game. Hector and Rob led their life with untroubled conscience and easy mind.

In a world of the devil, where the justification of existence lay in money on the one side, and work for money on the other, there could be no justification of the existence of these men; but this world does not belong to the devil, though it may often seem as if it did, and father and son lived and enjoyed life, as in a manner so to a decree unintelligible to him who, without his money and its consolations, would know himself in the hell he has not yet recog- nized. Neither of them could read or write; neither of them had a penny laid by for wet weather; neither of them would leave any memory beyond their generation; the will of neither would be laid up in Doctors' Commons; neither of the two would leave on record a single fact concerning one of the animals whose ways and habits they knew better than any other man in the highlands; that they were nothing, and worth nothing to anybody—even to themselves, would have been the judgment of most strangers concerning them; but God knew what a life of unspeakable pleasures it was that he had given them-a life the change from which to the life beyond, would scarce be distracting: neither would find himself much out of doors when he died. To Bob of the Angels tow could Abraham's bosom feel strange, accustomed to lie night after night, star-melted and soft-breathing, or snow-ghastly and howling, with his head on —the bosom of Hector of the Stags-an Abraham who could as ill do without his Isaac, as his Isaac without him!

The father trusted his son's hearing as implicitly as his own sight. When he saw a certain look come on his face, he would drop on the instant, and crouch as still as if he had ears and knew what noise was, watching Kob's face for news of some sound wandering through the vast of the night.

It seemed at times, however, as if either he was not quite deaf, or he had some gift that went toward compensation. To all motion about him he was sensitive as no other man. I am afraid to say from how far off the solid earth would convey to him the vibration of a stag's footstep. Bob sometimes thought his cheek must feel the wind of a sound to which his ear was irresponsive. Beyond a doubt he was occasionally aware of the proximity of an animal, and knew what animal it was, of which Rob had no intimation. His being, corporeal and spiritual, seemed, to the ceaseless vibrations of the great globe, a very seismograph. Often would he make his sign to Kob to lay his ear on the ground and listen, when no indication had reached the latter. I suspect the exceptional development in him of some sense rudimentary in us all.

He had the keenest eyes in Glenruadh, and was a dead shot. Even the chief was not his equal. Yet he never stalked a deer, never killed anything, for mere sport. I am not certain he never had, but for Rob of the Angels, he had the deep-rooted feeling of his chief in regard to the animals. What they wanted for food, they would kill; but it was not much they needed, for seldom can two men have lived on less, and they had positively not a greed of any kind between them. If their necessity was meal or potatoes, they would carry grouse or hares down the glen, or arrange with some farmer's wife, perhaps Mrs. Macruadh herself, for the haunches of a doe; but they never killed from pleasure in killing. Of creatures destructive to game they killed enough to do far more than make up for all the game they took; and for the skins of ermine and stoat and fox and otter they could always get money's worth; money itself they never sought or had. If the little birds be regarded as earning the fruit and seed they devour by the grubs and slugs they destroy, then Hector of the Stags and Rob of the Angels also thoroughly earned their food.

When a trustworthy messenger was wanted, and Rob was within reach, he was sure to be employed. But not even then were his father and he quite parted. Hector would shoulder his gun, and follow in the track of his fleet-footed son till he met him returning.

For what was life to Hector but to be with Rob! Was his Mary's son to go about the world unattended! He had a yet stronger feeling than any of the clan that his son was not of the common race of mortals. To Hector also, after their own fashion, would Rob of the Angels tell the tales that suggested the name his clanspeople gave him—wonderful tales of the high mountain-nights, the actors in them for the most part angels. Whether Rob believed he had intercourse with such beings, heard them speak, and saw them, do the things he reported, I cannot tell: it may be that, like any other poet of good things, he but saw and believed the things his tales meant, the things with which he represented the angels as dealing, and concerning which he told their sayings. To the eyes of those who knew him, Rob seemed just the sort of person with whom the angels might be well pleased to hold converse: was he not simplicity itself, truth, generosity, helpfulness? Did he not, when a child, all but lose his life in the rescue of an idiot from the swollen burn? Did he not, when a boy, fight a great golden eagle on its nest, thinking to deliver the lamb it had carried away? Knowing his father in want of a new bonnet, did not Rob with his bare hands seize an otter at the mouth of its hole, and carry it home, laughing merrily over the wounds it had given him?

His voice had in it a strangely peculiar tone, making it seem not of this world. Especially after he had been talking for some time, it would appear to come from far away, not from the lips of the man looking you in the face.

It was wonderful with what solemnity of speech, and purity of form he would tell his tales. So much in solitude with his dumb father, his speech might well be unlike the speech of other men; but whence the impression of cultivation it produced?

When the Christmas party broke up, most of the guests took the road toward the village, the chief and his brother accompanying them part of the way. Of these were Rob and his father, walking hand in hand, Hector looking straight before him, Rob gazing up into the heavens, as if holding counsel with the stars.

"Are you seeing any angels, Rob?" asked a gentle girl of ten.

"Well, and I'm not sure," answered Rob of the Angels.

"Sure you can tell whether you see anything!"

"Oh, yes, I see! but it is not easy to tell what will be an angel and what will not. There's so much all blue up there, it might be full of angels and none of us see one of them!"

"Do tell us what you see, Rob, dear Rob," said the girl.

"Well, and I will tell you. I think I see many heads close together, talking."

"And can you hear what they will be saying?"

"Some of it."

"Tell me, do tell me-some-just a little."

"Well then, they are saying, one to the other—not very plain, but I can hear —they are saying, 'I wonder when people will be good! It would be so easy, if only they would mean it, and begin when they are little!' That's what they are saying as they look down on us walking along."

"That will be good advice, Rob!" said one of the women.

"And," he resumed, "they are saying now—at least that is what it sounds to me—'I wish women were as good as they were when they were little girls!'"

"Now I know they are not saying that!" remarked the woman. "How should the angels trouble themselves about us! Rob, dear, confess you are making it up, because the child would be asking you."

Rob made no answer, but some saw him smile a curious smile. Rob would never defend anything he had said, or dispute anything another said. After a moment or two, he spoke again.

"Shall I be telling you what I heard them saying to each other this last night of all?" he asked.

"Yes, do, do!"

"It was upon Dorrachbeg; and there were two of them. They were sitting together in the moon—in the correi on the side of the hill over the village. I was lying in a bush near them, for I could not sleep, and came out, and the night was not cold. Now I would never be so bad-mannered as to listen where persons did not want me to hear."

"What were they like, Rob, dear?" interrupted the girl.

"That does not matter much," answered Rob; "but they were white, and their eyes not so white, but brighter; for so many sad things go in at their eyes when they come down to the earth, that it makes them dark."

"How could they be brighter and darker both at once?" asked the girl, very pertinently.

"I will tell you," answered Rob. "The dark things that go in at their eyes, they have to burn them in the fire of faith; and it is the fire of that burning that makes their eyes bright; it is the fire of their faith burning up the sad things they see."

"Oh, yes! I understand now!" said the girl. "And what were their clothes like, Rob?"

"When you see the angels, you don't think much about their clothes."

"And what were they saying?"

"I spoke first—the moment I saw them, for I was not sure they knew that I was there. I said, 'I am here, gentlemen.' 'Yes, we know that,' they answered. 'Are you far from home, gentlemen?' I asked. 'It is all one for that,' they answered. 'Well,' said I, 'it is true, gentlemen, for you seem as much at home here on the side of Dorrachbeg, as if it was a hill in paradise!' 'And how do you know it is not?' said they. 'Because I see people do upon it as they would not in paradise,' I answered. 'Ah!' said one of them, 'the hill may be in paradise, and the people not! But you cannot understand these things.' 'I think I do,' I said; 'but surely, if you did let them know they were on a hill in paradise, they would not do as they do!' 'It would be no use telling them,' said he; 'but, oh, how they spoil the house!' 'Are the red deer, and the hares, and the birds in paradise?' I asked. 'Certain sure!' he answered. 'Do they know it?' said I. 'No, it is not necessary for them; but they will know it one day.' 'You do not mind your little brother asking you questions?' I said. 'Ask a hundred, if you will, little brother,' he replied. 'Then tell me why you are down here to-night.' 'My friend and I came out for a walk, and we thought we would look to see when the village down there will have to be reaped.' 'What do you mean?' I said. 'You cannot see what we see,' they answered; 'but a human place is like a flower, or a field of corn, and grows ripe, or won't grow ripe, and then some of us up there have to sharpen our sickles.' 'What!' said I, for a great fear came upon me, 'they are not wicked people down there!' 'No, not very wicked, but slow and dull.' Then I could say nothing more for a while, and they did not speak either, but sat looking before them. 'Can you go and come as you please?' I asked at length. 'Yes, just as we are sent,' they answered. 'Would you not like better to go and come of yourselves, as my father and I do?' I said. 'No,' answered both of them, and something in their one voice almost frightened me; 'it is better than everything to go where we are sent. If we had to go and come at our own will, we should be miserable, for we do not love our own will.' 'Not love your own will?' 'No, not at all!' 'Why?' 'Because there is one—oh, ever so much better! When you and your father are quite good, you will not be left to go and come at your own will any more than we are.' And I cried out, and said, 'Oh, dear angel! you frighten me!' And he said, 'That is because you are only a man, and not a—' Now I am not sure of the word he said next; bat I think it was CHRISTIAN; and I do not quite know what the word meant."

"Oh, Rob, dear! everybody knows that!" exclaimed the girl.

But Rob said no more.

While he was talking, Alister had come up behind him, with Annie of the shop, and he said—

"Rob, my friend, I know what you mean, and I want to hear the rest of it: what did the angels say next?"

"They said," answered Rob, "—'Was it your will set you on this beautiful hill, with all these things to love, with such air to breathe, such a father as you've got, and such grand deer about you?' 'No,' I answered. 'Then,' said the angel, 'there must be a better will than yours, for you would never have even thought of such things!' 'How could I, when I wasn't made?' said I. 'There it is!' he returned, and said no more. I looked up, and the moon was shining, and there were no angels on the stone. But a little way off was my father, come out to see what had become of me."

"Now did you really see and hear all that, Rob?" said Alister.

Rob smiled a beautiful smile—with something in it common people would call idiotic—stopped and turned, took the chief's hand, and carried it to his lips; but not a word more would he speak, and soon they came where the path of the two turned away over the hill.

"Will you not come and sleep at our house?" said one of the company.

But they made kindly excuse.

"The hill-side would miss us; we are expected home!" said Rob—and away they climbed to their hut, a hollow in a limestone rock, with a front wall of turf, there to sleep side by side till the morning came, or, as Rob would have said, "till the wind of the sun woke them."

Rob of the Angels made songs, and would sing one sometimes; but they were in Gaelic, and the more poetic a thing, the more inadequate at least, if not stupid is its translation.

He had all the old legends of the country in his head, and many stories of ghosts and of the second sight. These stories he would tell exactly as he had heard them, showing he believed every word of them; but with such of the legends as were plainly no other than poetic inventions, he would take what liberties he pleased—and they lost nothing by it; for he not only gave them touches of fresh interest, but sent glimmering through them hints of something higher, of which ordinary natures perceived nothing, while others were dimly aware of a loftier intent: according to his listeners was their hearing. In Rob's stories, as in all the finer work of genius, a man would find as much as, and no more than, he was capable of. Ian's opinion of Rob was even higher than Alister's.

"What do you think, Ian, of the stories Rob of the Angels tells?" asked Alister, as they walked home.

"That the Lord has chosen the weak things of the world to confound the mighty," answered Ian.

"Tut! Rob confounds nobody."

"He confounds me," returned Ian.

"Does he believe what he tells?"

"He believes all of it that is to be believed," replied Ian.

"You are as bad as he!" rejoined Alister. "There is no telling, sometimes, what you mean!"

"Tell me this, Alister: can a thing be believed that is not true?"

"Yes, certainly!"

"I say, NO. Can you eat that which is not bread?"

"I have seen a poor fellow gnawing a stick for hunger!" answered Alister.

"Yes, gnawing! but gnawing is not eating. Did the poor fellow eat the stick? That is just it! Many a man will gnaw at a lie all his life, and perish of want. I mean LIE, of course, the real lie—a thing which is in its nature false. He may gnaw at it, he may even swallow it, but I deny that he can believe it. There is not that in it which can be believed; at most it can but be supposed to be true. Belief is another thing. Truth is alone the correlate of belief, just as air is for the lungs, just as form and colour are for the sight. A lie can no more be believed than carbonic acid can be breathed. It goes into the lungs, true, and a lie goes into the mind, but both kill; the one is not BREATHED, the other is not BELIEVED. The thing that is not true cannot find its way to the home of faith; if it could, it would be at once rejected with a loathing beyond utterance; to a pure soul, which alone can believe, nothing is so loathsome as a pretence of truth. A lie is a pretended truth. If there were no truth there could be no lie. As the devil upon God, the very being of a lie depends on that whose opposite and enemy it is. But tell me, Alister, do you believe the parables of our Lord?"

"With all my heart."

"Was there any real person in our Lord's mind when he told that one about the unjust judge?"

"I do not suppose there was; but there were doubtless many such."

"Many who would listen to a poor woman because she plagued them?"

"Well, it does not matter; what the story teaches is true, and that was what he wanted believed."

"Just so. The truth in the parables is what they mean, not what they say; and so it is, I think, with Rob of the Angels' stories. He believes all that can be believed of them. At the same time, to a mind so simple, the spirit of God must have freer entrance than to ours—perhaps even teaches the man by what we call THE MAN'S OWN WORDS. His words may go before his ideas—his higher ideas at least—his ideas follow after his words. As the half-thoughts pass through his mind—who can say how much generated by himself, how much directly suggested by the eternal thought in which his spirit lives and breathes!—he drinks and is refreshed. I am convinced that nowhere so much as in the highest knowledge of all—what the people above count knowledge—will the fulfilment of the saying of our Lord, "Many first shall be last, and the last first," cause astonishment; that a man who has been leader of the age's opinion, may be immeasurably behind another whom he would have shut up in a mad-house. Depend upon it, things go on in the soul of that Rob of the Angels which the angels, whether they come to talk with him or not, would gladly look into. Of such as he the angels may one day be the pupils."

A silence followed.

"Do you think the young ladies of the New House could understand Rob of the Angels, Ian?" at length asked Alister.

"Not a bit. I tried the younger, and she is the best.—They could if they would wake up."

"You might say that of anybody!"

"Yes; but there is this among other differences—that some people do not wake up, because they want a new brain first, such as they will get when they die, perhaps; while others do not wake up, because their whole education has been a rocking of them to sleep. And there is this difference between the girls, that the one is full of herself, and the other is not. The one has a close, the other an open mind."

"And yet," said Alister, "if they heard you say so, the open mind would imagine itself the close, and the close never doubt it was the open!"

CHAPTER III

AT THE NEW HOUSE.

The ladies of the New House were not a little surprised the next day when, as they sat waiting their guests, the door of the drawing-room opened, and they saw the young highlanders enter in ordinary evening dress. The plough-driving laird himself looked to Christina very much like her patterns of Grosvenor-square. It was long since he had worn his dress-coat, and it was certainly a little small for his more fully developed frame, but he carried himself as straight as a rush, and was nowise embarrassed with hands or feet. His hands were brown and large, but they were well shaped, and not ashamed of themselves, being as clean as his heart. Out of his hazel eyes, looking in the candle-light nearly as dark as Mercy's, went an occasional glance which an emergency might at once develop into a look of command.

For Ian, he would have attracted attention anywhere, if only from his look of quiet UNSELFNESS, and the invariable grace of the movement that broke his marked repose; but his entertainers would doubtless have honoured him more had they understood that his manner was just the same and himself as much at home in the grandest court of Europe.

The elder ladies got on together pretty well. The widow of the chief tried to explain to her hostess the condition of the country and its people; the latter, though knowing little and caring less about relations beyond those of the family and social circle, nor feeling any purely human responsibility, was yet interested enough to be able to seem more interested than she was; while her sweet smile and sweet manners were very pleasing to one who seldom now had the opportunity of meeting a woman so much on her own level.

The gentlemen, too, were tolerably comfortable together. Both Alister and Ian had plenty of talk and anecdote. The latter pleased the ladies with descriptions of northern ways and dresses and manners—perhaps yet more with what pleased the men also, tales of wolf-and bear-shooting. But it seemed odd that, when the talk turned upon the home-shooting called sport, both Alister and Ian should sit in unsmiling silence.

There was in Ian a certain playfulness, a subdued merriment, which made Mercy doubt her ears after his seriousness of the night before. Life seemed to flash from him on all sides, occasionally in a keen stroke of wit, oftener in a humorous presentation of things. His brother alone could see how he would check the witticism on his very lips lest it should hurt. It was in virtue of his tenderness toward everything that had life that he was able to give such narratives of what he had seen, such descriptions of persons he had met. When he told a story, it was with such quiet participation, manifest in the gleam of his gray eyes, in the smile that hovered like the very soul of Psyche about his lips, that his hearers enjoyed the telling more than the tale. Even the chief listened with eagerness to every word that fell from his brother.

The ladies took note that, while the manners of the laird and his mother were in a measure old-fashioned, those of Ian were of the latest: with social custom, in its flow of change, he seemed at home. But his ease never for a moment degenerated into the free-and-easy, the dry rot of manners; there was a stateliness in him that dominated the ease, and a courtesy that would not permit frendliness to fall into premature familiarity. He was at ease with his fellows because he respected them, and courteous because he loved them.

The ladies withdrew, and with their departure came the time that tests the man whether he be in truth a gentleman. In the presence of women the polish that is not revelation but concealment preserves itself only to vanish with them. How would not some women stand aghast to hear but a specimen of the talk of their heroes at such a time!

It had been remarked throughout the dinner that the highlanders took no wine; but it was supposed they were reserving their powers. When they now passed decanter and bottle and jug without filling their glasses, it gave offence to the very soul of Mr. Peregrine Palmer. The bettered custom of the present day had not then made progress enough to affect his table; he was not only fond of a glass of good wine, but had the ambition of the cellar largely developed; he would fain be held a connaisseur in wines, and kept up a good stock of distinguished vintages, from which he had brought of such to Glenruadh as would best bear the carriage. Having no aspiration, there was room in him for any number of petty ambitions; and it vexed him not to reap the harvest of recognition. "But of course," he said to himself, "no highlander understands anything but whisky!"

"You don't mean you're a teetotaler, Macruadh!" he said.

"No," answered the chief; "I do not call myself one; but I never drink anything strong."

"Not on Christmas-day? Of course you make an exception at times; and if at any time, why not on the merriest day of the year? You are under no pledge!"

"If that were a reason," returned Alister, laughing, "it would rather be one for becoming pledged immediately."

"Well, you surprise me! And highlanders too! I thought better of all highlanders; they have the reputation of good men at the bottle! You make me sorry to have brought my wine where it meets with no consideration.— Mr. Ian, you are a man of the world: you will not refuse to pledge me?"

"I must, Mr. Palmer! The fact is, my brother and I have seen so much evil come of the drinking habits of the country, which always get worse in a time of depression, that we dare not give in to them. My father, who was clergyman of the parish before he became head of the clan, was of the same mind before us, and brought us up not to drink. Throughout a whole Siberian winter I kept the rule."

"And got frost-bitten for your pains?"

"And found myself nothing the worse."

"It's mighty good of you, no doubt!" said the host, with a curl of his shaven lip.

"You can hardly call that good which does not involve any self-denial!" remarked Alister.

"Well," said Mr. Peregrine Palmer, "what IS the world coming to? All the pith is leaking out of our young men. In another generation we shall have neither soldiers nor sailors nor statesmen!"

"On what do you found such a sad conclusion?" inquired Ian.

"On the growth of asceticism in the young men. Believe me, it is necessary to manhood that men when they are young should drink a little, gamble a little, and sow a few wild oats—as necessary as that a nation should found itself by the law of the strongest. How else can we look for the moderation to follow with responsibilities? The vices that are more than excusable in the young, are very properly denied to the married man; the law for him is not the same as for the young man. I do not plead for license, you see; but it will never do for young men to turn ascetics! Let the clergy do as they please; they are hardly to be counted men; at least their calling is not a manly one! Depend upon it, young men who do not follow the dictates of nature—while they are young, I mean—will never make any mark in the world! They dry up like a nut, brain and all, and have neither spirit, nor wit, nor force of any kind. Nature knows best! When I was a young man, —"

"Pray spare us confession, Mr. Palmer," said Ian. "In our case your doctrine does not enter willing ears, and I should be sorry anything we might feel compelled to say, should have the appearance of personality."

"Do you suppose I should heed anything you said?" cried the host, betraying the bad blood in his breeding. "Is it manners here to prevent a man from speaking his mind at his own table? I say a saint is not a man! A fellow that will neither look at a woman nor drink his glass, is not cut out for man's work in the world!"

Like a sledge-hammer came the fist of the laird on the table, that the crystal danced and rang.

"My God!" he exclaimed, and rose in hugest indignation.

Ian laid his hand on his arm, and he sat down again.

"There may be some misunderstanding, Alister," said Ian, "between us and our host!—Pray, Mr. Palmer, let us understand each other: do you believe God made woman to be the slave of man? Can you believe he ever made a woman that she might be dishonoured?—that a man might caress and despise her?"

"I know nothing about God's intentions; all I say is, we must obey the laws of our nature."

"Is conscience then not a law of our nature? Or is it below the level of our instincts? Must not the lower laws be subject to the higher? It is a law—for ever broken, yet eternal—that a man is his brother's keeper: still more must he be his sister's keeper. Therein is involved all civilization, all national as well as individual growth."

Mr. Peregrine Palmer smiled a contemptuous smile. The other young men exchanged glances that seemed to say, "The governor knows what's what!"

"Such may be the popular feeling in this out-of-the-way spot," said Mr. Peregrine Palmer, "and no doubt it is very praiseworthy, but the world is not of your opinion, gentlemen."

"The world has got to come to our opinion," said the laird—at which the young men of the house broke into a laugh.

"May we join the ladies?" said Ian, rising.

"By all means," answered the host, with a laugh meant to be good-humoured; "they are the fittest company for you."

As the brothers went up the stair, they heard their host again holding forth; but they would not have been much edified by the slight change of front he had made—to impress on the young men the necessity of moderation in their pleasures.

There are two opposite classes related by a like unbelief—those who will not believe in the existence of the good of which they have apprehended no approximate instance, and those who will not believe in the existence of similar evil. I tell the one class, there are men who would cast their very being from them rather than be such as they; and the other, that their shutting of their eyes is no potent reason for the shutting of my mouth. There are multitudes delicate as they, who are compelled to meet evil face to face, and fight with it the sternest of battles: on their side may I be found! What the Lord knew and recognized, I will know and recognize too, be shocked who may. I spare them, however, any more of the talk at that dinner-table. Only let them take heed lest their refinement involve a very bad selfishness. Cursed be the evil thing, not ignored! Mrs. Palmer, sweet-smiled and clear-eyed, never showed the least indignation at her husband's doctrines. I fear she was devoid of indignation on behalf of others. Very far are such from understanding the ways of the all-pardoning, all-punishing Father!

The three from the cottage were half-way home ere the gentlemen of the New House rose from their wine. Then first the mother sought an explanation of the early departure they had suggested.

"Something went wrong, sons: what was it she said?"

"I don't like the men, mother; nor does Ian," answered Alister gloomily.

"Take care you are not unjust!" she replied.

"You would not have liked Mr. Palmer's doctrine any better than we did, mother."

"What was it?"

"We would rather not tell you."

"It was not fit for a woman to hear."

"Then do not tell me. I trust you to defend women."

"In God's name we will!" said Alister.

"There is no occasion for an oath, Alister!" said his mother.

"Alister meant it very solemnly!" said Ian.

"Yes; but it was not necessary—least of all to me. The name of our Lord God should lie a precious jewel in the cabinet of our hearts, to be taken out only at great times, and with loving awe."

"I shall be careful, mother," answered Alister; "but when things make me sorry, or glad, or angry, I always think of God first!"

"I understand you; but I fear taking the name of God in vain."

"It shall not be in vain, mother!" said the laird.

"Must it be a breach with our new neighbours?" asked the mother.

"It will depend on them. The thing began because we would not drink with them."

"You did not make any remark?"

"Not until our host's remarks called for our reasons. By the way, I should like to know how the man made his money."

CHAPTER IV.

THE BROTHERS.

Events, then, because of the deeper things whence they came, seemed sorely against any cordial approach of the old and the new houses of Glenruadh. But there was a sacred enemy within the stronghold of Mr. Peregrine Palmer, and that enemy forbade him to break with the young highlanders notwithstanding the downright mode in which they had expressed their difference with him: he felt, without knowing it, ashamed of the things he had uttered; they were not such as he would wish proclaimed from the house-tops out of the midst of which rose heavenward the spire of the church he had built; neither did the fact that he would have no man be wicked on Sundays, make him feel quite right in urging young men to their swing on other days.

Christian and Sercombe could not but admire the straightforwardness of the brothers; their conventionality could not prevent them from feeling the dignity with which they acted on their convictions. The quixotic young fellows ought not to be cut for their behaviour! They could not court their society, but would treat them with consideration! Things could not well happen to bring them into much proximity!

What had taken place could not definitely influence the ideas, feelings, or opinions of the young ladies. Their father would sooner have had his hand cut off than any word said over that fuliginous dessert reach the ears of his daughters. Is it not an absolute damnation of certain evil principles, that many men would be flayed alive rather than let those they love know that they hold them? But see the selfishness of such men: each looks with scorn on the woman he has done his part to degrade, but not an impure breath must reach the ears of HIS children! Another man's he will send to the devil!

Mr. Palmer did, however, communicate something of the conversation to his wife; and although she had neither the spirit, nor the insight, nor the active purity, to tell him he was in the wrong, she did not like the young highlanders the worse. She even thought it a pity the world should have been so made that they could not be in the right.

It is wonderful how a bird of the air will carry a matter, and some vaguest impression of what had occurred alighted on the minds of the elder girls—possibly from hints supposed unintelligible, passing between Mr. Sercombe and Christian: something in the social opinions of the two highlanders made those opinions differ much from the opinions prevailing in society! Now even Mercy had not escaped some notion of things of which the air about her was full; and she felt the glow of a conscious attraction towards men—somehow, she did not know how—like old-fashioned knights errant in their relations to women.

The attachment between the brothers was unusual both in kind and degree. Alister regarded Ian as his better self, through whom to rise above himself; Ian looked up to his brother as the head of the family, uniting in himself all ancestral claims, the representative of an ordered and harmonious commonwealth. He saw in Alister virtues and powers he did not recognize in himself. His love blossomed into the deeper devotion that he only had been sent to college: he was bound to share with his elder brother what he had learned. So Alister got more through Ian than he would have got at the best college in the world. For Ian was a born teacher, and found intensest delight, not in imparting knowledge—that is a comparatively poor thing—but in leading a mind up to see what it was before incapable of seeing. It was part of the same gift that he always knew when he had not succeeded. In Alister he found a wonderful docility—crossed indeed with a great pride, against which he fought sturdily.

It is not a good sign of any age that it should find it hard to believe in such simplicity and purity as that of these young men; it is perhaps even a worse sign of our own that we should find it difficult to believe in such love between men. I am sure of this, that a man incapable of loving another man with hearty devotion, can not be capable of loving a woman as a woman ought to be loved. From each other these two kept positively nothing secret.

Alister had a great love of music, which however had had little development except from the study of the violin, with the assistance of a certain poor enough performer in the village, and what criticism his brother could afford him, who, not himself a player, had heard much good music. But Alister was sorely hampered by the fact that his mother could not bear the sound of it. The late chief was one of the few clergymen who played the violin; and at the first wail of the old instrument in the hands of his son, his widow was seized with such a passion of weeping, that Alister took the utmost care she should never hear it again, always carrying it to some place too remote for the farthest-travelling tones to reach her. But this was not easy, for sound will travel very far among the hills. At times he would take it to the room behind Annie's shop, at times to the hut occupied by Hector of the Stags: there he would not excruciate his host at least, and Rob of the Angels would endure anything for his chief. The place which he most preferred was too distant to be often visited; but there, soon after Christmas, the brothers now resolved to have a day together, a long talk, and a conference with the violin. On a clear frosty morning in January they set out, provided for a night and two days.

The place was upon an upland pasture-ground, yet in their possession: no farm was complete without a range in some high valley for the sheep and cattle in summer. On the north of this valley stood a bare hilltop, whose crest was a limestone rock, rising from the heather about twenty feet. Every summer they had spent weeks of their boyhood with the shepherds, in the society of this hill, and one day discovered in its crest a shallow cave, to which thereafter they often took their food, and the book they were reading together. There they read the English Ossian, troubled by no ignorant unbelief; and there they made Gaelic songs, in which Alister excelled, while Ian did better in English.

When Ian was at home in the university-vacations, they were fonder than ever of going to the hill. There Ian would pour out to Alister of the fullness of his gathered knowledge, and there and then they made their first acquaintance with Shakspere. Ian had bought some dozen of his plays, in smallest compass and cleanest type, at a penny a piece, and how they revelled in them the long summer evenings! Ian had bought also, in a small thick volume, the poems of Shelley: these gave them not only large delight, but much to talk about, for they were quite capable of encountering his vague philosophy. Then they had their Euclid and Virgil—and even tried their mental teeth upon Dante, but found the Commedia without notes too hard a nut for them. Every fresh spring, Ian brought with him fresh books, and these they read in their cave. But I must not forget the cave itself, which also shared in the progress of its troglodytes.

The same week in which they first ate and read in it, they conceived and began to embody the idea of developing the hollow into a house. Foraging long ago in their father's library for mental pabulum, they had come upon Belzoni's quarto, and had read, with the avidity of imaginative boys, the tale of his discoveries, taking especial delight in his explorations of the tombs of the kings in the rocks of Beban el Malook: these it was that now suggested excavation.

They found serviceable tools about the place at home, and the rock was not quite of the hardest. Not a summer, for the last seventeen years, had passed without a good deal being done, Alister working alone when Ian was away, and the cave had now assumed notable dimensions. It was called by the people uamh an ceann, the cave of the chief, and regarded as his country house. All around it was covered with snow throughout the winter and spring, and supplied little to the need of man beyond the blessed air, and a glorious vision of sea and land, mountain and valley, falling water, gleaming lake, and shadowy cliff.

Crossing the wide space where so lately they had burned the heather that the sheep might have its young shoots in the spring, the brothers stood, and gazed around with delight.

"There is nothing like this anywhere!" said Ian.

"Do you mean nothing so beautiful?" asked Alister.

"No; I mean just what I say: there is nothing like it. I do not care a straw whether one scene be more or less beautiful than another; what I do care for is—its individual speech to my soul. I feel towards visions of nature as towards writers. If a book or a prospect produces in my mind a mood that no other produces, then I feel it individual, original, real, therefore precious. If a scene or a song play upon the organ of my heart as no other scene or song could, why should I ask at all whether it be beautiful? A bare hill may be more to me than a garden of Damascus, but I love them both. The first question as to any work of art is whether it puts the willing soul into any mood at all peculiar; the second, what that mood is. It matters to me little by whom our Ossian was composed, and it matters nothing whoever may in his ignorance declare that there never was an Ossian any more than a Homer: here is a something that has power over my heart and soul, works upon them as not anything else does. I do not ask whether its power be great or small; it is enough that it is a peculiar power, one by itself; that it puts my spiritual consciousness in a certain individual condition, such in character as nothing else can occasion. Either a man or a nation must have felt to make me so feel."

They were now climbing the last slope of the hill on whose top stood their playhouse, dearer now than in their boyhood. Alister occasionally went there for a few hours' solitude, and Ian would write there for days at a time, but in general when they visited the place it was together. Alister unlocked the door and they entered.

Unwilling to spend labour on the introductory, they had made the first chamber hardly larger than the room required for opening the door. Immediately within, another door opened into a room of about eight feet by twelve, with two small windows. Its hearth was a projection from the floor of the live stone; and there, all ready for lighting, was a large pile of peats. The chimney went up through the rock, and had been the most difficult part of their undertaking. They had to work it much wider than was necessary for the smoke, and then to reduce its capacity with stone and lime. Now and then it smoked, but peat-smoke is sweet.

The first thing after lighting the fire, was to fill their kettle, for which they had to take off the snow-lid of a small spring near at hand. Then they made a good meal of tea, mutton-ham, oatcakes and butter. The only seats in the room were a bench in each of two of the walls, and a chair on each side of the hearth, all of the live rock.

From this opened two rooms more—one a bedroom, with a bed in the rock-wall, big enough for two. Dry heather stood thick between the mattress and the stone. The third room, of which they intended making a parlour, was not yet more than half excavated; and there, when they had rested a while, they began to bore and chip at the stone. Their progress was slow, for the grain was close: never, even when the snow above was melting, had the least moisture come through. For a time they worked and talked: both talked better when using their hands. Then Alister stopped, and played while Ian went on; Ian stopped next, and read aloud from a manuscript he had brought, while his brother again worked. But first he gave Alister the history of what he was going to read. It was suggested, he said, by that strange poem of William Mayne's, called "The Dead Man's Moan," founded on the silly notion that the man himself is buried, and not merely his body.

"I   wish   I   were   up   to   straught   my   banes,
    And   drive   frae   my   face   the   cauld,   dead   air;
I   wish   I   were   up,   that   the   friendly   rains
    Micht wash the dark mould frae my tangled hair!"

quoted Ian, and added,

"I thought I should like to follow out the idea, and see what ought to come of it. I therefore supposed a person seized by something of the cataleptic kind, from which he comes to himself still in the body, but unable to hold communication with the outer world. He thinks therefore that he is dead and buried. Recovering from his first horror, he reflects that, as he did not make himself think and feel, nor can cease to think and feel if he would, there must be somewhere—and where but within himself?—the power by which he thinks and feels, a power whose care it must be, for it can belong to no other, to look after the creature he has made. Then comes to him the prayer of Job, 'Oh that thou wouldst hide me in the grave till thy anger with me was past! Then wouldst thou desire to see again the work of thy hands, the creature thou hadst made! Then wouldst thou call, and I would answer.' So grandly is the man comforted thereby, that he breaks out in a dumb song of triumph over death and the grave. As its last tone dies in him, a kiss falls upon his lips. It is the farewell of the earth; the same moment he bursts the bonds and rises above the clouds of the body, and enters into the joy of his Lord."

Having thus prepared Alister to hear without having to think as well as attend, which is not good for poetry, Ian read his verses. I will not trouble my reader with them; I am sure he would not think so well of them as did Alister. What Ian desired was sympathy, not admiration, but from Alister he had both.

Few men would care to hear the talk of those two, for they had no interest in anything that did not belong to the reality of things. To them the things most men count real, were the merest phantasms. They sought what would not merely last, but must go on growing. At strife with all their known selfishness, they were growing into strife with all the selfishness in them as yet unknown. There was for them no question of choice; they MUST choose what was true; they MUST choose life; they MUST NOT walk in the way of death.

They were very near to agreeing about EVERYthing they should ask. Few men are capable of understanding such love as theirs, of understanding the love of David and Jonathan, of Shakspere to W. H., of Tennyson and Hallam. Every such love, nevertheless, is a possession of the race; what has once been is, in possibility to come, as well as in fact that has come. A solitary instance of anything great is enough to prove it human, yea necessary to humanity. I have wondered whether the man in whom such love is possible, may not spring of an altogether happy conjunction of male and female—a father and mother who not only loved each other, but were of the same mind in high things, of the same lofty aims in life, so that their progeny came of their true man-and-woman-hood. If any unaccountable disruption or discord of soul appear in a man, it is worth while to ask whether his father and mother were of one aspiration. Might not the fact that their marriage did not go deep enough, that father and mother were not of one mind, only of one body, serve to account for the rude results of some marriages of personable people? At the same time we must not forget the endless and unfathomable perpetuations of ancestry. But however these things may be, those two men, brothers born, were also brothers willed.

They ceased quarrying, and returned to the outer room. Ian betook himself to drawing figures on one of the walls, with the intention of carving them in dipped relief. Alister proceeded to take their bedding from before the fire, and prepare for the night.

CHAPTER V.

THE PRINCESS.

While they were thus busied, Ian, with his face to the wall, in the dim light of the candle by which he was making his first rough sketches, began the story of his flight from Russia. Long ere he ended, Alister came close behind him, and there stood, his bosom heaving with emotion, his eyes burning with a dry fire. Ian was perfectly composed, his voice quiet and low.

I will not give his tale in the first person; and will tell of it only as much as I think it necessary my reader should know.

Having accepted a commission of the Czar, he was placed in a post of trust in the palace.

In one apartment of it, lived an imperial princess, the burden of whose rank had not even the alleviation of society. Her disclosure of a sympathy with oppressed humanity had wakened a doubt as to her politics, and she was virtually a prisoner, restricted to a corner of the huge dwelling, and allowed to see hardly any but her women. Her father had fallen into disgrace before her, and her mother was dead of grief. All around her were spies, and love was nowhere. Gladly would she have yielded every rag of her rank, to breathe the air of freedom. To be a peasant girl on her father's land, would be a life of rapture!

She knew little of the solace books might have given her. With a mind capable of rapid development, she had been ill taught except in music; and that, alone, cannot do much for spiritual development; it cannot enable the longing, the aspiration it rouses, to understand itself; it cannot lead back to its own eternal source.

She knew no one in whom to trust, or from whom to draw comfort; her confessor was a man of the world, incapable of leading her to any fountain of living water; she had no one to tell her of God and his fatherhood, the only and perfect refuge from the divine miseries of loneliness.

A great corridor went from end to end of one of the wings of the palace, and from this corridor another passage led toward the apartment of the princess, consisting of some five or six rooms. At certain times of the day, Ian had to be at the beginning of the corridor, at the head of a huge stair with a spacious hall-like landing. Along the corridor few passed, for the attendants used a back stair and passages. As he sat in the recess of a large window, where stood a table and chair for his use, Ian one morning heard a cry—whence, he never knew—and darted along the corridor, thinking assistance might be wanted. When about halfway down, he saw a lady enter, near the end of it, and come slowly along. He stood aside, respectfully waiting till she should pass. Her eyes were on the ground, but as she came near she raised them. The sadness of them went to his heart, and his soul rushed into his. The princess, I imagine, had never before met such an expression, and misunderstood it. Lonely, rejected, too helpless even to hope, it seemed full of something she had all her life been longing for—a soul to be her refuge from the wind, her covert from the tempest, her shadow as of a great rock in the weary land where no one cared for her. She stood and gazed at him.

Ian at once perceived who she must be, and stood waiting for some expression of her pleasure. But she appeared fascinated; her eyes remained on his, for they seemed to her to be promising help. Her fascination fascinated him, and for some moments they stood thus, regarding each other. Ian felt he must break the spell. It was her part to speak, his to obey, but he knew the danger of the smallest suspicion. If she was a princess and he but a soldier on guard, she was a woman and he was a man: he was there to protect her! "How may I serve your imperial highness?" he asked. She was silent yet a moment, then said, "Your name?" He gave it. "Your nation?" He stated it. "When are you here?" He told her his hours. "I will see you again," she said, and turned and went back.

From that moment she loved him, and thought he loved her. But, though he would willingly have died for her, he did not love her as she thought. Alister wondered to hear him say so. At such a moment, and heart-free, Alister could no more have helped falling in love with her than he could help opening his eyes when the light shone on their lids. Ian, with a greater love for his kind than even Alister, and with a tenderness for womankind altogether infinite, was not ready to fall in love. Accessible indeed he was to the finest of Nature's witcheries; ready for the response as of summer lightnings from opposing horizons; all aware of loveliest difference, of refuge and mysterious complement; but he was not prone to fall in love.

The princess, knowing the ways of the house, contrived to see him pretty often. He talked to her of the hest he knew; he did what he could to lighten her loneliness by finding her books and music; best of all, he persuaded her —without difficulty—to read the New Testament. In their few minutes of conference, he tried to show her the Master of men as he showed himself to his friends; but their time together was always so short, and their anxiety for each other so great, seeing that discovery would be ruin to both, that they could not go far with anything.

At length came an occasion when at parting they embraced. How it was Ian could not tell. He blamed himself much, but Alister thought it might not have been his fault. The same moment he was aware that he did not love her and that he could not turn back. He was ready to do anything, everything in honour; yet felt false inasmuch as he had given her ground for believing that he felt towards her as he could not help seeing she felt towards him. Had it been in his power to order his own heart, he would have willed to love, and so would have loved her. But the princess doubted nothing, and the change that passed upon her was wonderful. The power of human love is next to the power of Grod's love. Like a flower long repressed by cold, she blossomed so suddenly in the sunshine of her bliss, that Ian greatly dreaded the suspicion which the too evident alteration might arouse: the plain, ordinary-looking young woman with fine eyes, began to put on the robes of beauty. A softest vapour of rose, the colour of the east when sundown sets it dreaming of sunrise, tinged her cheek; it grew round like that of a girl; and ere two months were gone, she looked years younger than her age. But Ian could never be absolutely open with her; while she, poor princess, happy in her ignorance of the shows of love, and absorbed in the joy of its great deliverance, jealoused nothing of restraint, nothing of lack, either in his words or in the caresses of which he was religiously sparing. He was haunted by the dread of making her grieve who had already grieved so much, and was but just risen from the dead.

One evening they met as usual in the twilight; in five minutes the steps of the man would be heard coming to light the lamps of the corridor, his guard would be over, and he must retire. Few words passed, but they parted with more of lingering tenderness than usual, and the princess put a little packet in his hand. The same night his only friend in the service entered his room hurriedly, and urged immediate flight: something had been, or was imagined to be discovered, through which his liberty, perhaps his life, was compromised; he must leave at once by a certain coach which would start in an hour: there was but just time to disguise him; he must make for a certain port on the Baltic, and there lie concealed until a chance of getting away turned up!

Ian refused. He feared nothing, had done nothing to be ashamed of! What was it to him if they did take his life! he could die as well as another! Anxious about the princess, he persisted in his refusal, and the coach went without him. Every passenger in that coach was murdered. He saw afterward the signs of their fate in the snow.

In the middle of the night, a company of men in masks entered his room, muffled his head, and hurried him into a carriage, which drove rapidly away.

When it stopped, he thought he had arrived at some prison, but soon found himself in another carriage, with two of the police. He could have escaped had he been so minded, but he could do nothing for the princess, and did not care what became of him. At a certain town his attendants left him, with the assurance that if he did not make haste out of the country, he would find they had not lost sight of him.

But instead of obeying, he disguised himself, and took his way to Moscow, where he had friends. Thence he wrote to his friend at St. Petersburg. Not many letters passed ere he learned that the princess was dead. She had been placed in closer confinement, her health gave way, and by a rapid decline she had gained her freedom.

All the night through, not closing their eyes till the morning, the brothers, with many intervals of thoughtful silence, lay talking.

"I am glad to think," said Alister, after one of these silences, "you do not suffer so much, Ian, as if you had been downright in love with her."

"I suffer far more," answered Ian with a sigh; "and I ought to suffer more. It breaks my heart to think she had not so much from me as she thought she had."

They were once more silent. Alister was full of trouble for his brother. Ian at length spoke again.

"Alister," he said, "I must tell you everything! I know the truth now. If I wronged her, she is having her revenge!"

By his tone Alister seemed through the darkness to see his sad smile. He was silent, and Alister waited.

"She did not know much," Ian resumed. "I thought at first she had nothing but good manners and a good heart; but the moment the sun of another heart began to shine on her, the air of another's thought to breathe upon her, the room of another soul to surround her, she began to grow; and what more could God intend or man desire? As I told you, she grew beautiful, and what sign of life is equal to that!"

"But I want to know what you mean by her having her revenge on you?" said Alister.

"Whether I loved her then or not, and I believe I did, beyond a doubt I love her now. It needed only to be out of sight of her, and see other women beside the memory of her, to know that I loved her.—Alister, I LOVE HER!" repeated Ian with a strange exaltation.

"Oh, Ian!" groaned Alister; "how terrible for you!"

"Alister, you dear fellow!" returned Ian, "can you understand no better than that? Do you not see I am happy now? My trouble was that I did not love her—not that she loved me, but that I did not love her! Now we shall love each other for ever!"

"How do you know that, Ian?"

"By knowing that I love her. If I had not come to know that, I could not have said to myself I would love her for ever."

"But you can't marry her, Ian! The Lord said there would be no marrying there!"

"Did he say there would be no loving there, Alister? Most people seem to fancy he did, for how else could they forget the dead as they do, and look so little for their resurrection? Few can be said really to believe in any hereafter worth believing in. How many go against the liking of the dead the moment they are gone-behave as if they were nowhere, and could never call them to account! Their plans do not recognize their existence; the life beyond is no factor in their life here. If God has given me a hope altogether beyond anything I could have generated for myself, beyond all the likelihoods and fulfilments around me, what can I do but give him room to verify it—what but look onward! Some people's bodies get so tired that they long for the rest of the grave; it is my soul that gets tired, and I know the grave can give that no rest; I look for the rest of more life, more strength, more love. But God is not shut up in heaven, neither is there one law of life there and another here; I desire more life here, and shall have it, for what is needful for this world is to be had in this world. In proportion as I become one with God, I shall have it. This world never did seem my home; I have never felt quite comfortable in it; I have yet to find, and shall find the perfect home I have not felt this world, even my mother's bosom to be. Nature herself is not lovely enough to satisfy me. Nor can it be that I am beside myself, seeing I care only for the will of God, not for my own. For what is madness but two or more wills in one body? Does not the 'Bible itself tell us that we are pilgrims and strangers in the world, that here we have no abiding city? It is but a place to which we come to be made ready for another. Yet I am sure those who regard it as their home, are not half so well pleased with it as I. They are always grumbling at it. 'What wretched weather!' they say. 'What a cursed misfortune!' they cry. 'What abominable luck!' they protest. Health is the first thing, they say, and cannot find it. They complain that their plans are thwarted, and when they succeed, that they do not yield the satisfaction they expected. Yet they mock at him who says he seeks a better country!—But I am keeping you awake, Alister! I will talk no more. You must go to sleep!"

"It is better than any sleep to hear you talk, Ian," returned Alister. "What a way you are ahead of me! I do love this world! When I come to die, it will tear my heart to think that this cave which you and I have dug out together, must pass into other hands! I love every foot of the earth that remains to us —every foot that has been taken from us. When I stand on the top of this rock, and breathe the air of this mountain, I bless God we have still a spot to call our own. It is quite a different thing from the love of mere land; I could not feel the same toward any, however beautiful, that I had but bought. This, our own old land, I feel as if I loved in something the same way as I love my mother. Often in the hot summer-days, lying on my face in the grass, I have kissed the earth as if it were a live creature that could return my caresses! The long grass is a passion to me, and next to the grass I love the heather, not the growing corn. I am a fair farmer, I think, but I would rather see the land grow what it pleased, than pass into the hands of another. Place is to me sacred almost as body. There is at least something akin between the love we bear to the bodies of our friends, and that we bear to the place in which we were born and brought up."

"That is all very true, Alister. I understand your feeling perfectly; I have it myself. But we must be weaned, I say only weaned, from that kind of thing; we must not love the outside as if it were the inside! Everything comes that' we may know the sender-of whom it is a symbol, that is, a far-off likeness of something in him; and to him it must lead us-the self-existent, true, original love, the making love. But I have felt all you say. I used to lie in bed and imagine the earth alive and carrying me on her back, till I fell asleep longing to see the face of my nurse. Once, the fancy turned into a dream. I will try to recall a sonnet I made the same night, before the dream came: it will help you to understand it. I was then about nineteen, I believe. I did not care for it enough to repeat it to you, and I fear we shall find it very bad."

Stopping often to recall and rearrange words and lines, Ian completed at last the following sonnet:—

"She set me on my feet with steady hand, Among the crowding marvels on her face, Bidding me rise, and run a strong man's race; Swathed mo in circumstance's swaddling band; Fed me with her own self; then bade me stand MYself entire,—while she was but a place Hewn for my dwelling from the midst of space, A something better than HER sea or land. Nay, Earth! thou bearest me upon thy back, Like a rough nurse, and I can almost feel A touch of kindness in thy bands of steel, Although I cannot see thy face, and track An onward purpose shining through its black, Instinct with prophecy of future weal.

"There! It is not much, is it?"

"It is beautiful!" protested Alister.

"It is worth nothing," said Ian, "except between you and me-and that it will make you understand my dream. That I shall never forget. When a dream does us good we don't forget it.

"I thought I was home on the back of something great and strong-I could not tell what; it might be an elephant or a great eagle or a lion. It went sweeping swiftly along, the wind of its flight roaring past me in a tempest. I began to grow frightened. Where could this creature of such awful speed be carrying me? I prayed to God to take care of me. The head of the creature turned to me, and I saw the face of a woman, grand and beautiful. Never with my open eyes have I seen such a face! And I knew it was the face of this earth, and that I had never seen it before because she carries us upon her back. When I woke, I knew that all the strangest things in life and history must one day come together in a beautiful face of loving purpose, one of the faces of the living God. The very mother of the Lord did not for a long time understand him, and only through sorrow came to see true glory. Alister, if we were right with God, we could see the earth vanish and never heave a sigh; God, of whom it was but a shimmering revelation, would still be ours!"

In the morning they fell asleep, and it was daylight, late in the winter, when Alister rose. He roused the fire, asleep all through the night, and prepared their breakfast of porridge and butter, tea, oat-cake, and mutton-ham. When it was nearly ready, he woke Ian, and when they had eaten, they read together a portion of the Bible, that they might not forget, and start the life of the day without trust in the life-causing God.

"All that is not rooted in him," Ian would say, "all hope or joy that does not turn its face upward, is an idolatry. Our prayers must rise that our thoughts may follow them."

The portion they read contained the saying of the Lord that we must forsake all and follow him if we would be his disciples.

"I am sometimes almost terrified," said Ian, "at the scope of the demands made upon me, at the perfection of the self-abandonment required of me; yet outside of such absoluteness can be no salvation. In God we live every commonplace as well as most exalted moment of our being. To trust in him when no need is pressing, when things seem going right of themselves, may be harder than when things seem going wrong. At no time is there any danger except in ourselves, and the only danger is of trusting in something else than the living God, and so getting, as it were, outside of God. Oh Alister, take care you do not love the land more than the will of God! Take care you do not love even your people more than the will of God."

They spent the day on the hill-top, and as there was no sign of storm, remained till the dark night, when the moon came to light them home.

"Perhaps when we are dead," said Alister as they went, "we may be allowed to corne here again sometimes! Only we shall not be able to quarry any further, and there is pain in looking on what cannot go on."

"It may be a special pleasure," returned Ian, "in those new conditions, to look into such a changeless cabinet of the past. When we are one with our life, so that no prayer can be denied, there will be no end to the lovely possibilities."

"So I have the people I love, I think I could part with all things else, even the land!" said Alister.

"Be sure we shall not have to part with THEM. We shall yet walk, I think, with our father as of old, where the setting sun sent the shadows of the big horse-gowans that glowed in his red level rays, trooping eastward, as if they would go round the world to meet the sun that had banished them, and die in his glory; the wind of the twilight will again breathe about us like a thought of the living God haunting our goings, and watching to help us; the stars will yet call to us out of the great night, 'Love and be fearless.' 'Be independent!' cries the world from its' great Bible of the Belly;-says the Lord of men, 'Seek ye first the kingdom of God and his righteousness, and all these things shall be added unto you.' Our dependence is our eternity. We cannot live on bread alone; we need every word of God. We cannot live on air alone; we need an atmosphere of living souls. Should we be freer, Alister, if we were independent of each other? When I am out in the world, my heart is always with mother and you. We must be constantly giving ourselves away, we must dwell in houses of infinite dependence, or sit alone in the waste of a godless universe."

It was a rough walk in the moonlight over the hills, but full of a rare delight. And while they walked the mother was waiting them, with the joy of St. John, of the Saviour, of God himself in her heart, the joy of beholding how the men she loved loved each other.

CHAPTER VI.

THE TWO PAIRS.

The next morning, on the way to the village, the brothers overtook Christina and Mercy, and they walked along together.

The young men felt inclined to be the more friendly with the girls, that the men of their own family were so unworthy of them. A man who does not respect a woman because she is a woman, cannot have thorough respect for his own mother, protest as he pleases: he is incapable of it, and cannot know his own incapacity. Alas for girls in a family where the atmosphere of vile thinking, winnowed by the carrion wings of degraded and degrading judgments, infolds them! One of the marvels of the world is, that, with such fathers and brothers, there are so few wicked women. Type of the greater number stands Ophelia, poor, weak, and not very refined, yet honest, and, in all her poverty, immeasurably superior to father and brother.

Christina's condescension had by this time dwindled almost to the vanishing-point, and her talk was in consequence more natural: the company, conversation, and whole atmosphere of the young men, tended to wake in the girls what was best and sweetest. Reality appeals at once to the real, opens the way for a soul to emerge from the fog of the commonplace, the marsh of platitude, the Sahara of lies, into the colour and air of life. The better things of humanity often need the sun of friendship to wile them out. A girl, well-bred, tolerably clever, and with some genius of accommodation, will appear to a man possessed of a hundred faculties of which she knows nothing; but his belief will help to rouse them in her. A young man will see an angel where those who love her best see only a nice girl; but he sees not merely what she might be, but what one day she must be.

Christina had been at first rather taken with the ploughman, but she turned her masked batteries now mainly on the soldier. During the dinner she had noted how entirely Ian was what she chose to call a man of the world; and it rendered him in her eyes more worthy of conquest. Besides, as elder sister, must she not protect the inexperienced Mercy?

What is this passion for subjugation? this hunger for homage? Is it of hell direct, or what is there in it of good to begin with? Apparently it takes possession of such women as have set up each herself for the object of her worship: she cannot then rest from the effort to bring as many as possible to worship at the same shrine; and to this end will use means as deserving of the fire as any witchcraft.

Christina stopped short with a little cry, and caught Ian's arm.

"I beg your pardon," she said, "but I cannot bear it a moment longer! Something in my boot hurts me so!"

She limped to the road-side, sat down, accepted the service of Ian to unlace her boot, and gave a sigh of relief when he pulled it off. He inverted and shook it, then searched and found a nail which must have hurt her severely.

But how to get rid of the cruel projection! Ian's slender hand could but just reach with its finger-tips the haunted spot. In vain he tried to knock it down against a stone put inside. Alister could suggest nothing. But Mistress Conal's cottage was near: they might there find something to help! Only Christina could not be left behind, and how was she to walk in a silk stocking over a road frozen hard as glass? The chief would have carried her, but she would not let him. Ian therefore shod her with his Glengarry bonnet, tying it on with his handkerchief.

There was much merriment over the extemporized shoe, mingled with apologetic gratitude from Christina, who, laughing at her poulticed foot, was yet not displeased at its contrast with the other.

When the chief opened the door of the cottage, there was no one to be seen within. The fire was burning hot and flameless; a three-footed pot stood half in it; other sign of presence they saw none. As Alister stooped searching for some implement to serve their need, in shot a black cat, jumped over his back, and disappeared. The same instant they heard a groan, and then first discovered the old woman in bed, seemingly very ill. Ian went up to her.

"What is the matter with you, Mistress Conal?" he asked, addressing her in English because of the ladies.

But in reply she poured out a torrent of Gaelic, which seemed to the girls only grumbling, but was something stronger. Thereupon the chief went and spoke to her, but she was short and sullen with him. He left her to resume his search.

"Let alone," she cried. "When that nail leaves her brog, it will be for your heart."

Ian sought to soothe her.

"She will bring misery on you all!" she insisted.

"You have a hammer somewhere, I know!" said Alister, as if he had not heard her.

"She shall be finding no help in MY house!" answered the old woman in English.

"Very well, Mistress Conal!" returned the chief; "the lady cannot walk home; I shall have to carry her!"

"God forbid!" she cried. "Go and fetch a wheelbarrow."

"Mistress Conal, there is nothing for it but carry her home in my arms!"

"Give me the cursed brog then. I will draw the nail."

But the chief would not yield the boot; he went out and searched the hillside until he found a smooth stone of suitable size, with which and a pair of tongs, he beat down the nail. Christina put on the boot, and they left the place. The chief stayed behind the rest for a moment, but the old woman would not even acknowledge his presence.

"What a rude old thing she is! This is how she always treats us!" said Christina.

"Have you done anything to offend her?" asked Alister.

"Not that we know of. We can't help being lowlanders!"

"She no doubt bears you a grudge," said Ian, "for having what once belonged to us. I am sorry she is so unfriendly. It is not a common fault with our people."

"Poor old thing! what does it matter!" said Christina.

A woman's hate was to her no more than the barking of a dog.

They had not gone far, before the nail again asserted itself; it had been but partially subjugated. A consultation was held. It resulted in this, that Mercy and the chief went to fetch another pair of boots, while Ian remained with Christina.

They seated themselves on a stone by the roadside. The sun clouded over, a keen wind blew, and Christina shivered. There was nothing for it but go back to the cottage. The key was in the door, Ian turned it, and they went in. Certainly this time no one was there. The old woman so lately groaning on her bed had vanished. Ian made up the fire, and did what he could for his companion's comfort.

She was not pleased with the tone of his attentions, but the way she accepted them made her appear more pleased than Ian cared for, and he became colder and more polite. Piqued by his indifference, she took it nevertheless with a sweetness which belonged to her nature as God made it, not as she had spoiled it; and even such a butterfly as she, felt the influence of a man like Ian, and could not help being more natural in his presence. His truth elicited what there was of hers; the trae being drew to the surface what there was of true in the being that was not true. The longer she was in his company, the more she was pleased with him, and the more annoyed with her failure in pleasing him.

It is generally more or less awkward when a young man and maiden between whom is no convergent rush of spiritual currents, find themselves alone together. Ian was one of the last to feel such awkwardness, but he thought his companion felt it; he did his best, therefore, to make her forget herself and him, telling her story after story which she could not but find the more interesting that for the time she was quieted from self, and placed in the humbler and healthier position of receiving the influence of another. For one moment, as he was narrating a hair's-breadth escape he had had from a company of Tartar soldiers by the friendliness of a young girl, the daughter of a Siberian convict, she found herself under the charm of a certain potency of which he was himself altogether unconscious, but which had carried away hearts more indifferent than hers.

In the meantime, Alister and Mercy were walking toward the New House, and, walking, were more comfortable than those that sat waiting. Mercy indeed had not much to say, but she was capable of asking a question worth answering, and of understanding not a little. Thinking of her walk with Ian on Christmas day,—

"Would you mind telling me something about your brother?" she said.

"What would you like to know about him?" asked Alister.

"Anything you care to tell me," she answered.

Now there was nothing pleased Alister better than talking about Ian; and he talked so that Mercy could not help feeling what a brother he must be himself; while on his part Alister was delighted with the girl who took such an interest in Ian: for Ian's sake he began to love Mercy. He had never yet been what is called in love—had little opportunity indeed of falling in love. His breeding had been that of a gentleman, and notwithstanding the sweetness and gentleness of the maidens of his clan, there were differences which had as yet proved sufficient to prevent the first approaches of love, though, once entertained, they might have added to the depth of it. At the same time it was by no means impossible for Alister to fall in love with even an uneducated girl—so-called; neither would he, in that case, have felt any difficulty about marrying her; but the fatherly relation in which he stood toward his clan, had tended rather to prevent the thing. Many a youth falls to premature love-making, from the lack in his daily history of the womanly element. Matrons in towns should be exhorted to make of their houses a refuge. Too many mothers are anxious for what they count the welfare of their own children, and care nothing for the children of other women! But can we wonder, when they will wallow in mean- nesses to save their own from poverty and health, and damn them into comfort and decay.

Alister told Mercy how Ian and he used to spend their boyhood. He recounted some of their adventures in hunting and herding and fishing, and even in going to and from school, a distance of five miles, in all weathers. Then he got upon the poetry of the people, their legends, their ballads and their songs; and at last came to the poetry of the country itself—the delights of following the plough, the whispers and gleams of nature, her endless appeal through every sense. The mere smell of the earth in a spring morning, he said, always made him praise God.

"Everything we have," he went on, "must be shared with God. That is the notion of the Jewish thank-offering. Ian says the greatest word in the universe is ONE; the next greatest, ALL. They are but the two ends of a word to us unknowable—God's name for himself."

Mercy had read Mrs. Barbauld's Hymns, and they had been something to her; but most of the little poetry she had read was only platitude sweetened with sound; she had never read, certainly never understood a real poem. Who can tell what a nature may prove, after feeding on good food for a while? The queen bee is only a better fed working bee. Who can tell what it may prove when it has been ploughed with the plough of suffering, when the rains of sorrow, the frosts of pain, and the winds of poverty have moistened and swelled and dried its fallow clods?

Mercy had not such a sweet temper as her sister, but she was not so selfish. She was readier to take offence, perhaps just because she was less self-satisfied. Before long they might change places. A little dew from the eternal fountain was falling upon them. Christina was beginning to be aware that a certain man, neither rich nor distinguished nor ambitious, had yet a real charm for her. Not that for a moment she would think seriously of such a man! That would he simply idiotic! But it would be very nice to have a little innocent flirtation with him, or perhaps a "Platonic friendship! "—her phrase, not mine. What could she have to do with Plato, who, when she said I, was aware only of a neat bundle of foolish desires, not the God at her heart!

Mercy, on the other hand, was being drawn to the big, strong, childlike heart of the chief. There is always, notwithstanding the gulf of unlikeness between them, an appeal from the childish to the childlike. The childish is but the shadow of the childlike, and shadows are little like the things from which they fall. But to what save the heavenly shall the earthly appeal in its sore need, its widowhood, its orphanage? with what shall the childish take refuge but the childlike? to what shall ignorance cry but wisdom? Mercy felt no restraint with the chief as with Ian. His great, deep, yet refined and musical laugh, set her at ease. Ian's smile, with its shim—mering eternity, was no more than the moon on a rain-pool to Mercy. The moral health of the chief made an atmosphere of conscious safety around her. By the side of no other man had she ever felt so. With him she was at home, therefore happy. She was already growing under his genial influence. Every being has such influence who is not selfish.

When Christina was re-shod, and they were leaving the cottage, Ian, happening to look behind him, spied the black cat perched on the edge of the chimney in the smoke.

"Look at her," he said, "pretending innocence, when she has been watching you all the time!"

Alister took up a stone.

"Don't hurt her," said Ian, and he dropped it.

CHAPTER VII.

AN CABRACH MOR.

I have already said that the young men had not done well as hunters. They had neither experience nor trustworthy attendance: none of the chief's men would hunt with them. They looked on them as intruders, and those who did not share in their chiefs dislike to useless killing, yet respected it. Neither Christian nor Sercombe had yet shot a single stag, and the time was drawing nigh when they must return, the one to Glasgow, the other to London. To have no proof of prowess to display was humbling to Sercombe; he must show a stag's head, or hide his own! He resolved, therefore, one of the next moonlit nights, to stalk by himself a certain great, wide-horned stag, of whose habits he had received information.

At Oxford, where Valentine made his acquaintance, Sercombe belonged to a fast set, but had distinguished himself notwithstanding as an athlete. He was a great favourite with a few, not the best of the set, and admired by many for his confidence, his stature, and his regular features. These latter wore, however, a self-assertion which of others made him much disliked: a mean thing in itself, it had the meanest origin—the ability, namely, to spend money, for he was the favourite son of a rich banker in London. He knew nothing of the first business of life—self-restraint, had never denied himself anything, and but for social influences would, in manhood as infancy, have obeyed every impulse. He was one of the merest slaves in the universe, a slave in his very essence, for he counted wrong to others freedom for himself, and the rejection of the laws of his own being, liberty. The most righteous interference was insolence; his likings were his rights, and any devil that could whisper him a desire, might do with him as he pleased. From such a man every true nature shrinks with involuntary recoil, and a sick sense of the inhuman. But I have said more of him already than my history requires, and more than many a reader, partaking himself of his character to an unsuspected degree, will believe; for such men cannot know themselves. He had not yet in the eyes of the world disgraced himself: it takes a good many disgraceful things to bring a rich man to outward disgrace.

His sole attendant when shooting was a clever vagabond lad belonging to nowhere in particular, and living by any crook except the shepherd's. From him he heard of the great stag, and the spots which in the valleys he frequented, often scraping away the snow with his feet to get at the grass. He did not inform him that the animal was a special favourite with the chief of Clanruadh, or that the clan looked upon him. as their live symbol, the very stag represented as crest to the chief's coat of arms. It was the same Nancy had reported to her master as eating grass on the burn-side in the moonlight. Christian and Sercombe had stalked him day after day, but without success. And now, with one poor remaining hope, the latter had determined to stalk him at night. To despoil him of his life, his glorious rush over the mountain side, his plunge into the valley, and fierce strain up the opposing hill; to see that ideal of strength, suppleness, and joyous flight, lie nerveless and flaccid at his feet; to be able to call the thicket-like antlers of the splendid animal his own, was for the time the one ambition of Hilary Sercombe; for he was of the brood of Mephistopheles, the child of darkness, whose delight lies in undoing what God has done—the nearest that any evil power can come to creating.

There was, however, a reason for the failure of the young hunters beyond lack of skill and what they called their ill-luck. Hector of the Stags was awake; his keen, everywhere-roving eyes were upon them, seconded by the keen, all-hearkening ears of Bob of the Angels. They had discovered that the two men had set their hearts on the big stag, an cabrach mor by right of excellence, and every time they were out after him, Hector too was out with his spy-glass, the gift of an old sea-faring friend, searching the billowy hills. While, the southrons would be toiling along to get the wind of him unseen, for the old stag's eyes were as keen as his velvety nose, the father and son would be lying, perhaps close at hand, perhaps far away on some hill-side of another valley, watching now the hunters, now the stag. For love of the Macruadh, and for love of the stag, they had constituted themselves his guardians. Again and again when one of them thought he was going to have a splendid chance—perhaps just as, having reached a rock to which he had been making his weary way over stones and bogs like

Satan through chaos, and raised himself with weary slowness, he peeped at last over the top, and lo, there he was, well within range, quietly feeding, nought between the great pumping of his big joyous heart and the hot bullet but the brown skin behind his left shoulder!—a distant shot would forestall the nigh one, a shot for life, not death, and the stag, knowing instantly by wondrous combination of sense and judgment in what quarter lay the danger, would, without once looking round, measure straight a hundred yards of hillocks and rocks between the sight-taking and the pulling of the trigger. Another time it would be no shot, but the bark of a dog, the cry of a moorfowl, or a signal from watching hind that started him; for the creatures understand each the other's cries, and when an animal sees one of any sort on the watch to warn covey or herd or flock of its own kind, it will itself keep no watch, but feed in security. To Christian and Sercombe it seemed as if all the life in the glen were in conspiracy to frustrate their hearts' desire; and the latter at least grew ever the more determined to kill the great stag: he had begun to hate him.

The sounds that warned the stag were by no means always what they seemed, those of other wild animals; they were often hut imitations by Bob of the Angels. I fear the animal grew somewhat bolder and less careful from the assurance thus given him that he was watched over, and cultivated a little nonchalance. Not a moment, however, did he neglect any warning from quarter soever, but from peaceful feeder was instantaneously wind-like fleer, his great horns thrown back over his shoulders, and his four legs just touching the ground with elastic hoof, or tucking themselves almost out of sight as he skipped rather than leaped over rock and gully, stone and bush—whatever lay betwixt him and larger room. Great joy it was to his two guardians to see him, and great game to watch the motions of his discomfited enemies. For the sake of an cabrach Hector and Bob would go hungry for hours. But they never imagined the luxurious Sasunnach, incapable, as they thought, of hardship or sustained fatigue, would turn from his warm bed to stalk the lordly animal betwixt snow and moon.

One night, Hector of the Stags found he could not sleep. It was not for cold, for the night was for the season a mild one. The snow indeed lay deep around their dwelling, but they owed not a little of its warmth to the snow. It drifted up all about it, and kept off the terrible winds that swept along the side of the hill, like sharp swift scythes of death. They were in the largest and most comfortable of their huts—a deepish hollow in the limestone rock, lined with turf, and with wattles filled in with heather, the tops outward; its front a thick wall of turf, with a tolerable door of deal. It was indeed so snug as to be far from airy. Here they kept what little store of anything they had—some dried fish and venison; a barrel of oat-meal, seldom filled full; a few skins of wild creatures, and powder, ball, and shot.

After many fruitless attempts to catch the still fleeting vapour sleep, raising himself at last on his elbow, Hector found that Rob was not by his side.

He too had been unable to sleep, and at last discovered that he was uneasy about something-what, he could not tell. He rose and went out. The moon was shining very clear, and as there was much snow, the night, if not so bright as day, was yet brighter than many a day. The moon, the snow, the mountains, all dreaming awake, seemed to Rob the same as usual; but presently he fancied the hillside opposite had come nearer than usual: there must be a reason for that! He searched every yard of it with keenest gaze, but saw nothing.

They were high above Glenruadh, and commanded parts of it: late though it was, Rob thought he saw some light from the New House, which itself he could not see, reflected from some shadowed evergreen in the shrubbery. He was thinking some one might be ill, and he ought to run down and See whether a messenger was wanted, when his father joined him. He had brought his telescope, and immediately began to sweep the moonlight on the opposite hill. In a moment he touched Rob on the shoulder, and handed him the telescope, pointing with it. Rob looked and saw a dark speck on the snow, moving along the hill-side. It was the big stag. Now and then he would stop to snuff and search for a mouthful, but was evidently making for one of his feeding-places—most likely that by the burn on the chief's land. The light! could it imply danger? He had heard the young men were going to leave: were they about to attempt a last assault on the glory of the glen? He pointed out to his father the dim light in the shadow of the house. Hector turned his telescope thitherward, immediately gave the glass to Bob, went into the hut, and came out again with his gun. They had not gone far when they lost sight of the stag, but they held on towards the castle. At every point whence a peep could be had in the direction of the house, they halted to reconnoitre: if enemies were abroad, they must, if possible, get and keep sight of them. They did not stop for more than a glance, however, but made for the valley as fast as they could walk: the noise of running feet would, on such a still night, be heard too far. The whole way, without sound uttered, father and son kept interchanging ideas on the matter.

From thorough acquaintance with the habits of the animal, they were pretty certain he was on his way to the haunt aforementioned: if he got there, he would be safe; it was the chiefs ground, and no one would dare touch him. But he was not yet upon it, and was in danger; while, if he should leave the spot in any westward direction, he would almost at once be out of sanctuary! If they found him therefore at his usual feed, and danger threatening, they must scare him eastward; if no peril seemed at hand, they would watch him a while, that he might feed in safety. Swift and all but soundless on their quiet brogs they paced along: to startle the deer while the hunter was far off, might be to drive him within range of his shot.

They reached the root of the spur, and approached the castle; immediately beyond that, they would be in sight of the feeding ground. But they were yet behind it when Rob of the Angels bounded forward in terror at the sound of a gun. His father, however, who was in front, was off before him. Neither hearing anything, nor seeing Rob, he knew that a shot had been fired, and, caution being now useless, was in a moment at full speed. The smoke of the shot hung white in the moonlight over the end of the ridge. No red bulk shadowed the green pasture, no thicket of horns went shaking about over the sod. No lord of creation, but an enemy of life, stood regarding his work, a tumbled heap of death, yet saying to himself, like God when he made the world, "It is good." The noble creature lay disformed on the grass; shot through the heart he had leaped high in the air, fallen with his head under him, and broken his neck.

Rage filled the heart of Hector of the Stags. He could not curse, but he gave a roar like a wild beast, and raised his gun. But Rob of the Angels caught it ere it reached his shoulder. He yielded it, and, with another roar like a lion, bounded bare-handed upon the enemy. He took the descent in three leaps, and the burn in one. It was not merely that the enemy had killed an cabrach mor, the great stag of their love; he had killed him on the chief's own land! under the very eyes of the man whose business it was to watch over him! It was an offence unpardonable! an insult as well as a wrong to his chief! In the fierce majesty of righteous wrath he threw himself on the poacher. Sercombe met him with a blow straight from the shoulder, and he dropped.

Rob of the Angels, close behind him, threw down the gun. The devil all but got into Rob of the Angels. His knife flashed pale in the moonlight, and he darted on the Sasunnach. It would then have gone ill with the bigger man, for Bob was lithe as a snake, swift not only to parry and dodge but to strike; he could not have reached the body of his antagonist, but Sercombe's arm would have had at least one terrible gash from his skean-dhu, sharp as a razor, had not, at the moment, from the top of the ridge come the stern voice of the chief. Rob's knife, like Excalibur from the hand of Sir Bedivere, "made lightnings in the splendour of the moon," as he threw it from him, and himself down by his father. Then Hector came to himself and rose. Rob rose also; and his father, trembling with excitement, stood grasping his arm, for he saw the stalwart form of his chief on the ridge above them. Alister had been waked by the gun, and at the roar of his friend Hector, sprang from his bed. When he saw his beloved stag dead on his pasture, he came down the ridge like an avalanche.

Sercombe stood on his defence, wondering what devil was to pay, but beginning to think he might be in some wrong box. He had taken no trouble to understand the boundaries between Mr. Peregrine Palmer's land and that of the chief, and had imagined himself safe on the south side of the big burn.

Alister gazed speechless for a moment on the slaughtered stag, and heaved a great sigh.

"Mr. Sercombe," he said, "I would rather you had shot my best horse! Are you aware, sir, that you are a poacher?"

"I had supposed the appellation inapplicable to a gentleman!" answered Sercombe, with entire coolness. "But by all means take me before a magistrate."

"You are before a magistrate."

"All I have to answer then is, that I should not have shot the animal had I not believed myself within my rights."

"On that point, and on this very ground, I instructed you myself!" said the chief.

"I misunderstood you."

"Say rather you had not the courtesy to heed what I told you-had not faith enough to take the word of a gentleman! And for this my poor stag has suffered!"

He stood for some moments in conflict with himself, then quietly resumed.

"Of course, Mr. Sercombe, I have no intention of pushing the matter!" he said.

"I should hope not!" returned Sercombe scornfully. "I will pay whatever you choose to set on the brute."

It would be hard to say which was less agreeable to the chief-to have his stag called a brute, or be offered blood-money for him.

"Stag Ruadh priced like a bullock!" he said, with a slow smile, full of sadness; "—the pride of every child in the strath! Not a gentleman in the county would have shot Clanruadh's deer!"

Sercombe was by this time feeling uncomfortable, and it made him angry. He muttered something about superstition.

"He was taken when a calf," the chief went on, "and given to a great-aunt of mine. But when he grew up, he took to the hills again, and was known by his silver collar till he managed to rid himself of it. He shall he buried where he lies, and his monument shall tell how the stranger Sasunnach served the stag of Clanruadh!"

"Why the deuce didn't you keep the precious monster in a paddock, and let people know him for a tame animal?" sneered Sercombe.

"My poor Euadh!" said the chief; "he was no tame animal! He as well as I would have preferred the death you have given him to such a fate. He lived while he lived! I thank you for his immediate transit. Shot right through the heart! Had you maimed him I should have been angrier."

Sercombe felt flattered, and, attributing the chief's gentleness to a desire to please him, began to condescend.

"Well, come now, Macruadh!" he began; but the chief turned from him.

Hector stood with his arm on Rob's shoulder, and the tears rolling down his cheeks. He would not have wept but that the sobs of his son shook him.

"Rob of the Angels," Alister said in their mother-tongue, "you must make an apology to the Sasunnach gentleman for drawing the knife on him. That was wrong, if he had killed all the deer in Benruadh."

"It was not for that, Macruadh," answered Rob of the Angels. "It was because he struck my father, and laid a better man than himself on the grass."

The chief turned to the Englishman. "Did the old man strike you, Mr. Sercombe?"

"No, by Jove! I took a little care of that! If he had, I would have broke every bone in his body!"

"Why did you strike him then?"

"Because he rushed at me."

"It was his duty to capture a poacher!—But you did not know he was deaf and dumb!" Alister added, as some excuse.

"The deaf makes no difference!" protested Bob. "Hector of the Stags does not fight with his hands like a woman!"

"Well, what's done is done!" laughed Sercombe. "It wasn't a bad shot anyhow!"

"You have little to plume yourself upon, Mr. Sercombe!" said the chief. "You are a good shot, but you need not have been so frightened at an old man as to knock him down!"

"Come, come, Macruadh! enough's enough! It's time to drop this!" returned Sercombe. "I can't stand much more of it!—Take ten pounds for the head! —Come!"

The chief made one great stride towards him, but turned away, and said,

"Come along, Rob! Tell your father you must not go up the hill again to-night."

"No, sir," answered Bob; "there's nothing now to go up the hill for! Poor old Buadh! God rest his soul!"

"Amen!" responded the chief; "but say rather, 'God give him room to run!'"

"Amen! It is better.—But," added Kob, "we must watch by the body. The foxes and hooded crows are gathering already—I hear them on the hills;

and I saw a sea-eagle as white as silver yesterday! We cannot leave Ruadh till he is iznder God's plaid!"

"Then one of you come and fetch food and fire," said the chief. "I will be with you early."

Father and son communicated in silence, and Rob went with the chief.

"They worship the stag, these peasants, as the old Egyptians the bull!" said Sercombe to himself, walking home full of contempt.

CHAPTER VIII.

THE STAG'S HEAD.

Alister went straight to his brother's room, his heart bursting with indignation. It was some time before Ian could get the story from him in plain consecution; every other moment he would diverge into fierce denunciations.

"Hadn't you better tell your master what has happened?" at length said Ian. "He ought to know why you curse one of your fellows so bitterly."

Alister was dumb. For a moment he looked aghast.

"Ian!" he said: "You think he wants to be told anything? I always thought you believed in his divinity!"

"Ah!" returned Ian, "but do you? How am I to imagine it, when you go on like that in his hearing? Is it so you acknowledge his presence?"

"Oh, Ian! you don't know how it tortures me to think of that interloper, the low brute, killing the big stag, the Macruadh stag-and on my land too! I feel as if I could tear him in pieces. But for him I would have killed him on the spot! It is hard if I may not let off my rage even to you!"

"Let it off to him, Alister; he will give you fairer play than your small brother; he understands you better than I."

"But I could not let it off to him that way!"

"Then that is not a good way. The justice that, even in imagination, would tear and destroy and avenge, may be justice, but it is devil's justice. Come, begin now, and tell me all quietly-as if you had read it in a book."

"Word for word, then, with all the imprecations! "returned Alister, a little cooler; and Ian was soon in possession of the story.

"Now what do you think, Ian?" said the chief, ending a recital true to the very letter, and in a measure calm, but at various points revealing, by the merest dip of the surface, the boiling of the floods beneath.

"You must send him the head, Alister," answered Ian.

"Send-what-who-I don't understand you, Ian!" returned the chief, bewildered.

"Oh, well, never mind!" said Ian. "You will think of it presently!"

And therewith he turned his face to the wall, as if he would go to sleep.

It had been a thing understood betwixt the brothers, and that from so far back in the golden haze of childhood that the beginning of it was out of sight, that, the moment one of them turned his back, not a word more was to be said, until he who thus dropped the subject, chose to resume it: to break this unspoken compact would have been to break one of the strands in the ancient bond of their most fast brotherhood. Alister therefore went at once to his room, leaving Ian loving him hard, and praying for him with his face to the wall. He went as one knowing well the storm he was about to encounter, but never before had he had such a storm to meet.

He closed the door, and sat down on the side of his bed like one stunned. He did not doubt, yet could hardly allow he believed, that Ian, his oracle, had in verity told him to send the antlers of his cabrach mor, the late live type of his ancient crest, the pride of Clanruadh, to the vile fellow of a Sasunnach who had sent out into the deep the joyous soul of the fierce, bare mountains.

There were rushings to and fro in the spirit of Alister, wild and terrible, even as those in the Valley of the Shadow of Death. He never closed his eyes, but fought with himself all the night, until the morning broke. Could this thing be indeed his duty? And if not his duty, was he called to do it from mere bravado of goodness? How frightfully would not such an action be misunderstood by such a man! What could he take it for but a mean currying of favour with him! Why should he move to please such a fellow! Ian was too hard upon him! The more he yielded, the more Ian demanded! Every time it was something harder than the last! And why did he turn his face to the wall? Was he not fit to be argued with! Was he one that would not listen to reason! He had never known Ian ungenerous till now!

But all the time there lay at his door a thing calling out to be done! The thing he did not like was always the thing he had to do! he grumbled; but this thing he hated doing! It was abominable! What! send the grand head, with its horns spread wide like a half-moon, and leaning—like oaks from a precipice—send it to the man that made it a dead thing! Never! It must not be left behind! It must go to the grave with the fleet limbs! and over it should rise a monument, at sight of which every friendly highlandman would say, Feiich an cabracli mor de Clanruadli! What a mockery of fate to be exposed for ever to the vulgar Cockney gaze, the trophy of a fool, whose boast was to kill! Such a noble beast! Such a mean man! To mutilate his remains for the pride of the wretch who killed him! It was too horrible!

He thought and thought-until at last he lay powerless to think any more. But it is not always the devil that enters in when a man ceases to think. God forbid! The cessation of thought gives opportunity for setting the true soul thinking from another quarter. Suddenly Alister remembered a conversation he had had with Ian a day or two before. He had been saying to Ian that he could not understand what Jesus meant when he said, "Whosoever shall smite thee on thy right cheek, turn to him the other also;" and was dissatisfied with the way Ian had answered him. "You must explain it to yourself," Ian said. He replied, "If I could do that, I should not have to ask you." "There are many things," Ian rejoined, "—arithmetic is one—that can be understood only in the doing of them." "But how can I do a thing without understanding it?" objected Alister. "When you have an opportunity of doing this very thing," said Ian, "do it, and see what will follow!" At the time he thought Ian was refusing to come to the point, and was annoyingly indefinite and illogical; but now it struck him that here was the opportunity of which he had spoken.

"I see!" he said to himself. "It is not want of understanding that is in the way now! A thing cannot look hateful and reasonable at the same moment! This may be just the sort of thing Jesus meant! Even if I be in the right, I have a right to yield my right—and to HIM I will yield it. That was why Ian turned his face to the wall: he wanted me to discover that here was my opportunity! How but in the name of Jesus Christ could he have dared tell me to forgive Ruadh's death by sending his head to his murderer! It has to be done! I've got to do it! Here is my chance of turning the other cheek and being hurt again! What can come of it is no business of mine! To return evil is just to do a fresh evil! It MAY make the man ashamed of himself! It cannot hurt the stag; it only hurts my pride, and I owe my pride nothing! Why should not the fellow have what satisfaction he may—something to show for his shot! He shall have the head."

Thereupon rushed into his heart the joy of giving up, of deliverance from self; and pity, to leaven his contempt, awoke for Sercombe. No sooner had he yielded his pride, than he felt it possible to love the man—not for anything he was, but for what he might and must be.

"God let the man kill the stag," he said; "I will let him have the head."

Again and yet again swelled afresh the tide of wrath and unwillingness, making him feel as if he could not carry out his resolve; but all the time he knew the thing was as good as done—absolutely determined, so that nothing could turn it aside.

"To yield where one may, is the prerogative of liberty!" he said to himself. "God only can give; who would be his child must yield! Abroad in the fields of air, as Paul and the love of God make me hope, what will the wind-battling Ruadh care for his old head! Would he not say, 'Let the man have it; my hour was come, or the Some One would not have let him kill me!'?"

Thus argued the chief while the darkness endured—and as soon as the morning began to break, rose, took spade and pick and great knife, and went where Hector and Rob were watching the slain.

It was bitterly cold. The burn crept silent under a continuous bridge of ice. The grass-blades were crisp with frost. The ground was so hard it met iron like iron.

He sent the men to get their breakfast from Nancy: none but himself should do the last offices for Ruadh! With skilful hand he separated and laid aside the head—in sacrifice to the living God. Then the hard earth rang with mighty blows of the pickaxe. The labour was severe, and long ere the grave was deep enough, Hector and Rob had returned; but the chief would not get out of it to give them any share in the work. When he laid hold of the body, they did not offer to help him; they understood the heart of their chief. Not without a last pang that he could not lay the head beside it, he began to shovel in the frozen clods, and then at length allowed them to take a part. When the grave was full, they rolled great stones upon it, that it might not be desecrated. Then the chief went back to his room, and proceeded to prepare the head, that, as the sacrifice, so should be the gift.

"I suppose he would like glass eyes, the ruffian!" he muttered to himself, "but I will not have the mockery. I will fill the sockets and sew up the eyelids, and the face shall be as of one that sleeps."

Having done all, and written certain directions for temporary treatment, which he tied to an ear, he laid the head aside till the evening.

All the day long, not a word concerning it passed between the brothers; but when evening came, Alister, with a blue cotton handkerchief in his hand, hiding the head as far as the roots of the huge horns, asked Ian to go for a walk. They went straight to the New House. Alister left the head at the door, with his compliments to Mr. Sercombe.

As soon as they were out of sight of the house, Ian put his arm through his brother's, but did not speak.

"I know now about turning the other cheek!" said Alister. "—Poor Euadh!"

"Leave him to the God that made the great head and nimble feet of him," said Ian. "A God that did not care for what he had made, how should we believe in! but he who cares for the dying sparrow, may be trusted with the dead stag."

"Truly, yes," returned Alister.

"Let us sit down," said Ian, "and I will sing you a song I made last night; I could not sleep after you left me."

Without reply, Alister took a stone by the wayside, and Ian one a couple of yards from him. This was his song.

LOVE'S HISTORY.

Love, the baby,
  Toddled out to pluck a flower;
One said, "No, sir;" one said, "Maybe,
  At the evening hour!"

Love, the boy,
  Joined the boys and girls at play;
But he left them half his joy
  Ere the close of day.

Love, the youth,
  Roamed the country, lightning-laden;
But he hurt himself, and, sooth,
  Many a man and maiden!

Love, the man,
  Sought a service all about;
But he would not take their plan,
  So they cast him out.

Love,   the   aged,
  Walking,   bowed,   the   shadeless   miles,
Bead   a   volume   many-paged,
  Full of tears and smiles.

Love,   the   weary,
  Tottered   down   the   shelving   road:
At   its   foot,   lo,   night   the   starry
  Meeting him from God!

"Love,   the   holy!"
  Sang   a   music   in   her   dome,
Sang   it   softly,   sang   it   slowly,
  "—Love is coming home!"

Ere the week was out, there stood above the dead stag a growing cairn, to this day called Carn a' cabrach mor. It took ten men with levers to roll one of the boulders at its base. Men still cast stones upon it as they pass.

The next morning came a note to the cottage, in which Sercombe thanked the Macruadh for changing his mind, and said that, although he was indeed glad to have secured such a splendid head, he would certainly have stalked another deer, had he known the chief set such store by the one in question.

It was handed to Alister as he sat at his second breakfast with his mother and Ian: even in winter he was out of the house by six o'clock, to set his men to work, and take his own share. He read to the end of the first page with curling lip; the moment he turned the leaf, he sprang from his seat with an exclamation that startled his mother.

"The hound!—I beg my good dogs' pardon, one and all!" he cried. "—Look at this, Ian! See what comes of taking your advice!"

"My dear fellow, I gave you no advice that had the least regard to the consequence of following it! That was the one thing you had nothing to do with."

"READA," insisted Alister, as he pranced about the room. "No, don't read the letter; it's not worth, reading. Look at the paper in it."

Ian looked, and saw a cheque for ten pounds. He burst into loud laughter.

"Poor Ruadh's horns! they're hardly so long as their owner's ears!" he said.

"I told you so!" cried the chief.

"No, Alister! You never suspected such a donkey!"

"What is it all about?" asked the mother.

"The wretch who shot Ruadh," replied Alister, "—to whom I gave his head, all to please Ian,—"

"Alister!" said Ian.

The chief understood, and retracted.

"—no, not to please Ian, but to do what Ian showed me was right:—I believe it was my duty!—I hope it was!—here's the murdering fellow sends me a cheque for ten pounds!—I told you, Ian, he offered me ten pounds over the dead body!"

"I daresay the poor fellow was sorely puzzled what to do, and appealed to everybody in the house for advice!"

"You take the cheque to represent the combined wisdom of the New House?"

"You must have puzzled them all!" persisted Ian. "How could people with no principle beyond that of keeping to a bargain, understand you otherwise! First, you perform an action such persons think degrading: you carry a fellow's bag for a shilling, and then himself for nothing! Next, in the very fury of indignation with a man for killing the finest stag in the country on your meadow, you carry him home the head with your own hands! It all comes of that unlucky divine motion of yours to do good that good may come! That shilling of Mistress Conal's is at the root of it all!"

Ian laughed again, and right heartily. The chief was too angry to enter into the humour of the thing.

"Upon my word, Ian, it is too bad of you! What ARE you laughing at? It would become you better to tell me what I am to do! Am I free to break the rascal's bones?"

"Assuredly not, after that affair with the bag!"

"Oh, damn the bag!—I beg your pardon, mother."

"Am I to believe my ears, Alister?"

"What does it matter, mother? What harm can it do the bag? I wished no evil to any creature!"

"It was the more foolish."

"I grant it, mother. But you don't know what a relief it is sometimes to swear a little!—You are quite wrong, Ian; it all comes of giving him the head!"

"You wish you had not given it him?"

"No!" growled Alister, as from a pent volcano.

"You will break my ears, Alister!" cried the mother, unable to keep from laughing at the wrath in which he went straining through the room.

"Think of it," insisted Ian: "a man like could not think otherwise without a revolution of his whole being to which the change of the leopard's spots would he nothing.—What you meant, after all, was not cordiality; it was only generosity; to which his response, his countercheck friendly, was an order for ten pounds!—All is right between you!"

"Now, really, Ian, you must not go on teasing your elder brother so!" said the mother.

Alister laughed, and ceased fuming. "But I must answer the brute!" he said. "What am I to say to him?"

"That you are much obliged," replied Ian, "and will have the cheque framed and hung in the hall."

"Come, come! no more of that!"

"Well, then, let me answer the letter."

"That is just what I wanted!"

Ian sat down at his mother's table, and this is what he wrote.

"Dear sir,—My brother desires me to return the cheque which you unhappily thought it right to send him. Humanity is subject to mistake, but I am sorry for the individual who could so misunderstand his courtesy. I have the honour to remain, sir, your obedient servant, Ian Macruadh."

As Ian guessed, the matter had been openly discussed at the New House; and the money was sent with the approval of all except the two young ladies. They had seen the young men in circumstances more favourable to the understanding of them by ordinary people.

"Why didn't the chief write himself?" said Christian.

"Oh," replied Sercombe, "his little brother had been to school, and could write better!"

Christina and Mercy exchanged glances.

"I will tell you," Mercy said, "why Mr. lau answered the note: the chief had done with you!"

"Or," suggested Christina, "the chief was in such a rage that he would write nothing but a challenge."

"I wish to goodness he had! It would have given me the chance of giving the clodhopper a lesson."

"For sending you the finest stag's head and horns in the country!" remarked Mercy.

"I shot the stag! Perhaps you don't believe I shot him!"

"Indeed I do! No one else would have done it. The chief would have died sooner!"

"I'm sick of your chief!" said Christian. "A pretty chief without a penny to bless himself! A chief, and glad of the job of carrying a carpet-bag! You'll be calling him MY LORD, next!"

"He may at least write BARONET after his name when he pleases," returned Mercy.

"Why don't he then? A likely story!"

"Because," answered Christina, "both his father and himself were ashamed of how the first baronet got his title. It had to do with the sale of a part of the property, and they counted the land the clan's as well as the chief's. They regarded it as an act of treachery to put the clan in the power of a stranger, and the chief looks on the title as a brand of shame."

"I don't question the treachery," said Christian. "A highlander is treacherous."

Christina had asked a friend in Glasgow to find out for her anything known among the lawyers concerning the Macruadhs, and what she had just recounted was a part of the information she had thereby received.

Thenceforward silence covered the whole transaction. Sercombe neither returned the head, sent an apology, nor recognized the gift. That he had shot the stag was enough!

But these things wrought shaping the idea of the brothers in the minds of the sisters, and they were beginning to feel a strange confidence in them, such as they had never had in men before. A curious little halo began to shimmer about the heads of the young men in the picture-gallery of the girls' fancy. Not the less, however, did they regard them as enthusiasts, unfitted to this world, incapable of self-protection, too good to live—in a word, unpractical! Because a man would live according to the laws of his being as well as of his body, obeying simple, imperative, essential human necessity, his fellows forsooth call him UNPRACTICAL! Of the idiotic delusions of the children of this world, that of being practical is one of the most ludicrous.

Here is a translation, made by Ian, of one of Alister's Gaelic songs.

THE SUN'S DAUGHTER.

A bright drop of water
   In the gold tire
Of a sun's daughter
   Was laughing to her sire;

And from all the flowers about,
   That never toiled or spun,
The soul of each looked out,
   Clear laughing to the sun.

I saw them unfolding
   Their hearts every one!
Every soul holding
   Within it the sun!

But all the sun-mirrors
   Vanished anon;
And their flowers, mere starers,
   Grew dry in the sun.

"My soul is but water,
   Shining and gone!
She is but the daughter,"
   I said, "of the sun!"

My soul sat her down
   In a deep-shaded gloom;
Her glory was flown,
   Her earth was a tomb,

Till night came and caught her,
   And then out she shone;
And I knew her no daughter
   Of that shining sun—

Till night came down and taught her
   Of a glory yet unknown;
And I knew my soul the daughter
   Of a sun behind the sun.

Back, back to him that wrought her
   My soul shall haste and run;
Straight back to him, his daughter,
   To the sun behind the sun.

CHAPTER IX.

ANNIE OF THE SHOP.

At the dance in the chief's barn, Sercombe had paired with Annie of the shop oftener than with any other of the girls. That she should please him at all, was something in his favour, for she was a simple, modest girl, with the nicest feeling of the laws of intercourse, the keenest perception both of what is in itself right, and what is becoming in the commonest relation. She understood by a fine moral instinct what respect was due to her, and what respect she ought to show, and was therefore in the truest sense well-bred. There are women whom no change of circumstances would cause to alter even their manners a hair's-breadth: such are God's ladies; there are others in whom any outward change will reveal the vulgarity of a nature more conscious of claim than of obligation.

I need not say that Sercomhe, though a man of what is called education, was but conventionally a gentleman. If in doubt whether a man be a gentleman or not, hear him speak to a woman he regards as his inferior: his very tone will probably betray him. A true gentleman, that is a true man, will be the more carefully respectful. Sercombe was one of those who regard themselves as respectable because they are prudent; whether they are human, and their brother and sister's keeper, they have never asked themselves.

To some minds neither innocent nor simple, there is yet something attractive in innocence and simplicity. Perhaps it gives them a pleasing sense of their superiority—a background against which to rejoice in their liberty, while their pleasure in it helps to obscure the gulf between what the man would fain hold himself to be, and what in reality he is. There is no spectre so terrible as the unsuspected spectre of a man's own self; it is noisome enough to the man who is ever trying to better it: what must it appear to the man who sees it for the first time! Sercombe's self was ugly, and he did not know it; he thought himself an exceptionally fine fellow. No one knows what a poor creature he is but the man who makes it his business to be true. The only mistake worse than thinking well of himself, is for a man to think God takes no interest in him.

One evening, sorely in lack of amusement, Sercombe wandered out into a star-lit night, and along the road to the village. There he went into the general shop, where sat Annie behind the counter. Now the first attention he almost always paid a woman, that is when he cared and dared, was a compliment—the fungus of an empty head or a false heart; but with Annie he took no such initiative liberty, and she, accustomed to respectful familiarity from the chief and his brother, showed no repugnance to his friendly approach.

"Upon my word, Miss Annie," said Sercombe, venturing at length a little, "you were the best dancer on the floor that night!"

"Oh, Mr. Sercombe! how can you say so—with such dancers as the young ladies of your party!" returned Annie.

"They dance well," he returned, "but not so well as you."

"It all depends on the dance—whether you are used to it or not."

"No, by Jove! If you had a lesson or two such as they have been having all their lives, you would dance out of their sight in the twinkling of an eye. If I had you for a partner every night for a month, you would dance better than any woman I have ever seen—off the stage—any lady, that is."

The grosser the flattery, the surer with a country girl, he thought. But there was that in his tone, besides the freedom of sounding her praises in her own ears, which was unpleasing to Annie's ladyhood, and she held her peace.

"Come out and have a turn," he said thereupon. "It is lovely star-light. Have you had a walk to-day?"

"No, I have not," answered Annie, casting how to get rid of him.

"You wrong your beauty by keeping to the house."

"My beauty," said Annie, flushing, "may look after itself; I have nothing to do with it—neither, excuse me, sir, have you."

"Why, who has a right to be offended with the truth! A man can't help seeing your face is as sweet as your voice, and your figure, as revealed by your dancing, a match for the two!"

"I will call my mother," said Annie, and left the shop.

Sercombe did not believe she would, and waited. He took her departure for a mere coquetry. But when a rather grim, handsome old woman appeared, asking him—it took the most of her English—"What would you be wanting, sir?" as if he had just come into the shop, he found himself awkwardly situated. He answered, with more than his usual politeness, that, having had the pleasure of dancing with her daughter at the chief's hall, he had taken the liberty of looking in to inquire after her health; whereupon, perplexed, the old woman in her turn called Annie, who came at once, but kept close to her mother. Sercombe began to tell them about a tour he had made in Canada, for he had heard they had friends there; but the mother did not understand him, and Annie more and more disliked him. He soon saw that at least he had better say nothing more about a walk, and took himself off, not a little piqued at repulse from a peasant-girl in the most miserable shop he had ever entered.

Two days after, he went again—this time to buy tobacco. Annie was short with him, but he went yet again and yet sooner: these primitive people objected to strangers, he said; accustomed to him she would be friendly! he would not rest until he had gained some footing of favour with her! Annie grew heartily offended with the man. She also feared what might be said if he kept coming to the shop—where Mistress Conal had seen him more than once, and looked poison at him. For her own sake, for the sake of Lachlan, and for the sake of the chief, she resolved to make the young father of the ancient clan acquainted with her trouble. It was on the day after his rejection of the ten-pound note that she found her opportunity, for the chief came to see her.

"Was he rude to you, Annie?" he asked.

"No, sir—too polite, I think: he must have seen I did not want his company.—I shall feel happier now you know."

"I will see to it," said the chief.

"I hope it will not put you to any trouble, sir!"

"What am I here for, Annie! Are you not my clanswoman! Is not Lachlan my foster-brother!—He will trouble you no more, I think."

As Alister walked home, he met Sercombe, and after a greeting not very cordial on either side, said thus:

"I should be obliged to you, Mr. Sercombe, if you would send for anything you want, instead of going to the shop yourself. Annie Macruadh is not the sort of girl you may have found in such a position, and you would not wish to make her uncomfortable!"

Sercombe was, ashamed, I think; for the refuge of the fool when dissatisfied with himself, is offence with his neighbour, and Sercombe was angry.

"Are you her father—or her lover?" he said.

"She has a right to my protection—and claims it," rejoined Alister quietly.

"Protection! Oh!—What the devil would you protect her from?"

"From you, Mr. Sercombe."

"Protect her, then."

"I will. Force yourself on that young woman's notice again, and you will have to do with me."

They parted. Alister went home. Sercombe went straight to the shop.

He was doing what he could to recommend himself to Christina; but whether from something antagonistic between them, or from unwillingness on her part to yield her position of advantage and so her liberty, she had not given him the encouragement he thought he deserved. He believed himself in love with her, and had told her so; but the truest love such a man can feel, is a poor thing. He admired, and desired, and thought he loved her beauty, and that he called being in love with HER! He did not think much about her money, but had she then been brought to poverty, he would at least have hesitated about marrying her.

In the family he was regarded as her affianced, although she did not treat him as such, but merely went on bewitching him, pleased that at least he was a man of the world.

While one is yet only IN LOVE, the real person, the love-capable, lies covered with the rose-leaves of a thousand sleepy-eyed dreams, and through them come to the dreamer but the barest hints of the real person of whom is the dream. A thousand fancies fly out, approach, and cross, but never meet; the man and the woman are pleased, not with each other, but each with the fancied other. The merest common likings are taken for signs of a wonderful sympathy, of a radical unity—of essential capacity, therefore, of loving and being loved; at a hundred points their souls seem to touch, but their contacts are the merest brushings as of insect-antennae; the real man, the real woman, is all the time asleep under the rose-leaves. Happy is the rare fate of the true—to wake and come forth and meet in the majesty of the truth, in the image of God, in their very being, in the power of that love which alone is being. They love, not this and that about each other, but each the very other—a love as essential to reality, to truth, to religion, as the love of the very God. Where such love is, let the differences of taste, the unfitnesses of temperament be what they may, the two must by and by be thoroughly one.

Sercombe saw no reason why a gentleman should not amuse himself with any young woman he pleased. What was the chief to him! He was not his chief! If he was a big man in the eyes of his little clan, he was nothing much in the eyes of Hilary Sercombe.

CHAPTER X

THE ENCOUNTER.

Annie came again to her chief, with the complaint that Mr. Sercombe persisted in his attentions. Alister went to see her home. They had not gone far when Sercombe overtook them, and passed. The chief told Annie to go on, and called after him,

"I must have a word or two with you, Mr. Sercombe!"

He turned and came up with long steps, his hands in his coat-pockets.

"I warned you to leave that girl alone!" said the chief.

"And I warn you now," rejoined Sercombe, "to leave me alone!"

"I am bound to take care of her."

"And I of myself."

"Not at her expense!"

"At yours then!" answered Sercombe, provoking an encounter, to which he was the more inclined that he saw Ian coming slowly up the ridge.

"It was your deliberate intention then to forget the caution I gave you?" said the chief, restraining his anger.

"I make a point of forgetting what I do not think worth remembering."

"I forget nothing!"

"I congratulate you."

"And I mean to assist your memory, Mr. Sercombe."

"Mr. Macruadh!" returned Sercombe, "if you expect me not to open my lips to any hussy in the glen without your leave,—"

His speech was cut short by a box on the ear from the open hand of the chief. He would not use his fist without warning, but such a word applied to any honest woman of his clan demanded instant recognition.

Sercomhe fell back a step, white with rage, then darting forward, struck straight at the front of his adversary. Alister avoided the blow, but soon found himself a mere child at such play with the Englishman. He had not again touched Sercombe, and was himself bleeding fast, when Ian came up running.

"Damn you! come on!" cried Sercombe when he saw him; "I can do the precious pair of you!"

"Stop!" cried Ian, laying hold of his brother from behind, pinning his arms to his sides, wheeling him round, and taking his place. "Give over, Alister," he went on. "You can't do it, and I won't see you punished when it is he that deserves it. Go and sit there, and look on."

"YOU can't do it, Ian!" returned Alister. "It is my business. One blow in will serve. He jumps about like a goat that I can't hit him!"

"You are blind with blood!" said Ian, in a tone that gave Sercombe expectation of too easy a victory. "Sit down there, I tell you!"

"Mind, I don't give in!" said Alister, but turning went to the bank at the roadside. "If he speak once again to Annie, I swear I will make him repent it!"

Sercombe laughed insultingly.

"Mr. Sercombe," said Ian, "had we not better put off our bout till to-morrow? You have fought already!"

"Damn you for a coward, come on!"

"Would you not like to take your breath for a moment?"

"I have all I am likely to need."

"It is only fair," persisted Ian, "to warn you that you will not find my knowledge on the level of my brother's!"

"Shut up," said Sercombe savagely, "and come on."

For a few rounds Ian seemed to Alister to be giving Sercombe time to recover his wind; to Sercombe he seemed to be saving his own. He stood to defend, and did not attempt to put in a blow.

"Mr. Sercombe," he said at length, "you cannot serve me as you did my brother."

"I see that well enough. Come on!"

"Will you give your word to leave Annie of the shop alone?"

Sercombe answered with a scornful imprecation.

"I warn you again, I am no novice in this business!" said Ian.

Sercombe struck out, but did not reach his antagonist.

The fight lasted but a moment longer. As his adversary drew back from a failed blow, Alister saw Ian's eyes flash, and his left arm shoot out, as it seemed, to twice its length. Sercombe neither reeled nor staggered but fell supine, and lay motionless. The brothers were by his side in a moment.

"I struck too hard!" said Ian.

"Who can think about that in a fight!" returned Alister.

"I could have helped it well enough, and a better man would. Something shot through me—I hope it wasn't hatred; I am sure it was anger—and the man went down! What if the devil struck the blow!"

"Nonsense, Ian!" said Alister, as they raised Sercombe to carry him to the cottage. "It was pure indignation, and nothing to blame in it!"

"I wish I could be sure of that!"

They had not gone far before he began to come to himself.

"What are you about?" he said feebly but angrily. "Set me down."

They did so. He staggered to the road-side, and leaned against the bank.

"What's been the row?" he asked. "Oh, I remember!—Well, you've had the best of it!"

He held out his hand in a vague sort of way, and the gesture invaded their soft hearts. Each took the hand.

"I was all right about the girl though," said Sercombe. "I didn't mean her any harm."

"I don't think you did," answered Alister; "and I am sure you could have done her none; but the girl did not like it."

"There is not a girl of the clan, or in the neighbourhood, for whom my brother would not have done the same." said Ian.

"You're a brace of woodcocks!" cried Sercombe. "It's well you're not out in the world. You would be in hot water from morning to night! I can't think how the devil you get on at all!"

"Get on! Where?" asked Ian with a smile.

"Come now! You ain't such fools as you want to look! A man must make a place for himself somehow in the world!"

He rose, and they walked in the direction of the cottage.

"There is a better thing than that," said Ian!

"What?"

"To get clean out of it."

"What! cut your throats?"

"I meant that to get out of the world clean was better than to get on in it."

"I don't understand you. I don't choose to think the man that thrashed me a downright idiot!" growled Sercombe.

"What you call getting on," rejoined Ian, "we count not worth a thought. Look at our clan! it is a type of the world itself. Everything is passing away. We believe in the kingdom of heaven."

"Come, come! fellows like you must know well enough that's all bosh! Nobody nowadays—nobody with any brains—believes such rot!"

"We believe in Jesus Christ," said Ian, "and are determined to do what he will have us do, and take our orders from nobody else."

"I don't understand you!"

"I know you don't. You cannot until you set about changing your whole way of life."

"Oh, be damned! what an idea! a sneaking, impossible idea!"

"As to its being an impossible idea, we hold it, and live by it. How absurd it must seem to you, I know perfectly. But we don't live in your world, and you do not even see the lights of ours."

"'There is a world beyond the stars'!—Well, there may be; I know nothing about it; I only know there is one on this side of them,—a very decent sort of world too! I mean to make the best of it."

"And have not begun yet!"

"Indeed I have! I deny myself nothing. I live as I was made to live."

"If you were not made to obey your conscience or despise yourself, you are differently made from us, and no communication is possible between us. We must wait until what differences a man from a beast make its appearance in you."

"You are polite!"

"You have spoken of us as you think; now we speak of you as we think. Taking your representation of yourself, you are in the condition of the lower animals, for you claim inclination as the law of your life."

"My beast is better than your man!"

"You mean you get more of the good of life!"

"Right! I do."

The brothers exchanged a look and smile.

"But suppose," resumed Ian, "the man we have found in us should one day wake up in you! Suppose he should say, 'Why did you make a beast of me?'! It will not be easy for you to answer him!"

"That's all moonshine! Things are as you take them."

"So said Lady Macbeth till she took to walking in her sleep, and couldn't get rid of the smell of the blood!"

Sercombe said no more. He was silent with disgust at the nonsense of it all.

They reached the door of the cottage. Alister invited him to walk in. He drew back, and would have excused himself.

"You had better lie down a while," said Alister.

"You shall come to my room," said Ian. "We shall meet nobody."

Sercombe yielded, for he felt queer. He threw himself on Ian's bed, and in a few minutes was fast asleep.

When he woke, he had a cup of tea, and went away little the worse. The laird could not show himself for several days.

After this Annie had no further molestation. But indeed the young men's time was almost up—which was quite as well, for Annie of the shop, after turning a corner of the road, had climbed the hill-side, and seen all that passed. The young ladies, hearing contradictory statements, called upon Annie to learn the truth, and the intercourse with her that followed was not without influence on them. Through Annie they saw further into the character of the brothers, who, if they advocated things too fine for the world the girls had hitherto known, DID things also of which it would by no means have approved. They valued that world and its judgment not a straw!

CHAPTER XI.

A LESSON.

All the gentlemen at the New House left it together, and its ladies were once more abandoned to the society of Nature, who said little to any of them. For, though she recognized her grandchildren, and did what she could for them, it was now time they should make some move towards acquaintance with her. A point comes when she must stand upon her dignity, for it is great. If you would hear her wonderful tales, or see her marvellous treasures, you must not trifle with her; you must not talk as if you could rummage her drawers and cabinets as you pleased. You must believe in her; you must reverence her; else, although she is everywhere about the house, you may not meet her from the beginning of one year to the end of another.

To allude to any aspect of nature in the presence of the girls was to threaten to bore them; and I heartily confess to being bored myself with common talk about scenery; but these ladies appeared unaware of the least expression on the face of their grand-mother. Doubtless they received some good from the aspect of things—that they could not help; there Grannie's hidden, and therefore irresistible power was in operation; but the moment they had their thoughts directed to the world around them, they began to gape inwardly. Even the trumpet and shawm of her winds, the stately march of her clouds, and the torrent-rush of her waters, were to them poor facts, no vaguest embodiment of truths eternal. It was small wonder then that verse of any worth should be to them but sounding brass and clanging cymbals. What they called society, its ways and judgments, its decrees and condemnations, its fashions and pomps and shows, false, unjust, ugly, was nearly all they cared for. The truth of things, without care for which man or woman is the merest puppet, had hitherto been nothing to them. To talk of Nature was sentimental. To talk of God was both irreverent and ill-bred. Wordsworth was an old woman; St. Paul an evangelical churchman. They saw no feature of any truth, but, like all unthinkers, wrapped the words of it in their own foolishness, and then sneered at them. They were too much of ladies, however, to do it disagreeably; they only smiled at the foolish neighbour who believed things they were too sensible to believe. It must, however, be said for them, that they had not yet refused anything worth believing—as presented to them. They had not yet actually looked upon any truth and refused it. They were indeed not yet true enough in themselves to suspect the presence of either a truth or a falsehood.

A thaw came, and the ways were bad, and they found the time hang yet heavier on their unaided hands. An intercourse by degrees established itself between Mrs. Macruadh and the well-meaning, handsome, smiling Mrs. Palmer, and rendered it natural for the girls to go rather frequently to the cottage. They made themselves agreeable to the mother, and subject to the law of her presence showed to better advantage.

With their love of literature, it was natural also that the young men should at such times not only talk about books, but occasionally read for their entertainment from some favourite one; so that now, for the first time in their lives, the young ladies were brought under direct teaching of a worthy sort—they had had but a mockery of it at school and church—and a little light began to soak through their unseeking eyes. Among many others, however, less manifest, one obstruction to their progress lay in the fact that Christina, whose percep in some directions was quick enough, would always make a dart at the comical side of anything that could be comically turned, so disturbing upon occasion the whole spiritual atmosphere about some delicate epiphany: this to both Alister and Ian was unbearable. She offended chiefly in respect of Wordsworth—who had not humour enough always to perceive what seriously meant expression might suggest a ludicrous idea.

One time, reading from the Excursion, Ian came to the verse—not to be found, I think, in later editions—

"Perhaps it is not he but some one else":—

"Awful idea!" exclaimed Christina, with sepulchral tone; "—'some one else!' Think of it! It makes me shudder! Who might it not have been!"

Ian closed the book, and persistently refused to read more that day.

Another time he was reading, in illustration of something, Wordsworth's poem, "To a Skylark," the earlier of the two with that title: when he came to the unfortunate line,—

"Happy, happy liver!"—

"Oh, I am glad to know that!" cried Christina. "I always thought the poor lark must have a bad digestion—he was up so early!"

Ian refused to finish the poem, although Mercy begged hard.

The next time they came, he proposed to "read something in Miss Palmer's style," and taking up a volume of Hood, and avoiding both his serious and the best of his comic poems, turned to two or three of the worst he could find. After these he read a vulgar rime about an execution, pretending to be largely amused, making flat jokes of his own, and sometimes explaining elaborately where was no occasion.

"Ian!" said his mother at length; "have you bid farewell to your senses?"

"No, mother," he answered; "what I am doing is the merest consequence of the way you brought us up."

"I don't understand that!" she returned.

"You always taught us to do the best we could for our visitors. So when I fail to interest them, I try to amuse them."

"But you need not make a fool of yourself!"

"It is better to make a fool of myself, than let Miss Palmer make a fool of —a great man!"

"Mr. Ian," said Christina, "it is not of yourself but of me you have been making a fool.—I deserved it!" she added, and burst into tears.

"Miss Palmer," said Ian, "I will drop my foolishness, if you will drop your fun."

"I will," answered Christina.

And Ian read them the poem beginning—

"Three years she grew in sun and shower."

Scoffing at what is beautiful, is not necessarily a sign of evil; it may only indicate stupidity or undevelopment: the beauty is not perceived. But blame is often present in prolonged undevelopment. Surely no one habitually obeying his conscience would long be left without a visit from some shape of the beautiful!

CHAPTER XII.

NATURE.

The girls had every liberty; their mother seldom interfered. Herself true to her own dim horn-lantern, she had confidence in the discretion of her daughters, and looked for no more than discretion. Hence an amount of intercourse was possible between them and the young men, which must have speedily grown to a genuine intimacy had they inhabited even a neighbouring sphere of conscious life.

Almost unknown to herself, however, a change for the better had begun in Mercy. She had not yet laid hold of, had not yet perceived any truth; but she had some sense of the blank where truth ought to be. It was not a sense that truth was lacking; it was only a sense that something was not in her which was in those men. A nature such as hers, one that had not yet sinned against the truth, was not one long to frequent such a warm atmosphere of live truth, without approach to the hour when it must chip its shell, open its eyes, and acknowledge a world of duty around it.

One lovely star-lit night of keen frost, the two mothers were sitting by a red peat-fire in the little drawing-room of the cottage, and Ian was talking to the girls over some sketches he had made in the north, when the chief came in, bringing with him an air of sharp exhilaration, and proposed a walk.

"Come and have a taste of star-light!" he said.

The girls rose at once, and were ready in a minute.

The chief was walking between the two ladies, and Ian was a few steps in front, his head bent as in thought. Suddenly, Mercy saw him spread out his arms toward the starry vault, with his face to its serrated edge of mountain-tops. The feeling, almost the sense of another presence awoke in her, and as quickly vanished. The thought, IS HE A PANTHEIST? took its place. Had she not surprised him in an act of worship? In that wide outspreading of the lifted arms, was he not worshipping the whole, the Pan? Sky and stars and mountains and sea were his God! She walked aghast, forgetful of a hundred things she had heard him say that might have settled the point. She had, during the last day or two, been reading an article in which PANTHEISM was once and again referred to with more horror than definiteness. Recovering herself a little, she ventured approach to the subject.

"Macruadh," she said, "Mr. Ian and you often say things about NATURE that I cannot understand: I wish you would tell me what you mean by it."

"By what?" asked Alister.

"By NATURE" answered Mercy. "I heard Mr. Ian say, for instance, the other night, that he did not like Nature to take liberties with him; you said she might take what liberties with you she pleased; and then you went on talking so that I could not understand a word either of you said!"

While she spoke, Ian had turned and rejoined them, and they were now walking in a line, Mercy between the two men, and Christina on Ian's right. The brothers looked at each other: it would be hard to make her understand just that example! Something more rudimentary must prepare the way! Silence fell for a moment, and then Ian said—

"We mean by nature every visitation of the outside world through our senses."

"More plainly, please Mr. Ian! You cannot imagine how stupid I feel when you are talking your thinks, as once I heard a child call them."

"I mean by nature, then, all that you see and hear and smell and taste and feel of the things round about you."

"If that be all you mean, why should you make it seem so difficult?"

"But that is not all. We mean the things themselves only for the sake of what they say to us. As our sense of smell brings us news of fields far off, so those fields, or even the smell only that comes from them, tell us of things, meanings, thoughts, intentions beyond them, and embodied in them."

"And that is why you speak of Nature as a person?" asked Mercy.

"Whatever influences us must be a person. But God is the only real person, being in himself, and without help from anybody; and so we talk even of the world which is but his living garment, as if that were a person; and we call it SHE as if it were a woman, because so many of God's loveliest influences come to us through her. She always seems to me a beautiful old grandmother."

"But there now! when you talk of her influences, and the liberties she takes, I do not know what you mean. She seems to do and he something to you which certainly she does not and is not to me. I cannot tell what to make of it. I feel just as when our music-master was talking away about thorough bass: I could not get hold, head or tail, of what the man was after, and we all agreed there was no sense in it. Now I begin to suspect there must have been too much!"

"There is no fear of her!" said Ian to himself.

"My heart told me the truth about her!" thought Alister jubilant. "Now we shall have talk!"

"I think I can let you see into it, Miss Mercy," said Ian. "Imagine for a moment how it would be if, instead of having a roof like 'this most excellent canopy the air, this brave o'erhanging, this majestical roof, fretted with golden fire,'—"

"Are you making the words, or saying them out of a book?" interrupted Mercy.

"Ah! you don't know Hamlet? How rich I should feel myself if I had the first reading of it before me like you!—But imagine how different it would have been if, instead of such a roof, we had only clouds, hanging always down, like the flies in a theatre, within a yard or two of our heads!"

Mercy was silent for a moment, then said,

"It would be horribly wearisome."

"It would indeed be wearisome! But how do you think it would affect your nature, your being?"

Mercy held the peace which is the ignorant man's wisdom.

"We should have known nothing of astronomy," said Christina.

"True; and the worst would have been, that the soul would have had no astronomy—no notion of heavenly things."

"There you leave me out again!" said Mercy.

"I mean," said Ian, "that it would have had no sense of outstretching, endless space, no feeling of heights above, and depths beneath. The idea of space would not have come awake in it."

"I understand!" said Christina. "But I do not see that we should have been much the worse off. Why should we have the idea of more than we want? So long as we have room, I do not see what space matters to us!"

"Ah, but when the soul wakes up, it needs all space for room! A limit of thousands of worlds will not content it. Mere elbow-room will not do when the soul wakes up!"

"Then my soul is not waked up yet!" rejoined Christina with a laugh.

Ian did not reply, and Christina felt that he accepted the proposition, absurd as it seemed to herself.

"But there is far more than that," he resumed. "What notion could you have had of majesty, if the heavens seemed scarce higher than the earth? what feeling of the grandeur of him we call God, of his illimitation in goodness? For space is the body to the idea of liberty. Liberty is—God and the souls that love; these are the limitless room, the space, in which thoughts, the souls of things, have their being. If there were no holy mind, then no freedom, no spiritual space, therefore no thoughts; just as, if there were no space, there could be no things."

Ian saw that not even Alister was following him, and changed his key.

"Look up," he said, "and tell me what you see.—What is the shape over us?"

"It is a vault," replied Christina.

"A dome—is it not?" said Mercy.

"Yes; a vault or a dome, recognizable at the moment mainly by its shining points. This dome we understand to be the complement or completing part of a correspondent dome on the other side of the world. It follows that we are in the heart of a hollow sphere of loveliest blue, spangled with light. Now the sphere is the one perfect geometrical form. Over and round us then we have the one perfect shape. I do not say it is put there for the purpose of representing God; I say it is there of necessity, because of its nature, and its nature is its relation to God. It is of God's thinking; and that half-sphere above men's heads, with influence endlessly beyond the reach of their consciousness, is the beginning of all revelation of him to men. They must begin with that. It is the simplest as well as most external likeness of him, while its relation to him goes so deep that it represents things in his very nature that nothing else could."

"You bewilder me," said Mercy. "I cannot follow you. I am not fit for such high things!"

"I will go on; you will soon begin to see what I mean: I know what you are fit for better than you do yourself, Miss Mercy.—Think then how it would be if this blue sky were plainly a solid. Men of old believed it a succession of hollow spheres, one outside the other; it is hardly a wonder they should have had little gods. No matter how high the vault of the inclosing sphere; limited at all it could not declare the glory of God, it could only show his handiwork. In our day it is a sphere only to the eyes; it is a foreshortening of infinitude that it may enter our sight; there is no imagining of a limit to it; it is a sphere only in this, that in no one direction can we come nearer to its circumference than in another. This infinitive sphere, I say then, or, if you like it better, this spheric infinitude, is the only figure, image, emblem, symbol, fit to begin us to know God; it is an idea incomprehensible; we can only believe in it. In like manner God cannot by searching be found out, cannot be grasped by any mind, yet is ever before us, the one we can best know, the one we must know, the one we cannot help knowing; for his end in giving us being is that his humblest creature should at length possess himself, and be possessed by him."

"I think I begin," said Mercy—and said no more.

"If it were not for the outside world," resumed Ian, "we should have no inside world to understand things by. Least of all could we understand God without these millions of sights and sounds and scents and motions, weaving their endless harmonies. They come out from his heart to let us know a little of what is in it!"

Alister had been listening hard. He could not originate such things, but he could understand them; and his delight in them proved them his own, although his brother had sunk the shaft that laid open their lode.

"I never heard you put a thing better, Ian!" he said.

"You gentlemen," said Mercy, "seem to have a place to think in that I don't know how to get into! Could you not open your church-door a little wider to let me in? There must be room for more than two!"

She was looking up at Alister, not so much afraid of him; Ian was to her hardly of this world. In her eyes Alister saw something that seemed to reflect the starlight; but it might have been a luminous haze about the waking stars of her soul!

"My brother has always been janitor to me," replied Alister; "I do not know how to open any door. But here no door needs to be opened; you have just to step straight into the temple of nature, among all the good people worshipping."

"There! that is what I was afraid of!" cried Mercy: "you are pantheists!"

"Bless my soul, Mercy!" exclaimed Christina; "what do you mean?"

"Yes," answered Ian. "If to believe that not a lily can grow, not a sparrow fall to the ground without our Father, be pantheism, Alister and I are pantheists. If by pantheism you mean anything that would not fit with that, we are not pantheists."

"Why should we trouble about religion more than is required of us!" interposed Christina.

"Why indeed?" returned Ian. "But then how much is required?"

"You require far more than my father, and he is good enough for me!"

"The Master says we are to love God with all our hearts and souls and strength and mind."

"That was in the old law, Ian," said Alister.

"You are right. Jesus only justified it—and did it."

"How then can you worship in the temple of Nature?" said Mercy.

"Just as he did. It is Nature's temple, mind, for the worship of God, not of herself!"

"But how am I to get into it? That is what I want to know."

"The innermost places of the temple are open only to such as already worship in a greater temple; but it has courts into which any honest soul may enter."

"You wouldn't set me to study Wordsworth?"

"By no means."

"I am glad of that—though there must be more in him than I see, or you couldn't care for him so much!"

"Some of Nature's lessons you must learn before you can understand them."

"Can you call it learning a lesson if you do not understand it?"

"Yes—to a certain extent. Did you learn at school to work the rule of three?"

"Yes; and I was rather fond of it."

"Did you understand it?"

"I could work sums in it."

"Did you see how it was that setting the terms down so, and working out the rule, must give you a true answer. Did you perceive that it was safe to buy or sell, to build a house, or lay out a garden, by the rule of three?"

"I did not. I do not yet."

"Then one may so far learn a lesson without understanding it! All do, more or less, in Dame Nature's school. Not a few lessons must be so learned in order to be better learned. Without being so learned first, it is not possible to understand them; the scholar has not facts enough about the things to understand them. Keats's youthful delight in Nature was more intense even than Wordsworth's, but he was only beginning to understand her when he died. Shelley was much nearer understanding her than Keats, but he was drowned before he did understand her. Wordsworth was far before either of them. At the same time, presumptuous as it may appear, I believe there are regions to be traversed, beyond any point to which Wordsworth leads us."

"But how am I to begin? Do tell me. Nothing you say helps me in the least."

"I have all the time been leading you toward the door at which you want to go in. It is not likely, however, that it will open to you at once. I doubt if it will open to you at all except through sorrow."

"You are a most encouraging master!" said Christina, with a light laugh.

"It was Wordsworth's bitter disappointment in the outcome of the French revolution," continued Ian, "that opened the door to him. Yet he had gone through the outer courts of the temple with more understanding than any who immediately preceded him.—Will you let me ask you a question?"

"You frighten me!" said Mercy.

"I am sorry for that. We will talk of something else."

"I am not afraid of what you may ask me; I am frightened at what you tell me. I fear to go on if I must meet Sorrow on the way!"

"You make one think of some terrible secret society!" said Christina.

"Tell me then, Miss Mercy, is there anything you love very much? I don't say any PERSON, but any THING."

"I love some animals."

"An animal is not a thing. It is possible to love animals and not the nature of which we are speaking. You might love a dog dearly, and never care to see the sun rise!—Tell me, did any flower ever make you cry?

"No," answered Mercy, with a puzzled laugh; "how could it?"

"Did any flower ever make you a moment later in going to bed, or a moment earlier in getting out of it?"

"No, certainly!"

"In that direction, then, I am foiled!"

"You would not really have me cry over a flower, Mr. Ian? Did ever a flower make you cry yourself? Of course not! it is only silly women that cry for nothing!"

"I would rather not bring myself in at present," answered Ian smiling. "Do you know how Chaucer felt about flowers?"

"I never read a word of Chaucer."

"Shall I give you an instance?"

"Please."

"Chaucer was a man of the world, a courtier, more or less a man of affairs, employed by Edward III. in foreign business of state: you cannot mistake him for an effeminate or sentimental man! He does not anywhere, so far as I remember, say that ever he cried over a flower, but he shows a delight in some flowers so delicate and deep that it must have a source profounder than that of most people's tears. When we go back I will read you what he says about the daisy; but one more general passage I think I could repeat. There are animals in it too!"

"Pray let us hear it," said Christina.

He spoke the following stanzas—not quite correctly, but supplying for the moment's need where he could not recall:—

A	gardein	saw	I,	full	of	blosomed	bowis,
Upon	a	river,	in	a	grene	mede,
There	as	sweetnesse	evermore	inough	is,
With	floures	white,	blewe,	yelowe,	and	rede,
And	cold	welle	streames,	nothing	dede,
That	swommen	full	of	smale	fishes	light,

With finnes rede, and scales silver bright.

On   every   bough   the   birdes   heard   I   sing,
With   voice   of   angell,   in   hir   armonie,
That   busied   hem,   hir   birdes   forth   to   bring,
The   little   pretty   conies   to   hir   play   gan   hie,
And   further   all   about   I   gan   espie,
The   dredeful   roe,   the   buck,   the   hart,   and   hind,
Squirrels, and beastes small, of gentle kind.

Of   instruments   of   stringes   in   accorde,
Heard   I   so   play,   a   ravishing   swetnesse,
That   God,   that   maker   is   of   all   and   Lorde,
Ne   heard   never   better,   as   I   gesse,
Therewith   a   wind,   unneth   it   might   be   lesse,
Made   in   the   leaves   grene   a   noise   soft,
Accordant to the foules song on loft.

The   aire   of   the   place   so   attempre   was,
That   never   was   ther   grevance   of   hot   ne   cold,
There   was   eke   every   noisome   spice   and   gras,
Ne   no   man   may   there   waxe   sicke   ne   old,
Yet   was   there   more   joy   o   thousand   fold,
Than   I   can   tell   or   ever   could   or   might,
There is ever clere day, and never night.

He modernized them also a little in repeating them, so that his hearers missed nothing through failing to understand the words: how much they gained, it were hard to say.

"It reminds one," commented Ian, "of Dante's paradise on the top of the hill of purgatory."

"I don't know anything about Dante either," said Mercy regretfully.

"There is plenty of time!" said Ian.

"But there is so much to learn!" returned Mercy in a hopeless tone.

"That is the joy of existence!" Ian replied. "We are not bound to know; we are only bound to learn.—But to return to my task: a man may really love a flower. In another poem Chaucer tells us that such is his delight in his books that no other pleasure can take him from them—

Save   certainly,   when   that   the   month   of   May
Is   comen,   and   that   I   heare   the   foules   sing,
And   that   the   floures   ginnen   for   to   spring,
Farwell my booke, and my devotion!

Poor people love flowers; rich people admire them."

"But," said Mercy, "how can one love a thing that has no life?"

Ian could have told her that whatever grows must live; he could further have told her his belief that life cannot be without its measure of consciousness; but it would have led to more difficulty, and away from the end he had in view. He felt also that no imaginable degree of consciousness in it was commensurate with the love he had himself for almost any flower. His answer to Mercy's question was this:—

"The flowers come from the same heart as man himself, and are sent to be his companions and ministers. There is something divinely magical, because profoundly human in them. In some at least the human is plain; we see a face of childlike peace and confidence that appeals to our best. Our feeling for many of them doubtless owes something to childish associations; but how did they get their hold of our childhood? Why did they enter our souls at all? They are joyous, inarticulate children, come with vague messages from the father of all. If I confess that what they say to me sometimes makes me weep, how can I call my feeling for them anything but love? The eternal thing may have a thousand forms of which we know nothing yet!"

Mercy felt Ian must mean something she ought to like, if only she knew what it was; but he had not yet told her anything to help her! He had, however, neither reached his end nor lost his way; he was leading her on—gently and naturally.

"I did not mean," he resumed, "that you must of necessity begin with the flowers. I was only inquiring whether at that point you were nearer to Nature.—Tell me—were you ever alone?"

"Alone!" repeated Mercy, thinking. "—Surely everybody has been many times alone!"

"Could you tell when last you were alone?"

She thought, but could not tell.

"What I want to ask you," said Ian, "is—did you ever feel alone? Did you ever for a moment inhabit loneliness? Did it ever press itself upon you that there was nobody near—that if you called nobody would hear? You are not alone while you know that you can have a fellow creature with you the instant you choose."

"I hardly think I was ever alone in that way."

"Then what I would have you do," continued Ian, "is—to make yourself alone in one of Nature's withdrawing-rooms, and seat yourself in one of Grannie's own chairs.—I am coming to the point at last!—Upon a day when the weather is fine, go out by yourself. Tell no one where you are going, or that you are going anywhere. Climb a hill. If you cannot get to the top of it, go high on the side of it. No book, mind! nothing to fill your thinking-place from auother's! People are always saying 'I think,' when they are not thinking at all, when they are at best only passing the thoughts of others whom they do not even know.

"When you have got quite alone, when you do not even know the nearest point to anybody, sit down and be lonely. Look out on the loneliness, the wide world round you, and the great vault over you, with the lonely sun in the middle of it; fold your hands in your lap, and be still. Do not try to think anything. Do not try to call up any feeling or sentiment or sensation; just be still. By and by, it may be, you will begin to know something of

Nature. I do not know you well enough to be sure about it; but if you tell me afterwards how you fared, I shall then know you a little better, and perhaps be able to tell you whether Nature will soon speak to you, or not until, as Henry Vaughan says, some veil be broken in you."

They were approaching the cottage, and little more was said. They found Mrs. Palmer prepared to go, and Mercy was not sorry: she had had enough for a while. She was troubled at the thought that perhaps she was helplessly shut out from the life inhabited by the brothers. When she lay down, her own life seemed dull and poor. These men, with all their kindness, respect, attention, and even attendance upon them, did not show them the homage which the men of their own circle paid them!

"They will never miss us!" she said to herself. "They will go on with their pantheism, or whatever it is, all the same!"

But they should not say she was one of those who talk but will not do! That scorn she could not bear!

All the time, however, the thing seemed to savour more of spell or cast of magic than philosophy: the means enjoined were suggestive of a silent incantation!

CHAPTER XIII.

GRANNY ANGRY.

It must not be supposed that all the visiting was on the part of those of the New House. The visits thence were returned by both matron and men. But somehow there was never the same freedom in the house as in the cottage. The difference did not lie in the presence of the younger girls: they were well behaved, friendly, and nowise disagreeable children. Doubtless there was something in the absence of books: it was of no use to jump up when a passage occurred; help was not at hand. But it was more the air of the place, the presence of so many common-place things, that clogged the wheels of thought. Neither, with all her knowledge of the world and all her sweetness, did Mrs. Palmer understand the essentials of hospitality half so well as the widow of the late minister-chief. All of them liked, and confessed that they liked the cottage best. Even Christina felt something lacking in their reception. She regretted that the house was not grand enough to show what they were accustomed to.

Mrs. Palmer seldom understood the talk, and although she sat looking persistently content, was always haunted with a dim feeling that her husband would not be best pleased at so much intercourse between his rich daughters and those penniless country-fellows. But what could she do! the place where he had abandoned them was so dull, so solitary! the girls must not mope! Christina would wither up without amusement, and then good-bye to her beauty and all that depended upon it! In the purity of her motherhood, she more than liked the young men: happy mother she would think herself, were her daughters to marry such men as these! The relations between them and their mother delighted her: they were one! their hearts were together! they understood each other! She could never have such bliss with her sons! Never since she gave them birth had she had one such look from either of hers as she saw pass every now and then from these to their mother! It would be like being born again to feel herself loved in that way! For any danger to the girls, she thought with a sigh how soon in London they would forget the young highlanders. Was there no possibility of securing one of them? What chance was there of Mercy's marrying well!

she was so decidedly plain! Was the idea of marrying her into an old and once powerful family like that of the Macruadh, to her husband inconceivable? Could he not restore its property as the dowry of his unprized daughter! it would be to him but a trifle!—and he could stipulate that the chief should acknowledge the baronetcy and use his title! Mercy would then be a woman of consequence, and Peregrine would have the Bible-honour of being the repairer of the breach, the restorer of paths to dwell in!—Such were some of the thoughts that would come and go in the brain of the mother as she sat; nor were they without a share in her readiness to allow her daughters to go out with the young men: she had an unquestioning conviction of their safety with them.

The days went by, and what to Christina had seemed imprisonment, began to look like some sort of liberty. She had scarce come nearer to sympathy with those whose society consoled her, but their talk had ceased to sound repulsive. She was infinitely more than a well-modelled waxflower, and yet hardly a growing plant. More was needed to wake her than friends awake. It is wonderful how long the sleeping may go with the waking, and not discover any difference between them. But Grannie Nature was about to interfere.

The spring drew gently on. It would be long ere summer was summer enough to show. There seemed more of the destructive in the spring itself than of the genial—cold winds, great showers, days of steady rain, sudden assaults of hail and sleet. Still it was spring, and at length, one fine day with a bright sun, snow on the hills, and clouds in the east, but no sign of any sudden change, the girls went out for a walk, and took the younger girls with them.

A little way up the valley, out of sight of the cottage, a small burn came down its own dell to join that which flowed through the chiefs farm. Its channel was wide, but except in time of rain had little water in it. About half a mile up its course it divided, or rather the channel did, for in one of its branches there was seldom any water. At the fork was a low rocky mound, with an ancient ruin of no great size-three or four fragments of thick walls, within whose plan grew a slender birch-tree. Thither went the little party, wandering up the stream: the valley was sheltered; no wind but the south could reach it; and the sun, though it could not make it very warm, as it looked only aslant on its slopes, yet lighted both sides of it. Great white clouds passed slowly across the sky, with now and then a nearer black one threatening rain, but a wind overhead was carrying them quickly athwart.

Ian had seen the ladies pass, but made no effort to overtake them, although he was bound in the same direction: he preferred sauntering along with a book of ballads. Suddenly his attention was roused by a peculiar whistle, which he knew for that of Hector of the Stags: it was one of the few sounds he could make. Three times it was hurriedly repeated, and ere the third was over, Ian had discovered Hector high on a hill on the opposite side of the burn, waving his arms, and making eager signs to him. He stopped and set himself to understand. Hector was pointing with energy, but it was impossible to determine the exact direction: all that Ian could gather was, that his presence was wanted somewhere farther on. He resumed his walk therefore at a rapid pace, whereupon Hector pointed higher. There on the eastern horizon, towards the north, almost down upon the hills, Ian saw a congeries of clouds in strangest commotion, such as he had never before seen in any home latitude—a mass of darkly variegated vapours manifesting a peculiar and appalling unrest. It seemed tormented by a gyrating storm, twisting and contorting it with unceasing change. Now the gray came writhing out, now the black came bulging through, now a dirty brown smeared the ashy white, and now the blue shone calmly out from eternal distances. At the season he could hardly think it a thunderstorm, and stood absorbed in the unusual phenomenon. But again, louder and more hurried, came the whistling, and again he saw Hector gesticulating, more wildly than before. Then he knew that someone must be in want of help or succour, and set off running as hard as he could: he saw Hector keeping him in sight, and watching to give him further direction: perhaps the ladies had got into some difficulty!

When he arrived at the opening of the valley just mentioned, Hector's gesticulations made it quite plain it was up there he must go; and as soon as he entered it, he saw that the cloudy turmoil was among the hills at its head. With that he began to suspect the danger the hunter feared, and almost the same instant heard the merry voices of the children. Running yet faster, he came in sight of them on the other side of the stream,—not a moment too soon. The valley was full of a dull roaring sound. He called to them as he ran, and the children saw and came running down toward him, followed by Mercy. She was not looking much concerned, for she thought it only the grumbling of distant thunder. But Ian saw, far up the valley, what looked like a low brown wall across it, and knew what it was.

"Mercy!" he cried, "run up the side of the hill directly; you will be drowned—swept away if you do not."

She looked incredulous, and glanced up the hill-side, but carne on as if to cross the burn and join him.

"Do as I tell you," he cried, in a tone which few would have ventured to disregard, and turning darted across the channel toward her.

Mercy did not wait his coming, but took the children, each by a hand, and went a little way up the hill that immediately bordered the stream.

"Farther! farther!" cried Ian as he ran. "Where is Christina?"

"At the ruin," she answered.

"Good heavens!" exclaimed Ian, and darted off, crying, "Up the hill with you! up the hill!"

Christina was standing by the birch-tree in the ruin, looking down the burn. She had heard Ian calling, and saw him running, but suspected no danger.

"Come; come directly; for God's sake, come!" he cried. "Look up the burn!" he added, seeing her hesitate bewildered.

She turned, looked, and came running to him, down the channel, white with terror. It was too late. The charging water, whose front rank was turf, and hushes, and stones, was almost upon her. The solid matter had retarded its rush, but it was now on the point of dividing against the rocky mound, to sweep along both sides, and turn it into an island. Ian bounded to her in the middle of the channel, caught her by the arm, and hurried her back to the mound as fast as they could run: it was the highest ground immediately accessible. As they reached it, the water broke with a roar against its rocky base, rose, swelled—and in a moment the island was covered with a brown, seething, swirling flood.

"Where's Mercy and the children?" gasped Christina, as the water rose upon her.

"Safe, safe!" answered Ian. "We must get to the ruin!"

The water was halfway up his leg, and rising fast. Their danger was but beginning. Would the old walls, in greater part built without mortar, stand the rush? If a tree should strike them, they hardly would! If the flood came from a waterspout, it would soon be over—only how high it might first rise, who could tell! Such were his thoughts as they struggled to the ruin, and stood up at the end of a wall parallel with the current.

The water was up to Christina's waist, and very cold. Here out of the rush, however, she recovered her breath in a measure, and showed not a little courage. Ian stood between her and the wall, and held her fast. The torrent came round the end of the wall from both sides, but the encounter and eddy of the two currents rather pushed them up against it. Without it they could not have stood.

The chief danger to Christina, however, was from the cold. With the water so high on her body, and flowing so fast, she could not long resist it! Ian, therefore, took her round the knees, and lifted her almost out of the water.

"Put your arms up," he said, "and lay hold of the wall. Don't mind blinding me; my eyes are of little use at present. There—put your feet in my hands. Don't be frightened; I can hold you."

"I can't help being frightened!" she panted.

"We are in God's arms," returned Ian. "He is holding us."

"Are you sure we shall not be drowned?" she asked.

"No; but I am sure the water cannot take us out of God's arms."

This was not much comfort to Christina. She did not know anything about God—did not believe in him any more than most people. She knew God's arms only as the arms of Ian—and THEY comforted her, for she FELT them!

How many of us actually believe in any support we do not immediately feel? in any arms we do not see? But every help I from God; Ian's help was God's help; and though to believe in Ian was not to believe in God, it was a step on the road toward believing in God. He that believeth not in the good man whom he hath seen, how shall he believe in the God whom he hath not seen?

She began to feel a little better; the ghastly choking at her heart was almost gone.

"I shall break your arms!" she said.

"You are not very heavy," he answered; "and though I am not so strong as Alister, I am stronger than most men. With the help of the wall I can hold you a long time."

How was it that, now first in danger, self came less to the front with her than usual? It was that now first she was face to face with reality. Until this moment her life had been an affair of unrealities. Her selfishness had thinned, as it were vaporized, every reality that approached her. Solidity is not enough to teach some natures reality; they must hurt themselves against the solid ere they realize its solidity. Small reality, small positivity of existence has water to a dreaming soul, half consciously gazing through half shut eyes at the soft river floating away in the moonlight: Christina was shivering in its grasp on her person, its omnipresence to her skin; its cold made her gasp and choke; the push and tug of it threatened to sweep her away like a whelmed log! It is when we are most aware of the FACTITUDE of things, that we are most aware of our need of God, and most able to trust in him; when most aware of their presence, the soul finds it easiest to withdraw from them, and seek its safety with the maker of it and them. The recognition of inexorable reality in any shape, or kind, or way, tends to rouse the soul to the yet more real, to its relations with higher and deeper existence. It is not the hysterical alone for whom the great dash of cold water is good. All who dream life instead of living it, require some similar shock. Of the kind is every disappointment, every reverse, every tragedy of life. The true in even the lowest kind, is of the truth, and to be compelled to feel even that, is to be driven a trifle nearer to the truth of being, of creation, of God. Hence this sharp contact with Nature tended to make Christina less selfish: it made her forget herself so far as to care for her helper as well as herself.

It must be remembered, however, that her selfishness was not the cultivated and ingrained selfishness of a long life, but that of an uneducated, that is undeveloped nature. Her being had not degenerated by sinning against light known as light; it had not been consciously enlightened at all; it had scarcely as yet begun to grow. It was not lying dead, only unawaked. I would not be understood to imply that she was nowise to blame—but that she was by no means so much to blame as one who has but suspected the presence of a truth, and from selfishness or self-admiration has turned from it. She was to blame wherever she had not done as her conscience had feebly told her; and she had not made progress just because she had neglected the little things concerning which she had promptings. There are many who do not enter the kingdom of heaven just because they will not believe the tiny key that is handed them, fit to open its hospitable gate.

"Oh, Mr. Ian, if you should be drowned for my sake!" she faltered with white lips. "You should not have come to me!"

"I would not wish a better death," said Ian.

"How can you talk so coolly about it!" she cried.

"Well," he returned, "what better way of going out of the world is there than by the door of help? No man cares much about what the idiots of the world call life! What is it whether we live in this room or another? The same who sent us here, sends for us out of here!"

"Most men care very much! You are wrong there!"

"I don't call those who do, men! They are only children! I know many men who would no more cleave to this life than a butterfly would fold his wings and creep into his deserted chrysalis-case. I do care to live—tremendously, but I don't mind where. He who made this room so well worth living in, may surely be trusted with the next!"

"I can't quite follow you," stammered Christina. "I am sorry. Perhaps it is the cold. I can't feel my hands, I am so cold."

"Leave the wall, and put your arms round my neck. The change will rest me, and the water is already falling! It will go as rapidly as it came!"

"How do you know that?"

"It has sunk nearly a foot in the last fifteen minutes: I have been carefully watching it, you may be sure! It must have been a waterspout, and however much that may bring, it pours it out all at once."

"Oh!" said Christina, with a tremulous joyfulness; "I thought it would go on ever so long!"

"We shall get out of it alive!—God's will be done!"

"Why do you say that? Don't you really mean we are going to be saved?"

"Would you want to live, if he wanted you to die?"

"Oh, but you forget, Mr. Ian, I am not ready to die, like you!" sobbed Christina.

"Do you think anything could make it better for you to stop here, after God thought it better for you to go?"

"I dare not think about it."

"Be sure God will not take you away, if it be better for you to live here a little longer. But you will have to go sometime; and if you contrived to live after God wanted you to go, you would find yourself much less ready when the time came that you must. But, my dear Miss Palmer, no one can be living a true life, to whom dying is a terror."

Christina was silent. He spoke the truth! She was not worth anything! How grand it was to look death in the face with a smile!

If she had been no more than the creature she had hitherto shown herself, not all the floods of the deluge could have made her think or feel thus: her real self, her divine nature had begun to wake. True, that nature was as yet no more like the divine, than the drowsy, arm-stretching, yawning child is like the merry elf about to spring from his couch, full of life, of play, of love. She had no faith in God yet, but it was much that she felt she was not worth anything.

You are right: it was odd to hold such a conversation at such a time! But Ian was an odd man. He actually believed that God was nearer to him than his own consciousness, yet desired communion with him! and that Jesus Christ knew what he said when he told his disciples that the Father cared for his sparrows.

Only one human being witnessed their danger, and he could give no help. Hector of the Stags had crossed the main valley above where the torrent entered it, and coming over the hill, saw with consternation the flood-encompassed pair. If there had been help in man, he could have brought none; the raging torrent blocked the way both to the village and to the chief's house. He could only stand and gaze with his heart in his eyes.

Beyond the stream lay Mercy on the hillside, with her face in the heather. Frozen with dread, she dared not look up. Had she moved but ten yards, she would have seen her sister in Ian's arms.

The children sat by her, white as death, with great lumps in their throats, and the silent tears rolling down their cheeks. It was the first time death had come near them.

A sound of sweeping steps came through the heather. They looked up: there was the chief striding toward them.

The flood had come upon him at work in his fields, whelming his growing crops. He had but time to unyoke his bulls, and run for his life. The bulls, not quite equal to the occasion, were caught and swept away. They were found a week after on the hills, nothing the worse, and nearly as wild as when first the chief took them in hand. The cottage was in no danger; and Nancy got a horse and the last of the cows from the farm-yard on to the crest of the ridge, against which the burn rushed roaring, just as the water began to invade the cowhouse and stable. The moment he reached the ridge, the chief set out to look for his brother, whom he knew to be somewhere up the valley; and having climbed to get an outlook, saw Mercy and the girls, from whose postures he dreaded that something had befallen them.

The girls uttered a cry of welcome, and the chief answered, but Mercy did not lift her head.

"Mercy," said Alister softly, and kneeling laid his hand on her.

She turned to him such a face of blank misery as filled him with consternation.

"What has happened?" he asked.

She tried to speak, but could not.

"Where is Christina?" he went on.

She succeeded in bringing out the one word "ruin."

"Is anybody with her?"

"Ian."

"Oh!" he returned cheerily, as if then all would be right. But a pang shot through his heart, and it was as much for himself as for Mercy that he went on: "But God is with them, Mercy. If he were not, it would be bad indeed! Where he is, all is well!"

She sat up, and putting out her hand, laid it in his great palm.

"I wish I could believe that!" she said; "but you know people ARE drowned sometimes!"

"Yes, surely! but if God be with them what does it matter! It is no worse than when a mother puts her baby into a big bath."

"It is cruel to talk like that to me when my sister is drowning!"

She gave a stifled shriek, and threw herself again on her face.

"Mercy," said the chief—and his voice trembled a little, "you do not love your sister more than I love my brother, and if he be drowned I shall weep; but I shall not be miserable as if a mocking devil were at the root of it, and not one who loves them better than we ever shall. But come; I think we shall find them somehow alive yet! Ian knows what to do in an emergency; and though you might not think it, he is a very strong man."

She rose immediately, and taking like a child the hand he offered her, went up the hill with him.

The girls ran before them, and presently gave a scream of joy.

"I see Chrissy! I see Chrissy!" cried one.

"Yes! there she is! I see her too!" cried the other.

Alister hurried up with Mercy. There was Christina! She seemed standing on the water!

Mercy burst into tears.

"But where's Ian?" she said, when she had recovered herself a little; "I don't see him!"

"He is there though, all right!" answered Alister. "Don't you see his hands holding her out of the water?"

And with that he gave a great shout:—

"Ian! Ian! hold on, old boy! I'm coming!"

Ian heard him, and was filled with terror, but had neither breath nor strength to answer. Along the hillside went Alister bounding like a deer, then turning sharp, shot headlong down, dashed into the torrent—and was swept away like a cork. Mercy gave a scream, and ran down the hill.

He was not carried very far, however. In a moment or two he had recovered himself, and crept out gasping and laughing, just below Mercy. Ian did not move. He was so benumbed that to change his position an inch would, he well knew, be to fall.

And now Hector began to behave oddly. He threw a stone, which went in front of Ian and Christina. Then he threw another, which went behind them. Then he threw a third, and Christina felt her hat caught by a bit of string. She drew it toward her as fast as numbness would permit, and found at the end a small bottle. She managed to get it uncorked, and put it to Ian's lips. He swallowed a mouthful, and made her take some. Hector stood on one side, the chief on the other, and watched the proceeding.

"What would mother say, Alister!" cried Ian across the narrowing water.

In the joy of hearing his voice, Alister rushed again into the torrent; and, after a fierce struggle, reached the mound, where he scrambled up, and putting his arms round Ian's legs with a shout, lifted the two at once like a couple of babies.

"Come! come, Alister! don't be silly!" said Ian. "Set me down!"

"Give me the girl then."

"Take her!"

Christina turned on him a sorrowful gaze as Alister took her.

"I have killed you!" she said.

"You have done me the greatest favour," he replied.

"What?" she asked.

"Accepted help."

She burst out crying. She had not shed a tear before.

"Get on the top of the wall, Ian, out of the wet," said Alister.

"You can't tell what the water may have done to the foundations, Alister! I would rather not break my leg! It is so frozen it would never mend again!"

As they talked, the torrent had fallen so much, that Hector of the Stags came wading from the other side. A few minutes more, and Alister carried Christina to Mercy.

"Now," he said, setting her down, "you must walk."

Ian could not cross without Hector's help; he seemed to have no legs. They set out at once for the cottage.

"How will your crops fare, Alister?" asked Ian.

"Part will be spoiled," replied the chief; "part not much the worse."

The torrent had rushed half-way up the ridge, then swept along the flank of it, and round the end in huge bulk, to the level on the other side. The water lay soaking into the fields. The valley was desolated. What green things had not been uprooted or carried away with the soil, were laid flat.

Everywhere was mud, and scattered all over were lumps of turf, with heather, brushwood, and small trees. But it was early in the year, and there was hope!

I will spare the description of the haste and hurrying to and fro in the little house—the blowing of fires, the steaming pails and blankets, the hot milk and tea! Mrs. Macruadh rolled up her sleeves, and worked like a good housemaid. Nancy shot hither and thither on her bare feet like a fawn—you could not say she ran, and certainly she did not walk. Alister got Ian to bed, and rubbed him with rough towels—himself more wet than he, for he had been rolled over and over in the torrent. Christina fell asleep, and slept many hours. When she woke, she said she was quite well; but it was weeks before she was like herself. I doubt if ever she was quite as strong again. For some days Ian confessed to an aching in his legs and arms. It was the cold of the water, he said; but Alister insisted it was from holding Christina so long.

"Water could not hurt a highlander!" said Alister.

CHAPTER XIV

CHANGE.

Christina walked home without difficulty, but the next day did not leave her bed, and it was a fortnight before she was able to be out of doors. When Ian and she met, her manner was not quite the same as before. She seemed a little timid. As she shook hands with him her eyes fell; and when they looked up again, as if ashamed of their involuntary retreat, her face was rosy; but the slight embarrassment disappeared as soon as they began to talk. No affectation or formality, however, took its place: in respect of Ian her falseness was gone. The danger she had been in, and her deliverance through the voluntary sharing of it by Ian, had awaked the simpler, the real nature of the girl, hitherto buried in impressions and their responses. She had lived but as a mirror meant only to reflect the outer world: something of an operative existence was at length beginning to appear in her. She was growing a woman. And the first stage in that growth is to become as a little child.

The child, however, did not for some time show her face to any but Ian. In his presence Christina had no longer self-assertion or wile. Without seeking his notice she would yet manifest an almost childish willingness to please him. It was no sudden change. She had, ever since their adventure, been haunted, both awake and asleep, by his presence, and it had helped her to some discoveries regarding herself. And the more she grew real, the nearer, that is, that she came to being a PERSON, the more she came under the influence of his truth, his reality. It is only through live relation to others that any individuality crystallizes.

"You saved my life, Ian!" she said one evening for the tenth time.

"It pleased God you should live," answered Ian.

"Then you really think," she returned, "that God interfered to save us?"

"No, I do not; I don't think he ever interferes."

"Mr. Sercombe says everything goes by law, and God never interferes; my father says he does interfere sometimes."

"Would you say a woman interfered in the management of her own house? Can one be said to interfere where he is always at work? He is the necessity of the universe, ever and always doing the best that can be done, and especially for the individual, for whose sake alone the cosmos exists. If we had been drowned, we should have given God thanks for saving us."

"I do not understand you!"

"Should we not have given thanks to find ourselves lifted out of the cold rushing waters, in which we felt our strength slowly sinking?"

"But you said DROWNED! How could we have thanked God for deliverance if we were drowned?"

"What!—not when we found ourselves above the water, safe and well, and more alive than ever? Would it not be a dreadful thing to lie tossed for centuries under the sea-waves to which the torrent had borne us? Ah, how few believe in a life beyond, a larger life, more awake, more earnest, more joyous than this!"

"Oh, *I* do! but that is not what one means by LIFE; that is quite a different kind of thing!"

"How do you make out that it is so different? If I am I, and you are you, how can it be very different? The root of things is individuality, unity of idea, and persistence depends on it. God is the one perfect individual; and while this world is his and that world is his, there can be no inconsistency, no violent difference, between there and here."

"Then you must thank God for everything—thank him if you are drowned, or burnt, or anything!"

"Now you understand me! That is precisely what I mean."

"Then I can never be good, for I could never bring myself to that!"

"You cannot bring yourself to it; no one could. But we must come to it. I believe we shall all be brought to it."

"Never me! I should not wish it!"

"You do not wish it; but you may be brought to wish it; and without it the end of your being cannot be reached. No one, of course, could ever give thanks for what he did not know or feel as good. But what IS good must come to be felt good. Can you suppose that Jesus at any time could not thank his Father for sending him into the world?"

"You speak as if we and he were of the same kind!"

"He and we are so entirely of the same kind, that there is no bliss for him or for you or for me but in being the loving obedient child of the one Father."

"You frighten me! If I cannot get to heaven any other way than that, I shall never get there."

"You will get there, and you will get there that way and no other. If you could get there any other way, it would be to be miserable."

"Something tells me you speak the truth; but it is terrible! I do not like it."

"Naturally."

She was on the point of crying. They were alone in the drawing-room of the cottage, but his mother might enter any moment, and Ian said no more.

It was not a drawing toward the things of peace that was at work in Christina: it was an urging painful sense of separation from Ian. She had been conscious of some antipathy even toward him, so unlike were her feelings, thoughts, judgments, to his: this feeling had changed to its opposite.

A meeting with Ian was now to Christina the great event of day or week; but Ian, in love with the dead, never thought of danger to either.

One morning she woke from a sound and dreamless sleep, and getting out of bed, drew aside the curtains, looked out, and then opened her window. It was a lovely spring-morning. The birds were singing loud in the fast greening shrubbery. A soft wind was blowing. It came to her, and whispered something of which she understood only that it was both lovely and sad. The sun, but a little way up, was shining over hills and cone-shaped peaks, whose shadows, stretching eagerly westward, were yet ever shortening eastward. His light was gentle, warm, and humid, as if a little sorrowful, she thought, over his many dead children, that he must call forth so many more to the new life of the reviving year. Suddenly as she gazed, the little clump of trees against the hillside stood as she had never seen it stand before—as if the sap in them were no longer colourless, but red with human life; nature was alive with a presence she had never seen before; it was instinct with a meaning, an intent, a soul; the mountains stood against the sky as if reaching upward, knowing something, waiting for something; over all was a glory. The change was far more wondrous than from winter to summer; it was not as if a dead body, but a dead soul had come alive. What could it mean? Had the new aspect come forth to answer this glow in her heart, or was the glow in her heart the reflection of this new aspect of the world? She was ready to cry aloud, not with joy, not from her feeling of the beauty, but with a SENSATION almost, hitherto unknown, therefore nameless. It was a new and marvellous interest in the world, a new sense of life in herself, of life in everything, a recognition of brother-existence, a life-contact with the universe, a conscious flash of the divine in her soul, a throb of the pure joy of being. She was nearer God than she had ever been before. But she did not know this—might never in this world know it; she understood nothing of what was going on in her, only felt it go on; it was not love of God that was moving in her. Yet she stood in her white dress like one risen from the grave, looking in sweet bliss on a new heaven and a new earth, made new by the new opening of her eyes. To save man or woman, the next thing to the love of God is the love of man or woman; only let no man or woman mistake the love of love for love!

She started, grew white, stood straight up, grew red as a sunset:—was it—could it be?—"Is this love?" she said to herself, and for minutes she hardly moved.

It was love. Whether love was in her or not, she was in love—and it might get inside her. She hid her face in her hands, and wept.

With what opportunities I have had of studying, I do not say UNDERSTANDING, the human heart, I should not have expected such feeling from Christina—and she wondered at it herself. Till a child is awake, how tell his mood?—until a woman is awaked, how tell her nature? Who knows himself?—and how then shall he know his neighbour?

For who can know anything except on the supposition of its remaining the same? and the greatest change of all, next to being born again, is beginning to love. The very faculty of loving had been hitherto repressed in the soul of Christina—by poor education, by low family and social influences, by familiarity with the worship of riches, by vanity, and consequent hunger after the attentions of men; but now at length she was in love.

At breakfast, though she was silent, she looked so well that her mother complimented her on her loveliness. Had she been more of a mother, she might have seen cause for anxiety in this fresh bourgeoning of her beauty.

CHAPTER XV.

LOVE ALLODIAL.

While the chief went on in his humble way, enjoying life and his lowly position; seeming, in the society of his brother, to walk the outer courts of heaven; and, unsuspicious of the fact, growing more and more in love with the ill educated, but simple, open, and wise Mercy, a trouble was gathering for him of which he had no presentiment. We have to be delivered from the evils of which we are unaware as well as from those we hate; and the chief had to be set free from his unconscious worship of Mammon. He did not worship Mammon by yielding homage to riches; he did not make a man's money his pedestal; had he been himself a millionaire, he would not have connived at being therefore held in honour; but, ever consciously aware of the deteriorating condition of the country, and pitifully regarding the hundred and fifty souls who yet looked to him as their head, often turning it over in his mind how to shepherd them should things come to a crisis, his abiding, ever-recurring comfort was the money from the last sale of the property, accumulating ever since, and now to be his in a very few years: he always thought, I say, first of this money and not first of God. He imagined it an inexhaustible force, a power with which for his clan he could work wonders. It is the common human mistake to think of money as a force and not as a mere tool. But he never thought of it otherwise than as belonging to the clan; never imagined the least liberty to use it save in the direct service of his people. And all the time, the very shadow of this money was disappearing from the face of the earth!

It had scarcely been deposited where the old laird judged it as safe as in the Bank of England, when schemes and speculations were initiated by the intrusted company which brought into jeopardy everything it held, and things had been going from bad to worse ever since. Nothing of this was yet known, for the directors had from the first carefully muffled up the truth, avoiding the least economy lest it should be interpreted as hinting at any need of prudence; living in false show with the very money they were thus lying away, warming and banqueting their innocent neighbours with fuel and wine stolen from their own cellars; and working worse wrong and more misery under the robe of imputed righteousness, that is, respectability, than could a little army of burglars. Unawares to a trusting multitude, the vacant eyes of loss were drawing near to stare them out of hope and comfort; and annihilation had long closed in upon the fund which the chief regarded as the sheet-anchor of his clan: he trusted in Mammon, and Mammon had played him one of his rogue's-tricks. The most degrading wrong to ourselves, and the worst eventual wrong to others, is to trust in any thing or person but the living God: it was an evil thing from which the chief had sore need to be delivered. Even those who help us we must regard as the loving hands of the great heart of the universe, else we do God wrong, and will come to do them wrong also.

And there was more yet of what we call mischief brewing in another quarter to like hurt.

Mr. Peregrine Palmer was not now so rich a man as when he bought his highland property; also he was involved in affairs of doubtful result. It was natural, therefore, that he should begin to think of the said property not merely as an ornament of life, but as something to fall back upon. He feared nothing, however, more unpleasant than a temporary embarrassment. Had not his family been in the front for three generations! Had he not a vested right in success! Had he not a claim for the desire of his heart on whatever power it was that he pictured to himself as throned in the heavens! It never came into his head that, seeing there were now daughters in the family, it might he worth the while of that Power to make a poor man of him for their sakes; or that neither he, his predecessors, nor his sons, had ever come near enough to anything human to be fit for having their pleasures taken from them. But what I have to do with is the new aspect his Scotch acres now put on: he must see to making the best of them! and that best would be a deer-forest! He and his next neighbour might together effect something worth doing! Therefore all crofters or villagers likely to trespass must be got rid of—and first and foremost the shepherds, for they had endless opportunities of helping themselves to a deer. Where there were sheep there must be shepherds: they would make a clearance of both! The neighbour referred to, a certain Mr. Brander, who had made his money by sharp dealing in connection with a great Russian railway, and whom Mr. Peregrine Palmer knew before in London, had enlightened him on many things, and amongst others on the shepherds' passion for deer-stalking. Being in the company of the deer, he said, the whole day, and the whole year through, they were thoroughly acquainted with their habits, and were altogether too much both for the deer and for their owners. A shepherd would take the barrel of his gun from the stock, and thrust it down his back, or put it in a hollow crook, and so convey it to the vicinity of some spot frequented by a particular animal, to lie hidden there for his opportunity. In the hills it was impossible to tell with certainty whence came the sound of a shot; and no rascal of them would give information concerning another! In short, there was no protecting the deer without uprooting and expelling the peasantry!

The village of the Clanruadh was on Mr. Brander's land, and was dependent in part on the produce of small pieces of ground, the cultivators of which were mostly men with other employment as well. Some made shoes of the hides, others cloth and clothes of the wool of the country. Some were hinds on neighbouring farms, but most were shepherds, for there was now very little tillage. Almost all the land formerly cultivated had been given up to grass and sheep, and not a little of it was steadily returning to that state of nature from which it had been reclaimed, producing heather, ling, blueberries, cnowperts, and cranberries. The hamlet was too far from the sea for much fishing, but some of its inhabitants would join relatives on the coast and go fishing with them, when there was nothing else to be done. But many of those who looked to the sea for help had lately come through a hard time, in which they would have died but for the sea-weed and shellfish the shore afforded them; yet such was their spirit of independence that a commission appointed to inquire into their necessity, found scarcely one willing to acknowledge any want: such was the class of men and women now doomed, at the will of two common-minded, greedy men, to expulsion from the houses and land they had held for generations, and loved with a love unintelligible to their mean-souled oppressors.

Ian, having himself learned the lesson that, so long as a man is dependent on anything earthly, he is not a free man, was very desirous to have his brother free also. He could not be satisfied to leave the matter where, on their way home that night from THE TOMB, as they called their cave-house, their talk had left it. Alister's love of the material world, of the soil of his ancestral acres, was, Ian plainly saw, not yet one with the meaning and will of God: he was not yet content that the home of his fathers should fare as the father of fathers pleased. He was therefore on the outlook for the right opportunity of having another talk with him on the subject.

That those who are trying to be good are more continuously troubled than the indifferent, has for ages been a puzzle. "I saw the wicked spreading like a green bay tree," says king David; and he was far from having fathomed the mystery when he got his mind at rest about it. Is it not simply that the righteous are worth troubling? that they are capable of receiving good from being troubled? As a man advances, more and more is required of him. A wrong thing in the good man becomes more and more wrong as he draws nearer to freedom from it. His friends may say how seldom he offends; but every time he offends, he is the more to blame. Some are allowed to go on because it would be of no use to stop them yet; nothing would yet make them listen to wisdom. There must be many who, like Dives, need the bitter contrast between the good things of this life and the evil things of the next, to wake them up. In this life they are not only fools, and insist on being treated as fools, but would have God consent to treat them as if he too had no wisdom! The laird was one in whom was no guile, but he was far from perfect: any man is far from perfect whose sense of well-being could be altered by any change of circumstance. A man unable to do without this thing or that, is not yet in sight of his perfection, therefore not out of sight of suffering. They who do not know suffering, may well doubt if they have yet started on the way TO BE. If clouds were gathering to burst in fierce hail on the head of the chief, it was that he might be set free from yet another of the cords that bound him. He was like a soaring eagle from whose foot hung, trailing on the earth, the line by which his tyrant could at his will pull him back to his inglorious perch.

To worship truly is to treat according to indwelling worth. The highest worship of Nature is to worship toward it, as David and Daniel worshipped toward the holy place. But even the worship of Nature herself might be an ennobling idolatry, so much is the divine present in her. There is an intense, almost sensuous love of Nature, such as the chief confessed to his brother, which is not only one with love to the soul of Nature, but tends to lift the soul of man up to the lord of Nature. To love the soul of Nature, however, does not secure a man from loving the body of Nature in the low Mammon-way of possession. A man who loves the earth even as the meek love it, may also love it in a way hostile to such possession of it as is theirs. The love of possessing as property, must, unchecked, come in time to annihilate in a man the inheritance of the meek.

A few acres of good valley-land, with a small upland pasturage, and a space of barren hill-country, had developed in the chief a greater love of the land as a possession than would have come of entrance upon an undiminished inheritance. He clave to the ground remaining to him, as to the last remnant of a vanishing good.

One day the brothers were lying on the westward slope of the ridge, in front of the cottage. A few sheep, small, active, black-faced, were feeding around them: it was no use running away, for the chief's colley was lying beside him! The laird every now and then buried his face in the short sweet mountain-grass-like that of the clowns in England, not like the rich sown grass on the cultivated bank of the burn.

"I believe I love the grass," he said, "as much, Ian, as your Chaucer loved the daisy!"

"Hardly so much, I should think!" returned Ian.

"Why do you think so?"

"I doubt if grass can be loved so much as a flower."

"Why not?"

"Because the one is a mass, the other an individual."

"I understand."

"I have a fear, Alister, that you are in danger of avarice," said Ian, after a pause.

"Avarice, Ian! What can you mean?"

"You are as free, Alister, from the love of money, as any man I ever knew, but that is not enough. Did you ever think of the origin of the word AVARICE?"

"No."

"It comes—at least it seems to me to come—from the same root as the verb HAVE. It is the desire to call THINGS ours—the desire of company which is not of our kind—company such as, if small enough, you would put in your pocket and carry about with you. We call the holding in the hand, or the house, or the pocket, or the power, HAVING; but things so held cannot really be HAD; HAVING is but an illusion in regard to THINGS. It is only what we can be WITH that we can really possess—that is, what is of our kind, from God to the lowest animal partaking of humanity. A love can never be lost; it is a possession; but who can take his diamond ring into the somewhere beyond?—it is not a possession. God only can be ours perfectly; nothing called property can be ours at all."

"I know it—with my head at least," said Alister; "but I am not sure how you apply it to me."

"You love your country—don't you, Alister?"

"I do."

"What do you mean by LOVING YOUR COUNTRY?"

"It is hard to say all at once. The first thing that comes to me is, that I would rather live in it than in any other."

"Would you care to vaunt your country at the expense of any other?"

"Not if it did not plainly excel—and even then it might be neither modest nor polite!"

"Would you feel bound to love a man more because he was a fellow-countryman?"

"Other things being equal, I could not help it."

"Other things not being equal,—?"

"I should love the best man best—Scotsman or negro."

"That is as I thought of you. For my part, my love for my own people has taught me to love every man, be his colour or country what it may. The man whose patriotism is not leading him in that direction has not yet begun to be a true patriot. Let him go to St. Paul and learn, or stay in his own cellar and be an idiot.—But now, from loving our country, let us go down the other way:—Do you love the highlands or the lowlands best? You love the highlands, of course, you say. And what district do you like best? Our own. What parish? Your father's. What part of the parish? Why this, where at this moment we are lying. Now let me ask, have you, by your love for this piece of the world, which you will allow me to call ours, learned to love the whole world in like fashion?"

"I cannot say so. I do not think we can love the whole world in the same way as our own part of it—the part where we were born and bred! It is a portion of our very being."

"If your love to what we call our own land is a love that cannot spread, it seems to me of a questionable kind—of a kind involving the false notion of HAVING? The love that is eternal is alone true, and that is the love of the essential, which is the universal. We love indeed individuals, even to their peculiarities, but only BECAUSE of what lies under and is the life of them —what they share with every other, the eternal God-born humanity WHICH IS THE PERSON. Without this humanity where were your friend? Mind, I mean no abstraction, but the live individual humanity. Do

297

you see what I am driving at? I would extend my love of the world to all the worlds; my love of humanity to all that inhabit them. I want, from being a Scotsman, to be a Briton, then a European, then a cosmopolitan, then a dweller of the universe, a lover of all the worlds I see, and shall one day know. In the face of such a hope, I find my love for this ground of my father's—not indeed less than before, but very small. It has served its purpose in having begun in me love of the revelation of God. Wherever I see the beauty of the Lord, that shall be to me his holy temple. Our Lord was sent first to the lost sheep of the house of Israel:-how would you bear to be told that he loved them more than Africans or Scotsmen?"

"I could not bear it."

"Then, Alister, do you not see that the love of our mother earth is meant to be but a beginning; and that such love as yours for the land belongs to that love of things which must perish? You seem to me not to allow it to blossom, but to keep it a hard bud; and a bud that will not blossom is a coffin. A flower is a completed idea, a thought of God, a creature whose body is most perishable, bat whose soul, its idea, cannot die. With the idea of it in you, the withering of the flower you can bear. The God in it is yours always. Every spring you welcome the daisy anew; every time the primrose departs, it grows more dear by its death. I say there must be a better way of loving the ground on which we were born, than that whence the loss of it would cause us torture."

Alister listened as to a prophecy of evil.

"Rather than that cottage and those fields should pass into the hands of others," he said, almost fiercely, "I would see them sunk in a roaring tide!"

Ian rose, and walked slowly away.

Alister lay clutching the ground with his hands. For a passing moment Ian felt as if he had lost him.

"Lord, save him from this demon-love," he said, and sat down among the pines.

In a few minutes, Alister came to him.

"You cannot mean, Ian," he said-and his face was white through all its brown, "that I am to think no more of the fields of my fathers than of any other ground on the face of the earth!" "Think of them as the ground God gave to our fathers, which God may see fit to take from us again, and I shall be content—for the present," answered Ian.

"Do not be vexed with me," cried Alister. "I want to think as well as do what is right; but you cannot know how I feel or you would spare me. I love the very stones and clods of the land! The place is to me as Jerusalem to the Jews:—you know what the psalm says:—

Thy   saints   take   pleasure   in   her   stones,
    Her very dust to them is dear!"

"They loved their land as theirs," said Ian, "and have lost it!"

"I know I must be cast out of it! I know I must die and go from it; but I shall come back and wander about the fields and the hills with you and our father and mother!"

"And how about horse and dog?" asked Ian, willing to divert his thoughts for a moment,

"Well! Daoimean and Luath are so good that I'don't see why I should not have them!"

"No more do I!" responded Ian. "We may be sure God will either let you have them, or show you reason to content you for not having them. No love of any thing is to be put in the same thought-pocket with love for the poorest creature that has life. But I am sometimes not a little afraid lest your love for the soil get right in to your soul. We are here but pilgrims and strangers. God did not make the world to be dwelt in, but to be journeyed through. We must not love it as he did not mean we should. If we do, he may have great trouble and we much hurt ere we are set free from that love. Alister, would you willingly walk out of the house to follow him up and down for ever?"

"I don't know about willingly," replied Alister, "but if I were sure it was he calling me, I am sure I would walk out and follow him."

"What if your love of house and lands prevented you from being sure, when he called you, that it was he?"

"That would be terrible! But he would not leave me so. He would not forsake me in my ignorance!"

"No. Having to take you from everything, he would take everything from you!"

Alister went into the house.

He did not know how much of the worldly mingled with the true in him. He loved his people, and was unselfishly intent on helping them to the utmost; but the thought that he was their chief was no small satisfaction to him; and if the relation between them was a grand one, self had there the more soil wherein to spread its creeping choke-grass roots. In like manner, his love of nature nourished the parasite possession. He had but those bare hill-sides, and those few rich acres, yet when, from his ejrry on the hill-top, he looked down among the valleys, his heart would murmur within him, "From my feet the brook flows gurgling to water my fields! The wild moors around me feed my sheep! Yon glen is full of my people! "Even with the pure smell of the earth, mingled the sense of its possession. When, stepping from his cave-house, he saw the sun rise on the out- stretched grandeur of the mountain-world, and felt the earth a new creation as truly as when Adam first opened his eyes on its glory, his heart would give one little heave more at the thought that a portion of it was his own. But all is man's only because it is God's. The true possession of anything is to see and feel in it what God made it for; and the uplifting of the soul by that knowledge, is the joy of true having. The Lord had no land of his own. He did not care to have it, any more than the twelve legions of angels he would not pray for: his pupils must not care for things he did not care for. He had no place to lay his head in-had not even a grave of his own. For want of a boat he had once to walk the rough Galilean sea. True, he might have gone with the rest, but he had to stop behind to pray: he could not do without that. Once he sent a fish to fetch him money, but only to pay a tax. He had even to borrow the few loaves and little fishes from a boy, to feed his five thousand with.

The half-hour which Alister spent in the silence of his chamber, served him well: a ray as of light polarized entered his soul in its gloom. He returned to Ian, who had been all the time walking up and down the ridge.

"You are right, Ian!" he said. "I do love the world! If I were deprived of what I hold, I should doubt God! I fear, oh, I fear, Ian, he is going to take the land from me!"

"We must never fear the will of God, Alister! We are not right until we can pray heartily, not say submissively, 'Thy will be done!' We have not one interest, and God another. When we wish what he does not wish, we are not more against him than against our real selves. We are traitors to the human when we think anything but the will of God desirable, when we fear our very life."

It was getting toward summer, and the days were growing longer.

"Let us spend a night in the tomb!" said Ian; and they fixed a day in the following week.

CHAPTER XVI.

MEECY CALLS ON GEANNIE.

Although the subject did not again come up, Mercy had not forgotten what Ian had said about listening for the word of Nature, and had resolved to get away the first time she could, and see whether Grannie, as Ian had called her, would have anything to do with her. It were hard to say what she expected—something half magical rather than anything quite natural. The notions people have of spiritual influence are so unlike the facts, that, when it begins they never recognize it, but imagine something common at work. When the Lord came, those who were looking for him did not know him: —was he not a man like themselves! did they not know his father and mother!

It was a fine spring morning when Mercy left the house to seek an interview with Nature somewhere among the hills. She took a path she knew well, and then struck into a sheep-track she had never tried. Up and up she climbed, nor spent a thought on the sudden changes to which at that season, and amongst those hills, the weather is subject. With no anxiety as to how she might fare, she was yet already not without some awe: she was at length on her pilgrimage to the temple of Isis!

Not until she was beyond sight of any house, did she begin to feel alone. It was a new sensation, and of a mingled sort. But the slight sense of anxiety and fear that made part of it, was soon overpowered by something not unlike the exhilaration of a child escaped from school. This grew and grew until she felt like a wild thing that had been caught, and had broken loose. Now first, almost, she seemed to have begun to live, for now first was she free! She might lie in the heather, walk in the stream, do as she pleased! No one would interfere with her, no one say Don't! She felt stronger and fresher than ever in her life; and the farther she went, the greater grew the pleasure. The little burn up whose banks, now the one and now the other, she was walking, kept on welcoming her unaccustomed feet to the realms of solitude and liberty. For ever it seemed coming to meet her, hasting, running steep, as if straight out of the heaven to which she was drawing nearer and nearer. The wind woke now and then, and blew on her for a moment, as. if tasting her, to see what this young Psyche was that had floated up into the wild thin air of the hills. The incessant meeting of the brook made it a companion to her although it could not go her way, and was always leaving her. But it kept her from the utter loneliness she sought; for loneliness is imperfect while sound is by, especially a sing-sound, and the brook was one of Nature's self—playing song—instruments. But she came at length to a point where the ground was too rough to let her follow its path any more, and turning from it, she began to climb a steep ridge. The growing and deepening silence as she went farther and farther from the brook, promised the very place for her purpose on the top of the heathery ridge.

But when she reached it and looked behind her, lo, the valley she had left lay at her very feet! The world had rushed after and caught her! She had not got away from it! It was like being enchanted! She thought she was leaving it far behind, but the nature she sought to escape that she might find Nature, would not let her go! It kept following her as if to see that she fell into no snare, neither was too sternly received by the loftier spaces. She could distinguish one of the laird's men, ploughing in the valley below: she knew him by his red waistcoat! Almost fiercely she turned and made for the next ridge: it would screen her from the world she had left; it should not spy upon her! The danger of losing her way back never suggested itself. She had not learned that the look of things as you go, is not their look when you turn to go back; that with your attitude their mood will have altered. Nature is like a lobster-pot: she lets you easily go on, but not easily return.

When she gained the summit of the second ridge, she looked abroad on a country of which she knew nothing. It was like the face of an utter stranger. Not far beyond. rose yet another ridge: she must see how the world looked from that! On and on she went, crossing ridge after ridge, but no place invited her to stay and be still.

She found she was weary, and spying in the midst of some short heather a great stone, sat down, and gave herself up to the rest that stole upon her. Though the sun was warm, the air was keen, and, hot with climbing, she turned her face to it, and drank in its refreshing with delight. She looked around; not a trace of humanity was visible-nothing but brown and gray and green hills, with the clear sky over her head, and in the north a black cloud creeping up from the horizon. Another sense than that of rest awoke in her; now first in her life the sense of loneliness absolute began to possess her. And therewith suddenly descended upon her a farther something she had never known; it was as if the loneliness, or what is the same thing, the presence of her own being without another to qualify and make it reasonable and endurable, seized and held her. The silence gathered substance, grew as it were solid, and closing upon her, imprisoned her. Was it not rather that the Soul of Nature, unprevented, unthwarted by distracting influences, found a freer entrance to hers, but she, not yet in harmony with it, felt its con- tact as alien-as bondage therefore and not liberty? She was nearer than ever she had been to knowing the presence of the God who is always nearer to us than aught else. Yea, something seemed, through the very persistence of its silence, to say to her at last, and keep saying, "Here I am!" She looked behind her in sudden terror: 110 form was there. She sent out her gaze to the horizon: the huge waves of the solid earth stood up against the sky, sinking so slowly she could not see them sink: they stood mouldering away, biding their time. They were of those "who only stand and wait," fulfilling the will of him who set them to crumble till the hour of the new heavens and the new earth arrive. There was no visible life between her and the great silent mouldering hills. On her right hand lay a blue segment of the ever restless sea, but so far that its commotion seemed a yet deeper rest than that of the immovable hills.

She sat and sat, but nothing came, nothing seemed coming to her. The hope Ian had given her was not to be fulfilled! For here there was no revelation! She was not of the kind Nature could speak to!

She began to grow uncomfortable—to feel as if she had done something wrong—as if she was a child put into the corner—a corner of the great universe, to learn to be sorry for something. Certainly something was wrong with her-but what? Why did she feel so uncomfortable? Was she so silly as mind being alone? There was nothing in these mountains that would hurt her! The red deer were ^sometimes dangerous, but none were even within sight! Yet something like fear was growing in her! Why should she be afraid? Everything about her certainly did look strange, as if she had nothing to do with it, and it had nothing to do with her; but that was all! Ian Macruadh must be wrong! How could there be any such bond as he said between Nature and the human heart, when the first thing she felt when alone with her, was fear! The world was staring at her! She was the centre of a fixed, stony regard from all sides! The earth, and the sea, and the sky, were watching her! She did not like it! She would rise and shake off the fancy! But she did not rise; something held her to her thinking. Just so she would, when a child in the dark, stand afraid to move lest the fear itself, lying in wait like a tigress, should at her first motion pounce upon her. The terrible, persistent silence!—would nothing break it! And there was in herself a response to it—something that was in league with it, and kept telling her that things were not all right with her; that she ought not to be afraid, yet had good reason for being afraid; that she knew of no essential safety. There must be some refuge, some impregnable hiding-place, for the thing was a necessity, and she ought to know of it! There must be a human condition of never being afraid, of knowing nothing to be afraid of! She wondered whether, if she were quite good, went to church twice every Sunday, and read her bible every morning, she would come not to be afraid of-she did not know what. It would be grand to have no fear of person or thing! She was sometimes afraid of her own father, even when she knew no reason! How that mountain with the horn kept staring at her!

It was all nonsense! She was silly! She would get up and go home: it must be time!

But things were not as they should be! Something was required of her! Was it God wanting her to do something? She had never thought whether he required anything of her! She must be a better girl! Then she would have God with her, and not be afraid!

And all the time it was God near her that was making her unhappy. For, as the Son of Man came not to send peace on the earth but a sword, so the first visit of God to the human soul is generally in a cloud of fear and doubt, rising from the soul itself at his approach. The sun is the cloud-dispeller, yet often he must look through a fog if he would visit the earth at all. The child, not being a son, does not know his father. He may know he is what is called a father; what the word means he does not know. How then should he understand when the father comes to deliver him from his paltry self, and give him life indeed!

She tried to pray. She said, "Oh G—od! forgive me, and make me good. I want to be good!" Then she rose.

She went some little way without thinking where she was going, and then found she did not even know from what direction she had come. A sharp new fear, quite different from the former, now shot through her heart: she was lost! She had told no one she was going anywhere! No one would have a notion where to look for her! She had been beginning to feel hungry, but fear drove hunger away. All she knew was that she must not stay there. Here was nowhere; walking on she might come somewhere—that is, among human beings! So out she set on her weary travel from no-where to somewhere, giving Nature little thanks. She did not suspect that her grandmother had been doing anything for her by the space around her, or that now, by the tracklessness, the lostness, she was doing yet more. On and on she walked, climbing the one hillside and descending the other, going she knew not whither, hardly hoping she drew one step nearer home.

All at once her strength went from her. She sat down and cried. But with her tears came the thought how the chief and his brother talked of God. She remembered she had heard in church that men ought to cry to God in their troubles. Broken verses of a certain psalm came to her, saying God delivered those who cried to him even from things they had brought on themselves, and she had been doing nothing wrong! She tried to trust in him, but could not: he was as far from her as the blue heavens! True, it bent over all, but its one great eye was much too large to see the trouble she was in! What did it matter to the blue sky if she fell down and withered up to bones and dust! She well might-for here no foot of man might pass till she was a thing terrible to look at! If there was nobody where seemed to be nothing, how fearfully empty was the universe! Ah, if she had God for her friend! What if he was her friend, and she had not known it because she never spoke to him, never asked him to do anything for her? It was horrible to think it could be a mere chance whether she got home, or died there! She would pray to God! She would ask him to take her home!

A wintery blast came from the north. The black cloud had risen, and was now spreading over the zenith. Again the wind came with an angry burst and snarl. Snow carne swept upon it in hard sharp little pellets. She started up, and forgot to pray.

Some sound in the wind or some hidden motion of memory all at once let loose upon her another fear, which straight was agony. A rumour had reached the New House the night before, that a leopard had broken from a caravan, and got away to the hills. It was but a rumour; some did not believe it, and the owners contradicted it, but a party had set out with guns and dogs. It was true! it was true! There was the terrible creature crouching behind that stone! He was in every clump of heather she passed, swinging his tail, and ready to spring upon her! He must be hungry by this time, and there was nothing there for him to eat but her! By and by, however, she was too cold to be afraid, too cold to think, and presently, half-frozen and faint for lack of food, was scarce able to go a step farther. She saw a great rock, sank down in the shelter of it, and in a minute was asleep. She slept for some time, and woke a little refreshed. The wonder is that she woke at all. It was dark, and her first consciousness was ghastly fear. The wind had ceased, and the storm was over. Little snow had fallen. The stars were all out overhead, and the great night was round her, enclosing, watching her. She tried to rise, and could just move her limbs. Had she fallen asleep again, she would not have lived through the night. But it is idle to talk of what would have been; nothing could have been but what was. Mercy wondered afterwards that she did not lose her reason. She must, she thought, have been trusting somehow in God.

It was terribly dreary. Sure never one sorer needed God's help! And what better reason could there be for helping her than that she so sorely needed it! Perhaps God had let her walk into this trouble that she might learn she could not do without him! She—would try to be good! How terrible was the world, with such wide spaces and nobody in them!

And all the time, though she did not know it, she was sobbing and weeping.

The black silence was torn asunder by the report of a gun. She started up with a strange mingling of hope and terror, gave a loud cry, and sank senseless. The leopard would be upon her!

Her cry was her deliverance.

CHAPTER XVII.

IN THE TOMB.

The brothers had that same morning paid their visit to the tomb, and there spent the day after their usual fashion, intending to go home the same night, and as the old moon was very late in rising, to take the earlier and rougher part of the way in the twilight. Just as they were setting out, however, what they rightly judged a passing storm came on, and they delayed their departure. By the time the storm was over, it was dark, and there was no use in hurrying; they might as well stop a while, and have the moon the latter part of the way. When at length they were again on the point of starting, they thought they heard something like sounds of distress, but the darkness making search difficult and unsatisfactory, the chief thought of firing his gun, when Mercy's cry guided them to where she lay. Alister's heart, at sight of her, and at the thought of what she must have gone through, nearly stood still. They carried her in, laid her on the bed, and did what they could to restore her, till she began to come to herself. Then they left her, that she might not see them without preparation, and sat down by the fire in the outer room, leaving the door open between the two.

"I see how it is!" said Alister. "You remember, Ian, what you said to her about giving Nature an opportunity of exerting her influence? Mercy has been following your advice, and has lost her way among the hills!"

"That was so long ago!" returned Ian thoughtfully.

"Yes-when the weather was not fit for it. It is not fit now, but she has ventured!"

"I believe you are right! I thought there was some reality in her!-But she must not hear us talking about her!"

When Mercy came to herself, she thought at first that she lay where she had fallen, but presently perceived that she was covered, and had something hot at her feet: was she in her own bed? was it all a terrible dream, that she might know what it was to be lost, and think of God? .She put out her arm: her hand went against cold stone. The dread thought rushed in-that she was buried-was lying in her grave-to lie there till the trumpet should sound, and the dead be raised. She was not horrified; her first feeling was gladness that she had prayed before she died. She had been taught at church that an hour might come when it would be of no use to pray-the hour of an unbelieving death: it was of no use to pray now, but her prayer before she died might be of some avail! She wondered that she was not more frightened, for in sooth it was a dreary prospect before her: long and countless years must pass ere again she heard the sound of voices, again saw the light of the sun! She was half awake and half dreaming; the faintness of her swoon yet upon her, the repose following her great weariness, and the lightness of her brain from want of food, made her indifferent-almost happy. She could lie so a long time, she thought.

At length she began to hear sounds, and they were of human voices. She had companions then in the grave! she was not doomed to a solitary waiting for judgment! She must be in some family-vault, among strangers. She hoped they were nice people: it was very desirable to be buried with nice people!

Then she saw a reddish light. It was a fire—far off! Was she in the bad place? Were those shapes two demons, waiting till she had got over her dying? She listened:—"That will divide her between us," said one. "Yes," answered the other; "there will be no occasion to cut it! "What dreadful thing could they mean? But surely she had heard their voices before! She tried to speak, but could not.

"We must come again soon!" said one. "At this rate it will take a life-time to carve the tomb."

"If we were but at the roof of it!" said the other. "I long to tackle the great serpent of eternity, and lay him twining and coiling and undulating all over it! I dream about those tombs before ever they were broken into-royally furnished in the dark, waiting for the souls to come back to their old, brown, dried up bodies!"

Here one of them rose and came toward her, growing bigger and blacker as he came, until he stood by the bedside. He laid his hand on her wrist, and felt her pulse. It was Ian! She could not see his face for there was no light on it, but she knew his shape, his movements! She was saved!

He saw her wide eyes, two great spiritual nights, gazing up at him.

"All, you are better, Miss Mercy!" lie said cheerily. "Now you shall have some tea!"

Something inside her was weeping for joy, but her outer self was quite still. She tried again to speak, and uttered a few inarticulate sounds. Then came Alister on tip-toe, and they stood both by the bedside, looking down on her.

"I shall be all right presently!'" she managed at length to say. "I am so glad I'm not dead! I thought I was dead!"

"You would soon have been if we had not found you!" replied Alister.

"Was it you that fired the gun?"

"Yes."

"I was so frightened!"

"It saved your life, thank God! for then you cried out."

"Fright was your door out of fear!" said Ian.

"I thought it was the leopard!"

"I did bring my gun because of the leopard," said Alister.

"It was true about him then?"

"He is out."

"And now it is quite dark!"

"It doesn't signify; we'll take a lantern; I've got my gun, and Ian has his dirk!"

"Where are you going then?" asked Mercy, still confused.

"Home, of course."

"Oh, yes, of course! I will get up in a minute."

"There is plenty of time," said Ian. "You must eat something before you get up. We, have nothing but oat-cakes, I am sorry to say!"

"I think you promised me some tea!" said Mercy. "I don't feel hungry."

"You shall have the tea. When did you eat last?"

"Not since breakfast."

"It is a marvel you are able to speak! You must try to eat some oat-cake."

"I wish I hadn't taken that last slice of deer-ham!" said Alister, ruefully.

"I will eat if I can," said Mercy.

They brought her a cup of tea and some pieces of oat-cake; then, having lighted her a candle, they left her, and closed the door.

She sipped her tea, managed to eat a little of the dry but wholesome food, and found herself capable of getting up. It was the strangest bedroom! she thought. Everything was cut out of the live rock. The dressing-table might have been a sarcophagus! She kneeled by the bedside, and tried to thank God. Then she opened the door. The chief rose at the sound of it.

"I'm sorry," he said, "that we have no woman to wait on you."

"I want nothing, thank you!" answered Mercy, feeling very weak and ready to cry, but restraining her tears. "What a curious house this is!"

"It is a sort of doll's house my brother and I have been at work upon for nearly fifteen years. We meant, when summer was come, to ask you all to spend a day with us up here."

"Whhen first we went to work on it," said Ian, "we used to tell each other tales in which it bore a large share, and Alister's were generally about a lost princess taking refuge in it!"

"And now it is come true!" said Alister.

"What an escape I have had!"

"I do not like to hear you say that!" returned Ian. "You have been taken care of all the time. If you had died in the cold, it would not have been because God had forgotten you; you would not have been lost."

"I wanted to know," said Mercy, "whether Nature would speak to me. It was of no use! She never came near me!"

"I think she must have come without your knowing her," answered Ian. "But we shall have a talk about that afterwards, when you are quite rested; we must prepare for home now."

Mercy's heart sank within her—she felt so weak and sleepy! How was she to go back over all that rough mountain-way! But she dared not ask to be left-with the leopard about! He might come down the wide chimney!

She soon found that the brothers had never thought of her walking. They wrapt her in Ian's plaid. Then they took the chiefs, which was very strong, and having folded it twice lengthwise, drew each an end of it over his shoulders, letting it hang in a loop between them: in this loop they made her seat herself, and putting each as arm behind her, tried how they could all get on.

After a few shiftings and accommodations, they found the plan likely to answer. So they locked the door, and left the fire glowing on the solitary hearth.

To Mercy it was the strangest journey—an experience never to be forgotten. The tea had warmed her, and the air revived her. It was not very cold, for only now and then blew a little puff of wind. The stars were brilliant overhead, and the wide void of the air between her and the earth below seemed full of wonder and mystery. Now and then she fancied some distant sound the cry of the leopard: he might be coming nearer and nearer as they went! but it rather added to the eerie witchery of the night, making it like a terrible story read in the deserted nursery, with the distant noise outside of her brothers and sisters at play. The motion of her progress by and by became pleasant to her. Sometimes her feet would brush the tops of the heather; but when they came to rocky ground, they always shortened the loop of the plaid. To Mercy's inner ear came the sound of words she had heard at church: "He shall give his angels charge over thee, and in their hands they shall bear thee up, lest at any time thou dash thy foot against a stone." Were not these two men God's own angels!

They scarcely spoke, except when they stopped to take breath, but went on and on with a steady, rhythmic, silent trudge. Up and down the rough hill, and upon the hardly less rough hill-road, they had enough ado to heed their steps. Now and then they would let her walk a little way, but not far. She was neither so strong nor so heavy as a fat deer, they said.

They were yet high among the hills, when the pale, withered, waste shred of the old moon rose above the upheaved boat-like back of one of the battlements of the horizon-rampart. With disconsolate face, now lost, now found again, always reappearing where Mercy had not been looking for her, she accompanied them the rest of their journey, and the witch-like creature brought out the whole character of the night. Booked in her wonderful swing, Mercy was not always quite sure that she was not dreaming the strangest, pleasantest dream. Were they not fittest for a dream, this star and moon beset night-this wind that now and then blew so eerie and wild, yet did not wake her-this gulf around, above, and beneath her, through which she was borne as if she had indeed died, and angels were carrying her through wastes of air to some unknown region afar? Except when she brushed the heather, she forgot that the earth was near her. The arms around her were the arms of men and not angels, but how far above this lower world dwelt the souls that moved those strong limbs! What a small creature she was beside them! how unworthy of the labour of their deliverance! Her awe of the one kept growing; the other she could trust with heart as well as brain; she could never be afraid of him! To the chief she turned to shadow her from Ian.

When they came to the foot of the path leading up to Mistress Conal's cottage, there, although it was dark night, sat the old woman on a stone.

"It's a sorrow you are carrying home with you, chief!" she said in Gaelic. "As well have saved a drowning man!"

She did not rise or move, but spoke like one talking by the fireside.

"The drowning man has to be saved, mother!" answered the chief, also in Gaelic; "and the sorrow in your way has to be taken with you. It won't let you pass!"

"True, my son!" said the woman; "but it makes the heart sore that sees it!"

-"Thank you for the warning then, but welcome the sorrow!" he returned. "Good night."

"Good night, chiefs sons both!" she replied. "You're your father's anyway! Did he not one night bring home a frozen fox in his arms, to warm him by his fire! But when he had warmed him-lie turned him out!"

It was quite clear when last they looked at the sky, but the moment they left her, it began to rain heavily.

So fast did it rain, that the men, fearing for Mercy, turned off the road, and went down a steep descent, to make straight across their own fields for the cottage; and just as they reached the bottom of the descent, although they had come all the rough way hitherto without slipping or stumbling—once, the chief fell. He rose in consternation; but finding that Mercy, upheld by Ian, had simply dropped on her feet, and taken no hurt, relieved himself by un- sparing abuse of his clumsiness. Mercy laughed merrily, resumed her place in the plaid, and closed her eyes. She never saw where they were going, for she opened them again only when they stopped a little as they turned into the fir-clump before the door.

"Where are we?" she asked; but for answer they carried her straight into the house.

"We have brought you to our mother instead of yours," said Alister. "To get wet would have been the last straw on the back of such a day. We will let them know at once that you are safe."

Lady Macruadh, as the highlanders generally called her, made haste to receive the poor girl with that sympathetic pity which, of all good plants, flourishes most in the Celtic heart. Mercy's mother had come to her in consternation at her absence, and the only comfort she could give her was the suggestion that she had fallen in with her sons. She gave her a warm bath,-put her to bed, and then made her eat, so preparing her for a healthful sleep. And she did sleep, but dreamed of darkness and snow and leopards.

As men were out searching in all directions, Alister, while Ian went to the New House, lighted a beacon on the top of the old castle to bring them back. By the time Ian had persuaded Mrs. Palmer to leave Mercy in his mother's care for the night, it was blazing beautifully.

In the morning it was found that Mercy had a bad cold, and could not be moved. But the cottage, small as it was, had more than one guest-chamber, and Mrs. Macruadh was delighted to have her to nurse.

END OF VOL. II.

VOL. III.

CONTENTS OF VOL. III.

CHAPTER

WHAT'S MINE'S MINE

CHAPTER I

AT A HIGH SCHOOL.

When Mercy was able to go down to the drawing-room, she found the evenings pass as never evenings passed before; and during the day, although her mother and Christina came often to see her, she had time and quiet for thinking. And think she must; for she found herself in a region of human life so different from any she had hitherto entered, that in no other circumstances would she have been able to recognize even its existence. Everything said or done in it seemed to acknowledge something understood. Life went on with a continuous lean toward something rarely mentioned, plainly uppermost; it embodied a tacit reference of everything to some code so thoroughly recognized that occasion for alluding to it was unfrequent. Its inhabitants appeared to know things which her people did not even suspect. The air of the brothers especially was that of men at their ease yet ready to rise—of men whose loins were girded, alert for an expected call.

Under their influence a new idea of life, and the world, and the relations of men and things, began to grow in the mind of Mercy. There was a dignity, almost grandeur, about the simple life of the cottage, and the relation of its inmates to all they came near. No one of them seemed to live for self, but each to be thinking and caring for the others and for the clan. She awoke to see that manners are of the soul; that such as she had hitherto heard admired were not to be compared with the simple, almost peasant-like dignity and courtesy of the chief; that the natural grace, accustomed ease, and cultivated refinement of Ian's carriage, came out in attention and service to the lowly even more than in converse with his equals; while his words, his gestures, his looks, every expression born of contact, witnessed a directness and delicacy of recognition she could never have imagined. The moment he began to speak to another, he seemed to pass out of himself, and sit in the ears of the other to watch his own words, lest his thoughts should take such sound or shape as might render them unwelcome or weak. If they were not to be pleasant words, they should yet be no more unpleasant than was needful; they should not hurt save in the nature of that which they bore; the truth should receive no injury by admixture of his personality. He heard with his own soul, and was careful over the other soul as one of like kind. So delicately would he initiate what might be communion with another, that to a nature too dull or selfish to understand him, he gave offence by the very graciousness of his approach.

It was through her growing love to Alister that Mercy became able to understand Ian, and perceived at length that her dread, almost dislike of him at first, was owing solely to her mingled incapacity and unworthiness. Before she left the cottage, it was spring time in her soul; it had begun to put forth the buds of eternal life. Such buds are not unfrequently nipped; but even if they are, if a dull, false, commonplace frost close in, and numb the half wakened spirit back into its wintry sleep, that sleep will ever after be haunted with some fainting airs of the paradise those buds prophesied. In Mercy's case they were to grow into spiritual eyes—to open and see, through all the fogs and tumults of this phantom world, the light and reality of the true, the spiritual world everywhere around her—as the opened eyes of the servant of the prophet saw the mountains of Samaria full of horses of fire and chariots of fire around him. Every throb of true love, however mingled with the foolish and the false, is a bourgeoning of the buds of the life eternal—ah, how far from leaves! how much farther from flowers.

Ian was high above her, so high that she shrank from him; there seemed a whole heaven of height between them. It would fill her with a kind of despair to see him at times sit lost in thought: he was where she could never follow him! He was in a world which, to her childish thought, seemed not the world of humanity; and she would turn, with a sense of both seeking and finding, to the chief. She imagined he felt as she did, saw between his brother and him a gulf he could not cross. She did not perceive this difference, that Alister knew the gulf had to be crossed. At such a time, too, she had seen his mother regarding him with a similar expression of loss, but with a mingling of anxiety that was hers only. It was sweet to Mercy to see in the eyes of Alister, and in his whole bearing toward his younger brother, that he was a learner like herself, that they were scholars together in Ian's school.

A hunger after something beyond her, a something she could not have described, awoke in her. She needed a salvation of some kind, toward which she must grow! She needed a change which she could not understand until it came—a change the greatest in the universe, but which, man being created with the absolute necessity for it, can be no violent transformation, can be only a grand process in the divine idea of development.

She began to feel a mystery in the world, and in all the looks of it—a mystery because a meaning. She saw a jubilance in every sunrise, a sober sadness in every sunset; heard a whispering of strange secrets in the wind of the twilight; perceived a consciousness of unknown bliss in the song of the lark;—and was aware of a something beyond it all, now and then filling her with wonder, and compelling her to ask, "What does it, what can it mean?" Not once did she suspect that Nature had indeed begun to deal with her; not once suspect, although from childhood accustomed to hear the name of Love taken in vain, that love had anything to do with these inexplicable experiences.

Let no one, however, imagine he explains such experiences by suggesting that she was in love! That were but to mention another mystery as having introduced the former. For who in heaven or on earth has fathomed the marvel betwixt the man and the woman? Least of all the man or the woman who has not learned to regard it with reverence. There is more in this love to uplift us, more to condemn the lie in us, than in any other inborn drift of our being, except the heavenly tide Godward. From it flow all the other redeeming relations of life. It is the hold God has of us with his right hand, while death is the hold he has of us with his left. Love and death are the two marvels, yea the two terrors—but the one goal of our history.

It was love, in part, that now awoke in Mercy a hunger and thirst after heavenly things. This is a direction of its power little heeded by its historians; its earthly side occupies almost all their care. Because lovers are not worthy of even its earthly aspect, it palls upon them, and they grow weary, not of love, but of their lack of it. The want of the heavenly in it has caused it to perish: it had no salt. From those that have not is taken away that which they have. Love without religion is the plucked rose. Religion without love—there is no such thing. Religion is the bush that bears all the roses; for religion is the natural condition of man in relation to the eternal facts, that is the truths, of his own being. To live is to love; there is no life but love. What shape the love puts on, depends on the persons between whom is the relation. The poorest love with religion, is better, because truer, therefore more lasting, more genuine, more endowed with the possibility of persistence—that is, of infinite development, than the most passionate devotion between man and woman without it.

Thus together in their relation to Ian, it was natural that Mercy and the chief should draw yet more to each other. Mercy regarded Alister as a big brother in the same class with herself, but able to help her. Quickly they grew intimate. In the simplicity of his large nature, the chief talked with Mercy as openly as a boy, laying a heart bare to her such that, if the world had many like it, the kingdom of heaven would be more than at hand. He talked as to an old friend in perfect understanding with him, from whom he had nothing to gain or to fear. There was never a compliment on the part of the man, and never a coquetry on the part of the girl—a dull idea to such as without compliment or coquetry could hold no intercourse, having no other available means. Mercy had never like her sister cultivated the woman's part in the low game; and her truth required but the slightest stimulus to make her incapable of it. With such a man as Alister she could use only a simplicity like his; not thus to meet him would have been to decline the honouring friendship. Dark and plain, though with an interesting face and fine eyes, she had received no such compliments as had been showered upon her sister; it was an unspoiled girl, with a heart alive though not yet quite awake, that was brought under such good influences. What better influences for her, for any woman, than those of unselfish men? what influences so good for any man as those of unselfish women? Every man that hears and learns of a worthy neighbour, comes to the Father; every man that hath heard and learned of the Father comes to the Lord; every man that comes to the Lord, he leads back to the Father. To hear Ian speak one word about Jesus Christ, was for a true man to be thenceforth truer. To him the Lord was not a theological personage, but a man present in the world, who had to be understood and obeyed by the will and heart and soul, by the imagination and conscience of every other man. If what Ian said was true, this life was a serious affair, and to be lived in downright earnest! If God would have his creatures mind him, she must look to it! She pondered what she heard. But she went always to Alister to have Ian explained; and to hear him talk of Ian, revealed Alister to her.

When Mercy left the cottage, she felt as if she were leaving home to pay a visit. The rich house was dull and uninteresting. She found that she had immediately to put in practice one of the lessons she had learned—that the service of God is the service of those among whom he has sent us. She tried therefore to be cheerful, and even to forestall her mother's wishes. But life was harder than hitherto—so much more was required of her.

The chief was falling thoroughly in love with Mercy, but it was some time before he knew it. With a heart full of tenderness toward everything human, he knew little of love special, and was gradually sliding into it without being aware of it. How little are we our own! Existence is decreed us; love and suffering are appointed us. We may resist, we may modify; but we cannot help loving, and we cannot help dying. We need God to keep us from hating. Great in goodness, yea absolutely good, God must be, to have a right to make us—to compel our existence, and decree its laws! Without his choice the chief was falling in love. The woman was sent him; his heart opened and took her in. Relation with her family was not desirable, but there she was! Ian saw, but said nothing. His mother saw it too.

"Nothing good will come of it!" she said, with a strong feeling of unfitness in the thing.

"Everything will come of it, mother, that God would have come of it," answered Ian. "She is an honest, good girl, and whatever comes of it must be good, whether pleasant or not."

The mother was silent. She believed in God, but not so thoroughly as to abjure the exercise of a subsidiary providence of her own. The more people trust in God, the less will they trust their own judgments, or interfere with the ordering of events. The man or woman who opposes the heart's desire of another, except in aid of righteousness, is a servant of Satan. Nor will it avail anything to call that righteousness which is of Self or of Mammon.

"There is no action in fretting," Ian would say, "and not much in the pondering of consequences. True action is the doing of duty, come of it heartache, defeat, or success."

"You are a fatalist, Ian!" said his mother one day.

"Mother, I am; the will of God is my fate!" answered Ian. "He shall do with me what he pleases; and I will help him!"

She took him in her arms and kissed him. She hoped God would not he strict with him, for might not the very grandeur of his character be rooted in rebellion? Might not some figs grow on some thistles?

At length came the paternal summons for the Palmers to go to London. For a month the families had been meeting all but every day. The chief had begun to look deep into the eyes of the girl, as if searching there for some secret joy; and the girl, though she drooped her long lashes, did not turn her head away. And now separation, like death, gave her courage, and when they parted, Mercy not only sustained Alister's look, but gave him such a look in return that he felt no need, no impulse to say anything. Their souls were satisfied, for they knew they belonged to each other.

CHAPTER II

A TERRIBLE DISCOVERY.

So entirely were the chief and his family out of the world, that they had not yet a notion of the worldly relations of Mr. Peregrine Palmer. But the mother thought it high time to make inquiry as to his position and connections. She had an old friend in London, the wife of a certain vice-chancellor, with whom she held an occasional correspondence, and to her she wrote, asking if she knew anything of the family.

Mrs. Macruadh was nowise free from the worldliness that has regard to the world's regard. She would not have been satisfied that a daughter in law of hers should come of people distinguished for goodness and greatness of soul, if they were, for instance, tradespeople. She would doubtless have preferred the daughter of an honest man, whatever his position, to the daughter of a scoundrel, even if he chanced to be a duke; but she would not have been content with the most distinguished goodness by itself. Walking after Jesus, she would have drawn to the side of Joanna rather than Martha or Mary; and I fear she would have condescended—just a little—to Mary Magdalen: repentance, however perfect, is far from enough to satisfy the worldy squeamishness of not a few high-principled people who do not know what repentance means.

Mrs. Macruadh was anxious to know that the girl was respectable, and so far worthy of her son. The idea of such an inquiry would have filled Mercy's parents with scornful merriment, as a thing ludicrous indeed. People in THEIR position, who could do this and that, whose name stood so high for this and that, who knew themselves well bred, who had one relation an admiral, another a general, and a marriage-connection with some of the oldest families in the country—that one little better than a yeoman, a man who held the plough with his own big hands, should enquire into THEIR social standing! Was not Mr. Peregrine Palmer prepared to buy him up the moment he required to sell! Was he not rich enough to purchase an earl's daughter for his son, and an earl himself for his beautiful Christina! The thing would have seemed too preposterous.

The answer of the vice-chancellor's lady burst, nevertheless, like a bombshell in the cottage. It was to this effect:—The Palmers were known, if not just in the best, yet in very good society; the sons bore sign of a defective pedigree, but the one daughter out was, thanks to her mother, fit to go anywhere. For her own part, wrote the London correspondent, she could not help smelling the grains: in Scotland a distiller, Mr. Peregrine Palmer had taken to brewing in England—was one of the firm Pulp and Palmer, owning half the public-houses in London, therefore high in the regard of the English nobility, if not actually within their circle.—Thus far the satirical lady of the vice-chancellor.

Horror fell upon the soul of the mother. The distiller was to her as the publican to the ancient Jew. No dealing in rags and marine stores, no scraping of a fortune by pettifogging, chicane, and cheating, was to her half so abominable as the trade of a brewer. Worse yet was a brewer owning public-houses, gathering riches in half-pence wet with beer and smelling of gin. The brewer was to her a moral pariah; only a distiller was worse. As she read, the letter dropped from her hands, and she threw them up in unconscious appeal to heaven. She saw a vision of bloated men and white-faced women, drawing with trembling hands from torn pockets the money that had bought the wide acres of the Clanruadh. To think of the Macruadh marrying the daughter of such a man! In society few questions indeed were asked; everywhere money was counted a blessed thing, almost however made; none the less the damnable fact remained, that certain moneys were made, not in furthering the well-being of men and women, but in furthering their sin and degradation. The mother of the chief saw that, let the world wink itself to blindness, let it hide the roots of the money-plant in layer upon layer of social ascent, the flower for which an earl will give his daughter, has for the soil it grows in, not the dead, but the diseased and dying, of loathsome bodies and souls of God's men and women and children, which the grower of it has helped to make such as they are.

She was hot, she was cold; she started up and paced hurriedly about the room. Her son the son in law of a distiller! the husband of his daughter!

The idea was itself abhorrence and contempt! Was he not one of the devil's fishers, fishing the sea of the world for the souls of men and women to fill his infernal ponds withal! His money was the fungous growth of the devil's cellars. How would the brewer or the distiller, she said, appear at the last judgment! How would her son hold up his head, if he cast in his lot with theirs! But that he would never do! Why should she be so perturbed! in this matter at least there could be no difference between them! Her noble Alister would be as much shocked as herself at the news! Could the woman be a lady, grown on such a hothed! Yet, alas! love could tempt far —could subdue the impossible!

She could not rest; she must find one of them! Not a moment longer could she remain alone with the terrible disclosure. If Alister was in love with the girl, he must get out of it at once! Never again would she enter the Palmers' gate, never again set foot on their land! The thought of it was unthinkable! She would meet them as if she did not see them! But they should know her reason—and know her inexorable!

She went to the edge of the ridge, and saw Ian sitting with his book on the other side of the burn. She called him to her, and handed him the letter. He took it, read it through, and gave it her back.

"Ian!" she exclaimed, "have you nothing to say to that?"

"I beg your pardon, mother," he answered: "I must think about it. Why should it trouble you so! It is painfully annoying, but we have come under no obligation to them!"

"No; but Alister!"

"You cannot doubt Alister will do what is right!"

"He will do what he thinks right!"

"Is not that enough, mother?"

"No," she answered angrily; "he must do the thing that is right."

"Whether he knows it or not? Could he do the thing he thought wrong?"

She was silent.

"Mother dear," resumed Ian, "the only Way to get at what IS right is to do what seems right. Even if we mistake there is no other way!"

"You would do evil that good may come! Oh, Ian!"

"No, mother; evil that is not seen to be evil by one willing and trying to do right, is not counted evil to him. It is evil only to the person who either knows it to be evil, or does not care whether it be or not."

"That is dangerous doctrine!"

"I will go farther, mother, and say, that for Alister to do what you thought right, if he did not think it right himself—even if you were right and he wrong—would be for him to do wrong, and blind himself to the truth."

"A man may be to blame that he is not able to see the truth," said the mother.

"That is very true, but hardly such a man as Alister, who would sooner die than do the thing he believed wrong. But why should you take it for granted that Alister will think differently from you?"

"We don't always think alike."

"In matters of right and wrong, I never knew him or me think differently from you, mother!"

"He is very fond of the girl!"

"And justly. I never saw one more in earnest, or more anxious to learn."

"She might well be teachable to such teachers!"

"I don't see that she has ever sought to commend herself to either of us, mother. I believe her heart just opened to the realities she had never had shown her before. Come what may, she will never forget the things we have talked about."

"Nothing would make me trust her!"

"Why?"

"She comes of an' abominable breed."

"Is it your part, mother, to make her suffer for the sins of her fathers?"

"I make her suffer!"

"Certainly, mother—by changing your mind toward her, and suspecting her, the moment you learn cause to condemn her father."

"The sins of the fathers are visited on the children!—You will not dispute that?'

"I will grant more—that the sins of the fathers are often reproduced in the children. But it is nowhere said, 'Thou shalt visit the sins of the fathers on the children.' God puts no vengeance into our hands. I fear you are in danger of being unjust to the girl, mother!—but then you do not know her so well as we do!"

"Of course not! Every boy understands a woman better than his mother!"

"The thing is exceedingly annoying, mother! Let us go and find Alister at once!"

"He will take it like a man of sense, I trust!"

"He will. It will trouble him terribly, but he will do as he ought. Give him time and I don't believe there is a man in the world to whom the right comes out clearer than to Alister."

The mother answered only with a sigh.

"Many a man," remarked Ian, "has been saved through what men call an unfortunate love affair!"

"Many a man has been lost by having his own way in one!" rejoined the mother.

"As to LOST, I would not make up my mind about that for a few centuries or so!" returned lan. "A man may be allowed his own way for the discipline to result from it."

"I trust, lan, you will not encourage him in any folly!"

"I shall have nothing to do but encourage him in his first resolve, mother!"

CHAPTER III

HOW ALISTER TOOK IT.

They could not find Alister, who had gone to the smithy. It was tea-time before he came home. As soon as he entered, his mother handed him the letter.

He read it without a word, laid it on the table beside his plate, and began to drink his tea, his eyes gleaming with a strange light, Ian kept silence also. Mrs. Macruadh cast a quick glance, now at the one, now at the other. She was in great anxiety, and could scarce restrain herself. She knew her boys full of inbred dignity and strong conscience, but was nevertheless doubtful how they would act. They could not feel as she felt, else would the hot blood of their race have at once boiled over! Had she searched herself she might have discovered a latent dread that they might be nearer the right than she. Painfully she watched them, half conscious of a traitor in her bosom, judging the world's judgment and not God's. Her sons seemed on the point of concluding as she would not have them conclude: they would side with the young woman against their mother!

The reward of parents who have tried to be good, may be to learn, with a joyous humility from their children. Mrs. Macruadh was capable of learning more, and was now going to have a lesson.

When Alister pushed back his chair and rose, she could refrain no longer. She could not let him go in silence. She must understand something of what was passing in his mind!

"What do you think of THAT, Alister?" she said.

He turned to her with a faint smile, and answered,

"I am glad to know it, mother."

"That is good. I was afraid it would hurt you!"

"Seeing the thing is so, I am glad to be made aware of it. The information itself you cannot expect me to be pleased with!"

"No, indeed, my son! I am very sorry for you. After being so taken with the young woman,—"

Alister looked straight in his mother's face.

"You do not imagine, mother," he said, "it will make any difference as to Mercy?"

"Not make any difference!" echoed Mrs. Macruadh. "What is it possible you can mean, Alister?"

The anger that glowed in her dark eyes made her look yet handsomer, proving itself not a mean, though it might be a misplaced anger.

"Is she different, mother, from what she was before you had the letter?"

"You did not then know what she was!"

"Just as well as I do now. I have no reason to think she is not what I thought her."

"You thought her the daughter of a gentleman!"

"Hardly. I thought her a lady, and such I think her still."

"Then you mean to go on with it?"

"Mother dear," said Alister, taking her by the hand, "give ine a little time. Not that I am in any doubt—but the news has been such a blow to me that —"

"It must have been!" said the mother.

"—that I am afraid of answering you out of the soreness of my pride, and Ian says the Truth is never angry."

"I am quite willing you should do nothing in a hurry," said the mother.

She did not understand that he feared lest, in his indignation for Mercy, he should answer his mother as her son ought not.

"I will take time," he replied. "And here is Ian to help me!"

"Ah! if only your father were here!"

"He may be, mother! Anyhow I trust I shall do nothing he would not like!"

"He would sooner see son of his marry the daughter of a cobbler than of a brewer!"

"So would I, mother!" said Alister.

"I too," said Ian, "would much prefer that my sister-in-law's father were not a brewer."

"I suppose you are splitting some hair, Ian, but I don't see it," remarked his mother, who had begun to gather a little hope. "You will be back by supper-time, Alister, I suppose?"

"Certainly, mother. We are only going to the village."

The brothers went.

"I knew everything you were thinking," said Ian.

"Of course you did!" answered Alister.

"But I am very sorry!"

"So am I! It is a terrible bore!"

A pause followed. Alister burst into a laugh that was not merry.

"It makes me think of the look on my father's face," he said, "once at the market, as he was putting in his pocket a bunch of more than usually dirty bank-notes. The look seemed almost to be making apology that he was rny father—the notes were SO DIRTY! 'They're better than they look, lad!' he said."

"What ARE you thinking of, Alister?"

"Of nothing you are not thinking of, lan, I hope in God! Mr. Palmer's money is worse than it looks."

"You frightened me for a moment, Alister!"

"How could I, lan?"

"It was but a nervo-mechanical fright. I knew well enough you could mean nothing I should not like. But I see trouble ahead, Alister!"

"We shall be called a pack of fools, but what of that! We shall be told the money itself was clean, however dirty the hands that made it! The money-grubs!"

"I would rather see you hanged, than pocketing a shilling of it!"

"Of course you would! But the man who could pocket it, will be relieved to find it is only his daughter I care about."

"There will be difficulty, Alister, I fear. How much have you said to Mercy?"

"I have SAID nothing definite."

"But she understands?"

"I think—I hope so.—Don't you think Christina is much improved, lan?"

"She is more pleasant."

"She is quite attentive to you!"

"She is pleased with me for saving her life. She does not like me—and I have just arrived at not disliking her."

"There is a great change on her!"

"I doubt if there is any IN her though!"

"She may be only amusing herself with us in this outlandish place! Mercy, I am sure, is quite different!"

"I would trust her with anything, Alister. That girl would die for the man she loved!"

"I would rather have her love, though we should never meet in this world, than the lands of my fathers!"

"What will you do then?"

"I will go to Mr. Palmer, and say to him: 'Give me your daughter. I am a poor man, but we shall have enough to live upon. I believe she will be happy.'"

"I will answer for him: 'I have the greatest regard for you, Macruadh. You are a gentleman, and that you are poor is not of the slightest consequence; Mercy's dowry shall be worthy the lady of a chief!'—What then, Alister?"

"Fathers that love money must be glad to get rid of their daughters without a. dowry!"

"Yes, perhaps, when they are misers, or money is scarce, or wanted for something else. But when a poor man of position wanted to marry his daughter, a parent like Mr. Palmer would doubtless regard her dowry as a good investment. You must not think to escape that way, Alister! What would you answer him?"

"I would say, 'My dear sir,'—I may say 'My dear sir,' may I not? there is something about the man I like!—'I do not want your money. I will not have your money. Give me your daughter, and my soul will bless you.'"

"Suppose he should reply,' Do you think I am going to send my daughter from my house like a beggar? No, no, my boy! she must carry something with her! If beggars married beggars, the world would be full of beggars!'—what would you say then?"

"I would tell him I had conscientious scruples about taking his money."

"He would tell you you were a fool, and not to be trusted with a wife. 'Who ever heard such rubbish!' he would say. 'Scruples, indeed! You must get over them! What are they?'—What would you say then?"

"If it came to that, I should have no choice but tell him I had insuperable objections to the way his fortune was made, and could not consent to share it."

"He would protest himself insulted, and swear, if his money was not good enough for you, neither was his daughter. What then?"

"I would appeal to Mercy."

"She is too young. It would be sad to set one of her years at variance with her family. I almost think I would rather you ran away with her. It is a terrible thing to go into a house and destroy the peace of those relations which are at the root of all that is good in the world."

"I know it! I know it! That is my trouble! I am not afraid of Mercy's courage, and I am sure she would hold out. I am certain nothing would make her marry the man she did not love. But to turn the house into a hell about her—I shrink from that!—Do you count it necessary to provide against every contingency before taking the first step?"

"Indeed I do not! The first step is enough. When that step has landed us, we start afresh. But of all things you must not lose your temper with the man. However despicable his money, you are his suitor for his daughter! And he may possibly not think you half good enough for her."

"That would be a grand way out of the difficulty!"

"How?"

"It would leave me far freer to deal with her."

"Perhaps. And in any case, the more we can honestly avoid reference to his money, the better. We are not called on to rebuke."

"Small is my inclination to allude to it—so long as not a stiver of it seeks to cross to the Macruadh!"

"That is fast as fate. But there is another thing, Alister: I fear lest you should ever forget that her birth and her connections are no more a part of the woman's self than her poverty or her wealth."

"I know it, Ian. I will not forget it."

"There must never be a word concerning them!"

"Nor a thought, Ian! In God's name I will be true to her."

They found Annie of the shop in a sad way. She had just had a letter from Lachlan, stating that he had not been well for some time, and that there was little prospect of his being able to fetch her. He prayed her therefore to go out to him; and had sent money to pay her passage and her mother's.

"When do you go?" asked the chief.

"My mother fears the voyage, and is very unwilling to turn her back on her own country. But oh, if Lachlan die, and me not with him!"

She could say no more.

"He shall not die for want of you!" said the laird. "I will talk to your mother."

He went into the room behind. Ian remained in the shop.

"Of course you must go, Annie!" he said.

"Indeed, sir, I must! But how to persuade my mother I do not know! And I cannot leave her even for Lachlan. No one would nurse him more tenderly than she; but she has a horror of the salt water, and what she most dreads is being buried in it. She imagines herself drowning to all eternity!"

"My brother will persuade her."

"I hope so, sir. I was just coming to him! I should never hold up my head again—in this world or the next—either if I did not go, or if I went without my mother! Aunt Conal told me, about a month since, that I was going a long journey, and would never come back. I asked her if I was to die on the way, but she would not answer me. Anyhow I'm not fit to be his wife, if I'm not ready to die for him! Some people think it wrong to marry anybody going to die, but at the longest, you know, sir, you must part sooner than you would! Not many are allowed to die together!—You don't think, do you, sir, that marriages go for nothing in the other world?"

She spoke with a white face and brave eyes, and Ian was glad at heart.

"I do not, Annie," he answered. "'The gifts of God are without repentance.' He did not give you and Lachlan to each other to part you again! Though you are not married yet, it is all the same so long as you are true to each other."

"Thank you, sir; you always make me feel strong!"

Alister came from the back room.

"I think your mother sees it not quite so difficult now," he said.

The next time they went, they found them preparing to go.

Now Ian had nearly finished the book he was writing about Russia, and could not begin another all at once. He must not stay at home doing nothing, and he thought that, as things were going from bad to worse in the highlands, he might make a voyage to Canada, visit those of his clan, and see what ought to be done for such as must soon follow them. He would presently have a little money in his possession, and believed he could not spend it better. He made up his mind therefore to accompany Annie and her mother, which resolve overcame the last of the old woman's lingering reluctance. He did not like leaving Alister at such a critical point in his history; but he said to himself that a man might be helped too much; arid it might come that he and Mercy were in as much need of a refuge as the clan.

I cannot say NO worldly pride mingled in the chief's contempt for the distiller's money; his righteous soul was not yet clear of its inherited judgments as to what is dignified and what is not. He had in him still the prejudice of the landholder, for ages instinctive, against both manufacture and trade. Various things had combined to foster in him also the belief that trade at least was never free from more or less of unfair dealing, and was therefore in itself a low pursuit. He had not argued that nothing the Father of men has decreed can in its nature be contemptible, but must be capable of being nobly done. In the things that some one must do, the doer ranks in God's sight, and ought to rank among his fellow-men, according to how he does it. The higher the calling the more contemptible the man who therein pursues his own ends. The humblest calling, followed on the principles of the divine caller, is a true and divine calling, be it scavenging, handicraft, shop-keeping, or book-making. Oh for the day when God and not the king shall be regarded as the fountain of honour.

But the Macruadh looked upon the calling of the brewer or distiller as from the devil: he was not called of God to brew or distil! From childhood his mother had taught him a horror of gain by corruption. She had taught, and he had learned, that the poorest of all justifications, the least fit to serve the turn of gentleman, logician, or Christian, was—"If I do not touch this pitch, another will; there will be just as much harm done; AND

ANOTHER INSTEAD OF ME WILL HAVE THE BENEFIT; therefore it cannot defile me.—Offences must come, therefore I will do them!" "Imagine our Lord in the brewing trade instead of the carpentering!" she would say. That better beer was provided by the good brewer would not go far for brewer or drinker, she said: it mattered little that, by drinking good beer, the drunkard lived to be drunk the oftener. A brewer might do much to reduce drinking; but that would be to reduce a princely income to a modest livelihood, and to content himself with the baker's daughter instead of the duke's! It followed that the Macruadh would rather have robbed a church than touched Mr. Peregrine Palmer's money. To rifle the tombs of the dead would have seemed to him pure righteousness beside sharing in that. He could give Mercy up; he could NOT take such money with her! Much as he loved her, separate as he saw her, clearly as she was to him a woman undefiled and straight from God, it was yet a trial to him that she should be the daughter of a person whose manufacture and trade were such.

After much consideration, it was determined in the family conclave, that Ian should accompany the two women to Canada, note how things were going, and conclude what had best be done, should further exodus be found necessary. As, however, there had come better news of Lachlan, and it was plain he was in no immediate danger, they would not, for several reasons, start before the month of September. A few of the poorest of the clan resolved to go with them. Partly for their sakes, partly because his own provision would be small, Ian would take his passage also in the steerage.

CHAPTER IV

LOVE.

Christina went back to London considerably changed. Her beauty was greater far, for there was a new element in it—a certain atmosphere of distances and shadows gave mystery to her landscape. Her weather, that is her mood, was now subject to changes which to many made her more attractive. Fits of wild gaiety alternated with glooms, through which would break flashes of feline playfulness, where pat and scratch were a little mixed. She had more admirers than ever, for she had developed points capable of interesting men of somewhat higher development than those she had hitherto pleased. At the same time she was more wayward and imperious with her courtiers. Gladly would she have thrown all the flattery once so coveted into the rag-bag of creation, to have one approving smile from the grave-looking, gracious man, whom she knew happier, wandering alone over the hills, than if she were walking by his side. For an hour she would persuade herself that he cared for her a little; the next she would comfort herself with the small likelihood of his meeting another lady in Glenruadh. But then he had been such a traveller, had seen so much of the great world, that perhaps he was already lost to her! It seemed but too probable, when she recalled the sadness with which he seemed sometimes overshadowed: it could not be a religious gloom, for when he spoke of God his face shone, and his words were strong! I think she mistook a certain gravity, like that of the Merchant of Venice, for sorrowfulness; though doubtless the peculiarity of his loss, as well as the loss itself, did sometimes make him sad.

She had tried on him her little arts of subjugation, but the moment she began to love him, she not only saw their uselessness, but hated them. Her repellent behaviour to her admirers, and her occasional excitement and oddity, caused her mother some anxiety, but as the season came to a close, she grew gayer, and was at times absolutely bewitching. The mother wished to go northward by degrees, paying visits on the way; but her plan met with no approbation from the girls. Christina longed for the presence and voice of Ian in the cottage-parlour, Mercy for a hill-side with the chief;

both longed to hear them speak to each other in their own great way. And they talked so of the delights of their highland home, that the mother began to feel the mountains, the sea, and the islands, drawing her to a land of peace, where things went well, and the world knew how to live. But the stormiest months of her life were about to pass among those dumb mountains!

After a long and eager journey, the girls were once more in their rooms at the New House.

Mercy went to her window, and stood gazing from it upon the mountain-world, faint-lighted by the northern twilight. She might have said with Portia:—

"This   night   methinks   is   but   the   daylight   sick;
It   looks   a   little   paler: 'tis   a   day,
Such as the day is when the sun is hid."

She could see the dark bulk of the hills, sharpened to a clear edge against the pellucid horizon, but with no colour, and no visible featuring of their great fronts. When the sun rose, it would reveal innumerable varieties of surface, by the mottling of endless shadows; now all was smooth as an unawakened conscience. By the shape of a small top that rose against the greenish sky betwixt the parting lines of two higher hills, where it seemed to peep out over the marge into the infinite, as a little man through the gap between the heads of taller neighbours, she knew the roof of THE TOMB; and she thought how, just below there, away as it seemed in the high-lifted solitudes of heaven, she had lain in the clutches of death, all the time watched and defended by the angel of a higher life who had been with her ever since first she came to Glenruadh, waking her out of such a stupidity, such a non-existence, as now she could scarce see possible to human being. It was true her waking had been one with her love to that human East which first she saw as she opened her eyes, and whence first the light of her morning had flowed—the man who had been and was to her the window of God! But why should that make her doubt? God made man and woman to love each other: why should not the waking to love and the waking to truth come together, seeing both were of God? If the chief were never to speak to her again, she would never go back from what she had learned of him! If she ever became careless of truth and life and God, it would but show that she had never truly loved the chief!

As she stood gazing on the hill-top, high landmark of her history, she felt as if the earth were holding her up toward heaven, an offering to the higher life. The hill grew an altar of prayer on which her soul was lying, dead until taken up into life by the arms of the Father. A deep content pervaded her heart. She turned with her weight of peace, lay down, and went to sleep in the presence of her Life.

Christina looked also from her window, but her thoughts were not like Mercy's, for her heart was mainly filled, not with love of Ian, but with desire that Ian should love her. She longed to be his queen—the woman of all women he had seen. The sweet repose of the sleeping world wrought in her—not peace, but weakness. Her soul kept leaning towards Ian; she longed for his arms to start out the alien nature lying so self-satisfied all about her. To her the presence of God took shape as an emptiness—an absence. The resting world appeared to her cold, unsympathetic, heedless; its peace was but heartlessness. The soft pellucid chrysolite of passive heavenly thought, was a merest arrangement, a common fact, meaning nothing to her.

She was hungry, not merely after bliss, but after distinction in bliss; not after growth, but after acknowledged superiority. She needed to learn that she was nobody—that if the world were peopled with creatures like her, it would be no more worth sustaining than were it a world of sand, of which no man could build even a hut. Still, by her need of another, God was laying hold of her. As by the law is the knowledge of sin, so by love is selfishness rampantly roused—to be at last, like death, swallowed up in victory—the victory of the ideal self that dwells in God.

All night she dreamed sad dreams of Ian in the embrace of a lovely woman, without word or look for her. She woke weeping, and said to herself that it could not be. He COULD not be taken from her! it was against nature! Soul, brain, and heart, claimed him hers! How could another possess what, in the testimony of her whole consciousness, was hers and hers alone! Love asserts an innate and irreversible right of profoundest property in the person loved. It is an instinct—but how wrongly, undivinely, falsely interpreted! Hence so many tears! Hence a law of nature, deep written in the young heart, seems often set utterly at nought by circumstance!

But the girl in her dejection and doubt, was worth far more than in her content and confidence. She was even now the richer by the knowledge of sorrow, and she was on the way to know that she needed help, on the way to hate herself, to become capable of loving. Life could never be the same to her, and the farther from the same the better!

The beauty came down in the morning pale and dim and white-lipped, like a flower that had had no water. Mercy was fresh and rosy, with a luminous mist of loveliness over her plain unfinished features. Already had they begun to change in the direction of beauty. Christina's eyes burned; in Mercy's shone something of the light by which a soul may walk and not stumble. In the eyes of both was expectation, in the eyes of the one confident, in the eyes of the other anxious.

As soon as they found themselves alone together, eyes sought eyes, and met in understanding. They had not made confidantes of each other, each guessed well, and was well guessed at. They did not speculate; they understood. In like manner, Mercy and Alister understood each other, but not Christina and Ian. Neither of these knew the feelings of the other.

Without a word they rose, put on their hats, left the house, and took the road toward the valley.

About half-way to the root of the ridge, they came in sight of the ruined castle; Mercy stopped with a little cry.

"Look! Chrissy!" she said, pointing.

On the corner next them, close by the pepper-pot turret, sat the two men, in what seemed to loving eyes a dangerous position, but to the mountaineers themselves a comfortable coin of vantage. The girls thought, "They are looking out for us!" but Ian was there only because Alister was there.

The men waved their bonnets. Christina responded with her handkerchief. The men disappeared from their perch, and were with the ladies before they reached the ridge. There was no embarrassment on either side, though a few cheeks were rosier than usual. To the chief, Mercy was far beyond his memory of her. Not her face only, but her every movement bore witness to a deeper pleasure, a greater freedom in life than before.

"Why were you in such a dangerous place?" asked Christina.

"We were looking out for you," answered Alister." From there we could see you the moment you came out."

"Why didn't you come and meet us then?"

"Because we wanted to watch you coming."

"Spies!—I hope, Mercy, we were behaving ourselves properly! I had no idea we were watched!"

"We thought you had quarrelled; neither said a word to the other."

Mercy looked up; Christina looked down.

"Could you hear us at that height?" asked Mercy.

"How could we when there was not a word to hear!"

"How did you know we were silent?"

"We might have known by the way you walked," replied Alister. "But if you had spoken we should have heard, for sound travels far among the mountains!"

"Then I think it was a shame!" said Christina. "How could you tell that we might not object to your hearing us?"

"We never thought of that!" said Alister. "I am very sorry. We shall certainly not be guilty again!"

"What men you are for taking everything in downright earnest!" cried Christina; "—as if we could have anything to say we should wish YOU not to hear?"

She pat a little emphasis on the YOU, hut not much. Alister heard it as if Mercy had said it, and smiled a pleased smile.

"It will be a glad day for the world," he said, "when secrecy is over, and every man may speak out the thing that is in him, without danger of offence!"

In her turn, Christina heard the words as if spoken with reference to Ian though not by him, and took them to hint at the difficulty of saying what was in his heart. She had such an idea of her superiority because of her father's wealth and fancied position, that she at once concluded Ian dreaded rejection with scorn, for it was not even as if he were the chief. However poor, Alister was at least the head of a family, and might set SIR before, and BARONET after his name—not that her father would think that much of a dignity!—but no younger son of whatever rank, would be good enough for her in her father's eyes! At the same time she had a choice as well as her father, and he should find she too had a will of her own!

"But was it not a dangerous place to be in?" she said.

"It is a little crumbly!" confessed Ian. "—That reminds me, Alister, we must have a bout at the old walls before long!—Ever since Alister was ten years old," he went on in explanation to Christina, "he and I have been patching and pointing at the old hulk—the stranded ship of our poor fortunes. I showed you, did I not, the ship in our coat of arms—the galley at least, in which, they say, we arrived at the island?"

"Yes, I remember.—But you don't mean you do mason's work as well as everything else?" exclaimed Christina.

"Come; we will show you," said the chief.

"What do you do it for?"

The brothers exchanged glances.

"Would you count it sufficient reason," returned Ian, "that we desired to preserve its testimony to the former status of our family?"

A pang of pleasure shot through the heart of Christina. Passion is potent to twist in its favour whatever can possibly be so twisted. Here was an indubitable indication of his thoughts! He must make the most of himself, set what he could against the overwhelming advantages on her side! In the eyes of a man of the world like her father, an old name was nothing beside new money! still an old castle was always an old castle! and that he cared about it for her sake made it to her at least worth something!

Ere she could give an answer, Ian went on.

"But in truth," he said, "we have always had a vague hope of its resurrection. The dream of our boyhood was to rebuild the castle. Every year it has grown more hopeless, and keeps receding. But we have come to see how little it matters, and content ourselves with keeping up, for old love's sake, what is left of the ruin."

"How do you get up on the walls?" asked Mercy.

"Ah, that is a secret!" said Ian.

"Do tell us," pleaded Christina.

"If you want very much to know,—" answered Ian, a little doubtfully.

"I do, I do!"

"Then I suppose we must tell you!"

346

Yet more confirmation to the passion-prejudiced ears of Christina!

"There is a stair," Ian went on, "of which no one but our two selves knows anything. Such stairs are common in old houses—far commoner than people in towns have a notion of. But there would not have been much of it left by this time, if we hadn't taken care of it. We were little fellows when we began, and it needed much contrivance, for we were not able to unseat the remnants of the broken steps, and replace them with new ones."

"Do show it us," begged Christina.

"We will keep it," said Alister, "for some warm twilight. Morning is not for ruins. Yon mountain-side is calling to us. Will you come, Mercy?"

"Oh yes!" cried Christina; "that will be much better! Come, Mercy! You are up to a climb, I am sure!"

"I ought to be, after such a long rest."

"You may have forgotten how to climb!" said Alister.

"I dreamed too much of the hills for that! And always the noise of London was changed into the rush of waters."

They had dropped a little behind the other pair.

"Did you always climb your dream-hills alone?" asked Alister.

She answered him with just a lift of her big dark eyes.

They walked slowly down the road till they came to Mrs. Conal's path, passed her door unassailed, and went up the hill.

CHAPTER V

PASSION AND PATIENCE.

It was a glorious morning, and as they climbed, the lightening air made their spirits rise with their steps. Great masses of cloud hung beyond the edge of the world, and here and there towered foundationless in the sky— huge tumulous heaps of white vapour with gray shadows. The sun was strong, and poured down floods of light, but his heat was deliciously tempered by the mountain atmosphere. There was no wind—only an occasional movement as if the air itself were breathing—just enough to let them feel they moved in no vacuum, but in the heart of a gentle ocean.

They came to the hut I have already described as the one chiefly inhabited by Hector of the Stags and Bob of the Angels. It commanded a rare vision. In every direction rose some cone-shaped hill. The world lay in coloured waves before them, wild, rugged, and grand, with sheltering spots of beauty between, and the shine of lowly waters. They tapped at the door of the hut, but there was no response; they lifted the latch—it had no lock— and found neither within. Alister and Mercy wandered a little higher, to the shadow of a great stone; Christina went inside the hut and looked from its door upon the world; Ian leaned against the side of it, and looked up to the sky. Suddenly a few great drops fell—it was hard to say whence. The scattered clouds had been drawing a little nearer the sun, growing whiter as they approached him, and more had ascended from the horizon into the middle air, blue sky abounding between them. A swift rain, like a rain of the early summer, began to fall, and grew to a heavy shower. They were glorious drops that made that shower; for the sun shone, and every drop was a falling gem, shining, sparkling like a diamond, as it fell. It was a bounteous rain, coming from near the zenith, and falling in straight lines direct from heaven to earth. It wanted but sound to complete its charm, and that the bells of the heather gave, set ringing by the drops. The heaven was filled with blue windows, and the rain seemed to come from them rather than from the clouds. Into the rain rose the heads of the mountains, each clothed in its surplice of thin mist; they seemed rising on tiptoe heavenward, eager to drink of the high-born comfort; for the rain comes down, not upon the mown grass only, but upon the solitary and desert places also, where grass will never be—"the playgrounds of the young angels," Bob called them.

"Do come in," said Christina; "you will get quite wet!"

He turned towards her. She stepped back, and he entered. Like one a little weary, he sat down on Hector's old chair.

"Is anything the matter?" asked Christina, with genuine concern.

She saw that he was not quite like himself, that there was an unusual expression on his face. He gave a faint apologetic smile.

"As I stood there," he answered, "a strange feeling came over me—a foreboding, I suppose you would call it!"

He paused; Christina grew pale, and said, "Won't you tell me what it was?"

"It was an odd kind of conviction that the next time I stood there, it would not be in the body.—I think I shall not come back."

"Come back!" echoed Christina, fear beginning to sip at the cup of her heart. "Where are you going?"

"I start for Canada next week."

She turned deadly white, and put out her hands, feeling blindly after support. Ian started to his feet.

"We have tired you out!" he said in alarm, and took her by both hands to place her in the chair.

She did not hear him. The world had grown dark about her, a hissing noise was in her ears, and she would have fallen had he not put his arm round her. The moment she felt supported, she began to come to herself. There was no pretence, however, no coquetry in her faintness. Neither was it aught but misery and affection that made her lay her head on Ian's shoulder, and burst into a violent fit of weeping. Unused to real emotion, familiar only with the poverty-stricken, false emotion of conquest and gratified vanity, when the real emotion came she did not know how to deal with it, and it overpowered her.

"Oh! oh!" she cried at length between her sobs, "I am ashamed of myself! I can't help it! I can't help it! What will you think of me! I have disgraced myself!"

Ian had been far from any suspicion of the state of things, but he had had too much sorrowful experience to be able to keep his unwilling eyes closed to this new consternation. The cold shower seemed to flood his soul; the bright drops descending with such swiftness of beauty, instinct with sun-life, turned into points of icy steel that pierced his heart. But he must not heed himself! he must speak to her! He must say something through the terrible shroud that infolded them!

"You are as safe with me," he faltered, "—as safe as with your mother!"

"I believe it! I know it," she answered, still sobbing, but looking up with an expression of genuine integrity such as he had never seen on her face before. "But I AM sorry!" she went on. "It is very weak, and very, very un —un—womanly of me! But it came upon me all at once! If I had only had some warning! Oh, why did you not tell me before? Why did you not prepare me for it? You might have known what it would be to hear it so suddenly!"

More and more aghast grew Ian! What was to be done? What was to be said? What was left for a man to do, when a woman laid her soul before him? Was there nothing but a lie to save her from bitterest humiliation? To refuse any woman was to Ian a hard task; once he had found it impossible to refuse even where he could not give, and had let a woman take his soul! Thank God, she took it indeed! he yielded himself perfectly, and God gave him her in return! But that was once, and for ever! It could not be done again!

"I am very sorry!" he murmured; and the words and their tone sent a shiver through the heart of Christina.

But now that she had betrayed her secret, the pent up tide of her phantasy rushed to the door. She was reckless. Used to everything her own way, knowing nothing of disappointment, a new and ill understood passion dominating her, she let everything go and the torrent sweep her with it. Passion, like a lovely wild beast, had mastered her, and she never thought of trying to tame it. It was herself! there was not enough of her outside the passion to stand up against it! She began to see the filmy eyed Despair, and had neither experience to deal with herself, nor reticence enough to keep silence.

"If you speak to me like that," she cried, "my heart will break!—Must you go away?"

"Dear Miss Palmer,—" faltered Ian.

"Oh!" she ejaculated, with a world of bitterness in the protest.

"—do let us be calm!" continued Ian. "We shall not come to anything if we lose ourselves this way!"

The WE and the US gave her a little hope.

"How can I be calm!" she cried. "I am not cold-hearted like you!—You are going away, and I shall never see you again to all eternity!"

She burst out weeping afresh.

"Do love me a little before you go," she sobbed. "You gave me my life once, but that does not make it right to take it from me again! It only gives you a right to its best!"

"God knows," said Ian, "if my life could serve you, I should count it a small thing to yield!—But this is idle talk! A man must not pretend anything! We must not be untrue!"

She fancied he did not believe in her.

"I know! I know! you may well distrust me!" she returned. "I have often behaved abominably to you! But indeed I am true now! I dare not tell you a lie. To you I MUST speak the truth, for I love you with my whole soul."

Ian stood dumb. His look of consternation and sadness brought her to herself a little.

"What have I done!" she cried, and drawing back a pace, stood looking at him, and trembling. "I am disgraced for ever! I have told a man I love him, and he leaves me to the shame of it! He will not save me from it! he will not say one word to take it away! Where is your generosity, Ian?"

"I must be true!" said Ian, speaking as if to himself, and in a voice altogether unlike his own.

"You will not love me! You hate me! You despise me! But I will not live rejected! He brushes me like a feather from his coat!"

"Hear me," said Ian, trying to recover himself. "Do not think me insensible —"

"Oh, yes! I know!" cried Christina yet more bitterly; "—INSENSIBLE TO THE HONOUR *I* DO YOU, and all that world of nothing!—Pray use your victory! Lord it over me! I am the weed under your foot! I beg you will not spare me! Speak out what you think of me!"

Ian took her hand. It trembled as if she would pull it away, and her eyes flashed an angry fire. She looked more nearly beautiful than ever he had seen her! His heart was like to break. He drew her to the chair, and taking a stool, sat down beside her. Then, with a voice that gathered strength as he proceeded, he said:—

"Let me speak to you, Christina Palmer, as in the presence of him who made us! To pretend I loved you would be easier than to bear the pain of giving you such pain. Were I selfish enough, I could take much delight in your love; but I scorn the unmanliness of accepting gold and returning silver: my love is not mine to give."

It was some relief to her proud heart to imagine he would have loved her had he been free. But she did not speak.

"If I thought," pursued Ian, "that I had, by any behaviour of mine, been to blame for this,—" There he stopped, lest he should seem to lay blame on her.—"I think," he resumed, "I could help you if you would listen to me. Were I in like trouble with you, I would go into my room, and shut the door, and tell my Father in heaven everything about it. Ah, Christina! if you knew him, you would not break your heart that a man did not love you just as you loved him."

Had not her misery been so great, had she not also done the thing that humbled her before herself, Christina would have been indignant with the man who refused her love and dared speak to her of religion; but she was now too broken for resentment.

The diamond rain was falling, the sun was shining in his vaporous strength, and the great dome of heaven stood fathomless above the pair; but to Christina the world was black and blank as the gloomy hut in which they sat. When first her love blossomed, she saw the world open; she looked into its heart; she saw it alive—saw it burning with that which made the bush alive in the desert of Horeb—the presence of the living God; now, the vision was over, the desert was dull and dry, the bush burned no more, the glowing lava had cooled to unsightly stone! There was no God, nor any man more! Time had closed and swept the world into the limbo of vanity! For a time she sat without thought, as it were in a mental sleep. She opened her eyes, and the blank of creation stared into the very heart of her. The emptiness and loneliness overpowered her. Hardly aware of what she was doing, she slid to her knees at Ian's feet, crying,

"Save me, save me, Ian! I shall go mad! Pardon me! Help me!"

"All a man may be to his sister, I am ready to be to you. I will write to you from Canada; you can answer me or not as you please. My heart cries out to me to take you in my arms and comfort you, but I must not; it would not comfort you."

"You do not despise me, then?—Oh, thank you!"

"Despise you!—no more than my dead sister! I would cherish you as I would her were she in like sorrow. I would die to save you this grief— except indeed that I hope much from it."

"Forget all about me," said Christina, summoning pride to her aid.

"I will not forget you. It is impossible, nor would I if I could."

"You forgive me then, and will not think ill of me?"

"How forgive trust? Is that an offence?"

"I have lost your good opinion! How could I degrade myself so!"

"On the contrary, you are fast gaining iuy good opinion. You have begun to be a true woman!"

"What if it should be only for—"

"Whatever it may have been for, now you have tasted truth you will not turn back!"

"Now I know you do not care for me, I fear I shall soon sink back into my old self!"

"I do care for you, Christina, and you will not sink back into your old self. God means you to be a strong, good woman—able, with the help he will give you, to bear grief in a great-hearted fashion. Believe me, you and I may come nearer each other in the ages before us by being both true, than is possible in any other way whatever."

"I am miserable at the thought of what you must think of me! Everybody would say I had done a shameless thing in confessing my love!"

"I am not in the way of thinking as everybody thinks. There is little justice, and less sympathy, to be had from everybody. I would think and judge and feel as the one, my Master. Be sure you are safe with me."

"You will not tell anybody?"

"You must trust me."

"I beg your pardon! I have offended you!"

"Not in the least. But I will bind myself by no promises. I am bound already to be as careful over you as if you were the daughter of my father and mother. Your confession, instead of putting you in my power, makes me your servant."

By this time Christina was calm. There was a great load on her heart, but somehow she was aware of the possibility of carrying it. She looked up gratefully in Ian's face, already beginning to feel for him a reverence which made it easier to forego the right to put her arms round him. And therewith awoke in her the first movement of divine relationship—rose the first heave of the child-heart toward the source of its being. It appeared in the form of resistance. Complaint against God is far nearer to God than indifference about him.

"Ian Macruadh," said Christina solemnly, and she looked him in the eyes as she said it, "how can you believe there is a God? If there were, would he allow such a dreadful thing to befall one of his creatures? How am I to blame? I could not help it!"

"I see in it his truth and goodness toward his child. And he will let you see it. The thing is between him and you."

"It will be hard to convince me it is either good or loving to make anyone suffer like this!" protested Christina, her hand unconsciously pressed on her heart; "—and all the disgrace of it too!" she added bitterly.

"I will not allow there is any disgrace," returned Ian. "But I will not try to con vince you of anything about God. I cannot. You must know him. I only say I believe in him with all my heart. You must ask him to explain himself to you, and not take it for granted, because he has done what you do not like, that he has done you a wrong. Whether you seek him or not, he will do you justice; but he cannot explain himself except you seek him."

"I think I understand. Believe me, I am willing to understand."

A few long seconds of silence followed. Christina came a little nearer. She was still on her knees.

"Will you kiss me once," she said, "as you would a little child!"

"In the name of God!" answered Ian, and stooping kissed her gently and tenderly.

"Thank you!" she said; "—and now the rain is over, let us join Mercy and the chief. I hope they have not got very wet!"

"Alister will have taken care of that. There is plenty of shelter about here."

They left the cottage, drew the door close, and through the heather, sparkling with a thousand rain-drops, the sun shining hotter than ever through the rain-mist, went up the hill.

They found the other pair sheltered by the great stone, which was not only a shadow from the heat, but sloped sufficiently to be a covert from the rain. They did not know it had ceased; perhaps they did not know it had rained.

On a fine morning of the following week, the emigrants began the first stage of their long journey; the women in two carts, with their small impedimenta, the men walking—Ian with them, a stout stick in his hand. They were to sail from Greenock.

Ian and Christina met several times before he left, but never alone. No conference of any kind, not even of eyes, had been sought by Christina, and Ian had resolved to say nothing more until he reached Canada. Thence he would write things which pen and ink would say better and carry nearer home than could speech; and by that time too the first keenness of her pain would have dulled, and left her mind more capable of receiving them. He was greatly pleased with the gentle calm of her behaviour. No one else could have seen any difference toward himself. He read in her carriage that of a child who had made a mistake, and was humbled, not vexed. Her mother noted that her cheek was pale, and that she seemed thoughtful; but farther she did not penetrate. To Ian it was plain that she had set herself to be reasonable.

CHAPTER VI

LOVE GLOOMING.

Ian, the light of his mother's eyes, was gone, and she felt forsaken. Alister was too much occupied with Mercy to feel his departure as on former occasions, yet he missed him every hour of the day. Mercy and he met, but not for some time in open company, as Christina refused to go near the cottage. Things were ripening to a change.

Alister's occupation with Mercy, however, was far from absorption; the moment Ian was gone, he increased his attention to his mother, feeling she had but him. But his mother was not quite the same to him now. At times she was even more tender; at other times she seemed to hold him away from her, as one with whom she was not in sympathy. The fear awoke in him that she might so speak to some one of the Palmers as to raise an insuperable barrier between the families; and this fear made him resolve to come at once to an understanding with Mercy. The resulting difficulties might be great; he felt keenly the possible alternative of his loss of Mercy, or Mercy's loss of her family; but the fact that he loved her gave him a right to tell her so, and made it his duty to lay before her the probability of an obstacle. That his mother did not like the alliance had to be braved, for a man must leave father and mother and cleave to his wife—a saying commonly by male presumption inverted. Mercy's love he believed such that she would, without a thought, leave the luxury of her father's house for the mere plenty of his. That it would not be to descend but to rise in the true social scale he would leave her to discover. Had he known what Mr. Palmer was, and how his money had been made, he would neither have sought nor accepted his acquaintance, and it would no more have been possible to fall in love with one of his family than to covet one of his fine horses. But that which might, could, would, or should have been, affected in no way that which was. He had entered in ignorance, by the will of God, into certain relations with "the young woman," as his mother called her, and those relations had to be followed to their natural and righteous end.

Talking together over possibilities, Mr. Peregrine Palmer had agreed with his wife that, Mercy being so far from a beauty, it might not be such a bad match, would not at least be one to be ashamed of, if she did marry the impoverished chief of a highland clan with a baronetcy in his pocket. Having bought the land cheap, he could afford to let a part, perhaps even the whole of it, go back with his daughter, thus restoring to its former position an ancient and honourable family. The husband of his younger daughter would then be head of one of the very few highland families yet in possession of their ancestral acres—a distinction he would owe to Peregrine Palmer! It was a pleasant thought to the kindly, consequential, common little man. Mrs. Palmer, therefore, when the chief called upon her, received him with more than her previous cordiality.

His mother would have been glad to see him return from his call somewhat dejected; he entered so radiant and handsome, that her heart sank within her. Was she actually on the point of being allied through the child of her bosom to a distiller and brewer—a man who had grown rich on the ruin of thousands of his fellow countrymen? To what depths might not the most ancient family sink! For any poverty, she said to herself, she was prepared —but how was she to endure disgrace! Alas for the clan, whose history was about to cease—smothered in the defiling garment of ill-gotten wealth! Miserable, humiliating close to ancient story! She had no doubt as to her son's intention, although he had said nothing; she KNEW that his refusal of dower would be his plea in justification; but would that deliver them from the degrading approval of the world? How many, if they ever heard of it, would believe that the poor, high-souled Macruadh declined to receive a single hundred from his father-in-law's affluence! That he took his daughter poor as she was born—his one stipulation that she should be clean from her father's mud! For one to whom there would even be a chance of stating the truth of the matter, a hundred would say, "That's your plan! The only salvation for your shattered houses! Point them up well with the bird-lime of the brewer, the quack, or the money-lender, and they'll last till doom'sday!"

Thus bitterly spoke the mother. She brooded and scorned, raged inwardly, and took to herself dishonour, until evidently she was wasting. The chief's heart was troubled; could it be that she doubted his strength to resist temptation? He must make haste and have the whole thing settled! And first of all speak definitely to Mercy on the matter!

He had appointed to meet her the same evening, and went long before the hour to watch for her appearing. He climbed the hill, and lay down in the heather whence he could see the door of the New House, and Mercy the moment she should come out of it. He lay there till the sun was down, and the stars began to appear. At length—and even then it was many minutes to the time—he saw the door open, and Mercy walk slowly to the gate. He rose and went down the hill. She saw him, watched him descending, and the moment he reached the road, went to meet him. They walked slowly down the road, without a word spoken, until they felt themselves alone.

"You look so lovely!" said the chief.

"In the twilight, I suppose!" said Mercy.

"Perhaps; you are a creature of the twilight, or the night rather, with your great black eyes!"

"I don't like you to speak to me so! You never did before! You know I am not lovely! I am very plain!"

She was evidently not pleased.

"What have I done to vex you, Mercy?" he rejoined. "Why should you mind my saying what is true?"

She bit her lip, and could hardly speak to answer him. Often in London she had been morally sickened by the false rubbish talked to her sister, and had boasted to herself that the chief had never paid her a compliment. Now he had done it!

She took her hand from his arm.

"I think I will go home!" she said.

Alister stopped and turned to her. The last gleam of the west was reflected from her eyes, and all the sadness of the fading light seemed gathered into them.

"My child!" he said, all that was fatherly in the chief rising at the sight, "who has been making you unhappy?"

"You," she answered, looking him in the face.

"How? I do not understand!" he returned, gazing at her bewildered.

"You have just paid me a compliment—a thing you never did before—a thing I never heard before from any but a fool! How could you say I was beautiful! You know I am not beautiful! It breaks my heart to think you could say what you didn't believe!"

"Mercy!" answered the chief, "if I said you were beautiful, and to my eyes you were not, it would yet be true; for to my heart, which sees deeper than my eyes, you are more beautiful than any other ever was or ever will be. I know you are not beautiful in the world's meaning, but you are very lovely —and it was lovely I said you were!"

"Lovely because you love me? Is that what you meant?"

"Yes, that and more. Your eyes are beautiful, and your hair is beautiful, and your expression is lovely. But I am not flattering you—I am not even paying you compliments, for those things are not yours; God made them, and has given them to me!"

She put her hand in his arm again, and there was no more love-making.

"But Mercy," said the chief, when they had walked some distance without speaking, "do you think you could live here always, and never see London again?"

"I would not care if London were scratched out."

"Could you be content to be a farmer's wife?"

"If he was a very good farmer," she answered, looking up archly.

"Am I a good enough farmer, then, to serve your turn?"

"Good enough if I were ten times better. Do you really mean it, Macruadh?"

"With all my heart. Only there is one thing I am very anxious about."

"What is that?"

"How your father will take my condition."

"He will allow, I think, that it is good enough for me—and more than I deserve."

"That is not what I mean; it is that I have a certain condition to make."

"Else you won't marry me? That seems strange! Of course I will do anything you would wish me to do! A condition!" she repeated, ponderingly, with just a little dissatisfaction in the tone.

Alister wondered she was not angry. But she trusted him too well to take offence readily.

"Yes," he rejoined, "a real condition! Terms belong naturally to the giver, not the petitioner; I hope with all my heart it will not offend him. It will not offend you, I think."

"Let me hear your condition," said Mercy, looking at him curiously, her honest eyes shining in the faint light.

"I want him to let me take you just as you are, without a shilling of his money to spoil the gift. I want you in and for yourself."

"I dare not think you one who would rather not be obliged to his wife for anything!" said Mercy. "That cannot be it!"

She spoke with just a shadow of displeasure. He did not answer. He was in great dread of hurting her, and his plain reason could not fail to hurt her.

"Well," she resumed, as he did not reply, "there are fathers, I daresay, who would not count that a hard condition!"

"Of course your father will not like the idea of your marrying so poor a man!"

"If he should insist on your having something with me, you will not refuse, will you? Why should you mind it?"

Alister was silent. The thing had already begun to grow dreadful! How could he tell her his reasons! Was it necessary to tell her? If he had to explain, it must be to her father, not to her! How, until absolutely compelled, reveal the horrible fact that her father was despised by her lover! She might believe it her part to refuse such love! He trembled lest she should urge him. But Mercy, thinking she had been very bold already, also held her peace.

They tried to talk about other things, but with little success, and when they parted, it was with a sense on both sides that something had got between them. The night through Mercy hardly slept for trying to discover what his aversion to her dowry might mean. No princedom was worth contrasting with poverty and her farmer-chief, but why should not his love be able to carry her few thousands? It was impossible his great soul should grudge his wife's superiority in the one poor trifle of money! Was not the whole family superior to money! Had she, alas, been too confident in their greatness? Must she be brought to confess that their grand ways had their little heart of pride? Did they not regard themselves as the ancient aristocracy of the country! Yes, it must be! The chief despised the origin of her father's riches!

But, although so far in the direction of the fact, she had no suspicion of anything more than landed pride looking down upon manufacture and trade. She suspected no moral root of even a share in the chief's difficulty.

Naturally, she was offended. How differently Christina would have met the least hint of a CONDITION, she thought. She had been too ready to show and confess her love! Had she stood off a little, she might have escaped this humiliation! But would that have been honest? Must she not first of all be true? Was the chief, whatever his pride, capable of being ungenerous? Questions like these kept coming and going throughout the night. Hither and thither went her thoughts, refusing to be controlled. The morning came, the sun rose, and she could not find rest. She had come to see how ideally delightful it was just to wait God's will of love, yet, in this her first trouble, she actually forgot to think of God, never asked him to look after the thing for her, never said, "Thy will be done!" And when at length weariness overpowered her, fell asleep like a heathen, without a word from her heart to the heart.

Alister missed Ian sorely. He prayed to God, but was too troubled to feel him near. Trouble imagined may seem easy to meet; trouble actual is quite another thing! His mother, perhaps, was to have her desire; Mercy, perhaps, would not marry a man who disapproved of her family! Between them already was what could not be talked about! He could not set free his heart to her!

When Mercy woke, the old love was awake also; let Alister's reason be what it might, it was not for her to resent it! The life he led was so much grander than a life spent in making money, that he must feel himself superior! Throned in the hearts, and influencing the characters of men, was he not in a far nobler position than money could give him? From her night of doubt and bitterness Mercy issued more loving and humble. What should she be now, she said to herself, if Alister had not taught her? He had been good to her as never father or brother! She would trust him! She would believe him right! Had he hurt her pride? It was well her pride should be hurt! Her mind was at rest.

But Alister must continue in pain and dread until he had spoken to her father. Knowing then the worst, he might use argument with Mercy; the moment for that was not yet come! If he consented that his daughter should leave him undowered, an explanation with Mercy might be postponed. When the honour of her husband was more to her than the false credit of her family, when she had had time to understand principles which, born and brought up as she had been, she might not yet be able to see into, then it would be time to explain! One with him, she would see things as he saw them! Till her father came, he would avoid the subject!

All the morning he was busy in the cornyard—with his hands in preparing new stances for ricks, with his heart in try ing to content himself beforehand with whatever fate the Lord might intend for him. As yet he was more of a Christian philosopher than a philosophical Christian. The thing most disappointing to him he would treat as the will of God for him, and try to make up his mind to it, persuading himself it was the right and best thing—as if he knew it the will of God. He was thus working in the region of supposition, and not of revealed duty; in his own imagination, and not in the will of God. If this should not prove the will of God concerning him, then he was spending his strength for nought. There is something in the very presence and actuality of a thing to make one able to bear it; but a man may weaken himself for bearing what God intends him to bear, by trying to bear what God does not intend him to bear. The chief was forestalling the morrow like an unbeliever—not without some moral advantage, I dare say, but with spiritual loss. We have no right to school ourselves to an imaginary duty. When we do not know, then what he lays upon us is NOT TO KNOW, and to be content not to know. The philosopher is he who lives in the thought of things, the Christian is he who lives in the things themselves. The philosopher occupies himself with Grod's decree, the Christian with God's will; the philosopher with what God may intend, the Christian with what God wants HIM TO DO.

The laird looked up and there were the young ladies! It was the first time Christina had come nigh the cottage since Ian's departure.

"Can you tell me, Macruadh," she said, "what makes Mrs. Conal so spiteful always? When we bade her good morning a few minutes ago, she overwhelmed us with a torrent of abuse!"

"How did you know it was abuse?"

"We understand enough of Gaelic to know it was not exactly blessing us she was. It is not necessary to know cat-language to distinguish between purring and spitting! What harm have we done? Her voice was fierce, and her eyes were like two live peats flaming at us! Do speak to her."

"It would be of no use!"

"Where's the good of being chief then? I don't ask you to make the old woman civil, but I think you might keep her from insulting your friends! I begin to think your chiefdom a sham!"

"I doubt indeed if it reaches to the tongues of the clan! But let us go and tell my mother. She may be able to do something with her!"

Christina went into the cottage; the chief drew Mercy back.

"What do you think the first duty of married people, Mercy—to each other, I mean," he said.

"To be always what they look," answered Mercy.

"Yes, but I mean actively. What is it their first duty to do towards each other?"

"I can't answer that without thinking."

"Is it not each to help the other to do the will of God?"

"I would say YES if I were sure I really meant it."

"You will mean it one day."

"Are you sure God will teach me?"

"I think he cares more to do that than anything else."

"More than to save us?"

"What is saving but taking us out of the dark into the light? There is no salvation but to know God and grow like him."

CHAPTER VII

A GENEROUS DOWRY.

The only hope of the chief's mother was in what the girl's father might say to her son's proposal. Would not his pride revolt against giving his daughter to a man who would not receive his blessing in money?

Mr. Peregrine Palmer arrived, and the next day Alister called upon him.

Not unprepared for the proposal of the chief, Mercy's father had nothing to urge against it. Her suitor's name was almost an historical one, for it stood high in the home-annals of Scotland. And the new laird, who had always a vague sense of injury in the lack of an illustrious pedigree of his own to send forward, was not un willing that a man more justly treated than himself should supply the SOLATIUM to his daughter's children. He received the Macruadh, therefore, if a little pompously, yet with kindness. And the moment they were seated Alister laid his request before him.

"Mr. Palmer," he said, "I come to ask the hand of your daughter Mercy. I have not much beyond myself to offer her, but I can tell you precisely what there is."

Mr. Peregrine Palmer sat for a moment looking important. He seemed to see much to ponder in the proposal.

"Well, Macruadh," he said at length, hesitating with hum and with haw, "the thing is—well, to speak the truth, you take me a good deal by surprise! I do not know how the thing may appear to Mrs. Palmer. And then the girl herself, you will allow, ought, in a free country, to have a word in the matter! WE give our girls absolute liberty; their own hearts must guide them—that is, where there is no serious exception to be taken. Honestly, it is not the kind of match we should have chosen! It is not as if things were with you now as once, when the land was all your own, and—and—you—pardon me, I am a father—did not have to work with your own hands!"

Had he been there on any other errand the chief would have stated his opinion that it was degrading to a man to draw income from anything he would count it degrading to put his own hand to; but there was so much he might be compelled to say to the displeasure of Mr. Palmer while asking of him the greatest gift he had to bestow, that he would say nothing unpalatable which he was not compelled to say.

"My ancestors," he answered, willing to give the objection a pleasant turn, "would certainly have preferred helping themselves to the produce of lowland fields! My great-great-grandfather, scorning to ask any man for his daughter, carried her off without a word!"

I am glad the peculiarity has not shown itself hereditary," said Mr. Palmer laughing.

"But if I have little to offer, I expect nothing with her," said the chief abruptly. "I want only herself!"

"A very loverly mode of speaking! But it is needless to say no daughter of mine shall leave me without a certainty, one way or the other, of suitable maintenance. You know the old proverb, Macruadh,—'When poverty comes in at the door,'—?"

"There is hardly a question of poverty in the sense the proverb intends!" answered the chief smiling.

"Of course! Of course! At the same time you cannot keep the wolf too far from the door. I would not, for my part, care to say I had given my daughter to a poor farmer in the north. Two men, it is, I believe, you employ, Macruadh?"

The chief answered with a nod.

"I have other daughters to settle—not to mention my sons," pursued the great little man, "—but—but I will find a time to talk the matter over with Mrs. Palmer, and see what I can do for you. Meanwhile you may reckon you have a friend at court; all I have seen makes me judge well of you. Where we do not think alike, I can yet say for you that your faults lean to virtue's side, and are such as my daughter at least will be no loser by. Good morning, Macruadh."

Mr. Peregrine Palmer rose; and the chief, perplexed and indignant, but anxious not to prejudice, his very doubtful cause, rose also.

"You scarcely understand me, Mr. Palmer," he said. "On the possibility of being honoured with your daughter's hand, you must allow me to say distinctly beforehand, that I must decline receiving anything with her. When will you allow me to wait upon you again?"

"I will write. Good morning."

The interview was certainly not much to the assuagement of the chief's anxiety. He went home with the feeling that he had submitted to be patronized, almost insulted by a paltry fellow whose consequence rested on his ill-made money—a man who owed everything to a false and degrading appetite in his neighbours! Nothing could have made him put up with him but the love of Mercy, his dove in a crow's nest! But it would be all in vain, for he could not lie! Truth, indeed, if not less of a virtue, was less of a heroism in the chief than in most men, for he COULD NOT lie. Had he been tempted to try, he would have reddened, stammered, broken down, with the full shame, and none of the success of a falsehood.

For a week, he heard nothing; there seemed small anxiety to welcome him into the Palmer family! Then came a letter. It implied, almost said that some difficulty had been felt as to his reception by EVERY member of the family—which the chief must himself see to have been only natural! But while money was of no con sequence to Mr. Palmer, it was of the greatest consequence that his daughter should seem to make a good match; therefore, as only in respect of POSITION was the alliance objectionable, he had concluded to set that right, and in giving him his daughter, to restore the chief's family to its former dignity, by making over to him the Clanruadh property now in his possession by purchase. While he thus did his duty by his daughter, he hoped the Macruadh would accept the arrangement as a mark of esteem for himself. Two conditions only he would make—the first, that, as long as he lived, the shooting should be Mr. Palmer's, to use or to let, and should extend over the whole estate; the second, that the chief should assume the baronetcy which belonged to him.

My reader will regard the proposition as not ungenerous, however much the money value of the land lay in the shooting.

As Alister took leave of his mother for the night, he gave her the letter.

She took it, read it slowly, laughed angrily, smiled scornfully, wept bitterly, crushed it in her hand, and walked up to her room with her head high. All the time she was preparing for her bed, she was talking in her spirit with her husband. When she lay down she became a mere prey to her own thoughts, and was pulled, and torn, and hurt by them for hours ere she set herself to rule them. For the first time in her life she distrusted her son. She did not know what he would do! The temptation would surely be too strong for him! Two good things were set over against one evil thing—an evil thing, however, with which nobody would associate blame, an evil thing which would raise him high in the respect of everyone whose respect was not worth having!—the woman he loved and the land of his ancestors on the one side, and only the money that bought the land for him on the other!—would he hold out? He must take the three together, or have none of them! Her fear for him grew and possessed her. She grew cold as death. Why did he give her the letter, and go without saying a word? She knew well the arguments he would adduce! Henceforward and for ever there would be a gulf between them! The poor religion he had would never serve to keep him straight! What was it but a compromise with pride and self-sufficiency! It could bear no such strain! He acknowledged God, but not God reconciled in Christ, only God such as unregenerate man would have him! And when Ian came home, he would be sure to side with Alister!

There was but one excuse for the poor boy—and that a miserable one: the blinding of love! Yes there was more excuse than that: to be lord of the old lands, with the old clan growing and gathering again about its chief! It was a temptation fit to ruin an archangel! What could he not do then for his people! What could he not do for the land! And for her, she might have her Ian always at home with her! God forbid she should buy even such bliss at such a cost! She was only thinking, she said to herself, how, if the thing had to be, she would make the best of it: she was bound as a mother to do that!

But the edge of the wedge was in. She said to herself afterwards, that the enemy of her soul must have been lying in wait for her that night; she almost believed in some bodily presence of him in her room: how otherwise could she account for her fall! he must have been permitted to tempt her, because, in condemning evil, she had given way to contempt and worldly pride. Her thoughts unchecked flowed forward. They lingered brooding for a time on the joys that might be hers—the joys of the mother of a chief over territory as well as hearts. Then they stole round, and began to flow the other way. Ere the thing had come she began to make the best of it for the sake of her son and the bond between them; then she began to excuse it for the sake of the clan; and now she began to justify it a little for the sake of the world! Everything that could favour the acceptance of the offer came up clear before her. The land was the same as it always had been! it had never been in the distillery! it had never been in the brew-house! it was clean, whoever had transacted concerning it, through whatever hands it had passed! A good cow was a good cow, had she been twenty times reaved! For Mr. Palmer to give and Alister to take the land back, would be some amends to the nation, grievously injured in the money of its purchase! The deed would restore to the redeeming and uplifting influence of her son many who were fast perishing from poverty and whisky; for, their houses and crofts once more in the power of their chief, he would again be their landlord as well! It would be a pure exercise of the law of compensation! Hundreds who had gone abroad would return to replenish the old glens with the true national wealth—with men and women, and children growing to be men and women, for the hour of their country's need! These were the true, the golden crops! The glorious time she had herself seen would return, when Strathruadh could alone send out a regiment of the soldiers that may be defeated, but will not live to know it. The dream of her boys would come true! they would rebuild the old castle, and make it a landmark in the history of the highlands!

But while she stood elate upon this high-soaring peak of the dark mountains of ambition, sudden before her mind's eye rose the face of her husband, sudden his voice was in her ear; he seemed to stand above her in the pulpit, reading from the prophet Isaiah the four Woes that begin four contiguous chapters:—"Woe to the crown of pride, to the drunkards of Ephraim, whose glorious beauty is a fading flower, which are on the head of the fat valleys of them that are overcome with wine!"—"Woe to Ariel, to Ariel, the city where David dwelt! Add ye year to year; let them kill sacrifices; yet I will distress Ariel."—"Woe to the rebellious children, saith the Lord, that take counsel, but not of me; and that cover with a covering, but not of my spirit, that they may add sin to sin!"—" Woe to them that go down to Egypt for help; and stay on horses, and trust in chariots, because they are many; and in horsemen, because they are very strong; but they look not unto the holy one of Israel, neither seek the Lord!" Then followed the words opening the next chapter:—"Behold, a king shall reign in righteousness, and princes shall rule in judgment. And a man shall be as an hiding place from the wind, and a covert from the tempest." All this, in solemn order, one woe after the other, she heard in the very voice of her husband; in awful spiritual procession, they passed before her listening mind! She grew cold as the dead, and shuddered and shivered. She looked over the edge into the heart of a black gulf, into which she had been on the point of casting herself—say rather, down whose side, searching for an easy descent, she had already slid a long way, when the voice from above recalled her! She covered her face with her hands and wept—ashamed before God, ashamed before her husband. It was a shame unutterable that the thing should even have looked tempting! She cried for forgiveness, rose, and sought Alister's room.

Seldom since he was a man had she visited her elder son in his chamber. She cherished for him, as chief, something of the reverence of the clan. The same familiarity had never existed between them as between her and Ian. Now she was going to wake him, and hold a solemn talk with him. Not a moment longer should he stand leaning over the gulf into which she had herself well nigh fallen!

She found him awake, and troubled, though not with an eternal trouble such as hers.

"I thought I should find you asleep, Alister!" she said.

"It was not very likely, mother!" he answered gently.

"You too have been tried with terrible thoughts?"

"I have been tried, but ha^ly with terrible thoughts: I know that Mercy loves me!"

"Ah, my son, my dear son! love itself is the terrible thing! It has drawn many a man from the way of peace!"

"Did it draw you and my father from the way of peace?" asked Alister.

"Not for a moment!" she answered. "It made our steps firmer in the way."

"Then why should you fear it will draw me from it? I hope I have never made you think I was not following my father and you!"

"Who knows what either of us might have done, with such a temptation as yours!"

"Either you say, mother, that my father was not so good as I think him, or that he did what he did in his own strength!"

"' Let him that thinketh '—you know the rest!" rejoined the mother.

"I don't think I am tempted to anything just now."

"There it is, you see!—the temptation so subtle that you do not suspect its character!"

"I am confident my father would have done just as I mean to do!"

"What do you mean to do?"

"Is it my own mother asks me? Does she distrust her husband and her son together?"

It began to dawn on the mother that she had fallen into her own temptation through distrust of her son. Because she-distrusted him, she sought excuse for him, and excuse had turned to all but justification: she had given place to the devil! But she must be sure about Alister! She had had enough of the wiles of Satan: she must not trust her impressions! The enemy might even now be bent on deceiving her afresh! For a moment she kept silence, then said:—

"It would be a grand thing to have the whole country-side your own again —wouldn't it, Alister?"

"It would, mother!" he answered.

"And have all your people quite under your own care?"

"A grand thing, indeed, mother!"

"How can you say then it is no temptation to you?"

"Because it is none."

"How is that?"

"I would not have my clan under a factor of Satan's, mother!"

"I do not understand you!"

"What else should I be, if I accepted the oversight of them on terms of allegiance to him! That was how he tempted Jesus. I will not be the devil's steward, to call any land or any people mine!"

His mother kissed him on the forehead, walked erect from the room, and went to her own to humble herself afresh.

In the morning, Alister took his dinner of bread and cheese in his pocket, and set out for the tomb on the hill-top. There he remained until the evening, and wrote his answer, sorely missing Ian.

He hegged Mr. Peregrine Palmer to dismiss the idea of enriching him, thanked him for his great liberality, but declared himself entirely content, and determined not to change his position. He could not and would not avail himself of his generosity.

Mr. Palmer, unable to suspect the reasons at work in the chief's mind, pleased with the genuineness of his acknowledgment, and regarding him as a silly fellow who would quixotically outdo him in magnanimity, answered in a more familiar, almost jocular strain. He must not be unreasonable, he said; pride was no doubt an estimable weakness, but it might be carried too far; men must act upon realities not fancies; he must learn to have an eye to the main chance, and eschew heroics: what was life without money! It was not as if he gave it grudgingly, for he made him heartily welcome. The property was in truth but a flea-bite to him! He hoped the Macruadh would live long to enjoy it, and make his father-in-law the great grandfather of chiefs, perpetuating his memory to ages unborn. There was more to the same effect, void neither of eloquence nor of a certain good-heartedness, which the laird both recognized and felt.

It was again his painful turn. He had now to make his refusal as positive as words could make it. He said he was sorry to appear headstrong, perhaps uncivil and ungrateful, but he could not and would not accept anything beyond the priceless gift of Mercy's hand.

Not even then did Peregrine Palmer divine that his offered gift was despised; that idea was to him all but impossible of conception. He read merely opposition, and was determined to have his way. Next time he too wrote positively, though far from unkindly:—the Macruadh must take the land with his daughter, or leave both!

The chief replied that he could not yield his claim to Mercy, for he loved her, and believed she loved him; therefore begged Mr. Peregrine Palmer, of his generosity, to leave the decision with his daughter.

The next was a letter from Mercy, entreating Alister not to hurt her father by seeming to doubt the kindness of his intentions. She assured him her father was not the man to interfere with his management of the estate, the shooting was all he cared about; and if that was the difficulty, she imagined even that might be got over. She ended praying that he would, for her sake, cease making much of a trifle, for such the greatest property in the world must be betwixt them. No man, she said, could love a woman right, who would not be under the poorest obligation to her people!

The chief answered her in the tenderest way, assuring her that if the property had been hers he would only have blessed her for it; that he was not making much ado about nothing; that pride, or unwillingness to be indebted, had nothing to do with his determination; that the thing was with him in very truth a matter of conscience. He implored her therefore from the bottom of his heart to do her best to persuade her father—if she would save him who loved her more than his own soul, from a misery God only could make him able to bear.

Mercy was bewildered. She neither understood nor suspected. She wrote again, saying her father was now thoroughly angry; that she found herself without argument, the thing being incomprehensible to her as to her father; that she could not see where the conscience of the thing lay. Her terror was, that, if he persisted, she would be driven to think he did not care for her; his behaviour she had tried in vain to reconcile with what he had taught her; if he destroyed her faith in him, all her faith might go, and she be left without God as well as without him!

Then Alister saw that necessity had culminated, and that it was no longer possi ble to hold anything back. Whatever other suffering he might cause her, Mercy must not be left to think him capable of sacrificing her to an absurdity! She must know the truth of the matter, and how it was to him of the deepest conscience! He must let her see that if he allowed her to persuade him, it would be to go about thenceforward consumed of self-contempt, a slave to the property, no more its owner than if he had stolen it, and in danger of committing suicide to escape hating his wife!

For the man without a tender conscience, cannot imagine the state to which another may come, who carries one about with him, stinging and accusing him all day long.

So, out of a heart aching with very fullness, Alister wrote the truth to Mercy. And Mercy, though it filled her with grief and shame, had so much love for the truth, and for the man who had waked that love, that she understood him, and loved him through all the pain of his words; loved him the more for daring the risk of losing her; loved him yet the more for cleaving to her while loathing the mere thought of sharing her wealth; loved him most of all that he was immaculate in truth.

She carried the letter to her father's room, laid it before him without a word, and went out again.

The storm gathered swiftly, and burst at once. Not two minutes seemed to have passed when she heard his door open, and a voice of wrathful displeasure call out her name. She returned—in fear, but in fortitude.

Then first she knew her father!—for although wrath and injustice were at home in him, they seldom showed themselves out of doors. He treated her as a willing party to an unspeakable insult from a highland boor to her own father. To hand him such a letter was the same as to have written it herself! She identified herself with the writer when she became the bearer of the mangy hound's insolence! He raged at Mercy as in truth he had never raged before. If once she spoke to the fellow again, he would turn her out of the house!

She would have left the room. He locked the door, set a chair before his writing table, and ordered her to sit there and write to his dictation. But no power on earth or under it would have prevailed to make Mercy write as her own the words that were not hers.

"You must excuse me, papa!" she said in a tone unheard from her before.

This raising of the rampart of human dignity, crowned with refusal, between him and his own child, galled him afresh.

"Then you shall be compelled!" he said, with an oath through his clenched teeth.

Mercy stood silent and motionless.

"Go to your room. By heaven you shall stay there till you do as I tell you!"

He was between her and the door.

"You need not think to gain your point by obstinacy," he added. "I swear that not another word shall pass between you and that blockhead of a chief —not if I have to turn watch-dog myself!"

He made way for her, but did not open the door. She left the room too angry to cry, and went to her own. Her fear of her father had vanished. With Alister on her side she could stand against the world! She went to her window. She could not see the cottage from it, but she could see the ruin, and the hill of the crescent fire, on which she had passed through the shadow of death. Gazing on the hill she remembered what Alister would have her do, and with her Father in heaven sought shelter from her father on earth.

CHAPTER VIII

MISTRESS CONAL.

Mr. Peregrine Palmer's generosity had in part rested on the idea of securing the estate against reverse of fortune, sufficiently possible though not expected; while with the improvements almost in hand, the shooting would make him a large return. He felt the more wronged by the ridiculous scruples of the chief—in which after all, though he could not have said why, he did not quite believe. It never occurred to him that, even had the land been so come by that the chief could accept a gift of it, he would, upon the discovery that it had been so secured from the donor's creditors, at once have insisted on placing it at their disposal.

His wrath proceeded to vent itself in hastening the realization of his schemes of improvement, for he was well aware they would be worse than distasteful to the Macruadh. Their first requirement was the removal of every peasant within his power capable of violating the sanctity of the deer forest into which he and his next neighbour had agreed to turn the whole of their property. While the settlement of his daughter was pending, he had seen that the point might cause trouble unless previously understood between him and the chief; but he never doubted the recovery of the land would reconcile the latter to the loss of the men. Now he chuckled with wrathful chuckle to think how entirely he had him in his power for justifiable annoyance; for he believed himself about to do nothing but good to THE COUNTRY in removing from it its miserable inhabitants, whom the sentimental indulgence of their so-called chief kept contented with their poverty, and with whom interference must now enrage him. How he hated the whole wretched pack!

Mr. Palmer's doing of good to the country consisted in making the land yield more money into the pockets of Mr. Brander and himself by feeding wild animals instead of men. To tell such land-owners that they are simply running a tilt at the creative energy, can be of no use: they do not believe in God, however much they may protest and imagine they do.

The next day but one, he sent Mistress Conal the message that she must be out of her hut, goods and gear, within a fortnight. He was not sure that the thing was legally correct, but he would risk it. She might go to law if she would, but he would make a beginning with her! The chief might take up her quarrel if he chose: nothing would please Mr. Palmer more than to involve him in a law-suit, clear him out, and send him adrift! His money might be contemptible, but the chief should find it at least dangerous! Contempt would not stave off a land-slip!

Mistress Conal, with a rage and scorn that made her feel every inch a witch, and accompanied by her black cat, which might or might not be the innocent animal the neighbours did not think him, hurried to the Macruadh, and informed him that "the lowland thief" had given her notice to quit the house of her fathers within a fortnight.

"I fear much we cannot help it! the house is on his land!" said the chief sorrowfully.

"His land!" echoed the old woman. "Is the nest of the old eagle his land? Can he make his heather white or his ptarmigan black? Will he dry up the lochs, and stay the rivers? Will he remove the mountains from their places, or cause the generations of men to cease from the earth? Defend me, chief! I come to you for the help that was never sought in vain from the Macruadh!"

"What help I have is yours without the asking," returned the chief. "I cannot do more than is in my power! One thing only I can promise you— that you shall lack neither food nor shelter."

"My chief will abandon me to the wolf!" she cried.

"Never! But I can only protect you, not your house. He may have no right to turn you out at such short notice; but it could only be a matter of weeks. To go to law with him would but leave me without a roof to shelter you when your own was gone!"

"The dead would have shown him into the dark, ere he turned me into the cold!" she muttered, and turning, left him.

The chief was greatly troubled. He had heard nothing of such an intention on the part of his neighbour. Could it be for revenge? He had heard nothing yet of his answer to Mercy! All he could do was to represent to Mr. Palmer the trouble the poor woman was in, and let him know that the proceeding threatened would render him very unpopular in the strath. This he thought it best to do by letter.

It could not enrage Mr. Palmer more, but it enraged him afresh. He vowed that the moment the time was up, out the old witch should go, neck and crop; and with the help of Mr. Brander, provided men for the enforcement of his purpose who did not belong to the neighbourhood.

The chief kept hoping to hear from the New House, but neither his letter to Mercy nor to her father received any answer. How he wished for Ian to tell him what he ought to do! His mother could not help him. He saw nothing for it but wait events.

Day after day passed, and he heard nothing. He would have tried to find out the state of things at the New House, but until war was declared that would not be right! Mr. Palmer might be seeking how with dignity to move in the matter, for certainly the chief had placed him in a position yet more unpleasant than his own! He must wait on!

The very day fortnight after the notice given, about three o'clock in the afternoon, came flying to the chief a ragged little urchin of the village, too breathless almost to make intelligible his news—that there were men at Mistress Conal's who would not go out of her house, and she and her old black cat were swearing at them.

The chief ran: could the new laird be actually unhousing the aged, helpless woman? It was the part of a devil and not of a man! As he neared the place —there were her poor possessions already on the roadside!—her one chair and stool, her bedding, her three-footed pot, her girdle, her big chest, all that she could call hers in the world! and when he came in sight of the cottage, there she was being brought out of it, struggling, screaming, and cursing, in the grasp of two men! Fierce in its glow was the torrent of Gaelic that rushed from the crater of her lips, molten in the volcanic depths of her indignant soul.

When one thinks of the appalling amount of rage exhausted by poor humans upon wrong, the energy of indignation, whether issued or suppressed, and how little it has done to right wrong, to draw acknowledgment or amends from self-satisfied insolence, he naturally asks what becomes of so much vital force. Can it fare differently from other forces, and be lost? The energy of evil is turned into the mill-race of good; but the wrath of man, even his righteous wrath, worketh not the righteousness of God! What becomes of it? If it be not lost, and have but changed its form, in what shape shall we look for it?

"Set her down," cried the chief. "I will take care of her."

When she heard the voice of her champion, the old woman let go a cat-like screech of triumph, and her gliding Gaelic, smoothness itself in articulation, flowed yet firier in word, and fiercer in tone. But the who were thus ejecting her—hangers on of the sheriff-court in the county town, employed to give a colour of law to the doubtful proceeding—did not know the chief.

"Oh, we'll set her down," answered one of them insolently, "—and glad enough too! but we'll have her on the public road with her sticks first!"

Infuriated by the man's disregard of her chief, Mistress Conal struck her nails into his face, and with a curse he flung her from him. She turned instantly on the other with the same argument ad hominem, and found herself staggering on her own weak limbs to a severe fall, when the chief caught and saved her. She struggled hard to break from him and rush again into the hut, declaring she would not leave it if they burned her alive in it, but he held her fast.

There was a pause, for one or two who had accompanied the men employed, knew the chief, and their reluctance to go on with the ruthless deed in his presence. influenced the rest. Report of the ejection had spread, and the neighbours came running from the village. A crowd seemed to be gathering. Again and again Mistress Conal tried to escape from Alister and rush into the cottage.

"You too, my chief!" she cried. "You turned against the poor of your people!"

"No, Mistress Conal," he answered. "I am too much your friend to let you kill yourself!"

"We have orders, Macruadh, to set fire to the hovel," said one of the men, touching his hat respectfully.

"They'll roast my black one!" shrieked the old woman.

"Small fear for him," said a man's voice from the little crowd, "if half be true—!"

Apparently the speaker dared no more.

"Fire won't singe a hair of him, Mistress Conal," said another voice. "You know it; he's used to it!"

"Come along, and let's get it over!" cried the leader of the ejection-party. "It—won't take many minutes once it's well a going, and there's fire enough on the hearth to set Ben Cruachan in a blaze!"

"Is everything out of it?" demanded the chief.

"All but her cat. We've done our best, sir, and searched everywhere, but he's not to be found. There's nothing else left."

"It's a lie!" screamed Mistress Conal. "Is there not a great pile of peats, carried on my own back from the moss! Ach, you robbers! Would you burn the good peats?"

"What good will the peats be to you, woman," said one of them not unkindly, "when you have no hearth?"

She gave a loud wail, but checked it.

"I will burn them on the road," she said. "They will keep me a few hours from the dark! When I die I will go straight up to God and implore his curse upon you, on your bed and board, your hands and tools, your body and soul. May your every prayer be lost in the wide murk, and never come at his ears! May—"

"Hush! hush!" interposed the chief with great gentleness. "You do not know what you are saying. But you do know who tells us to forgive our enemies!"

"It's well for HIM to forgive," she screamed, "sitting on his grand throne, and leaving me to be turned out of my blessed house, on to the cold road!"

"Nannie!" said the chief, calling her by her name, "because a man is unjust to you, is that a reason for you to be unjust to him who died for you? You know as well as he, that you will not be left out on the cold road. He knows, and so do you, that while I have a house over my head, there is a warm corner in it for you! And as for his sitting on his throne, you know that all these years he has been trying to take you up beside him, and can't get you to set your foot on the first step of it! Be ashamed of yourself, Nannie!"

She was silent.

"Bring out her peats," he said, turning to the bystanders; "we have small need, with winter on the road, to waste any of God's gifts!"

They obeyed. But as they carried them out, and down to the road, the number of Mistress Conal's friends kept growing, and a laying together of heads began, and a gathering of human fire under glooming eyebrows. It looked threatening. Suddenly Mistress Conal broke out in a wild yet awful speech, wherein truth indeed was the fuel, but earthly wrath supplied the prophetic fire. Her friends suspended their talk, and her foes their work, to listen.

English is by no means equally poetic with the Gaelic, regarded as a language, and ill-serves to represent her utterance. Much that seems natural in the one language, seems forced and unreal amidst the less imaginative forms of the other. I will nevertheless attempt in English what can prove little better than an imitation of her prophetic outpouring. It was like a sermon in this, that she began with a text:—

"Woe unto them," she said—and her voice sounded like the wind among the great stones of a hillside—" that join house to house, that lay field to field, till there be no place, that they may be placed alone in the midst of the earth!"

This woe she followed with woe upon woe, and curse upon curse, now from the Bible, now from some old poem of the country, and now from the bitterness of her own heart. Then she broke out in purely native eloquence:—

"Who art thou, O man, born of a woman, to say to thy brother, 'Depart from this earth: here is no footing for thee: all the room had been taken for me ere thou wast heard of! What right hast thou in a world where I want room for the red deer, and the big sheep, and the brown cattle? Go up, thou infant bald-head! Is there not room above, in the fields of the air? Is there not room below with the dead? Verily there is none here upon the earth!' Who art thou, I say, to speak thus to thy fellow, as if he entered the world by another door than thyself! Because thou art rich, is he not also a man?— a man made in the image of the same God? Who but God sent him? And who but God, save thy father was indeed the devil, hath sent thee? Thou hast to make room for thy brother! What brother of thy house, when a child is born into it, would presume to say, 'Let him begone, and speedily! I do not want him! There is no room for him! I require it all for myself!' Wilt thou say of any man, 'He is not my brother,' when God says he is! If thou say, 'Am I therefore his keeper?' God for that saying will brand thee with the brand of Cain. Yea, the hour will come when those ye will not give room to breathe, will rise panting in the agony, yea fury of their need, and cry, 'If we may neither eat nor lie down by their leave, lo, we are strong! let us take what they will not give! If we die we but die!' Then shall there be blood to the knees of the fighting men, yea, to the horses' bridles; and the earth shall be left desolate because of you, foul feeders on the flesh and blood, on the bodies and souls of men! In the pit of hell you will find room enough, but no drop of water; and it will comfort you little that ye lived merrily among pining men! Which of us has coveted your silver or your gold? Which of us has stretched out the hand to take of your wheat or your barley? All we ask is room to live! But because ye would see the dust of the earth on the head of the poor, ye have crushed and straitened us till we are ready to cry out, 'God, for thy mercy's sake, let us die, lest we be guilty of our own blood!'"

A solitary man had come down the hill behind, and stood alone listening. It was the mover of the wickedness. In the old time the rights of the people in the land were fully recognized; but when the chiefs of Clanruadh sold it, they could not indeed sell the rights that were not theirs, but they forgot to secure them for the help- less, and they were now in the grasp of the selfish and greedy, the devourers of the poor. He did not understand a word the woman was saying, but he was pleased to look on her rage, and see the man who had insulted him suffer with her. When he began to note the glances of lurid fire which every now and then turned upon him during Mistress Conal's speech, he scorned the indication: such poor creatures dared venture nothing, he thought, against the mere appearance of law. Under what he counted the chiefs contempt, he had already grown worse; and the thought that perhaps the great world might one day look upon him with like contempt, wrought in him bitterly; he had not the assurance of rectitude which makes contempt hurtless. He was crueller now than before the chief's letter to his daughter.

When Mistress Conal saw him, she addressed herself to him directly. What he would have felt had he understood, I cannot tell. Never in this life did he know how the weak can despise the strong, how the poor can scorn the rich!

"Worm!" she said, "uncontent with holding the land, eating the earth that another may not share! the worms eat but what their bodies will hold, and thou canst devour but the fill of thy life! The hour is at hand when the earth will swallow thee, and thy fellow worms will eat thee, as thou hast eaten men. The possessions of thy brethren thou hast consumed, so that they are not! The holy and beautiful house of my fathers,—" She spoke of her poor little cottage, but in the words lay spiritual fact. "—mock not its poverty!" she went on, as if forestalling contempt; "for is it not to me a holy house where the woman lay in the agony whence first I opened my eyes to the sun? Is it not a holy house where my father prayed morning and evening, and read the words of grace and comfort? Is it not to me sacred as the cottage at Nazareth to the poor man who lived there with his peasants? And is not that a beautiful house in which a woman's ear did first listen to the words of love? Old and despised I am, but once I was younger than any of you, and ye will be old and decrepit as I, if the curse of God do not cut you off too soon. My Alister would have taken any two of you and knocked your heads together. He died fighting for his country; and for his sake the voice of man's love has never again entered my heart! I knew a true man, and could be true also. Would to God I were with him! You man-trapping, land-reaving, house-burning Sasunnach, do your worst! I care not." She ceased, and the spell was broken. "Come, come!" said one of the men impatiently. "Tom, you get a peat, and set it on the top of the wall, under the roof. You, too, George!—and be quick. Peats all around! there are plenty on the hearth!—How's the wind blowing?—You, Henry, make a few holes in the wall here, outside, and we'll set live peats in them. It's time there was an end to this!"

"You're right; but there's a better way to end it!" returned one of the clan, and gave him a shove that sent him to the ground.

"Men, do your duty!" cried Mr. Palmer from behind. "*I* am here—to see you do it! Never mind the old woman! Of course she thinks it hard; but hard things have got to be done! it's the way of the world, and all for the best."

"Mr. Palmer," said another of the clan, "the old woman has the right of you: she and hers have lived there, in that cottage, for nigh a hundred years."

"She has no right. If she thinks she has, let her go to the law for it. In the meantime I choose to turn her off my land. What's mine's mine, as I mean every man jack of you to know—chief and beggar!"

The Macruadh walked up to him.

"Pardon me, sir," he said: "I doubt much if you have a legal right to disturb the poor woman. She has never paid rent for her hut, and it has always been looked upon as her property."

"Then the chief that sold it swindled both me and her!" stammered Mr. Palmer, white with rage. "But as for you who call yourself a chief, you are the most insolent, ill-bred fellow I ever had to do with, and I have not another word to say to you!"

A silence like that before a thunderstorm succeeded: not a man of the clan could for the moment trust his hearing. But there is nothing the Celtic nature resents like rudeness: half a dozen at once of the Macruadhs rushed upon the insulter of their chief, intent on his punishment.

"One of you touch him," cried Alister, "and I will knock him down. I would if he were my foster-brother!"

Each eager assailant stood like a block.

"Finish your work, men!" shouted Mr. Palmer.

To do him justice, he was no coward.

"Clansmen," said the chief, "let him have his way. I do not see how to resist the wrong without bringing more evil upon us than we can meet. We must leave it to him who says 'Vengeance is mine.'"

The Macruadhs murmured their obedience, and stood sullenly looking on. The disseizors went into the hut, and carried out the last of the fuel. Then they scooped holes in the turf walls, inside to leeward, outside to windward, and taking live peats from the hearth, put them in the holes. A few minutes, and poor Nannie's "holy and beautiful house" was a great fire.

When they began to apply the peats, Alister would at once have taken the old woman away, but he dreaded an outbreak, and lingered. When the fire began to run up the roof, Mistress Conal broke from him, and darted to the door. Every one rushed to seize her, Mr. Palmer with the rest.

"Blackie! Blackie! Blackie!" she shrieked like a madwoman.

While the men encumbered each other in their endeavours to get her away, down shot the cat from the blazing roof, a fizz of fire in his black fur, his tail as thick as his neck, an infernal howling screech of hatred in his horrible throat, and, wild with rage and fear, flung himself straight upon Mr. Palmer. A roar of delighted laughter burst forth. He bawled out—and his bawl was mingled with a scream—to take the brute off him, and his own men hurried to his rescue; but the fury-frantic animal had dug his claws and teeth into his face, and clung to him so that they had to choke him off. The chief caught up Mistress Conal and carried her away: there was no danger of any one hurting Mr. Palmer now!

He bore her on one arm like a child, and indeed she was not much heavier. But she kept her face turned and her eyes fixed on her burning home, and leaning over the shoulder of the chief, poured out, as he carried her farther and farther from the scene of the outrage, a flood of maledictory prophecy against the doers of the deed. The laird said never a word, never looked behind him, while she, almost tumbling down his back as she cursed with outstretched arms, deafened him with her raging. He walked steadily down the path to the road, where he stepped into the midst of her goods and chattels. The sight of them diverted a little the current of her wrath.

"Where are you going, Macruadh?" she cried, as he walked on. "See you not my property lying to the hand of the thief? Know you not that the greedy Sasunnach will sweep everything away!"

"I can't carry them and you too, Mistress Conal!" said the chief gayly.

"Set me down then. Who ever asked you to carry me! And where would you be carrying me? My place is with my things!"

"Your place is with me, Mistress Conal! I belong to you, and you belong to me, and I am taking you home to my mother."

At the word, silence fell, not on the lips, but on the soul of the raving prophetess: the chief she loved, his mother she feared.

"Set me down, Macruadh!" she pleaded in gentle tone. "Don't carry me to her empty-handed! Set me down straight; I will load my back with my goods, and bear them to my lady, and throw them at her feet."

"As soon as we get to the cottage," said the chief, striding on with his reluctant burden, "I will send up two men with wheelbarrows to bring them home."

"HOME, said you?" cried the old woman, and burst into the tearless wailing of a child; "there is a home for me no more! My house was all that was left me of my people, and it is your own that make a house a home! In the long winter nights, when I sat by the fire and heard the wind howl, and the snow pat, pat like the small hands of my little brothers on the window, my heart grew glad within me, and the dead came back to my soul! When I took the book, I heard the spirit of my father reading through my own lips! And oh, my mother! my mother!"

She ceased as if in despair.

"Surely, Nannie, you will be at home with your chief!" said Alister. "My house is your house now, and your dead will come to it and be welcome!"

"It is their chief's house, and they will!" she returned hopefully. "They loved their chief.—Shall we not make a fine clan when we're all gathered, we Macmadhs! Man nor woman can say I did anything to disgrace it!"

"Lest we should disgrace it," answered the chief, "we must bear with patience what is sent upon it."

He carried her into the drawing-room and told her story, then stood, to the delighted amusement of his mother, with his little old sister in his arms, waiting her orders, like a big boy carrying the baby, who now and then moaned a little, but did not speak.

Mrs. Macruadh called Nancy, and told her to bring the tea-tray, and then, get ready for Mistress Conal the room next Nancy's own, that she might be near to wait on her; and thither, when warmed and fed, the chief carried her.

But the terrible excitement had so thinned the mainspring of her time-watch, that it soon broke. She did not live many weeks. From the first she sank into great dejection, and her mind wandered. She said her father never came to see her now; that he was displeased with her for leaving the house; and that she knew now she ought to have stayed and been burned in it. The chief reminded her that she had no choice, but had been carried bodily away.

"Yes, yes," she answered; "but they do not know that! I must make haste and tell them! Who can bear her own people to think ill of her!—I'm coming! I'm coming! I'll tell you all about it! I'm an honest woman yet!"

Another thing troubled her sorely, for which she would hear no consolation; Blackie had vanished!—whether he was killed at the time of his onslaught on Mr. Palmer, or was afterwards shot; whether, disgusted with the treatment of his old home, or the memory of what he had there suffered, he had fled the strath, and gone to the wild cats among the hills, or back to the place which some averred he came from, no one could tell. In her wanderings she talked more of her cat than of anything else, and would say things that with some would have gone far to justify the belief that the animal was by nature on familiar terms with the element which had yet driven him from his temporary home.

Nancy was more than uneasy at having the witch so near, but by no means neglected her duty to her. One night she woke, and had for some time lain listening whether she stirred or not, when suddenly quavered through the dark the most horrible cat-cry she had ever heard. In abject terror she covered her head, and lay shuddering. The cry came again, and kept coming at regular intervals, but drawing nearer and nearer. Its expression was of intense and increasing pain. The creature whence it issued seemed to come close to the house, then with difficulty to scramble up on the roof, where it went on yowling, and screeching, and throwing itself about as if tying itself in knots, Nancy said, until at last it gave a great choking, gobbling scream, and fell to the ground, after which all was quiet. Persuading herself it was only a cat, she tried to sleep, and at length succeeded. When she woke in the morning, the first thing she did was to go out, fully expecting to find the cat lying at the foot of the wall. No cat was there. She went then as usual to attend to the old woman. Mistress Conal was dead and cold.

The clan followed her body to the grave, and the black cat was never seen.

CHAPTER IX

THE MARCHES.

It was plainly of no use for the chief to attempt mollifying Mr. Palmer. So long as it was possible for him to be what he was, it must be impossible for him to understand the conscience that compelled the chief to refuse participation in the results of his life. Where a man's own conscience is content, how shall he listen to the remonstrance of another man's! But even if he could have understood that the offence was unavoidable, that would rather have increased than diminished the pain of the hurt; as it was, the chief's determination must seem to Mr. Palmer an unprovoked insult! Thus reflecting, Alister tried all he could to be fair to the man whom he had driven to cut his acquaintance.

It was now a lonely time for Alister, lonelier than any ever before. Ian was not within reach even by letter; Mercy was shut up from him: he had not seen or heard from her since writing his explanation; and his mother did not sympathize with his dearest earthly desire: she would be greatly relieved, yea heartily glad, if Mercy was denied him! She loved Ian more than the chief, yet could have better borne to see him the husband of Mercy; what was wanting to the equality of her love was in this regard more than balanced by her respect for the chief of the clan and head of the family. Alister's light was thus left to burn in very darkness, that it might burn the better; for as strength is made perfect through weakness, so does the light, within grow by darkness. It was the people that sat in darkness that saw a great light. He was brought closer than ever to first principles; had to think and judge more than ever of the right thing to do—first of all, the right thing with regard to Mercy. Of giving her up, there was of course no thought; so long as she would be his, he was hers as entirely as the bonds of any marriage could make him! But she owed something to her father! and of all men the patriarchal chief was the last to dare interfere with the RIGHTS of a father. BUT THEY MUST BE RIGHTS, not rights turned into, or founded upon wrongs. With the first in acknowledging true, he would not be with the last even, in yielding to false rights! The question was, what were the rights of a father? One thing was clear, that it was the duty, therefore the right of a father, to prevent his child from giving herself away before she could know what she did; and Mercy was not yet of age. That one woman might be capable of knowing at fifteen, and another not at fifty, left untouched the necessity for fixing a limit. It was his own duty and right, on the other hand, to do what he could to prevent her from being in any way deceived concerning him. It was essential that nothing should be done, resolved, or yielded, by the girl, through any misunderstanding he could forestall, or because of any falsehood he could frustrate. He must therefore contrive to hold some communication with her!

First of all, however, he must learn how she was treated! It was not only in fiction or the ancient clan-histories that tyrannical and cruel things were done! A tragedy is even more a tragedy that it has not much diversity of incident, that it is acted in commonplace surroundings, and that the agents of it are commonplace persons— fathers and mothers acting from the best of low or selfish motives. Where either Mammon or Society is worshipped, in love, longing, or fear, there is room for any falsehood, any cruelty, any suffering.

There were several of the clan employed about the New House of whom Alister might have sought information; but he was of another construction from the man of fashion in the old plays, whose first love-strategy is always to bribe the lady's maid: the chief scorned to learn anything through those of a man's own household. He fired a gun, and ran up a flag on the old castle, which brought Rob of the Angels at full speed, and comforted the heart of Mercy sitting disconsolate at her window: it was her chiefs doing, and might have to do with her!

Having told Rob the state of matters between him and the New House—

"I need not desire you, Rob," he concluded, "to be silent! You may of course let your father know, but never a soul besides. From this moment, every hour your father does not actually need you, be somewhere on the hills where you can see the New House. I want to learn first whether she goes out at all. With the dark you must draw nearer the house. But I will have no questioning of the servants or anyone employed about it; I will never use a man's pay to thwart his plans, nor yet make any man even unconsciously a traitor."

Rob understood and departed; but before he had news for his master an event occurred which superseded his service.

The neighbours, Mr. Peregrine Palmer and Mr. Brander, had begun to enclose their joint estates for a deer-forest, and had engaged men to act as curators. They were from the neighbourhood, but none of them belonged to Strathruadh, and not one knew the boundaries of the district they had to patrol; nor indeed were the boundaries everywhere precisely determined: why should they be, where all was heather and rock? Until game-sprinkled space grew valuable, who would care whether this or that lump of limestone, rooted in the solid earth, were the actual property of the one or the other! Either would make the other welcome to blast and cart it away!

There was just one person who knew all about the boundaries that was to be known; he could not in places draw their lines with absolute assurance, but he had better grounds for his conclusions than anyone else could have; this was Hector of the Stags. For who so likely to understand them as he who knew the surface within them as well as the clay-floor of his own hut? If he did not everywhere know where the marchline fell, at least he knew perfectly where it ought to fall.

It happened just at this time that THE MISTRESS told Hector she would be glad of a deer, intending to cure part for winter use; the next day, therefore,—the first of Rob of the Angels' secret service—he stalked one across the hill-farm, got a shot at it near the cave-house, brought it down, and was busy breaking it, when two men who had come creeping up behind, threw themselves upon him, and managed, well for themselves, to secure him before he had a chance of defending himself. Finding he was deaf and dumb, one of them knew who he must be, and would have let him go; but the other, eager to ingratiate himself with the new laird, used such, argument to the contrary as prevailed with his companion, and they set out for the New House, Hector between them with his hands tied. Annoyed and angry at being thus treated like a malefactor, he yet found amusement in the notion of their mistake. But he found it awkward to be unable to use that readiest weapon of human defence, the tongue. If only his EARS AND MOUTH, as he called Rob in their own speech, had been with him! When he saw, however, where they were taking him, he was comforted, for Rob was almost certain to see him: wherever he was, he was watching the New House! He went composedly along with them therefore, fuming and snorting, not caring to escape.

When Rob caught sight of the three, he could not think how it was that his father walked so unlike himself. He could not be hurt, for his step was strong and steady as ever; not the less was there something of the rhythm gone out of his motion! there was "a broken music" in his gait! He took the telescope which the chief had lent him, and turned it upon him. Discovering then that his father's hands were bound behind his back, fiercest indignation overwhelmed the soul of Rob of the Angels. His father bound like a criminal!—his father, the best of men! What could the devils mean? Ah, they were taking him to the New House! He shut up his telescope, laid it down by a stone, and bounded to meet them, sharpening his knife on his hand as he went.

The moment they were near enough, signs, unintelligible to the keepers, began to pass between the father and son: Rob's meant that he must let him pass unnoticed; Hector's that he understood. So, with but the usual salutation of a stranger, Rob passed them. The same moment he turned, and with one swift sweep of his knife, severed the bonds of his father. The old man stepped back, and father and son stood fronting the enemy.

"Now," said Eob, "if you are honest men, stand to it! How dared you bind Hector of the Stags?"

"Because he is not an honest man," replied one of them.

Rob answered him with a blow. The man made at him, but Hector stepped between.

"Say that again of my father," cried Rob, "who has no speech to defend himself, and I will drive my knife into you."

"We are only doing our duty!" said the other. "We came upon him there cutting up the deer he had just killed on the new laird's land."

"Who are you to say which is the stranger's, and which the Macruadh's? Neither my father nor I have ever seen the faces of you in the country! Will you pretend to know the marches better than my father, who was born and bred in the heather, and knows every stone on the face of the hills?"

"We can't help where he was born or what he knows! he was on our land!"

"He is the Macruadh's keeper, and was on his own land. You will get yourselves into trouble!"

"We'll take our chance!"

"Take your man then!"

"If he try to escape, I swear by the bones of my grandfather," said the more inimical of the two, inheritor of a clan-feud with the Macruadhs, "I will shoot him."

Bob of the Angels burst into a scornful laugh.

"You will! will you?"

"I will not kill him; I don't want to be hanged for him! but I will empty my shot-barrel into the legs of him! So take your chance; you are warned!"

They had Hector's gun, and Rob had no weapon but his knife. Nor was he inclined to use either now he had cooled a little. He turned to his father. The old man understood perfectly what had passed between them, and signed to Rob that he would go on to the New House, and Rob might run and let the chief know what had happened. The same thing was in Rob's mind, for he saw how it would favour the desires of his chief, bringing them all naturally about the place. But he must first go with his father on the chance of learning something.

"We will go with you," he said.

"We don't want YOU!"

"But I mean to go!—My father is not able to speak for himself!"

"You know nothing."

"I know what he knows. The lie does not grow in our strath."

"You crow high, my cock!"

"No higher than I strike," answered Rob.

In the eyes of the men Rob was small and weak; but there was something in him notwithstanding that looked dangerous, and, though far from cowards, they thought it as well to leave him alone.

Mercy at her window, where was her usual seat now, saw them coming, and instinctively connected their appearance with her father's new measures of protection; and when the men turned toward the kitchen, she ran down to learn what she could. Rob greeted her with a smile as he entered.

"I am going to fetch the Macruadh," he whispered, and turning went out again.

He told the chief that at the word her face lighted up as with the rise of the moon.

One of the maids went and told her master that they had got a poacher in the kitchen.

Mr. Palmer's eyes lightened under his black brows when he saw the captive, whom he knew by sight and by report. His men told him the story their own way, never hinting a doubt as to whose was the land on which the deer had been killed.

"Where is the nearest magistrate?" he inquired with grand severity.

"The nearest is the Macruadh, sir!" answered a highlander who had come from work in the garden to see what was going on.

"I cannot apply to him; the fellow is one of his own men!"

"The Macruadh does what is just!" rejoined the man.

His master vouchsafed him no reply. He would not show his wrath against the chief: it would be undignified!

"Take him to the tool-house, and lock him up till I think what to do with him. Bring me the key."

The butler led the way, and Hector followed between his captors. They might have been showing him to his bed-room, so calm was he: Bob gone to fetch the chief, his imprisonment could not last!—and for the indignity, was he not in the right!

As Mr. Palmer left the kitchen, his eye fell on Mercy.

"Go to your room," he said angrily, and turned from her.

She obeyed in silence, consoling herself that from her window she could see the arrival of the chief. Nor had she watched long when she saw him coming along the road with Rob. At the gate she lost sight of them. Presently she heard voices in the hall, and crept down the stair far enough to hear.

"I could commit you for a breach of the peace, Mr. Palmer," she heard the chief say. "You ought to have brought the man to me. As a magistrate I order his release. But I give my word he shall be forthcoming when legally required."

"Your word is no bail. The man was taken poaching; I have him, and I will keep him."

"Let me see him then, that I may learn from himself where he shot the deer."

"He shall go before Mr. Brander."

"Then I beg you will take him at once. I will go with him. But listen a moment, Mr. Palmer. When this same man, my keeper, took your guest poaching on my ground, I let Mr. Sercombe go. I could have committed him as you would commit Hector. I ask you in return to let Hector go. Being deaf and dumb, and the hills the joy of his life, confinement will be terrible to him."

"I will do nothing of the kind. You could never have committed a gentleman for a mistake. This is quite a different thing!"

"It is a different thing, for Hector cannot have made a mistake. He could not have followed a deer on to your ground without knowing it!"

"I make no question of that!"

"He says he was not on your property."

"Says!"

"He is not a man to lie!"

Mr. Palmer smiled.

"Once more I pray you, let us see him together."

"You shall not see him."

"Then take him at once before Mr. Brander."

"Mr. Brander is not at home."

"Take him before SOME magistrate—I care not who. There is Mr. Chisholm!"

"I will take him when and where it suits me."

"Then as a magistrate I will set him at liberty. I am sorry to make myself unpleasant to you. Of all things I would have avoided it. But I cannot let the man suffer unjustly. Where have you put him?"

"Where you will not find him."

"He is one of my people; I must have him!"

"Your people! A set of idle, poaching fellows! By heaven, the strath shall be rid of the pack of them before another year is out!"

"While I have land in it with room for them to stand upon, the strath shall not be rid of them!—But this is idle! Where have you put Hector of the Stags?"

Mr. Palmer laughed.

"In safe keeping. There is no occasion to be uneasy about him! He shall have plenty to eat and drink, be well punished, and show the rest of the rascals the way out of the country!"

"Then I must find him! You compel me!"

So saying, the chief, with intent to begin his search at the top of the house in the hope of seeing Mercy, darted up the stair. She heard him coming, went a few steps higher, and waited. On the landing he saw her, white, with flashing eyes. Their hands clasped each other—for a moment only, but the moment was of eternity, not of time.

"You will find Hector in the tool-house," she said aloud.

"You shameless hussey!" cried her father, following the chief in a fury.

Mercy ran up the stair. The chief turned and faced Mr. Palmer.

"You have no business in my house!"

"I have the right of a magistrate."

"You have no right. Leave it at once."

"Allow me to pass."

"You ought to be ashamed of yourself—making a girl turn traitor to her own father!"

"You ought to be proud of a daughter with the conscience and courage to turn against you!"

The chief passed Mr. Palmer, and running down the stair, joined Rob of the Angels where he stood at the door in a group composed of the keepers and most of the servants.

"Do you know the tool-house?" he said to Rob.

"Yes, Macruadh."

"Lead the way then. Your father is there."

"On no account let them open the door," cried Mr. Palmer. "They may hold through it what communication they please."

"You will not be saying much to a deaf man through inch boards!" remarked the clansman from the garden.

Mr. Palmer hurried after them, and his men followed.

Alister found the door fast and solid, without handle. He turned a look on his companion, and was about to run his weight against the lock.

"It is too strong," said Rob. "Hector of the Stags must open it!"

"But how? You cannot even let him know what you want!"

Rob gave a smile, and going up to the door, laid himself against it, as close as he could stand, with his face upon it, and so stood silent.

Mr. Palmer coming up with his attendants, all stood for a few moments in silence, wondering at Rob: he must be holding communication with his father—but how?

Sounds began inside—first a tumbling of tools about, then an attack on the lock.

"Come! come! this won't do!" said Mr. Palmer, approaching the door.

"Prevent it then," said the chief. "Do what you will you cannot make him hear you, and while the door is between you, he cannot see you! If you do not open it, he will!"

"Run," said Mr. Palmer to the butler; "you will find the key on my table! I don't want the lock ruined!"

But there was no stopping the thing! Before the butler came back, the lock fell, the door opened, and out came Hector, wiping his brow with his sleeve, and looking as if he enjoyed the fun.

The keepers darted forward.

"Stand off!" said the chief stepping between. "I don't want to hurt you, but if you attempt to lay hands on him, I will."

One of the men dodged round, and laid hold of Hector from behind; the other made a move towards him in front. Hector stood motionless for an instant, watching his chief, but when he saw him knock down the man before him, he had his own assailant by the throat in an instant, gave him a shake, and threw him beside his companion.

"You shall suffer for this, Macruadh!" cried Mr. Palmer, coming close up to him, and speaking in a low, determined tone, carrying a conviction of unchangeableness.

"Better leave what may not be the worst alone!" returned the chief. "It is of no use telling you how sorry I am to have to make myself disagreeable to you; but I give you fair warning that I will accept no refusal of the hand of your daughter from any but herself. As you have chosen to break with me,

I accept your declaration of war, and tell you plainly I will do all I can to win your daughter, never asking your leave in respect of anything I may think it well to do. You will find there are stronger forces in the world than money. Henceforward I hold myself clear of any personal obligation to you except as Mercy's father and my enemy."

From very rage Mr. Palmer was incapable of answering him. Alister turned from him, and in his excitement mechanically followed Rob, who was turning a corner of the house. It was not the way to the gate, but Rob had seen Mercy peeping round that same corner—anxious in truth about her father; she feared nothing for Alister.

He came at once upon Mercy and Rob talking together. Rob withdrew and joined his father a little way off; they retired a few more paces, and stood waiting their chief's orders.

"How AM I to see you again, Mercy?" said the chief hurriedly. "Can't you think of some way? Think quick."

Now Mercy, as she sat alone at her window, had not unfrequently imagined the chief standing below on the walk, or just beyond in the belt of shrubbery; and now once more in her mind's eye suddenly seeing him there, she answered hurriedly,

"Come under my window to-night."

"I do not know which it is."

"You see it from the castle. I will put a candle in it."

"What hour?"

"ANY time after midnight. I will sit there till you come."

"Thank you," said the chief, and departed with his attendants.

Mercy hastened into the house by a back door, but had to cross the hall to reach the stair. As she ran up, her father came in at the front door, saw her, and called her. She went down again to meet the tempest of his rage, which now broke upon her in gathered fury. He called her a treacherous, unnatural child, with every name he thought bad enough to characterize her conduct. Had she been to him as Began or Goneril, he could hardly have found worse names for her. She stood pale, but looked him in the face. Her mother came trembling as near as she dared, withered by her terror to almost twice her age. Mr. Palmer in his fury took a step towards Mercy as if he would strike her. Mercy did not move a muscle, but stood ready for the blow. Then love overcame her fear, and the wife and mother threw herself between, her arms round her husband, as if rather to protect him from the deed than her daughter from its hurt.

"Go to your room, Mercy," she said.

Mercy turned and went. She could not understand herself. She used to be afraid of her father when she knew no reason; now that all the bad in his nature and breeding took form and utterance, she found herself calm! But the thing that quieted her was in reality her sorrow that he should carry himself so wildly. What she thought was, if the mere sense of not being in the wrong made one able to endure so much, what must not the truth's sake enable one to bear! She sat down at her window to gaze and brood.

When her father cooled down, he was annoyed with himself, not that he had been unjust, but that he had behaved with so little dignity. With brows black as evil, he sat degraded in his own eyes, resenting the degradation on his daughter. Every time he thought of her, new rage arose in his heart. He had been proud of his family autocracy. So seldom had it been necessary to enforce his authority, that he never doubted his wishes had but to be known to be obeyed. Born tyrannical, the characterless submission of his wife had nourished the tyrannical in him. Now, all at once, a daughter, the ugly one, from whom no credit was to be looked for, dared to defy him for a clown figuring in a worn-out rag of chieftainship—the musty fiction of a clan— half a dozen shepherds, crofters, weavers, and shoemakers, not the shadow of a gentleman among them!—a man who ate brose, went with bare knees, worked like any hind, and did not dare offend his wretched relations by calling his paltry farm his own!—for the sake of such a fellow, with a highland twang that disgusted his fastidious ear, his own daughter made a mock of his authority, treated him as a nobody! In his own house she had risen against him, and betrayed him to the insults of his enemy! His conscious importance, partly from doubt in itself, boiled and fumed, bubbled and steamed in the caldron of his angry brain. Not one, but many suns would go down upon such a wrath!

"I wish I might never set eyes on the girl again!" he said to his wife. "A small enough loss the sight of her would be, the ugly, common-looking thing! I beg you will save me from it in future as much as you can. She makes me feel as if I should go out of my mind!—so calm, forsooth! so meek! so self-sufficient!—oh, quite a saint!—and so strong-minded!— equal to throwing her father over for a fellow she never saw till a year ago!"

"She shall have her dinner sent up to her as usual," answered his wife with a sigh. "But, really, Peregrine, my dear, you must compose yourself! Love has driven many a woman to extremes!"

"Love! Why should she love such a fellow? I see nothing in him to love! WHY should she love him? Tell me that! Give me one good reason for her folly, and I will forgive her—do anything for her!— anything but let her have the rascal! That I WILL NOT! Take for your son-in-law an ape that loathes your money, calls it filthy lucre—and means it! Not if I can help it! —Don't let me see her! I shall come to hate her! and that I would rather not; a man must love and cherish his own flesh! I shall go away, I must!— to get rid of the hateful face of the minx, with its selfrighteous, injured look staring at you!"

"If you do, you can't expect me to prevent her from seeing him!"

"Lock her up in the coal-hole—bury her if you like! I shall never ask what you have done with her! Never to see her again is all I care about!"

"Ah, if she were really dead, you would want to see her again—after a while!"

"I wish then she was dead, that I might want to see her again! It won't be sooner! Ten times rather than know her married to that beast, I would see her dead and buried!"

The mother held her peace. He did not mean it, she said to herself. It was only his anger! But he did mean it; at that moment he would with joy have heard the earth fall on her coffin.

Notwithstanding her faculty for shutting out the painful, her persistent self-assuring that it would blow over, and her confidence that things would by and by resume their course, Mrs. Palmer was in those days very unhappy. The former quiet once restored, she would take Mercy in hand, and reasoning with her, soon persuade her to what she pleased! It was her husband's severity that had brought it to this!

The accomplice of her husband, she did not understand that influence works only between such as inhabit the same spiritual sphere: the daughter had been lifted into a region far above all the arguments of her mother—arguments poor in life, and base in reach.

CHAPTER X

MIDNIGHT.

Mercy sat alone but not lonely at her window. A joy in her heart made her independent for the time of human intercourse. Life at the moment was livable without it, for there was no bar between her and her lover.

The evening drew on. They sent her food. She forgot to eat it, and sat looking, till the lines of the horizon seemed grown into her mind like an etching. She watched the slow dusk swell and gather—with such delicate, soft-blending gradations in the birth of night as Edwin Waugh loves to seize and word-paint. Through all its fine evanescent change of thought and feeling she watched unconsciously; and the growth, death, and burial of that twilight were ever after a substratum to all the sadness and all the hope that visited her. Through palest eastern rose, through silvery gold and golden green and brown, the daylight passed into the shadow of the light, and the stars, like hope in despair, began to show themselves where they always were, and the night came on, and deeper and deeper sank the silence. Household sound expired, and no step came near her door. Her father had given orders, and was obeyed. Christina has stolen indeed from her own room and listened at hers, but hearing nor sound nor motion, had concluded it better for Mercy as well as safer for herself, to return. So she sat the sole wakeful thing in the house, for even her father slept.

The earth had grown vague and dim, looking as it must look to the dead. Its oppressive solidity, its obtrusive HERENESS, dissolved in the dark, it left the soul to live its own life. She could still trace the meeting of earth and sky, each the evidence of the other, but the earth was content to be and not assert, and the sky lived only in the points of light that dotted its vaulted quiet. Sound itself seemed asleep, and filling the air with the repose of its slumber. Absolute silence the soul cannot grasp; therefore deepest silence seems ever, in Wordsworth's lovely phrase, wandering into sound, for silence is but the thin shadow of harmony—say rather creation's ear agape for sound, the waiting matrix of interwoven melodies, the sphere-bowl standing empty for the wine of the spirit. There may be yet another reason beyond its too great depth or height or strength, why we should be deaf to the spheral music; it may be that the absolute perfection of its harmony can take to our ears but the shape of silence.

Content and patient, Mercy sat watching.

It was just past midnight, but she had not yet lighted a candle, when something struck the window as with the soft blow of a moth's wing. Her heart gave a great leap. She listened breathless. Nothing followed. It must have been some flying night-thing, though surely too late in the year for a moth!

It came again! She dared not speak. She softly opened the window. The darkness had thinned on the horizon, and the half-moon was lifting a corner above the edge of the world. Something in the shrubbery answered her shine, and without rustle of branch, quiet as a ghost, the chief stepped into the open space. Mercy leaned toward him and said,

"Hush! speak low."

"There is no need to say much," he answered." I come only to tell you that, as man may, I am with you always."

"How quietly you came! I did not hear a sound!"

"I have been two hours here in the shrubbery."

"And I not once to suspect it! You might have given me some hint! A very small one would have been enough! Why did you not let me know?"

"It was not your hour; it is twelve but now; the moon comes to say so. I came for the luxury of expectation, and the delight of knowing you better attended than you thought: you knew me with you in spirit; I was with you in the body too!"

"My chief!" she said softly. "I shall always find you nearer and better than I was able to think! I know I do not know how good you are."

"I am good toward you, Mercy! I love you!"

A long silence, save of shining eyes, followed.

"We are waiting for God!" said Alister at length.

"Waiting is loving," answered Mercy.

She leaned out, looking down to her heaven.

The moon had been climbing the sky, veiled in a little cloud. The cloud vanished, and her light fell on the chief.

"Have you been to a ball?" said Mercy.

"No, Mercy. I doubt if there will be any dancing more in Strathruadh!"

"Then why are you in court dress?"

"When should a Celt, who of all the world loves radiance and colour, put on his gay attire? For the multitude, or for the one?"

"Thank you. Is it a compliment?—But after your love, everything fine seems only natural!"

"In love there are no compliments; truth only walks the sacred path between the two doors. I will love you as my father loved my mother, and loves her still."

"I do like to see you shining! It was kind of you to dress for the moon and me!"

"Whoever loves the truth must love shining things! God is the father of lights, even of the lights hid in the dark earth—sapphires and rubies, and all the families of splendour."

"I shall always see you like that!"

"There is one thing I want to say to you, Mercy:—you will not think me indifferent however long I may be in proposing a definite plan for our future! We must wait upon God!"

"I shall think nothing you would not have me think. A little while ago I might have dreamed anything, for I was fast asleep. I was dead till you waked me. If I were what girls call IN LOVE, I should be impatient to be with you; but I love you much more than that, and do not need to be always with you. You have made me able to think, and I can think about you! I was but a child, and you made a woman of me!"

"God and Ian did," said Alister.

"Yes, but through you, and I want to be worthy of you. A woman to whom a man's love was so little comfort that she pined away and died because she could not be married to him, would not be a wife worthy of my chief!"

"Then you will always trust me?"

"I will. When one really knows another, then all is safe!"

"How many people do you know?" asked the chief.

She thought a moment, and with a little laugh, replied,

"You."

"Pardon me, Mercy, but I do want to know how your father treats you!"

"We will not talk about him, please. He is my father!—and so far yours that you are bound to make what excuse you can for him."

"That I am bound to do, if he were no father to either of us. It is what God is always doing for us!—only he will never let us off."

"He has had no one to teach him, Alister! and has always been rich, and accustomed to have his own way! I begin to think one punishment of making money in a wrong manner is to be prosperous in it!"

"I am sure you are right! But will you be able to bear poverty, Mercy?"

"Yes," she answered, but so carelessly that she seemed to speak without having thought.

"You do not know what poverty means!" rejoined Alister. "We may have to endure much for our people!"

"It means YOU any way, does it not? If you and poverty come together, welcome you and your friend!—I see I must confess a thing! Do you remember telling me to read Julius Caesar?"

"Yes."

"Do you remember how Portia gave herself a wound, that she might prove to her husband she was able to keep a secret?"

"Yes, surely!"

"I have my meals in my room now, so I can do as I please, and I never eat the nice things dear mother always sends me, but potatoes, and porridge, and bread and milk."

"What IS that for, Mercy?"

"To show you I am worthy of being poor—able at least to be poor. I have not once tasted anything VERY nice since the letter that made my father so angry."

"You darling!"

Of all men a highlander understands independence of the KIND of food.

413

"But," continued Alister, "you need not go on with it; I am quite convinced; and we must take with thanksgiving what God gives us. Besides, you have to grow yet!"

"Alister! and me like a May-pole!"

"You are tall enough, but we are creatures of three dimensions, and need more than height. You must eat, or you will certainly be ill!"

"Oh, I eat! But just as you please! Only it wouldn't do me the least harm so long as you didn't mind! It was as much to prove to myself I could, as to you! But don't you think it must he nearly time for people to wake from their first sleep?"

The same instant there was a little noise—like a sob. Mercy started, and when she looked again Alister had vanished—as noiselessly as he came. For a moment she sat afraid to move. A wind came blowing upon her from the window: some one had opened her door! What if it were her father! She compelled herself to turn her head. It was something white!—it was Christina! She came to her through the shadow of the moonlight, put her arms round her, and pressed to her face a wet cheek. For a moment or two neither spoke.

"I heard a little, Mercy!" sobbed Christina. "Forgive me; I meant no harm; I only wanted to know if you were awake; I was coming to see you."

"Thank you, Chrissy! That was good of you!"

"You are a dear!—and so is your chief! I am sorry I scared him! It made me so miserable to hear you so happy that I could not help it! Would you mind forgiving me, dear?"

"I don't mind your hearing a bit. I am glad you should know how the chief loves me!"

But you must be careful, dear! Papa might pretend to take him for a robber, and shoot him!"

"Oh, no, Chrissy! He wouldn't do that!"

"I would not be too sure! I hadn't an idea before what papa was like! Oh what men are, and what they can be! I shall never hold up my head again!"

With this incoherent speech, to Mercy's astonishment and consternation she burst into tears. Mercy tried to comfort her, but did not know how. She had seen for some time that there was a difference in her, that something was the matter, and wondered whether she could be missing Ian, but it was merest surmise. Perhaps now she would tell her!

She was weeping like a child on her shoulder. Presently she began to tremble. Mercy coaxed her into her bed, and undressing quickly, lay down beside her, and took her in her arms to make her warm. Before the morning, with many breaks of sobbing and weeping, Christina had told Mercy her story.

"I wish you would let me tell the chief!" she said. "He would know how to comfort you."

"Thank you!" said Christina, with not a little indignation. "I forgot I was talking to a girl as good as married, who would not keep my secrets any more than her own!"

She would have arisen at once to go to her own room, and the night that had brought such joy to Mercy threatened to end very sadly. She threw her arms round Christina's waist, locked her hands together, and held her fast.

"Hear me, Chrissy, darling! I am a great big huge brute," she cried. "But I was only stupid. I would not tell a secret of yours even to Alister—not for worlds! If I did, he would be nearer despising me than I should know how to bear. I will not tell him. Did I ever break my word to you, Chrissy?"

"No, never, Mercy!" responded Christina, and turning she put her arms round her.

"Besides," she went on, "why should I go to anyone for counsel? Could I have a better counsellor than Ian? Is he not my friend? Oh, he is! he is! he said so! he said so!"

The words prefaced another storm of tears.

"He is going to write to me," she sobbed, as soon as she could again speak.

"Perhaps he will love you yet, Chrissy!"

"No, no; he will never love me that way! For goodness' sake don't hint at such a thing! I should not be able to write a word to him, if I thought that! I should feel a wolf in sheep's clothing! I have done with tricks and pretendings! Ian shall never say to himself, 'I wish I had not trusted that girl! I thought she was going to be honest! But what's bred in the bone—!' I declare, Mercy, I should blush myself out of being to learn he thought of me like that! I mean to be worthy of his friendship! His friendship is better than any other man's love! I will be worthy of it!"

The poor girl burst yet again into tears—not so bitter as before, and ended them all at once with a kiss to Mercy.

"For his sake," she said, "I am going to take care of Alister and you!"

"Thank you! thank you, Chrissy! Only you must not do anything to offend papa! It is hard enough on him as it is! I cannot give up the chief to please him, for he has been a father to my better self; but we must do nothing to trouble him that we can help!"

CHAPTER XI

SOMETHING STRANGE.

Alister did not feel inclined to go home. The night was more like Mercy, and he lingered with the night, inhabiting the dream that it was Mercy's house, and she in the next room. He turned into the castle, climbed the broken steps, and sat on the corner of the wall, the blank hill before him, asleep standing, with the New House on its shoulder, and the moonlight reflected from Mercy's window under which he had so lately stood. He sat for an hour, and when he came down, was as much disinclined to go home as before: he could not rest in his chamber, with no Ian on the other side of its wall! He went straying down the road, into the valley, along the burnside, up the steep beyond it, and away to the hill-farm and the tomb.

The moon was with him all the way, but she seemed thinking to herself rather than talking to him. Why should the strange, burnt-out old cinder of a satellite be the star of lovers? The answer lies hid, I suspect, in the mysteries of light reflected.

He wandered along, careless of time, of moonset, star-shine, or sunrise, brooding on many things in the rayless radiance of his love, and by the time he reached the tomb, was weary with excitement and lack of sleep. Taking the key from where it was cunningly hidden, he unlocked the door and entered.

He started back at sight of a gray-haired old man, seated on one of the stone chairs, and leaning sadly over the fireless hearth: it must be his uncle! The same moment he saw it was a ray from the sinking moon, entering by the small, deep window, and shining feebly on the chair. He struck a light, kindled the peats on the hearth, and went for water. Returning from the well he found the house dark as before; and there was the old man again, cowering over the extinguished fire! The idea lasted but a moment; once more the level light of the moon lay cold and gray upon the stone chair! He tried to laugh at his fancifulness, but did not quite succeed. Several times on the way up, he had thought of his old uncle: this must have given the shape to the moonlight and the stone! He made many attempts to recall the illusion, but in vain. He relighted the fire, and put on the kettle. Going then for a book to read till the water boiled, he remembered a letter which, in the excitement of the afternoon, he had put in his pocket unread, and forgotten. It was from the family lawyer in Glasgow, informing him that the bank in which his uncle had deposited the proceeds of his sale of the land, was in a state of absolute and irrecoverable collapse; there was not the slightest hope of retrieving any portion of the wreck.

Alister did not jump up and pace the room in the rage of disappointment; neither did he sit as one stunned and forlorn of sense. He felt some bitterness in the loss of the hope of making up to his people for his uncle's wrong; but it was clear that if God had cared for his having the money, he would have cared that he should have it. Here was an opportunity for absolute faith and contentment in the will that looks after all our affairs, the small as well as the great.

Those who think their affairs too insignificant for God's regard, will justify themselves in lying crushed under their seeming ruin. Either we live in the heart of an eternal thought, or we are the product and sport of that which is lower than we.

"It was evil money!" said the chief to himself; "it was the sale of a birthright for a mess of pottage! I would have turned it back into the right channel, the good of my people! but after all, what can money do? It was discontent with poverty that began the ruin of the highlands! If the heads of the people had but lived pure, active, sober, unostentatious lives, satisfied to be poor, poverty would never have overwhelmed them! The highlands would have made Scotland great with the greatness of men dignified by high-hearted contentment, and strong with the strength of men who could do without!" Therewith it dawned upon Alister how, when he longed to help his people, his thoughts had always turned, not to God first, but to the money his uncle had left him. He had trusted in a fancy—no less a fancy when in his uncle's possession than when cast into the quicksand of the bank; for trust in money that is, is no less vain, and is farther from redress, than trust in money that is not. In God alone can trust repose. His heart had been so faithless that he did not know it was! He thought he loved God as the first and last, the beginning, middle, and end of all things, and he had been trusting, not in God, but in uncertain riches, that is in vile Mammon! It was a painful and humiliating discovery. "It was well," he said, "that my false deity should be taken from me! For my idolatry perhaps, a good gift has failed to reach my people! I must be more to them than ever, to make up to them for their loss with better than money!"

He fell on his knees, and thanked God for the wind that had blown cold through his spirit, and slain at least one evil thing; and when he rose, all that was left of his trouble was a lump in his throat, which melted away as he walked home through the morning air on the hills. For he could not delay; he must let his mother know their trouble, and, as one who had already received help from on high, help her to bear it! If the messenger of Satan had buffeted him, he had but broken a way for strength!

But at first he could not enjoy as he was wont the glory of the morning. It troubled him. Would a single note in the song of the sons of the morning fail because God did or would not do a thing? Could God deserve less than thanks perfect from any one of his creatures? That man could not know God who thanked him but for what men call good things, nor took the evil as from the same love! He scorned himself, and lifted up his heart. As he reached the brow of his last descent, the sun rose, and with it his soul arose and shone, for its light was come, and the glory of the Lord was risen upon it. "Let God," he said, "take from us what he will: himself he can only give!" Joyful he went down the hill. God was, and all was well!

CHAPTER XII

THE POWER OF DARKNESS.

He found his mother at breakfast, wondering what had become of him.

"Are you equal to a bit of bad news, mother?" he asked with a smile.

The mother's thoughts flew instantly to Ian.

"Oh, it's nothing about Ian!" said the chief, answering her look.

Its expression changed; she hoped now it was some fresh obstacle between him and Mercy.

"No, mother, it is not that either!" said Alister, again answering her look—with a sad one of his own, for the lack of his mother's sympathy was the sorest trouble he had. "It is only that uncle's money is gone—all gone."

She sat silent for a moment, gave a little sigh, and said,

"Well, it will all be over soon! In the meantime things are no worse than they were! His will be done!"

"I should have liked to make a few friends with the mammon of unrighteousness before we were turned out naked!"

"We shall have plenty," answered the mother, "—God himself, and a few beside! If you could make friends with the mammon, you can make friends without it!"

"Yes, that is happily true! Ian says it was only a lesson for the wise and prudent with money in their pockets—a lesson suited to their limited reception!"

As they spoke, Nancy entered.

"Please, laird, she said, "Donal shoemaker is wanting to see you."

"Tell him to come in," answered the chief.

Donal entered and stood up by the door, with his bonnet under his arm—a little man with puckered face, the puckers radiating from or centering in the mouth, which he seemed to untie like a money-hag, and pull open by means of a smile, before he began to speak. The chief shook hands with him, and asked how he could serve him.

"It will not be to your pleasure to know, Macruadh," said Donal, humbly declining to sit, "that I have received this day notice to quit my house and garden!"

The house was a turf-cottage, and the garden might grow two bushels and a half of potatoes.

"Are you far behind with your rent?"

"Not a quarter, Macruadh."

"Then what does it mean?"

"It means, sir, that Strathruadh is to be given to the red deer, and the son of man have nowhere to lay his head. I am the first at your door with my sorrow, but before the day is over you will have—"

Here he named four or five who had received like notice to quit.

"It is a sad business!" said the chief sorrowfully.

"Is it law, sir?"

"It is not easy to say what is law, Donal; certainly it is not gospel! As a matter of course you will not be without shelter, so long as I may call stone or turf mine, but things are looking bad! Things as well as souls are in God's hands however!"

"I learn from the new men on the hills," resumed Donal, "that the new lairds have conspired to exterminate us. They have discovered, apparently, that the earth was not made for man, but for rich men and beasts!" Here the little man paused, and his insignificant face grew in expression grand. "But the day of the Lord will come," he went on, "as a thief in the night. Vengeance is his, and he will know where to give many stripes, and where few.—What would you have us do, laird?"

"I will go with you to the village."

"No, if you please, sir! Better men will be at your door presently to put the same question, for they will do nothing without the Macruadh. We are no more on your land, great is our sorrow, chief, but we are of your blood, you are our lord, and your will is ours. You have been a nursing father to us, Macruadh!"

"I would fain be!" answered the chief.

"They will want to know whether these strangers have the right to turn us out; and if they have not the right to disseize, whether we have not the right to resist. If you would have us fight, and will head us, we will fall to a man —for fall we must; we cannot think to stand before the redcoats."

"No, no, Donal! It is not a question of the truth; that we should be bound to die for, of course. It is only our rights that are concerned, and they are not worth dying for. That would be mere pride, and denial of God who is fighting for us. At least so it seems at the moment to me!"

"Some of us would fain fight and have done with it, sir!"

The chief could not help smiling with pleasure at the little man's warlike readiness: he knew it was no empty boast; what there was of him was good stuff.

"You have a wife and children, Donal!" he said; "what would become of them if you fell?"

"My sister was turned out in the cold spring," answered Donal, "and died in Glencalvu! It would be better to die together!"

"But, Donal, none of yours will die of cold, and I can't let you fight, because the wives and children would all come on my hands, and I should have too many for my meal! No, we must not fight. We may have a right to fight, I do not know; but I am sure we have at least the right to abstain from fighting. Don't let us confound right and duty, Donal—neither in thing nor in word!"

"Will the law not help us, Macruadh?"

"The law is such a slow coach! our enemies are so rich! and the lawyers have little love of righteousness! Most of them would see the dust on our heads to have the picking of our bones! Stick nor stone would be left us before anything came of it!"

"But, sir," said Donal, "is it the part of brave men to give up their rights?"

"No man can take from us our rights," answered the chief, "but any man rich enough may keep us from getting the good of them. I say again we are not bound to insist on our rights. We may decline to do so, and that way leave them to God to look after for us."

"God does not always give men their rights, sir! I don't believe he cares about our small matters!"

"Nothing that God does not care about can be worth our caring about. But, Donal, how dare you say what you do? Have you lived to all eternity? How do you know what you say? GOD DOES care for our rights. A day is coming, as you have just said, when he will judge the oppressors of their brethren."

"We shall be all dead and buried long before then!"

"As he pleases, Donal! He is my chief. I will have what he wills, not what I should like! A thousand years I will wait for my rights if he chooses. I will trust him to do splendidly for me. No; I will have no other way than my chief's! He will set everything straight!"

"You must be right, sir! only I can't help wishing for the old times, when a man could strike a blow for himself!"

With all who came Alister held similar talk; for though they were not all so warlike as the cobbler, they keenly felt the wrong that was done them, and would mostly, but for a doubt of its rectitude, have opposed force with force. It would at least bring their case before the country!

"The case is before a higher tribunal," answered the laird; "and one's country is no incarnation of justice! How could she be, made up mostly of such as do not love fair play except in the abstract, or for themselves! The wise thing is to submit to wrong."

It is in ordering our own thoughts and our own actions, that we have first to stand up for the right; our business is not to protect ourselves from our neighbour's wrong, but our neighbour from our wrong. This is to slay evil; the other is to make it multiply. A man who would pull out even a mote from his brother's eye, must first pull out the beam from his own eye, must be righteous against his own selfishness. That is the only way to wound the root of evil. He who teaches his neighbour to insist on his rights, is not a teacher of righteousness. He who, by fulfilling his own duties, teaches his neighbour to give every man the fair play he owes him, is a fellow-worker with God.

But although not a few of the villagers spoke in wrath and counselled resistance, not one of them rejoiced in the anticipation of disorder. Heartily did Rob of the Angels insist on peace, but his words had the less force that he was puny in person, and, although capable of great endurance, unnoted for deeds of strength. Evil birds carried the words of natural and righteous anger to the ears of the new laird; no good birds bore the words of appeasement: he concluded after his kind that their chief countenanced a determined resistance.

On all sides the horizon was dark about the remnant of Clanruadh. Poorly as they lived in Strathruadh, they knew no place else where they could live at all. Separated, and so disabled from making common cause against want, they must perish! But their horizon was not heaven, and God was beyond it.

It was a great comfort to the chief that in the matter of his clan his mother agreed with him altogether: to the last penny of their having they must help their people! Those who feel as if the land were their own, do fearful wrong to their own souls! What grandest opportunities of growing divine they lose! Instead of being man-nobles, leading a sumptuous life until it no longer looks sumptuous, they might be God-nobles—saviours of men, yielding themselves to and for their brethren! What friends might they not make with the mammon of unrighteousness, instead of passing hence into a region where no doors, no arms will be open to them! Things are ours that we may use them for all—sometimes that we may sacrifice them. God had but one precious thing, and he gave that!

The chief, although he saw that the proceedings of Mr. Palmer and Mr. Brander must have been determined upon while his relation to Mercy was yet undeclared, could not help imagining how differently it might have gone with his people, had he been married to Mercy, and in a good understanding with her father. Had he crippled his reach toward men by the narrowness of his conscience toward God? So long as he did what seemed right, he must regret no consequences, even for the sake of others! God would mind others as well as him! Every sequence of right, even to the sword and fire, are God's care; he will justify himself in the eyes of the true, nor heed the judgment of the false.

One thing was clear—that it would do but harm to beg of Mr. Palmer any pity for his people: it would but give zest to his rejoicing in iniquity! Something nevertheless must be determined, and speedily, for winter was at hand.

The Macruadh had to consider not only the immediate accommodation of the ejected but how they were to be maintained. Such was his difficulty that he began to long for such news from Ian as would justify an exodus from their own country, not the less a land of bondage, to a home in the wilderness. But ah, what would then the land of his fathers without its people be to him! It would be no more worthy the name of land, no longer fit to be called a possession! He knew then that the true love of the land is one with the love of its people. To live on it after they were gone, would be like making a home of the family mausoleum. The rich "pant after the dust of the earth on the head of the poor," but what would any land become without the poor in it? The poor are blessed because by their poverty they are open to divine influences; they are the buckets set out to catch the rain of heaven; they are the salt of the earth! The poor are to be always with a nation for its best blessing, or for its condemnation and ruin. The chief saw the valleys desolate of the men readiest and ablest to fight the battles of his country. For the sake of greedy, low-minded fellows, the summons of her war-pipes would be heard in them no more, or would sound in vain among the manless rocks; from sheilin, cottage, or clachan, would spring no kilted warriors with battle response! The red deer and the big sheep had taken the place of men over countless miles of mountain and moor and strath! His heart bled for the sufferings and wrongs of those whose ancestors died to keep the country free that was now expelling their progeny. But the vengeance had begun to gather, though neither his generation nor ours has seen it break. It must be that offences come, but woe unto them by whom they come!

CHAPTER XIII.

THE NEW STANCE.

The Macruadh cast his mind's and his body's eye too upon the small strip of ground on the west side of the castle-ridge, between it and the tiny tributary of the strath burn which was here the boundary between the lands of the two lairds. The slope of the ridge on this side was not so steep, and before the rock sank into the alluvial soil of the valley, it became for a few yards nearly level—sufficiently so, with a little smoothing and raising, to serve for a foundation; while in front was a narrow but rich piece of ground, the bank of the little brook. Before many days were over, men were at work there, in full sight of the upper windows of the New House. It was not at first clear what they were about; but soon began to rise, plain enough, the walls of cottages, some of stone, and some of turf; Mr. Palmer saw a new village already in process of construction, to take the place of that about to be destroyed! The despicable enemy had moved his camp, to pitch it under his very walls! It filled him with the rage of defeat. The poor man who scorned him was going to be too much for him! Not yet was he any nearer to being placed alone in the midst of the earth. He thought to have rid himself of all those hateful faces, full of their chiefs contempt, he imagined, ever eyeing him as an intruder on his own land; but here instead was their filthy little hamlet of hovels growing like a fungus just under his nose, expressly to spite him! Thinking to destroy it, he had merely sent for it! When the wind was in the east, the smoke of their miserable cabins would be blown right in at his dining-room windows! It was useless to expostulate! That he would not like it was of course the chief's first reason for choosing that one spot as the site of his new rookery! The fellow had stolen a march upon him! And what had he done beyond what was absolutely necessary for the improvement of his property! The people were in his way, and he only wanted to get rid of them! And here their chief had brought them almost into his garden! Doubtless if his land had come near enough, he would have built his sty at the very gate of his shrubbery!—the fellow could not like having them so near himself!

He let his whole household see how annoying the thing was to him. He never doubted it was done purely to irritate him. Christina ventured the suggestion that Mr. Brander and not the chief was the author of the inconvenience. What did that matter! he returned. What right had the chief, as she called him, to interfere between a landlord and his tenants? Christina hinted that, evicted by their landlord, they ceased to be his tenants, and even were he not their chief, he could not be said to interfere in giving help to the destitute. Thereupon he burst at her in a way that terrified her, and she had never even been checked by him before, had often been impertinent to him without rebuke. The man seemed entirely changed, but in truth he was no whit changed: things had but occurred capable of bringing out the facts of his nature. Her mother, who had not dared to speak at the time, expostulated with her afterward.

"Why should papa never be told the truth?" objected Christina.

Her mother was on the point of replying, "Because he will not hear it," but saw she owed it to her husband not to say so to his child.

Mercy said to herself, "It is not to annoy my father he does it, but to do what he can for his people! He does not even know how unpleasant it is to my father to have them so near! It must be one of the punishments of riches that they make the sight of poverty so disagreeable! To luxury, poverty is a living reproach." She longed to see Alister: something might perhaps be done to mitigate the offence. But her father would never consent to use her influence! Perhaps her mother might!

She suggested therefore that Alister would do nothing for the sake of annoying her father, and could have no idea how annoying this thing was to him: if her mother would contrive her seeing him, she would represent it to him!

Mrs. Palmer was of Mercy's opinion regarding the purity of Alister's intent, and promised to think the matter over.

The next night her husband was going to spend at Mr. Brander's: the project might be carried out in safety!

The thing should be done! They would go together, in the hope of persuading the chief to change the site of his new village!

When it was dark they walked to the cottage, and knocking at the door, asked Nancy if the chief were at home. The girl invited them to enter, though not with her usual cordiality; but Mrs. Palmer declined, requesting her to let the chief know they were there, desirous of a word with him.

Alister was at the door in a moment, and wanted them to go in and see his mother, but an instant's reflection made him glad of their refusal.

"I am so sorry for all that has happened!" said Mrs. Palmer. "You know I can have had nothing to do with it! There is not a man I should like for a son-in-law better than yourself, Macruadh; but I am helpless."

"I quite understand," replied the chief, "and thank you heartily for your kindness. Is there anything I can do for you?"

"Mercy has something she wants to speak to you about."

"It was so good of you to bring her!—What is it, Mercy?"

Without the least hesitation, Mercy told him her father's fancy that he was building the new village to spite him, seeing it could not be a pleasure to himself to have the smoke from its chimneys blowing in at door and windows as often as the wind was from the sea.

"I am sorry but not surprised your father should think so, Mercy. To trouble him is as much against my feelings as my interests. And certainly it is for no convenience or comfort to ourselves, that my mother and I have determined on having the village immediately below us."

"I thought," said Mercy, "that if you knew how it vexed papa, you would— But I am afraid it may be for some reason that cannot be helped!"

"Indeed it is; I too am afraid it cannot be helped! I must think of my people! You see, if I put them on the other side of the ridge, they would be exposed to the east wind—and the more that every door and window would have to be to the east. You know yourselves how bitterly it blows down the strath! Besides, we should there have to build over good land much too damp to be healthy, every foot of which will be wanted to feed them! There they are on the rock. I might, of course, put them on the hillside, but I have no place so sheltered as here, and they would have no gardens. And then it gives me an opportunity, such as chief never had before, of teaching them some things I could not otherwise. Would it be reasonable, Mercy, to sacrifice the good of so many poor people to spare one rich man one single annoyance, which is yet no hurt? Would it be right? Ought I not rather to suffer the rise of yet greater obstacles between you and me?"

"Yes, Alister, yes!" cried Mercy. "You must not change anything. I am only sorry my father cannot be taught that you have no ill will to him in what you do."

"I cannot think it would make much difference. He will never give you to me, Mercy. But be true, and God will."

"Would you mind letting the flag fly, Alister? I should have something to look at!"

"I will; and when I want particularly to see you, I will haul it down. Then, if you hang a handkerchief from your window, I will come to you."

CHAPTER XIV

THE PEAT-MOSS.

For the first winter the Clanruadh had not much to fear—hardly more than usual: they had their small provision of potatoes and meal, and some a poor trifle of money. But "Lady Macruadh" was anxious lest the new cottages should not be quite dry, and gave a general order that fires were to be burned in them for some time before they were occupied: for this they must use their present stock of dry peats, and more must be provided for the winter. The available strength of the clan would be required to get the fresh stock under cover before the weather broke.

The peat-moss from which they cut their fuel, was at some distance from the castle, on the outskirts of the hill-farm. It was the nearest moss to the glen, and the old chief, when he parted with so much of the land, took care to except it, knowing well that his remaining people could not without it live through a winter. But as, of course, his brother, the minister, who succeeded him, and the present chieftain, had freely allowed all the tenants on the land sold to supply themselves from it as before, the notion had been generated that the moss was not part of the chief's remaining property.

When the report was carried to Mr. Peregrine Palmer, that the tenants Mr. Brander and he were about to eject, and who were in consequence affronting him with a new hamlet on the very verge of his land, were providing themselves with a stock of fuel greatly in excess of what they had usually laid in for the winter—that in fact they were cutting large quantities of peat, besides the turf for their new cottages; without making the smallest inquiry, or suspecting for a moment that the proceeding might be justifiable, he determined, after a brief consultation with men who knew nothing but said anything, to put a stop to the supposed presumption.

A few of the peats cut in the summer had not yet been removed, not having dried so well as the rest, and the owners of some of these, two widows, went one day to fetch them home to the new village, when, as it happened, there were none of the clan besides in the moss.

They filled their creels, helped each other to get them on their backs, and were setting out on their weary tramp home, when up rose two of Mr. Palmer's men, who had been watching them, cut their ropes and took their loads, emptied the peats into a moss-hag full of water, and threw the creels after them. The poor women poured out their wrath on the men, telling them they would go straight to the chief, but were answered only with mockery of their chief and themselves. They turned in despair, and with their outcry filled the hollows of the hills as they went, bemoaning the loss of their peats and their creels, and raging at the wrong they had received. One of them, a characterless creature in the eyes of her neighbours, harmless, and always in want, had faith in her chief, for she had done nothing to make her ashamed, and would go to him at once: he had always a word and a smile and a hand-shake for her, she said; the other, commonly called Craftie, was unwilling: her character did not stand high, and she feared the face of the Macruadh.

"He does not like me!" said Craftie.

"When a woman is in trouble," said the other, "the Macruadh makes no questions. You come with me! He will be glad of something to do for you."

In her confidence she persuaded her companion, and together they went to the chief.

Having gathered courage to appear, Craftie needed none to speak: where that was the call, she was never slow to respond.

"Craftie," said the chief, "is what you are telling me true?"

"Ask HER," answered Craftie, who knew that asseveration on her part was not all-convincing.

"She speaks the truth, Macruadh," said the other. "I will take my oath to it."

"Your word is enough," replied the chief, "—as Craftie knew when she brought you with her."

"Please, laird, it was myself brought Craftie; she was not willing to come!"

"Craftie," said the chief, "I wish I could make a friend of you! But you know I can't!"

"I do know it, Macruadh, and I am sorry for it, many is the good time! But my door never had any latch, and the word is out before I can think to keep it back!"

"And so you send another and another to back the first! Ah, Craftie! If purgatory don't do something for you, then—!"

"Indeed and I hope I shall fall into it on my way farther, chief!" said Craftie, who happened to be a catholic.

"But now," resumed the chief, "when will you be going for the rest of your peats?"

"They're sure to be on the watch for us; and there's no saying what they mightn't do another time!" was the indirect and hesitating answer.

"I will go with you."

"When you please, then, chief."

So the next day the poor women went again, and the chief went with them, their guard and servant. If there were any on the watch, they did not appear. The Macruadh fished out their creels, and put them to dry, then helped them to fill those they had borrowed for the occasion. Returning, he carried now the one, now the other creel, so that one of the women was always free. The new laird met them on the road, and recognized with a scornful pleasure the chief bending under his burden. That was the fellow who would so fain be HIS son-in-law!

About this time Sercombe and Valentine came again to the New House. Sercombe, although he had of late had no encouragement from Christina, was not therefore prepared to give her up, and came "to press the siege." He found the lady's reception of him so far from cordial, however, that he could not but suspect some new adverse influence. He saw too that Mercy was in disgrace; and, as Ian was gone, concluded there must have been something between them: had the chief been "trying it on with" Christina? The brute was always getting in his way! But some chance of serving him out was certain to turn, up!

For the first suitable day Alister had arranged an expedition from the village, with all the carts that could be got together, to bring home as many peats as horses and men and women could together carry. The company was seen setting out, and report of it carried at once to Mr. Palmer; for he had set watch on the doings of the clan. Within half an hour he too set out with the messenger, accompanied by Sercombe, in grim delight at the prospect of a row. Valentine went also, willing enough to see what would happen, though with no ill will toward the chief. They were all furnished as for a day's shooting, and expected to be joined by some of the keepers on their way.

The chief, in view of possible assault, had taken care that not one of his men should have a gun. Even Hector of the Stags he requested to leave his at home.

They went in little groups, some about the creeping carts, in which were the older women and younger children, some a good way ahead, some scattered behind, but the main body attending the chief, who talked to them as they went. They looked a very poor company, but God saw past their poverty. The chief himself, save in size and strength, had not a flourishing appearance. He was very thoughtful: much lay on his shoulders, and Ian was not there to help! His clothes, all their clothes were shabby, with a crumpled, blown-about look—like drifts, in their many faded colours, of autumnal leaves. They had about them all a forgotten air—looked thin and wan like a ghostly funeral to the second sight—as if they had walked so long they had forgotten how to sleep, and the grave would not have them. Except in their chief, there was nothing left of the martial glance and gait and show, once so notable in every gathering of the Clanruadh, when the men were all soldiers born, and the women were mothers, daughters, and wives of soldiers. Their former stately grace had vanished from the women; they were weather-worn and bowed with labour too heavy for their strength, too long for their endurance; they were weak from lack of fit human food, from lack of hope, and the dreariness of the outlook, the ever gray spiritual horizon; they were numbed with the cold that has ceased to be felt, the deadening sense of life as a weight to be borne, not a strength to rejoice in. But they were not abject yet; there was one that loved them— their chief and their friend! Below their level was a deeper depth, in which, alas, lie many of like heart and, passions with them, trodden into the mire by Dives and his stewards!

The carts were small, with puny horses, long-tailed and droop-necked, in harness of more rope than leather. They had a look of old men, an aspect weirdly venerable, as of life and labour prolonged after due time, as of creatures kept from the grave and their last sleep to work a little longer. Scrambling up the steep places they were like that rare sea-bird which, unable to fly for shortness of wing, makes of its beak a third leg, to help it up the cliff: these horses seemed to make fifth legs of their necks and noses. The chief's horses alone, always at the service of the clan, looked well fed, well kept, and strong, and the clan was proud of them.

"And what news is there from Ian?" asked an old man of his chief.

"Not much news yet, but I hope for more soon. It will be so easy to let you hear all his letters, when we can meet any moment in the barn!"

"I fear he will be wanting us all to go after the rest!" said one of the women.

"There might be a worse thing!" answered her neighbour.

"A worse thing than leave the hills where we were born?—No! There is no worse for me! I trust in God I shall be buried where I grew up!"

"Then you will leave the hills sure enough!" said the chief.

"Not so sure, Macruadh! We shall rest in our graves till the resurrection!" said an old man.

"Only our bodies," returned Alister.

"Well, and what will my body be but myself! Much I would make of myself without my body! I will stay with my body, and let my soul step about, waiting for me, and craving a shot at the stags with the big branches! No, I won't be going from my own strath!"

"You would not like to be left in it alone, with none but unfriendly Sasunnachs about you—not one of your own people to close your eyes?"

"Indeed it would not be pleasant. But the winds would be the same; and the hills would be the same; and the smell of the earth would be the same; and they would be our own worms that came crawling over me to eat me! No; I won't leave the strath till I die—and I won't leave it then!"

"That is very well, John!" said the woman; "but if you were all day with your little ones—all of them all day looking hunger in your face, you would think it a blessed country wherever it was that gave you bread to put in their mouths!"

"And how to keep calling this home!" said another. "Why, it will soon be everywhere a crime to set foot on a hill, for frightening of the deer! I was walking last month in a part of the county I did not know, when I came to a wall that went out of my sight, seeming to go all round a big hill. I said to myself, 'Is no poor man to climb to heaven any more?' And with that I came to a bill stuck on a post, which answered me; for it said thus: 'Any well-dressed person, who will give his word not to leave the path, may have permission to go to the top of the hill, by applying to—'—I forget the name of the doorkeeper, but sure he was not of God, seeing his door was not to let a poor man in, but to keep him out!"

"They do well to starve us before they choke us: we might else fight when it comes to the air to breathe!"

"Have patience, my sons," said the chief. "God will not forget us."

"What better are we for that? It would be all the same if he did forget us!" growled a young fellow shambling along without shoes.

"Shame! Shame!" cried several voices. "Has not God left us the Macruadh? Does he not share everything with us?"

"The best coat in the clan is on his own back!" muttered the lad, careless whether he were heard or not.

"You scoundrel!" cried another; "yours is a warmer one!"

The chief heard all, and held his peace. It was true he had the best coat!

"I tell you what," said Donal shoemaker, "if the chief give you the stick, not one of us will say it was more than you deserved! If he will put it into my hands, not to defile his own, I will take and give it with all my heart. Everybody knows you for the idlest vagabond in the village! Why, the chief with his own hands works ten times as much!"

"That's how he takes the bread out of my mouth—doing his work himself!" rejoined the youth, who had been to Glasgow, and thought he had learned a thing or two.

The chief recovered from his impulse to pull off his coat and give it him.

"I will make you an offer, my lad," he said instead: "come to the farm and take my place. For every fair day's work you shall have a fair day's wages, and, for every bit of idleness, a fair thrashing. Do you agree?"

The youth pretended to laugh the thing off, but slunk away, and was seen no more till eating time arrived, and "Lady Macruadh's" well-filled baskets were opened.

"And who wouldn't see a better coat on his chief!" cried the little tailor. "I would clip my own to make lappets for his!"

They reached the moss. It lay in a fold of the hills, desert and dreary, full of great hollows and holes whence the peat had been taken, now filled with water, black and terrible,—a land hideous by day, and at night full of danger and lonely horror. Everywhere stood piles of peats set up to dry, with many openings through and through, windy drains to gather and remove their moisture. Here and there was a tuft of dry grass, a bush of heather, or a few slender-stalked, hoary heads of CANNACH or cotton-grass; it was a land of devoted desolation, doing nothing for itself, this bountiful store of life and warmth for the winter-sieged houses of the strath.

They went heartily to work. They cut turf for their walls and peats for their fires; they loaded the carts from the driest piles, and made new piles of the fresh wet peats they dug. It was approaching noon, and some of the old women were getting the food out of "my lady's" baskets, when over the nearest ridge beyond rose men to the number of seven, carrying guns. Rob of the Angels was the first to spy them. He pointed them out to his father, and presently they two disappeared together. The rest went on with their work, but the chief could see that, stooping to their labour, they cast upward and sidelong glances at them, reading hostility in their approach. Suddenly, as by common consent, they all ceased working, stood erect, and looked out like men on their guard. But the chief making them a sign, they resumed their labour as if they saw nothing.

Mr. Peregrine Palmer had laid it upon himself to act with becoming calmness and dignity. But it would amaze most people to be told how little their order is self-restraint, their regular conduct their own—how much of the savage and how little of the civilized man goes to form their being—how much their decent behaviour is owing to the moral pressure, like that of the atmosphere, of the laws and persons and habits and opinions that surround them. Witness how many, who seemed respectable people at home, become vulgar, self- indulgent, ruffianly, cruel even, in the wilder parts of the colonies! No man who has not, through restraint, learned not to need restraint, but be as well behaved among savages as in society, has yet become a true man. No perfection of mere civilization kills the savage in a man: the savage is there all the time till the man pass through the birth from above. Till then, he is no certain hiding-place from the wind, no sure covert from the tempest.

Mr. Palmer was in the worst of positions as to protection against himself. Possessed of large property, he owed his position to evil and not to good. Not only had he done nothing to raise those through whom he made his money, but the very making of their money his, was plunging them deeper and deeper in poverty and vice: his success was the ruin of many. Yet was he full of his own imagined importance—or had been full until now that he felt a worm at the root of his gourd—the contempt of one man for his wealth and position. Well might such a man hate such another—and the more that his daughter loved him! All the chief's schemes and ways were founded on such opposite principles to his own that of necessity they annoyed him at every point, and, incapable of perceiving their true nature, he imagined his annoyance their object and end. And now here was his enemy insolently daring, as Mr. Palmer fully believed, to trespass in person on his land!

Add to all this, that here Mr. Peregrine Palmer was in a place whose remoteness lightened the pressure of conventional restraints, while its wildness tended to rouse all the old savage in him—its very look suggesting to the city-man its fitness for an unlawful deed for a lawful end. Persons more RESPECTABLE than Mr. Palmer are capable of doing the most wicked and lawless things when their selfish sense of their own right is uppermost. Witness the occasionally iniquitous judgments of country magistrates in their own interest—how they drive law even to cruelty!

"Are you not aware you are trespassing on my land, Macruadh?" cried the new laird, across several holes full of black water which obstructed his nearer approach.

"On the contrary, Mr. Palmer," replied the chief, "I am perfectly aware that I am not!"

"You have no right to cut peats there without my permission!"

"I beg your pardon: you have no right to stand where you speak the words without my permission. But you are quite welcome."

"I am satisfied there is not a word of truth in what you say," rejoined Mr. Palmer. "I desire you to order your people away at once."

"That I cannot do. It would be to require their consent to die of cold."

"Let them die! What are they to me—or to anybody! Order them off, or it will be the worse for them—and for you too!"

"Excuse me; I cannot."

"I give you one more warning. Go yourself, and they will follow."

"I will not."

"Go, or I will compel you."

As he spoke, he half raised his gun.

"You dare not!" said the chief, drawing himself up indignantly.

Together Mr. Palmer and Mr. Sercombe raised their guns to their shoulders, and one of them fired. To give Mr. Palmer the benefit of a doubt, he was not quite at home with his gun, and would use a hair-trigger. The same instant each found himself, breath and consciousness equally scant, floundering, gun and all, in the black bog water on whose edge he had stood. There now stood Rob of the Angels, gazing after them into the depth, with the look of an avenging seraph, his father beside him, grim as a gratified Fate.

Such a roar of rage rose from the clansmen with the shot, and so many came bounding with sticks and spades over the rough ground, that the keepers, knowing, if each killed his two men, they would not after escape with their lives, judged it more prudent to wait orders. Only Valentine came running in terror to the help of his father.

"Don't be frightened," said Rob; "we only wanted to wet their powder!"

"But they'll be drowned!" cried the lad, almost weeping.

"Not a hair of them!" answered Bob. "We'll have them out in a moment! But please tell your men, if they dare to lift a gun, we'll serve them the same. It wets the horn, and it cools the man!"

A minute more, and the two men lay coughing and gasping on the crumbly bank, for in their utter surprizal they had let more of the nasty soft water inside than was good for them. With his first breath Sercombe began to swear.

"Drop that, sir, if you please," said Rob, "or in you go again!"

He began to reply with a volley of oaths, but began only, for the same instant the black water was again choking him. Might Hector of the Stags have had his way, he would have kept there the murderer of AN CABRACH MOR till he had to be dived for. Rob on his part was determined he should not come out until he gave his word that he would not swear.

"Come! Come!" gasped Sercombe at length, after many attempts to get out which, the bystanders easily foiled—" you don't mean to drown me, do you?"

"We mean to drown your bad language. Promise to use no more on this peat-moss," returned Rob.

"Damn the promise you get from me!" he gasped.

"Men must have patience with a suffering brother!" remarked Bob, and seated himself, with a few words in Gaelic which drew a hearty laugh from the men about him, on a heap of turf to watch the unyielding flounder in the peat-hole, where there was no room to swim. He had begun to think the man would drown in his contumacy, when his ears welcomed the despairing words—

"Take me out, and I will promise anything."

He was scarcely able to move till one of the keepers gave him whisky, but in a few minutes he was crawling homeward after his host, who, parent of little streams, was doing his best to walk over rocks and through bogs with the help of Valentine's arm, chattering rather than muttering something about "proper legal fashion."

In the mean time the chief lay shot in the right arm and chest, but not dangerously wounded by the scattering lead.

He had lost a good deal of blood, and was faint—a sensation new to him. The women had done what they could, but that was only binding his arm, laying him in a dry place, and giving him water. He would not let them recall the men till the enemy was gone.

When they knew what had happened they were in sad trouble—Rob of the Angels especially that he had not been quick enough to prevent the firing of the gun. The chief would have him get the shot out of his arm with his knife; but Rob, instead, started off at full speed, running as no man else in the county could run, to fetch the doctor to the castle.

At the chief's desire, they made a hurried meal, and then resumed the loading of the carts, preparing one of them for his transport. When it was half full, they covered the peats with a layer of dry elastic turf, then made on that a bed of heather, tops uppermost; and more to please them than that he could not walk, Alister consented to be laid on this luxurious invalid-carriage, and borne home over the rough roads like a disabled warrior.

They arrived some time before the doctor.

CHAPTER XV

A DARING VISIT.

Mercy soon learned that some sort of encounter had taken place between her father's shooting party and some of the clan; also that the chief was hurt, but not in what manner—for by silent agreement that was not mentioned: it might seem to put them in the wrong! She had heard enough, however, to fill her with anxiety. Her window commanding the ridge by the castle, she seated herself to watch that point with her opera-glass. When the hill-party came from behind the ruin, she missed his tall figure amongst his people, and presently discovered him lying very white on one of the carts. Her heart became as water within her. But instant contriving how she could reach him, kept her up.

By and by Christina came to tell her she had just heard from one of the servants that the Macruadh was shot. Mercy, having seen him alive, heard the frightful news with tolerable calmness. Christina said she would do her best to discover before the morning how much he was hurt; no one in the house seemed able to tell her! Mercy, to avoid implicating her sister, held her peace as to her own intention.

As soon as it was dark she prepared to steal from the house, dreading nothing but prevention. When her dinner was brought her, and she knew they were all safe in the dining-room, she drew her plaid over her head, and leaving her food untasted, stole half down the stair, whence watching her opportunity between the comings and goings of the waiting servants, she presently got away unseen, crept softly past the windows, and when out of the shrubbery, darted off at her full speed. Her breath was all but gone when she knocked at the drawing-room door of the cottage.

It opened, and there stood the mother of her chief! The moment Mrs. Macruadh saw her, leaving her no time to say a word, she bore down upon her like one vessel that would sink another, pushing her from the door, and pulling it to behind her, stern as righteous Fate. Mercy was not going to be put down, however: she was doing nothing wrong!

"How is the Macruadh, please?" she managed to say.

"Alive, but terribly hurt," answered his mother, and would have borne her out of the open door of the cottage, towards the latch of which she reached her hand while yet a yard from it. Her action said, "Why WILL Nancy leave the door open!"

"Please, please, what is it?" panted Mercy, standing her ground. "How is he hurt?"

She turned upon her almost fiercely.

"This is what YOU have done for him!" she said, with right ungenerous reproach. "Your father fired at him, on my son's own land, and shot him in the chest."

"Is he in danger?" gasped Mercy, leaning against the wall, and trembling so she could scarcely stand.

"I fear he is in GREAT danger. If only the doctor would come!"

"You wouldn't mind my sitting in the kitchen till he does?" whispered Mercy, her voice all but gone.

"I could not allow it. I will not connive at your coming here without the knowledge of your parents! It is not at all a proper thing for a young lady to do!"

"Then I will wait outside!" said Mercy, her quick temper waking in spite of her anxiety: she had anticipated coldness, but not treatment like this! "There is one, I think, Mrs. Macruadh," she added, "who will not find fault with me for it!"

"At least he will not tell you so for some time!"

The door had not been quite closed, and it opened noiselessly.

"She does not mean me, mother," said Alister; "she means Jesus Christ. He would say to you, LET HER ALONE. He does not care for Society. Its ways are not his ways, nor its laws his laws. Come in, Mercy. I am sorry my mother's trouble about me should have made her inhospitable to you!"

"I cannot come in, Alister, if she will not let me!" answered Mercy.

"Pray walk in!" said Mrs. Macruadh.

She would have passed Mercy, going toward the kitchen, but the TRANCE was narrow, and Mercy did not move.

"You see, Alister, I cannot!" she insisted. "That would not please, would it?" she added reverently. "Tell me how you are, and I will go, and come again to-morrow."

Alister told her what had befallen, making little of the affair, and saying he suspected it was an accident.

"Oh, thank you!" she said, with a sigh of relief. "I meant to sit by the castle wall till the doctor came; but now I shall get back before they discover I am gone."

Without a word more, she turned and ran from the house, and reached her room unmissed and unseen.

The next was a dreary hour—the most painful that mother and son had ever passed together. The mother was all this time buttressing her pride with her grief, and the son was cut to the heart that he should have had to take part against his mother. But when the doctor came at length, and the mother saw him take out his instruments, the pride that parted her from her boy melted away.

"Forgive me, Alister!" she whispered; and his happy kiss comforted her repentant soul.

When the small operations were over, and Alister was in bed, she would have gone to let Mercy know all she could tell her. But she must not: it would work mischief in the house! She sat down by Alister's bedside, and watched him all night.

He slept well, being in such a healthful condition of body that his loss of blood, and the presence of the few shot that could not be found, did him little harm. He yielded to his mother's entreaties to spend the morning in bed, but was up long before the evening in the hope of Mercy's coming, confident that his mother would now be like herself to her. She came; the mother took her in her arms, and begged her forgiveness; nor, having thus embraced her, could she any more treat her relation to her son with coldness. If the girl was ready, as her conduct showed, to leave all for Alister, she had saved her soul alive, she was no more one of the enemy!

Thus was the mother repaid for her righteous education of her son: through him her pride received almost a mortal blow, her justice grew more discriminating, and her righteousness more generous.

In a few days the chief was out, and looking quite himself.

CHAPTER XVI

THE FLITTING.

The time was drawing nigh when the warning of ejection would doubtless begin to be put in force; and the chief hearing, through Rob of the Angels, that attempts were making to stir the people up, determined to render them futile: they must be a trick of the enemy to get them into trouble! Taking counsel therefore with the best of the villagers, both women and men, he was confirmed in the idea that they had better all remove together, before the limit of the earliest notice was expired. But his councillors agreed with him that the people should not be told to get themselves in readiness except at a moment's notice to move. In the meantime he pushed on their labour at the new village.

In the afternoon preceding the day on which certain of the clan were to be the first cast out of their homes, the chief went to the village, and going from house to house, told his people to have everything in order for flitting that very night, so that in the morning there should not be an old shoe left behind; and to let no rumour of their purpose get abroad. They would thus have a good laugh at the enemy, who was reported to have applied for military assistance as a precautionary measure. His horses should be ready, and as soon as it was dark they would begin to cart and carry, and be snug in their new houses before the morning!

All agreed, and a tumult of preparation began. "Lady Macruadh" came with help and counsel, and took the children in charge while the mothers bustled. It was amazing how much had to be done to remove so small an amount of property. The chief's three carts were first laden; then the men and women loaded each other. The chief took on his hack the biggest load of all, except indeed it were Hector's. To and fro went the carts, and to and fro went the men and women, I know not how many journeys, upheld by companionship, merriment, hope, and the clan-mother's plentiful provision of tea, coffee, milk, bread and butter, cold mutton and ham—luxurious fare to all. As the sun was rising they closed every door, and walked for the last time, laden with the last of their goods, out of the place of their oppression, leaving behind them not a cock to crow, a peat to burn, or a scrap that was worth stealing—all removed in such order and silence that not one, even at the New House, had a suspicion of what was going on. Mercy, indeed, as she sat looking from her window like Daniel praying toward Jerusalem, her constant custom now, even when there was no moon to show what lay before her, did think she heard strange sounds come faintly through the night from the valley below—even thought she caught shadowy glimpses of a shapeless, gnome-like train moving along the road; but she only wondered if the Highlands had suddenly gifted her with the second sight, and these were the brain-phantasms of coming events. She listened and gazed, but could not be sure that she heard or saw.

When she looked out in the morning, however, she understood, for the castle-ridge was almost hidden in the smoke that poured from every chimney of the new village. Her heart swelled with joy to think of her chief with all his people under his eyes, and within reach of his voice. From her window they seemed so many friends gathered to comfort her solitude, or the camp of an army come to set her free.

Hector and Rob, with one or two more of the clan, hid themselves to watch those who came to evict the first of the villagers. There were no military. Two sheriff's officers, a good many constables, and a few vagabonds, made up the party. Rob's keen eye enabled him to distinguish the very moment when first they began to be aware of something unusual about the place; he saw them presently halt and look at each other as if the duty before them were not altogether CANNY. At no time would there be many signs of life in the poor hamlet, but there would always be some sounds of handicraft, some shuttle or hammer going, some cries of children weeping or at play, some noises of animals, some ascending smoke, some issuing or entering shape! They feared an ambush, a sudden onslaught. Warily they stepped into the place, sharply and warily they looked about them in the street, slowly and with circumspection they opened door after door, afraid of what might be lurking behind to pounce upon them at unawares. Only after searching every house, and discovering not the smallest sign of the presence of living creature, did they recognize their fool's-errand. And all the time there was the new village, smoking hard, under the very windows, as he chose himself to say, of its chief adversary!

CHAPTER XVII

THE NEW VILLAGE.

The winter came down upon them early, and the chief and his mother had a sore time of it. Well as they had known it before, the poverty of their people was far better understood by them now. Unable to endure the sight of it, and spending more and more to meet it, they saw it impossible for them to hold out. For a long time their succour had been draining if not exhausting the poor resources of the chief; he had borne up in the hope of the money he was so soon to receive; and now there was none, and the need greater than ever! He was not troubled, for his faith was simple and strong; but his faith made him the more desirous of doing his part for the coming deliverance: faith in God compels and enables a man to be fellow-worker with God. He was now waiting the judgment of Ian concerning the prospects of the settlers in that part of Canada to which he had gone, hoping it might help him to some resolve in view of the worse difficulties at hand.

In the meantime the clan was more comfortable, and passed the winter more happily, than for many years. First of all, they had access to the chief at any moment. Then he had prepared a room in his own house where were always fire and light for such as would read what books he was able to lend them, or play at quiet games. To them its humble arrangements were sumptuous. And best of all, he would, in the long dark fore-nights, as the lowland Scotch call them, read aloud, at one time in Gaelic, at another in English, things that gave them great delight. Donal shoemaker was filled with joy unutterable by the Rime of the Ancient Mariner. If only this state of things could be kept up—with Ian back, and Mercy married to the chief! thought the mother. But it was not to be; that grew plainer every day.

Mr. Palmer would gladly have spent his winter elsewhere, leaving his family behind him; but as things were, he could not leave them, and as certain other things were, he did not care to take them to London. Besides, for them all to leave now, would be to confess defeat; and who could tell what hurt to his forest might not follow in his absence from the cowardly hatred of the peasants! He was resolved to see the thing out. But above all, he must keep that worthless girl, Mercy, under his own eye!

"That's what comes of NOT drinking!" he would say to himself; "a man grows as proud as Satan, and makes himself a curse to his neighbours!"

Then he would sigh like a man ill-used and disconsolate.

Both Mercy and the chief thought it better not to venture much, but they did occasionally contrive to meet for a few minutes—by the help of Christina generally. Twice only was Mercy's handkerchief hung from the window, when her longing for his voice had grown almost too strong for her to bear. The signal brought him both times through the wild wintry storm, joyous as a bird through the summer air. Once or twice they met just outside the gate, Mercy flying like a snow-bird to the tryst, and as swiftly back through the keen blue frost, when her breath as she ran seemed to linger in the air like smoke, and threaten to betray her.

At length came the much desired letter from Ian, full of matter for the enabling of the chief's decision.

Two things had long been clear to Alister—that, even if the ground he had could keep his people alive, it certainly could not keep them all employed; and that, if they went elsewhere, especially to any town, it might induce for many, and ensure for their children, a lamentable descent in the moral scale. He was their shepherd, and must lose none of them! therefore, first of all, he must not lose sight of them! It was now clear also, that the best and most desirable thing was, that the poor remnant of the clan should leave their native country, and betake themselves where not a few of their own people, among them Lachlan and Annie, would welcome them to probable ease and comfort. There he would buy land, settle with them, and build a village. Some would cultivate the soil under their chief; others would pursue their trades for the good of the community and themselves!

And now came once more the love of land face to face with the love of men, and in the chief's heart paled before it. For there was but one way to get the needful money: the last of the Macruadh property must go! Not for one moment did it rouse a grudging thought in the chief: it was for the sake of the men and women and children whose lives would be required of him! The land itself must yield, them wings to forsake it withal, and fly beyond the sea!

CHAPTER XVIII

A FRIENDLY OFFER

It was agreed between mother and son to submit the matter to Ian, and if he should, be of the same mind, at once to negotiate the sale of the land, in order to carry the clan to Canada. They wrote therefore to Ian, and composed themselves to await his answer.

It was a sorrowful thing to Alister to seem for a moment to follow the example of the recreant chiefs whose defection to feudalism was the prelude to their treachery toward their people, and whose faithlessness had ruined the highlands. But unlike Glengarry or "Esau" Reay, he desired to sell his land that he might keep his people, care for them, and share with them: his people safe, what mattered the acres!

Reflecting on the thing, he saw, in the case of Ian's approval of the sale, no reason why he should not show friendliness where none was expected, and give Mr. Peregrine Palmer the first chance of purchase. He thought also, with his usual hopefulness, that the time might come when the clan, laying its savings together, would be able to redeem its ancient homesteads, and then it might be an advantage that they were all in the possession of one man. Such things had been, and might be again! The Lord could bring again the captivity of Clanruahd as well as that of Zion!

Two months passed, and they had Ian's answer—when it was well on into the spring, and weather good for a sea-voyage was upon its way. Because of the loss of their uncle's money, and the good prospect of comfort in return for labour, hard but not killing, Ian entirely approved of the proposal. From that moment the thing was no longer discussed, but how best to carry it out. The chief assembled the clan in the barn, read his brother's letter, and in a simple speech acquainted them with the situation. He told them of the loss of the money to which he had looked for the power to aid them; reminded them that there was neither employment nor subsistence enough on the land—not even if his mother and he were to live like the rest of them, which if necessary they were quite prepared to do; and stated his resolve to part with the remnant of it in order to provide the means of their migrating in a body to Canada, where not a few old friends were eager to welcome them. There they would buy land, he said, of which every man that would cultivate it should have a portion enough to live upon, while those with trades should have every facility for following them. All, he believed, would fare well in return for hard work, and they would be in the power of no man. There was even a possibility, he hoped, that, if they lived and laboured well, they might one day buy back the home they had left; or if not they, their sons and daughters might return from their captivity, and restore the house of their fathers. If anyone would not go, he would do for him what seemed fair.

Donal shoemaker rose, unpuckered his face, slackened the purse-strings of his mouth, and said,

"Where my chief goes, I will go; where my chief lives, I will live; and where my chief is buried, God grant I may be buried also, with all my family!"

He sat down, covered his face with his hands, and wept and sobbed.

One voice rose from all present:

"We'll go, Macruadh! We'll go! Our chief is our home!"

The chief's heart swelled with mingled gladness and grief, but he answered quietly,

"Then you must at once begin your preparations; we ought not to be in a hurry at the last."

An immediate stir, movement, bustle, followed. There was much talking, and many sunny faces, over which kept sweeping the clouds of sorrow.

The next morning the chief went to the New House, and desired to see Mr. Palmer. He was shown into what the new laird called his study. Mr.

Palmer's first thought was that he had come to call him to account for firing at him. He neither spoke nor advanced a step to meet him. The chief stood still some yards from him, and said as pleasantly as he could,—

"You are surprised to see me, Mr. Palmer!"

"I am."

"I come to ask if you would like to buy my land?"

"Already!" said Mr. Palmer, cast on his enemy a glare of victory, and so stood regarding him. The chief did not reply.

"Well!" said Mr. Palmer.

"I wait your answer," returned the chief.

"Did it never strike you that insolence might be carried too far?"

"I came for your sake more than my own," rejoined the chief, without even a shadow of anger. "I have no particular desire you should take the land, but thought it reasonable you should have the first offer."

"What a dull ox the fellow must take me for!" remarked the new laird to himself. "It's all a dodge to get into the house! As if he would sell ME his land! Or could think I would hold any communication with him! Buy his land! It's some trick, I'll lay my soul! The infernal scoundrel! Such a mean-spirited wretch too! Takes an ounce of shot in the stomach, and never says 'What the devil do you mean by it?' I don't believe the savage ever felt it!"

Something like this passed with thought's own swiftness through the mind of Mr. Palmer, as he stood looking the chief from head to foot, yet in his inmost person feeling small before him.

"If you cannot at once make up your mind," said Alister, "I will give you till to-morrow to think it over."

"When you have learned to behave like a gentleman," answered the new laird, "let me know, and I will refer you to my factor."

He turned and rang the hell. Alister bowed, and did not wait for the servant.

It must be said for Mr. Palmer, however, that that morning Christina had positively refused to listen to a word more from Mr. Sercombe.

In the afternoon, Alister set out for London.

CHAPTER XIX

ANOTHER EXPULSION.

Mr. Peregrine Palmer brooded more and more upon what he counted the contempt of the chief. It became in him almost a fixed idea. It had already sent out several suckers, and had, amongst others, developed the notion that he was despised by those from whom first of all he looked for the appreciation after which his soul thirsted—his own family. He grew therefore yet more moody, and his moodiness and distrust developed suspicion. It is scarce credible what a crushing influence the judgment he pretended to scorn, thus exercised upon him. It was not that he acknowledged in it the smallest justice; neither was it that he cared altogether for what such a fanatical fool as the chief might think; but he reflected that if one could so despise his money because of its source, there might be others, might be many who did so. At the same time, had he been sure of the approbation of all the world beside, it would have troubled him not a little, in his thirst after recognition, that any gentleman, one of family especially, however old-fashioned and absurd he might be, should look down upon him. His smouldering, causelessly excited anger, his evident struggle to throw off an oppression, and the fierce resentment of the chief's judgment which he would now and then betray, revealed how closely the offence clung to his consciousness.

Flattering himself from her calmness that Mercy had got over her foolish liking for the "boor," as he would not unfrequently style the chief, he had listened to the prayers of her mother, and submitted to her company at the dinner-table; but he continued to treat her as one who had committed a shameful fault.

That evening, the great little man could hardly eat for recurrent wrathful memories of the interview of the morning. Perhaps his most painful reflection was that he had not been quick enough to embrace the opportunity of annihilating his enemy. Thunder lowered portentous in his black brows, and not until he had drunk several glasses of wine did a word come from his lips. His presence was purgatory without the purifying element.

"What do you think that fellow has been here about this morning?" he said at length.

"What fellow?" asked his wife unnecessarily, for she knew what visitor had been shown into the study.

"The highland fellow," he answered, "that claims to do what he pleases on my property!"

Mercy's face grew hot.

"—Came actually to offer me the refusal of his land!—the merest trick to get into the house—confound him! As much as told me, if I did not buy it off-hand, I should not have the chance again! The cheek of the brute! To dare show his face in my house after trifling with my daughter's affections on the pretence that he could not marry a girl whose father was in trade!"

Mercy felt she would be false to the man she loved, and whom she knew to be true, if she did not speak. She had no thought of defending him, but simply of witnessing to him.

"I beg your pardon, papa," she said, "but the Macruadh never trifled with me. He loves me, and has not given me up. If he told you he was going to part with his land, he is going to part with it, and came to you first because he must return good for evil. I saw him from my window ride off as if he were going to meet the afternoon coach."

She would not have been allowed to say so much, had not her father been speechless with rage. This was more than he or any man could bear! He rose from the table, his eyes blazing.

"Return ME good for evil!" he exclaimed; "—a beast who has done me more wrong than ever I did in all my life! a scoundrel bumpkin who loses not an opportunity of insulting me as never was man insulted before! You are an insolent, heartless, depraved girl!—ready to sacrifice yourself, body and soul, to a man who despises you and yours with the pride of a savage! You hussey, I can scarce keep my hands off you!"

He came toward her with a threatful stride. She rose, pushed back her chair, and stood facing him.

"Strike me," she said with a choking voice, "if you will, papa; but mamma knows I am not what you call me! I should be false and cowardly if I did not speak the truth for the man to whom I owe"—she was going to say "more than to any other human being," but she checked herself.

"If the beggar is your god," said her father, and struck her on the cheek with his open hand, "you can go to him!"

He took her by the arm, and pushed her before him out of the room, and across the hall; then opening the door, shoved her from him into the garden, and flung the door to behind her. The rain was falling in torrents, the night was very dark, and when the door shut, she felt as if she had lost her eyesight.

It was terrible!—but, thank God, she was free! Without a moment's hesitation—while her mother wept and pleaded, Christina stood burning with indignation, the two little ones sat white with open mouths, and the servants hurried about scared, but trying to look as if nothing had happened —Mercy fled into the dark. She stumbled into the shrubbery several times, but at last reached the gate, and while they imagined her standing before the house waiting to be let in, was running from it as from the jaws of the pit, in terror of a voice calling her back. The pouring rain was sweet to her whole indignant person, and especially to the cheek where burned the brand of her father's blow. The way was deep in mud, and she slipped and fell more than once as she ran.

Mrs. Macruadh was sitting in the little parlour, no one but Nancy in the house, when the door opened, and in came the wild-looking girl, draggled and spent, and dropped kneeling at her feet. Great masses of long black hair hung dripping with rain about her shoulders. Her dress was torn and wet, and soiled with clay from the road and earth from the shrubbery. One cheek was white, and the other had a red patch on it.

"My poor child!" cried the mother; "what has happened? Alister is away!"

"I know that," panted Mercy. "I saw him go, but I thought you would take me in—though you do not like me much!"

"Not like you, my child!" echoed the mother tenderly. "I love you! Are you not my Alister's choice? There are things I could have wished otherwise, but—"

"Well could I wish them otherwise too!" interposed Mercy. "I do not wish another father; and I am not quite able to wish he hadn't struck me and put me out into the dark and the rain, but—"

"Struck you and put you out! My child! What did he do it for?"

"Perhaps I deserved it: it is difficult to know how to behave to a father! A father is supposed to be one whom you not only love, as I do mine, but of whom you can be proud as well! I can't be proud of mine, and don't know quite how to behave to him. Perhaps I ought to have held my peace, but when he said things that were not—not correct about Alister, misinterpreting him altogether, I felt it cowardly and false to hold my tongue. So I said I did not believe that was what Alister meant. It is but a quarter of an hour ago, and it looks a fortnight! I don't think I quite know what I am saying!"

She ceased, laid her head on Mrs. Macruadh's knee, then sank to the floor, and lay motionless. All the compassion of the woman, all the protective pride of the chieftainess, woke in the mother. She raised the girl in her arms, and vowed that not one of her house should set eyes on her again without the consent of her son. He should see how his mother cared for what was his!—how wide her arms, how big her heart, to take in what he loved! Dear to him, the daughter of the man she despised should be as the apple of her eye! They would of course repent and want her back, but they should not have her; neither should a sound of threat or demand reach the darling's ears. She should be in peace until Alister came to determine her future. There was the mark of the wicked hand on the sweet sallow cheek! She was not beautiful, but she would love her the more to make up! Thank God, they had turned her out, and that made her free of them! They should not have her again; Alister should have her!—and from the hand of his mother!

She got her to bed, and sent for Rob of the Angels. With injunctions to silence, she told him to fetch his father, and be ready as soon as possible to drive a cart to the chief's cave, there to make everything comfortable for herself and Miss Mercy Palmer.

Mercy slept well, and as the day was breaking Mrs. Macruadh woke her and helped her to dress. Then they walked together through the lovely spring morning to the turn of the valley-road, where a cart was waiting them, half-filled with oat-straw. They got in, and were borne up and up at a walking-pace to the spot Mercy knew so well. Never by swiftest coach had she enjoyed a journey so much as that slow crawl up the mountains in the rough springless cart of her ploughman lover! She felt so protected, so happy, so hopeful. Alister's mother was indeed a hiding place from the wind, a covert from the tempest! Having consented to be her mother, she could mother her no way but entirely. An outcast for the sake of her Alister, she should have the warmest corner of her heart next to him and Ian!

Into the tomb they went, and found everything strangely comfortable—the stone-floor covered with warm and woolly skins of black-faced sheep, a great fire glowing, plenty of provisions hung and stored, and the deaf, keen-eyed father with the swift keen-eared son for attendants.

"You will not mind sharing your bed with me—will you, my child?" said Mrs. Macruadh: "Our accommodation is scanty. But we shall be safe from intrusion. Only those two faithful men know where we are."

"Mother will be terribly frightened!" said Mercy.

"I thought of that, and left a note with Nancy, telling her you were safe and well, but giving no hint of where. I said that her dove had flown to my bosom for shelter, and there she should have it."

Mercy answered with a passionate embrace.

CHAPTER XX

ALISTER'S PRINCESS.

Ten peaceful days they spent in the cave-house. It was cold outside, but the clear air of the hill-top was delicious, and inside it was warm and dry. There were plenty of books, and Mercy never felt the time a moment too long. The mother talked freely of her sons, and of their father, of the history of the clan, of her own girlhood, and of the hopes and intentions of her sons.

"Will you go with him, Mercy?" she asked, laying her hand on hers.

"I would rather be his servant," answered Mercy, "than remain at home: there is no life there!"

"There is life wherever there is the will to live—that is, to do the thing that is given one to do," said the mother.

In writing she told Alister nothing of what had happened: he might hurry home without completing his business! Undisturbed by fresh anxiety, he settled everything, parted with his property to an old friend of the family, and received what would suffice for his further intents. He also chartered a vessel to take them over the sea, and to save weariness and expense, arranged for it to go northward as far as a certain bay on the coast, and there take the clan on board.

When at length he reached home, Nancy informed him that his mother was at the hill-house, and begged he would go there to her. He was a good deal perplexed: she very seldom went there, and had never before gone for the night! and it was so early in the season! He set out immediately.

It was twilight when he reached the top of the hill, and no light shone from the little windows of the tomb.

That day Mercy had been amusing her protectress with imitations, in which kind she had some gift, of certain of her London acquaintance: when the mother heard her son's approaching step, a thought came to her.

"Here! Quick!" she said; "Put on my cap and shawl, and sit in this chair. I will go into the bedroom. Then do as you like."

When the chief entered, he saw the form of his mother, as he thought, bending over the peat-fire, which had sunk rather low: in his imagination he saw again the form of his uncle as on that night in the low moonlight. She did not move, did not even look up. He stood still for a moment; a strange feeling possessed him of something not being as it ought to be. But he recovered himself with an effort, and kneeling beside her, put his arms round her—not a little frightened at her continued silence.

"What is the matter, mother dear?" he said. "Why have you come up to this lonely place?"

When first Mercy felt his arms, she could not have spoken if she would— her heart seemed to grow too large for her body. But in a moment or two she controlled herself, and was able to say—sufficiently in his mother's tone and manner to keep up the initiated misconception:

"They put me out of the house, Alister."

"Put you out of the house!" he returned, like one hearing and talking in a dream. "Who dared interfere with you, mother? Am I losing my senses? I seem not to understand my own words!"

"Mr. Palmer."

"Mr. Palmer! Was it to him I sold the land in London? What could he have to do with you, mother? How did they allow him to come near the house in my absence? Oh, I see! He came and worried you so about Mercy that you were glad to take refuge from him up here!—I understand now!"

He ended in a tone of great relief: he felt as if he had just recovered his senses.

"No, that was not it. But we are going so soon, there would have been no good in fighting it out. We ARE going soon, are we not?"

"Indeed we are, please God!" replied the chief, who had relapsed into bewilderment.

"That is well—for you more than anybody. Would you believe it—the worthless girl vows she will never leave her mother's house!"

"Ah, mother, YOU never heard her say so! I know Mercy better than that! She will leave it when I say COME. But that won't be now. I must wait, and come and fetch her when she is of age."

"She is not worthy of you."

"She is worthy of me if I were twenty times worthier! Mother, mother! What has turned you against us again? It is not like you to change about so! I cannot bear to find you changeable! I should have sworn you were just the one to understand her perfectly! I cannot bear you should let unworthy reasons prejudice you against anyone!—If you say a word more against her, I will go and sit outside with the moon. She is not up yet, but she will be presently —and though she is rather old and silly, I shall find her much better company than you, mother dear!"

He spoke playfully, but was grievously puzzled.

"To whom are you talking, Alister?—yourself or a ghost?"

Alister started up, and saw his mother coming from the bedroom with a candle in her hand! He stood stupefied. He looked again at the seated figure, still bending over the fire. Who was it if not his mother?

With a wild burst of almost hysteric laughter, Mercy sprang to her feet, and threw herself in his arms. It was not the less a new bewilderment that it was an unspeakably delightful change from the last. Was he awake or dreaming? Was the dream of his boyhood come true? or was he dreaming it on in manhood? It was come true! The princess was arrived! She was here in his cave to be his own!

A great calm and a boundless hope filled the heart of Alister. The night was far advanced when he left them to go home. Nor did he find his way home, but wandered all night about the tomb, making long rounds and still returning like an angel sent to hover and watch until the morning. When he astonished them by entering as they sat at breakfast, and told them how he had passed the night, it thrilled Mercy's heart to know that, while she slept and was dreaming about him, he was awake and thinking about her.

"What is only dreaming in me, is thinking in you, Alister!" she said.

"I was thinking," returned Alister, "that as you did not know I was watching you, so, when we feel as if God were nowhere, he is watching over us with an eternal consciousness, above and beyond our every hope and fear, untouched by the varying faith and fluctuating moods of his children."

After breakfast he went to see the clergyman of the parish, who lived some miles away; the result of which visit was that in a few days they were married. First, however, he went once more to the New House, desiring to tell Mr. Palmer what had been and was about to be done. He refused to see him, and would not allow his wife or Christina to go to him.

The wedding was solemnized at noon within the ruined walls of the old castle. The withered remnant of the clan, with pipes playing, guns firing, and shouts of celebration, marched to the cave-house to fetch thence the bride. When the ceremony was over, a feast was ready for all in the barn, and much dancing followed.

When evening came, with a half-moon hanging faint in the limpid blue, and the stars looking large through the mist of ungathered tears—those of nature, not the lovers; with a wind like the breath of a sleeping child, sweet and soft, and full of dreams of summer; the mountains and hills asleep around them like a flock of day- wearied things, and haunted by the angels of Rob's visions—the lovers, taking leave only of the mother, stole away to walk through the heavenly sapphire of the still night, up the hills and over the rushing streams of the spring, to the cave of their rest—no ill omen but lovely symbol to such as could see in the tomb the porch of paradise. Where should true lovers make their bed but on the threshold of eternity!

CHAPTER XXI

THE FAREWELL.

A month passed, and the flag of their exile was seen flying in the bay. The same hour the chief's horses were put to, the carts were loaded, their last things gathered. Few farewells had to be made, for the whole clan, except two that had gone to the bad, turned out at the minute appointed. The chief arranged them in marching column. Foremost went the pipes; the chief, his wife, and his mother, came next; Hector of the Stags, carrying the double-barrelled rifle the chief had given him, Rob of the Angels, and Donal shoemaker, followed. Then came the women and children; next, the carts, with a few, who could not walk, on the top of the baggage; the men brought up the rear. Four or five favourite dogs were the skirmishers of the column.

The road to the bay led them past the gate of the New House. The chief called a halt, and went with his wife to seek a last interview. Mr. Peregrine Palmer kept his room, but Mrs. Palmer bade her daughter a loving farewell —more relieved than she cared to show, that the cause of so much discomfort was going so far away. The children wept. Christina bade her sister good-bye with a hopeless, almost envious look: Mercy, who did not love him, would see Ian! She who would give her soul for him was never to look on him again in this world!

Kissing Mercy once more, she choked down a sob, and whispered,

"Give my love—no, my heart, to Ian, and tell him I AM trying."

They all walked together to the gate, and there the chief's mother took her leave of the ladies of the New House. The pipes struck up; the column moved on.

When they came to the corner which would hide from them their native strath, the march changed to a lament, and with the opening wail, all stopped and turned for a farewell look. Men and women, the chief alone excepted, burst into weeping, and the sound of their lamentation went wandering through the hills with an adieu to every loved spot. And this was what the pipes said:

We shall never see you more, Never more, never more! Till the sea be dry, and the world be bare, And the dews have ceased to fall, And the rivers have ceased to run, We shall never see you more, Never more, never more!

They stood and gazed, and the pipes went on lamenting, and the women went on weeping.

"This is heathenish!" said Alister to himself, and stopped the piper.

"My friends," he cried, in Gaelic of course, "look at me: my eyes are dry! Where Jesus, the Son of God, is—there is my home! He is here, and he is over the sea, and my home is everywhere! I have lost my land and my country, but I take with me my people, and make no moan over my exile! Hearts are more than hills. Farewell Strathruadh of my childhood! Place of my dreams, I shall visit you again in my sleep! And again I shall see you in happier times, please God, with my friends around me!"

He took off his bonnet. All the men too uncovered for a moment, then turned to follow their chief. The pipes struck up Macrimmon's lament, Till an crodh a Dhonnachaidh (TURN THE KINE, DUNCAN). Not one looked behind him again till they reached the shore. There, out in the bay, the biggest ship any of the clan had ever seen was waiting to receive them.

When Mr. Peregrine Palmer saw that the land might in truth be for sale, he would gladly have bought it, but found to his chagrin that he was too late. It was just like the fellow, he said, to mock him with the chance of buying it! He took care to come himself, and not send a man he could have believed!

The clan throve in the clearings of the pine forests. The hill-men stared at their harvests as if they saw them growing. Their many children were strong and healthy, and called Scotland their home.

In an outlying and barren part of the chief's land, they came upon rock oil. It was so plentiful that as soon as carriage became possible, the chief and his people began to grow rich.

News came to them that Mr. Peregrine Palmer was in difficulties, and desirous of parting with his highland estate. The chief was now able to buy it ten times over. He gave his agent in London directions to secure it for him, with any other land conterminous that might come into the market. But he would not at once return to occupy it, for his mother dreaded the sea, and thought to start soon for another home. Also he would rather have his boys grow where they were, and as men face the temptations beyond: where could they find such teaching as that of their uncle Ian! Both father and uncle would have them ALIVE before encountering what the world calls LIFE.

But the Macruadh yet dreams of the time when those of the clan then left in the world, accompanied, he hopes, by some of those that went out before them, shall go back to repeople the old waste places, and from a wilderness of white sheep and red deer, make the mountain land a nursery of honest, unambitious, brave men and strong-hearted women, loving God and their neighbour; where no man will think of himself at his brother's cost, no man grow rich by his neighbour's ruin, no man lay field to field, to treasure up for himself wrath against the day of wrath.

George MacDonald

Made in the USA
Monee, IL
15 November 2023

46613808R00260